D0177178

This bo
be rene
date, a

0

HEIRESS *in*
Regency
Society

HELEN
DICKSON

Published in Great Britain 2014
by Mills & Boon, an imprint of Harlequin (UK) Limited,
Eton House, 18-24 Paradise Road, Richmond, Surrey, TW9 1SR

HEIRESS IN REGENCY SOCIETY
© 2014 Harlequin Books S.A.

The Defiant Debutante © 2006 Helen Dickson
From Governess to Society Bride © 2008 Helen Dickson

ISBN: 978-0-263-25012-1

052-0315

Harlequin (UK) policy is to use papers that are natural, renewable and recyclable products and made from wood grown in sustainable forests. The logging and manufacturing processes conform to the legal environmental regulations of the country of origin.

Printed and bound
by CPI Group (UK) Ltd, Croydon, CR0 4YY

Helen Dickson was born and lives in South Yorkshire, with her retired farm manager husband. Having moved out of the busy farmhouse where she raised their two sons, she has more time to indulge in her favourite pastimes. She enjoys being outdoors, travelling, reading and music. An incurable romantic, she writes for pleasure. It was a love of history that drove her to writing historical fiction.

The Defiant Debutante

HELEN DICKSON

Chapter One

London, May 1812

Birds were stirring in the trees and dew was still on the grass as dawn began to spread its watery grey light over the deserted park. Two men shrouded in long black cloaks rode towards the seclusion of a group of trees and dismounted.

Cursing at his own folly, Alexander Montgomery, the seventh Earl of Arlington and taller of the two, glanced irritably at Sir Nathan Beresford. The two men were as close as friends could be, and as different as night and day. Nathan, with his ash-blond hair and blue eyes, was well liked, good natured and easy-going, and he lacked the aura of authority and power that seemed to surround Alex. Nathan was to act as Alex's second, when the other party deigned to arrive for the duel.

Three inches over six feet tall, Alex was a man diverse and complex, and could be utterly ruthless when the need arose. There was a hard set to his firm jaw, and his wide, well-shaped mouth was held in a stern line. His face was clean shaven and one of arrogant handsomeness, dark brows slashed his forehead and his hair was thick and ebony black. In the midst of so much darkness his eyes were dove grey, striking and piercing. Hidden deep in them was a cynicism, watchful, mocking, as though he found the world a dubious place to be.

He possessed a haughty reserve that was not inviting and set him apart from others in society. There was an aggressive confidence and strength of purpose in his features, and he had an air of a man who succeeds in all he sets out to achieve. From the arrogant lift of his dark head and casual stance, he was a man with many shades to his nature, a man with a sense of his own infallibility.

'You've tied yourself into some knots in your time, Alex, but this is by far the tightest,' Nathan remarked, tethering his horse to a branch and scanning the park for the arrival of Alex's opponent. 'I only hope you can extricate yourself from this mess with some modicum of honour.'

'I agree. It's a damned unfortunate business, Nathan, and I bear the entire weight of this incident on my own conscience.'

'Surely Amelia Fairhurst must shoulder some of the blame.'

'The responsibility is all mine,' Alex replied curtly, dismissing Nathan's well-meaning attempt to absolve him. 'But if ever I am stupid enough to fall prey to another pretty face, remind me to scrutinise her credentials for hidden husbands.'

'Knowing how assiduous you are to detail, I am surprised you didn't vet her more carefully.'

'I must have taken leave of my senses,' Alex replied, contemplating the irony of the situation. Here he was, one of the most eligible bachelors in England, and yet he had made the fatal mistake of taking to bed a married woman. His stupidity galled him, and he cursed himself for being a dim-witted fool.

Nathan cast him an arch look. 'The delectable Amelia Fairhurst must be quite something for you to have overlooked the fact that she has an aging husband tucked conveniently out of the way in Yorkshire.'

Alex's firm lips curved in a slight smile when he remembered the stunningly vivacious brunette, who had taken no persuading to jump into his bed. 'She's certainly an interesting, unconventional female.'

Nathan chuckled, giving his friend a conspiratorial wink. 'And I seem to recall you saying on more than one occasion that unconventional women are always more exciting between the sheets.'

'Exactly,' Alex replied with a wry grin. 'Providing one doesn't happen to be married to one.'

His words were flippant, but Nathan heard an edge to his voice. Alex was a self-proclaimed single man. Past experiences had forged him into a hardened cynic, and he discarded all women as being dispensable and irrelevant. Age and experience had taught him that women couldn't be trusted, and the first lady to show him this had been his own mother. Her affairs had been notorious and had hurt him badly. They had also been the reason why his father had sought oblivion in alcohol before blowing out his brains. Alex's mother, the beautiful and immoral Margaret Montgomery, had married her Spanish lover soon after and had gone to live in Spain. Whether she lived or had died Alex neither knew nor cared.

'Thank God Fairhurst is in his dotage. With any luck his eyesight will be impaired and his brain addled. I am merely one in a long line of Amelia's lovers. Why the devil he's singled me out is quite beyond me.'

'Maybe it's because you're the only one he knows about.'

'I doubt it. But whatever the reason, remind me not to stray from Caroline from now on. She's more than enough to satisfy my needs.'

Alex was always careful to choose a mistress whose company he enjoyed. She had to be intelligent and sophisticated, who would not mistake lovemaking and desire with love, and, moreover, she had to be a woman who made no demands and expected no promises.

For these reasons she would be kept in the lap of luxury. She could expect a smart town house, a beautiful carriage and horses, servants, gowns, furs and jewels that would be the envy of every other woman.

'Does Caroline know about your affair with Amelia?'

'Yes, but she understands not to ask for an explanation. However, I must admit that I've been unfair to her.'

Nathan quirked a brow, his blue eyes twinkling with light mockery. 'What's this? Are you becoming sentimental?'

'I am never sentimental,' Alex snapped. 'But for the life of me I can't understand why someone as stunning as Amelia married old Fairhurst in the first place. It's disgraceful that so much beauty is wasted on such a pathetic old man.'

Nathan regarded his friend with mild cynicism. 'Yes, you can. You know the type of woman she is. She's a scheming fortune-hunter who likes to drink the finest champagne and wear the most expensive jewels. She openly and shamelessly admits she married Fairhurst for his title and wealth and flaunts it with aplomb.'

'So she does, but you must admit she is more pleasing than those simpering young misses, who swoon at the merest hint of a stolen kiss, their mamas hovering over them like hawks, ready to latch on to me if I show any sign of compromising their precious daughters.'

Alex was aware that he was a fantastic matrimonial prize— top of the list of every ambitious matchmaking mama, whom he treated with amused condescension. They were women whose only ambition in life was to form an alliance with the powerful and illustrious Montgomery family. His ancestors on his mother's side had been rewarded for their loyalty to the crown through the ages with estates and riches enough to make him one of the wealthiest men in England.

Alex's attitude to the female sex was highly critical, his opinion low, but his own popularity among them was high. He was unattached, unattainable, and he would stay that way.

'Perhaps if you were to give marriage some serious thought it might put a stop to the hunt.'

Alex threw Nathan a look that would have stopped a race-horse in its tracks. 'When I want some of your logic, Nathan,' he retorted tersely, 'I'll ask for it.'

'Nevertheless, it would solve the problem,' Nathan went on

imperturbably, ignoring Alex's black look. Nathan was one of the few people who could argue with him and escape unscathed.

'Marriage and love are for fools,' Alex stated caustically.

'I never mentioned love. Besides, where you are concerned, since when has love anything to do with marriage or anything else for that matter?' Nathan proclaimed.

'You're right. I despise the romantic ideal of love. I've seen enough of it in the past to know of its destructive effects. Desire I understand. It's a more honest emotion. Passion and desire are easily appeased—fleeting—and easily doused.'

'It's a good thing we're not all as cynical as you are,' Nathan chuckled. 'Not every woman is as ambitious and devious as you seem to think they are. I am fortunate to be married to one, don't forget.'

That was true. Twelve months ago Nathan had found wedded bliss with the lovely Verity Fortesque, a woman with whom even Alex had been unable to find fault. Alex and Verity were cousins, Verity being the only daughter of his Aunt Patience, Uncle Henry's younger sister. Patience's husband had died after just a few short yet happy years of marriage. She had never remarried and still lived in the house they had shared at Richmond.

'Verity is a sweet thing, I grant you. But she is the exception. However, unlike you, I do not find marriage a desirable institution.'

Nathan shot him an exasperated look. 'I agree it can be heaven or hell. Thankfully I chose my wife wisely. Our marriage will be long lasting, based on caring—and love. And you may scoff at that all you like.'

Alex looked at his friend, suddenly serious. 'I'm not scoffing, Nathan. In a way I envy you.'

'You do?'

Alex nodded and looked away.

'You know, Alex, you Montgomerys have become thin on the ground; if you want to continue the line, you really should give some thought to producing an heir. You don't have to marry for love—but I suspect that one day you will fall prey to what you consider to be a debilitating emotion, and it will come as the greatest shock in your life.'

Alex favoured him with a look of absolute disdain, but Nathan ignored it. 'I don't think so,' he answered coldly, his tone suggesting that the subject was closed. But as he turned away he frowned, his thoughts reverting to the matter of an heir. Nathan was right. He was heir to his uncle, the Duke of Mowbray, and Alex knew how anxious his uncle was for him to marry. If he didn't produce a legitimate heir, the title would become extinct. It troubled him more than anyone realised, and he knew he couldn't go on ignoring the issue.

He had stayed a bachelor far longer than most of his contemporaries, and the truth of it was that he was beginning to tire of courtesans and mistresses, and all the jealousies and petty tantrums they brought with them. This latest affair with Amelia Fairhurst had made him see that he was susceptible to women of a certain type, and a wave of disgust swept over him. There had to be an easier way of satisfying his physical needs. Perhaps Nathan was right and a marriage of convenience was the answer after all. In fact, it might have much to offer, and, further, the ideal woman was waiting in the wings.

Lavinia Howard was the eldest daughter of Lord Howard of Springfield Hall in Kent. She was eminently suitable and available. He would dwell on the prospect and invite her—along with a party of friends—to Arlington, his estate in Hertfordshire. If he offered for her, marriage would be a comfortable arrangement that would suit them both. A union between two civilised people who knew what to expect from each other might be just what he needed. He could still enjoy pleasant intrigues, providing he had a compliant wife.

Cursing softly under his breath, impatiently he moved away and began pacing to and fro. 'Fairhurst's late. Where the devil is the man?' Annoyed, Alex thought of the impending duel with distaste. He hoped Fairhurst would achieve satisfaction by merely wounding him—or preferably missing him completely. Alex would fire into the air, and, in so doing, would be admitting his guilt—then the affair would be ended. This was how duels were usually settled between gentlemen. If a death should occur, it would draw the attention of the law, and neither of them wanted that.

'Tell me, Alex. Does your uncle know that Fairhurst has challenged you to a duel?'

Alex's mouth narrowed into a thin line of annoyance. 'No. At this very moment my uncle is en route to America.'

'Really?' Nathan expressed profound surprise. 'I say! That's a bit sudden—and reckless, considering the present situation. It's highly probably that America will declare war on us very soon.'

Alex knew this to be true and his irritation about the situation had increased considerably. 'I know it's only a matter of time before the situation ignites. His decision to go was all rather sudden. He has a cousin, Lydia Hamilton, in Boston who is dying. Her husband is dead and she's fallen on hard times. It appears she has appealed to my uncle to make her daughter his ward. The girl is a minor and Lydia wants him to bring her to England and offer her a home.'

'And you're not pleased, I can see that,' Nathan stated.

'No. When I returned to London from Arlington and read his note, my first impulse was to take the next ship and go after him to bring him back.'

'Thank God common sense prevailed. Do you think your uncle will bring the girl back with him?'

'Uncle Henry is far too sensible to do anything irrational, but from what I recall, his feelings for Lydia were far stronger than just cousinly fondness. Their mothers were sisters, and Henry and Lydia created a scandal that embroiled both families at the time. I believe she is the reason why my uncle never married. I don't know the gist of it, but what I do know makes me decidedly reluctant and uneasy about admitting that woman's daughter into our lives.'

'Why did she go to America?'

'Against her father's wishes, Lydia married an adventurer by the name of Richard Hamilton with undue haste and went with him to Boston. I believe they went west and settled in Ohio. Apparently, her father was outraged and cut her off without a penny. As far as I am aware, nothing has been heard of her since—until my uncle received a letter from her three weeks ago.'

'And no doubt you're afraid he'll be taken in.'

'Yes. He is not a man who shirks his responsibilities, and he obviously thinks of his cousin's daughter as just that, otherwise he would not have gone tearing halfway across the world without discussing the matter with me first. But why go at all? He could have written or sent someone to escort the girl to England.'

'It occurs to me that this grand gesture might be your uncle's way of telling Lydia Hamilton that where she is concerned his feelings are no different to what they were all those years ago.'

It was a possibility that Alex refused to dwell upon.

'Alex, your uncle may have a soft heart, but, contrary to what you believe, he is no fool.'

'You're right. But to saddle himself with a ward at his time of life could be disastrous.'

Nathan arched a sceptical brow. 'For whom? Him or you?'

Alex shot him an icy glance. 'All right, damn you. Me,' he answered curtly.

Nathan grinned, arching a brow at his grim-faced friend. 'It needn't be. I think it's rather touching. But is there no one in America who can look after the girl?'

'Apparently not. My uncle is Lydia Hamilton's next of kin, and I suspect she will take advantage of that. It's years since he last saw her and I'm afraid she might turn out to be a scheming opportunist.'

'Never having met the woman, don't you think you do her an injustice? Come, Alex. I doubt her daughter will bring any real changes to your life,' Nathan argued.

Alex's eyes were full of distaste when he looked at Nathan.

'I hope you're right. But a girl from the wilds of America will have no social skills and find it hard to adjust to the kind of world we inhabit. If so she'll be nothing but a damned nuisance and an embarrassment.'

'Good Lord, Alex! What are you expecting? An ill-bred barbarian? A girl who is half-savage, with brown skin and feathers in her hair?'

Alex shrugged. 'Why not? She could be anything. We know absolutely nothing about her.'

'Nevertheless, having met several colonists both on my travels and here in London, on the whole they are extremely civilised, pleasant people.'

'Several of my acquaintances are Americans, Nathan, so I would be grateful if you did not lecture me on their attributes,' Alex replied drily. 'If my uncle brings the girl to England, he will have legal control over her until she is twenty-one.'

'Are you afraid that she'll be a drain on your resources?'

'No. We can afford it,' Alex bit out.

'Not only will you have to feed her, but you will be faced with the enormous expense of clothing her and introducing her to society.'

'I don't need reminding.' His eyes like dagger thrusts, Alex glared with deadly menace at the amusement Nathan was unable to conceal in his eyes. 'Damn it, Nathan! I do believe you're enjoying my predicament,' he flared in exasperation.

Blithely ignoring his friend's ill humour, Nathan grinned good-naturedly. 'No, not really. I merely find it odd that a girl you have never met, a girl you know nothing about, is capable of rousing so much ire in you. It appears to me that you have already made up your mind not to like her, and have no intention of being charitable or accommodating.'

Alex's eyes impaled Nathan like sharp flints. 'I cannot be accused of being either uncharitable or unaccommodating in this instance. And contrary to what you may think, I have formed no opinion of her whatsoever.'

'I am glad to hear it. You may be pleasantly surprised. Why, she might be a pretty young thing with a sweet disposition and excellent manners.'

'Let us hope so—for all our sakes,' Alex drawled, scanning the park for Lord Fairhurst, his annoyance increasing by the minute the longer he was kept waiting.

'Nevertheless, try to imagine how she might feel,' Nathan persisted. 'Her mother is dying, you say, and she has no relatives in America. Maybe she doesn't want to come to England. My fear is that when she is faced with your formidable manner—a daunting prospect for any girl—it will alienate her from the start. Has it not entered that arrogant, stubborn head of yours that you might like her, Alex? And, if so, will it wound your pride to admit it?'

'Even for an arrogant, stubborn male like me it is not beyond the realms of possibility,' Alex conceded with sarcasm. 'I am protective of my uncle; as you are aware, he does not always enjoy the best of health. He is renowned for his generosity and I am naturally concerned that he is not taken advantage of.'

'Yes, I can understand that. How old is the girl?'

'I really have no idea, but it is my intention to marry her off to the first prospective suitor.'

Nathan watched an inexplicable smile trace its way across the other man's face. 'In which case, you do realise that you will have to provide a somewhat generous dowry?'

Alex regarded Nathan in casual, speculative silence, one dark brow lifted in amused mockery. 'If she turns out to be a wilful hoyden with outrageous manners,' he said drily, 'it will be worth it to get her off our hands.'

Alex had been trained to discipline as soon as he had drawn breath. Already the American girl had caused a rift in his routine—a disturbance that had brought a feeling of unease which had begun to trouble him. It was like a pebble breaking the calm surface of a pond. Once thrown there was nothing to prevent the ripple widening in ever-increasing circles.

The quiet of the park was interrupted. Hearing the measured thud of horses' hooves on the soft turf and the creaking of wheels, they turned to see a closed carriage bearing down on them. It came to a halt and they saw it had only one occupant, a man in middle age. He climbed out and calmly told an astonished Alex that Lord Fairhurst had died suddenly of a seizure during the night.

When Angelina and her mother, Lydia, had left Ohio, never in her life had Angelina known such grief. It broke her heart to think that as well as her father, all the people she had known in the settlement were dead, that whole families had been wiped out by the Shawnee.

Will Casper had accompanied them to Boston. He was a loner, a man of few words, who helped Angelina's father on the land when needed. Will had become a good and loyal friend to them over the years. He had found a doctor to tend to Lydia after she was badly wounded in the Shawnee attack, but he could give them little hope that she would live beyond the next few weeks.

With a horse and wagon, a few meagre possessions and a rifle, they had faced east, pushing themselves hard on well-worn trails. The months of trekking through Pennsylvania and across the mountains were a harsh and emotional time for Angelina, during which she was veiled in a curtain of shock. Her pain defied release. It hid itself in a hollow place inside her heart, beyond the reach of understanding.

Will silently watched her battle to be brave and grown up. He showed her she wasn't alone, and together they made it to the state of Massachusetts, making their home in a shack on the outskirts of Boston. The land round about was wild, and fast-flowing water cut its way through a steep rocky gorge beside the shack, moving north to the Charles River.

The night of the massacre and her own treatment at the hands of the Shawnee had scorched its memory on Angelina's soul. Even now, two years later, she felt defiled and beyond redemption. The terrible, haunting nightmares had pursued her all the way back east. At first they happened every night, but now they were less frequent. But no matter how much time passed, she could not swallow her feeling of outrage and pretend the incident had never happened. She would never be able to come to terms with it, never be able to speak of it. Her terrible secret would remain a burden she would never be able to put into more manageable proportions.

Angelina galloped so hard towards Henry Montgomery that he half-expected a troop of Amazons to materialise from the trees in her wake. Riding the forest pathways on a pony as energetic as herself, she was reckless, like an Indian, and as refreshing as a cool, invigorating wind. With long bouncing braids sticking out from beneath a battered old beaver hat with an eagle's feather stuck in its brim, she pulled her lathered pony to an abrupt halt in front of him, unconcerned by the clouds of dust that the restless animal sent into the air with its hooves, which covered his fine clothes.

Dressed in a worn brown jerkin, ill-fitting deerskin trousers and dull brown boots that no amount of rubbing would bring a shine to, Angelina levelled a steady dark gaze at the tall, silver-haired man. Silently they took stock of each other. She was guarded, wary, looking at him with a wordless resentment.

Henry Montgomery possessed a commanding presence. He had the poise and regal bearing of a man who has lived a thoroughly privileged life. With Angelina he aroused a curious inspection. He looked cool and contained in his immaculate charcoal grey suit and pristine white stock. He was the sort of gentleman her mother had told her about—his rather austere mien and noble bearing out of place here in the backwoods of New England.

Despite the unease and resentment his unexpected arrival caused her, knowing how much her mother was looking forward to meeting him, she had primed herself to be gracious.

'You're the Englishman,' she stated without preamble, her pronunciation clear and distinct. Taking note of this, Henry smiled inwardly. He would have expected nothing less from Lydia's daughter. Swinging her leg over her pony she jumped down like an Indian—lithe, supple and long limbed.

Henry inclined his silver head with amusement and quite without resentment on being confronted by the bold and forthright manner of the girl, who positively oozed energy and vitality. Somehow it came as no surprise to see the butt of a rifle sticking out of a saddle pouch on the side of her pony.

She held out a slim hand. 'It is most kind of you to come all this way.'

Taking her hand in both of his, Henry held it, gazing with complete absorption into the darkest eyes he had ever seen. Set in a face burnt golden by the sun, they slanted slightly and were fringed with sooty black lashes. Her cheekbones were high, her nose pert, and an attractive little cleft dented her delicately rounded chin. Dainty and fine though her features were, her face could possibly pass for a boy's, and with a baggy shirt and jerkin concealing her adolescent breasts, the same could be said of her body. But the mouth was much too soft and pink, too delicate, to belong to a boy. There was something inexpressibly dainty about her, which aroused vague feelings of chivalry.

'I am Henry Montgomery—the Duke of Mowbray. And you are Lydia's daughter.' The likeness almost cut his heart in two.

'My name is Angelina Hamilton,' she replied, withdrawing her hand, completely unfazed by the stranger's grand title and fancy clothes. 'You've come a long way.'

If Angelina did but know it, Henry would walk through hell fire and promise to live in eternal damnation if Lydia asked him to. Even though he was fifty-five and a veteran of hundreds of dispassionate affairs, this girl's mother was the only woman to have captivated his heart. He had loved her as much as it was possible to love another human being, but, because their parents had considered their relationship to be incestuous, he'd had to resign himself to letting her go. Yet, despite the distance, their hearts were still entwined, and neither separation nor time had lessened the pain or their love for each other.

'I came in response to your mother's letter.'

'I know.'

Her eyes were questioning and direct, and her voice was steady, but there was something in it of a frustrated, frightened child.

'How is she? In her letter she mentioned that she was ill—that she was wounded when Indians attacked your home.'

'My mother is dying, sir.'

Carefully Henry schooled his features as he took note of the pain showing naked on Angelina's young face upturned to his. A hint of tears brightened her translucent eyes, which were like windows laying bare the suffering and many hardships of her young life.

'I'm so very sorry, my dear. How dreadful this must be for you.'

'Mother knows she's dying, but she set her mind on not doing so until she heard from you. She didn't know if you would come in person. She didn't expect you to. She thought that perhaps you would write in response to her letter.'

'We used to be very close, your mother and I, before she married your father and came to live in America.' He averted his eyes when Angelina gave him a curious, questioning look. 'Come—walk with me back to the hotel. Mr Phipps, the proprietor, has kindly offered me the use of his buggy. You can take me to her.'

Mr Phipps was a man who liked to talk. All Henry had had to do was sit back and listen when he made it known that he was here to see Mrs Hamilton and her daughter, Angelina.

'Real nice is Miss Angelina,' Mr Phipps had told him. 'Shame about her ma an' pa, though—what the Indians did an' all. After the attack an' when she'd buried her pa, she brought her ma back here an' bought the old McKay place down by the gorge. It was a wreck of a place so it didn't cost much.'

'Did Angelina see what happened?' Henry had asked him.

'She saw all right—more than is right for a child to see. Done killed the Indian who killed her pa, she did. Stabbed him right through the heart, accordin' to Will.'

Unable to comprehend what Angelina must have suffered

during the Indian attack, Henry's expression remained unchanged as he absorbed this shocking piece of information. 'Will?'

'Will Casper. He was out west at the time an' came back east with her and her ma. Been right good to them, too. Don't know what they'd 'ave done without him.'

'How do they manage?'

'Miss Angelina spends all her time huntin' an fishin' an' lookin' after her ma, while Will does all the work about the place—when he's not off trappin' beaver. They 'aven't much—but what they do 'ave they make the best of.'

Moving towards the door through which the Englishman had disappeared, Angelina stopped on the threshold, suddenly feeling like an outsider in her own home. Knowing her mother wanted to be alone with him, she would go no further, but before the bedroom door closed she saw the Englishman bend and pick her mother's limp hand up off the patchwork quilt and place it to his lips. At the same time her mother raised her free hand and gently placed it on his silver head, as if bestowing a title on the Duke of Mowbray. It was a scene that would remain indelibly printed on her mind for all time.

When he emerged from Lydia's room after what seemed like an eternity, Henry passed through the house to the veranda, welcoming the cool air after the heat of the sick room. Night had fallen and a languid breeze stirred the trees. The air carried a heavy fragrance of jasmine, wood smoke and cedar wood.

Henry had been taken aback at first to see how ill Lydia was, and he knew she wasn't long for this world. As fragile as a plucked wildflower, she lay still and as white as death against the pillows. But when he'd gazed once more into those glorious dark eyes, he had seen that the years had not quenched their glow.

Lydia had been his *grande passion,* the woman he had been prepared to relinquish his title and his family to marry. She had been part of his flesh and his spirit, and a large part of him had died when she left him. Without warning and without his knowledge she had married Richard Hamilton, sacrificing herself for his own sake, and gone to America. In a brooding silence he was conscious of the girl standing silently behind him, waiting for him to speak, her dog, Mr Boone, at her feet.

Henry turned and looked at her. The soft, silvery moonlight washed over her, touching the delicate, pensive features of her face. He saw the questioning black eyes in cheeks pale with apprehension, and it was only then, upon meeting that dark, misty gaze, that he realised the enormity of the responsibility Lydia had placed in his hands.

'You know why your mother wrote to me, Angelina,' Henry said, sitting in one of two battered old wicker chairs. 'You also know that I am her cousin and closest kin. It is most unfortunate that on your late father's side there are no close relatives. It is your mother's wish that I take charge of you, and take you back with me to England. Would you like that?'

Angelina's reaction to say no was instinctive, but, realising that this gentleman had travelled a long way to help her mother and herself, she could not be so discourteous. It wasn't that she disliked the Englishman, but the question of being forced into something she had no control over that troubled her. Independence had become a part of everyday life, and she had no wish to renounce that.

'I don't know.'

'I have promised your mother that before we leave America I will legally make you my ward. When she is gone, as your next of kin your responsibility rests entirely with me.'

'Are you really my only living relative?'

Henry frowned. It was one question he had anticipated, and since he now knew what Lydia had told Angelina about her grandparents—that they were dead and nothing more—he was capable of answering. He would rather not, because it meant having to lie. However, he didn't see how it could be evaded if he was to abide by his promise to Lydia.

'Your grandparents on your mother's side were killed in a carriage accident some years ago,' he told her in a gentle, straightforward voice, praying she would never discover the truth.

'My grandparents never wrote to her, and she would never speak of them. Do you know why?'

He nodded, silently cursing Jonathan Adams, Lydia's father. Anne, his wife and Henry's own aunt, had been a gentle woman, who had lived in awe of her husband, and had been unable to stand against him when he had coldly cut Lydia out of their lives.

'When your mother married your father and left England, Angelina, it was against your grandfather's wishes. He was a hard, unforgiving man and meant to punish her for disobeying him. He cut off all connection with her—and insisted that your grandmother did the same. You mother never forgave them.'

How true this was, Henry thought sadly. Lydia's lack of forgiveness was no temporary state of affairs. With great intensity she had insisted that there must be no connection between Angelina and her grandmother. Not wishing to distress her further, Henry had promised he would abide by her wishes.

Angelina sat on the top step of the veranda with her back propped against a wooden rail. 'Won't someone like me be a burden to you in England—a financial one?'

Henry was mildly amused at her words so innocently and frankly spoken. 'I can well afford it. It will be a pleasure. And you are far too lovely and independent to be a burden. You will learn to be a fine lady,' he told her, wanting to tell her not to change, that she was just perfect the way she was. But, if she was to live in the social world he inhabited, regretfully it was necessary.

'How should I address you? For me to call you "my Lord" every time I speak to you is too formal and quite ridiculous.'

'I couldn't agree more. Uncle Henry will be appropriate.'

She considered this for a moment and then nodded. 'Yes. Uncle Henry it is then.'

Angelina's new uncle had a warmth of manner that made

her feel as if she had known him a long time. His physical impression might be one of age, yet his twinkling eyes and willing smile were the epitome of eternal youth. Over the distance they smiled at each other, comfortable together, sharing a moment of accord on the veranda that seemed to bind them together.

'It is obvious to me that your education seems to have been taken care of, so we'll have no trouble in that quarter,' Henry remarked at length. 'Your pronunciation of the English language is excellent.'

'Thank you. I am also conversant in French, Latin and some Greek, too,' Angelina confessed proudly. 'Despite the everyday hardships of living in Ohio, my mother saw to that.'

Henry's admiration for her was growing all the time.

'Do you have a wife?' Angelina asked suddenly, with the natural curiosity of a child.

'No,' he answered, startled by the abruptness of her question, but not offended by it. 'I never found a woman I wanted to spend the rest of my life with—except, perhaps, one,' he said softly, his eyes clouding with memory, wondering how Angelina would feel if she knew that her beloved father had been accepted by her mother as a hasty second best.

'But isn't it the custom for gentlemen of your standing to marry to beget an heir?'

'I had no intention of adhering to custom by chaining myself to any woman I might only have a passing fancy for, in order to beget an heir. Besides, I have a perfectly acceptable heir in my nephew, Alex—my brother's son.'

Angelina's eyes became alert. 'Alex?'

'Alexander Henry Frederick Montgomery, the seventh Earl of Arlington and Lord Montgomery—which are just two of his titles. His friends call him Alex.'

Angelina's eyes widened in awe. 'Gracious me! What an awesome responsibility it must be to have so many names. Doesn't he feel weighted down by so many titles?'

'Not in the least. He was born to them and learned to accept and ignore them from an early age. One day he will become the sixth Duke of Mowbray—following my demise, you understand. His title as the seventh Earl of Arlington he inherited from his mother's family. The sixth earl died several years ago, and as the estate is unentailed he left it directly to Alex—with provision made for his mother, who was an only child. He made representations to the King that Alex be given the title of seventh Earl on his demise. You'll meet him when we get to England. He is the only son of my brother, who died when Alex was fifteen. Alex is now twenty-eight—and I swear that young man is the reason for my hair turning white,' he chuckled softly.

'Is he married?'

'Despite being one of the most eligible bachelors in England, I've all but despaired of ever seeing him suitably married.'

'Why? What's wrong with him?'

'Nothing. He hasn't got two heads or anything like that.' Henry chuckled aloud. 'It is his unequivocal wish to remain a bachelor and childless. I cannot hide the fact that he's an exacting man, who insists on the highest standards from all those he employs. However, he can be quite charming, when it suits him.'

'What does he do?' Angelina asked, already in awe of Alex Montgomery.

'Alex handles all my business and financial affairs—as well as his own. He has a brilliant mind and a head for figures that shames me. He drives himself hard, demanding too much of himself—and others. Ever since he took over he's increased all my holdings considerably. Now I'm in my dotage I'm perfectly content to sit back and let him handle everything. Oh, he consults me now and then, but business is not my forte.'

'And do you trust him?'

'Implicitly. Besides, my dear…' he chuckled softly, his grey eyes twinkling merrily '…if I didn't, I wouldn't dare tell him so.'

Angelina frowned. He sounds quite formidable. He's bound to resent me. How do you think he'll react?'

Henry grinned. 'He'll be outraged when he finds out I have made myself your guardian—but he'll soon get used to having you around. Besides, there's not a lot he can do about it.' He relaxed, regarding her warmly. 'Don't worry, my dear. You'll soon get used to Alex.'

Just two days after Henry Montgomery had come to Boston, Lydia slipped quietly away in her sleep.

Angelina's heart was heavy with sadness, but she didn't give in to her grief. Her mother had suffered greatly, and now she was at peace. Henry gave no outward sign to Angelina of his own private emotions, but his face was lined, his eyes dull with a deep sorrow.

It was difficult for Will to stand on the bustling quayside and watch Angelina board the ship. Her leaving would leave a huge hole in his heart.

Feeling quite forlorn, a hard lump of tears formed in Angelina's throat as she looked into Will's rheumy eyes. He looked lost and torn and old. Although it broke her heart to do so, she had decided to leave Mr Boone behind, in the hope that he would help console Will and that it would ease their parting. Will had carved her a wonderful likeness of Mr Boone out of ebony. It was packed in her trunk and she would cherish it always.

'Goodbye, Will. I'll never forget you, you know that. I promise I'll write and let you know what it's like in England.'

'You go and make your ma proud,' Will said, his voice hoarse with emotion, wondering where she would send her letters to when he had disappeared into the backwoods of North America. 'You're going to do all those things she talked about. You'll dazzle all those English gents—you see if you don't. Remember it's what your ma wanted. She told you that.'

'I do remember, Will, and I'll never forget. Ever.'

Will's eyes met those of Henry Montgomery in mutual concern. Unbeknown to Angelina, Will had told the Englishman what had happened to her on the night of the Shawnee massacre, and how he had rescued her. He hoped that, in knowing, the English duke would have a deeper understanding of his ward.

Henry had listened to all Will had said with a sense of horror. Will had told him that there was still something about that night Angelina refused to speak of. It was like an inner wound that was bleeding. The secret lurked in her gaze. Was it the shock of the massacre and her father's death that caused it— or something else? Whatever it was might be eased when she reached England. A new country, a new home—a new life.

Chapter Two

The sky was overcast as the carriage ventured north towards Mayfair. Angelina devoured the sights and sounds of what her mother had told her was the most exciting city in the world. On reaching Brook Street she gaped in awe when the door of one of the impressive houses was opened by a servant meticulously garbed in white wig, mulberry coat edged in gold and white breeches. His face was impassive as he stepped aside to let them enter.

'Welcome to Brook Street,' Henry said, smiling as he watched his ward's reaction.

Angelina was completely overwhelmed by the beauty and wealth of the house. Standing in the centre of the white marble floor she looked dazedly about her, wondering if she had not been brought to some royal palace by mistake. She wasn't to know that compared to Mowbray Park, Henry's home in Sussex, this house on Brook Street was considered to be of moderate proportions. Craning her neck and looking upward, she was almost dazzled by the huge chandelier suspended from the ceiling, dripping with hundreds of tiny crystal pieces.

A superior-looking man with a dignified bearing and dressed all in black stepped forward. 'Welcome back, your Grace. You are expected. I trust you had a pleasant crossing from America.'

'Yes, thank you, Bramwell. Is my nephew at home?'

The butler replied, 'No, your Grace. He's out of town for a few days, staying with Sir Nathan and his wife in Surrey.'

'I see.' Henry smiled at Angelina, who looked visibly relieved by the reprieve. 'Perhaps you would like to see your room and freshen up before dinner, my dear. Show Miss Hamilton to her room, will you, Bramwell.'

'Certainly, your Grace. The green room has been prepared. I'm certain it will meet with Miss Hamilton's approval. It's quiet and overlooks the garden,' he told Angelina, before leading her up the elegant staircase.

Entering a large room on the first floor, Angelina blinked at the extravagance and unaccustomed luxury. The walls were lined with mirrors and pictures depicting placid rural scenes, and the bed hangings were in the same pale green brocade embroidered with ivory silk as the windows.

'Oh, what a lovely room,' she gasped.

'I thought you'd like it.' Bramwell directed his gaze towards the dressing room when a fresh-faced young maid emerged, her arms full of linen. 'This is Miss Bates, Miss Hamilton. She has been appointed your personal maid.'

When Bramwell had departed Angelina smiled warmly at her maid, who bobbed a curtsy. Two or three years older than Angelina, she was quite pretty, small and rather plump, with the majority of her dark brown hair concealed beneath a modest white cap.

'I've never had a personal maid before,' Angelina confessed. 'What does it mean?' She saw surprise register on Miss Bates's face, which was replaced by an indulgent little smile. No doubt she had decided that, as she was from America, her new mistress's ignorance could be excused, that perhaps people over there weren't as civilised or refined as they were in England.

'Why—I see to all your personal needs—take care of your clothes—everything, really,' she explained cheerfully.

'Well, it seems you will have to teach me—and I have much

to learn. Where I come from, unless you are very rich, one doesn't have personal maids.'

Miss Bates seemed to be lost for words at this candid admission. 'I'm sure you'll soon get used to having me do things for you.'

'Perhaps, but I simply refuse to call you Miss Bates. What is your Christian name?'

'Pauline, miss.'

'Then since we are to spend a good deal of time together, I shall address you as Pauline,' she said, as two footmen entered with her trunk.

The following afternoon while her uncle was resting, and feeling hemmed in and restless at having to remain indoors because of the rain that continued to pour down, Angelina wandered through the house. Her uneducated eye was unable to place a value on the things she saw, but she was able to appreciate and admire the quality of the beautifully furnished rooms.

The library, with its highly polished floor and vividly coloured oriental carpets, was like an Aladdin's cave—a treasure trove of precious leatherbound tomes. It was a room which, to Angelina, encapsulated every culture and civilisation of the universe, where bookshelves stretched from floor to ceiling, broken only by a huge white marble fireplace and long windows. Happily she browsed along the shelves, looking for a book to suit her mood, eventually finding just what she was looking for.

Unaccustomed to being indoors for such a long period, she placed her books on the desk and went to the window, leaning her shoulder against the window frame, gazing in a somewhat disconsolate manner at the garden, glad to see it had stopped raining and envying the gardener pottering about among the flower beds. Unable to resist the temptation to join him, but not wishing to dirty her dainty slippers, she dashed to her room and donned an old pair of stout boots she had brought with her.

She entered the garden by the long French windows in the library, and spent half an hour chatting to the gardener and helping him debud some of the sodden roses—which Jarvis thought highly irregular considering who she was. Then the rain came down again and the wind rose with a vengeance, so she made a dash for the house. On entering the library she was unable to prevent the sudden gust that sent some loose papers blowing off the desk all over the place and a tiny figurine from crashing to the floor.

'You stupid, reckless little fool. Do you have to enter the house like a bloody whirlwind?' a voice thundered.

Angelina's face was a frozen mask. In her struggle to keep the door from blowing off its hinges, she hadn't seen the man sitting at the desk with damp, unruly locks of raven black hair tumbling wildly over his head. Scraping his chair back, he stood up and strode towards her, his face livid.

Like an animal on the defensive, Angelina's eyes narrowed and flashed. 'You are just about the rudest man I have ever come across and you have a foul mouth for such a well-bred gentleman—I assume you are Lord Montgomery.'

'Precisely, and I know who you are—Miss Hamilton.' He seemed to lose control of his expression momentarily as his gaze passed over her, from the top of her shining head to her boots, where it froze.

Angelina followed his gaze and saw her mud-caked boots dirtying the parquet flooring. Soil clung to the front of her skirt, resisting all her efforts to brush it away. Despairing, she groaned inwardly with frustration. For two days dressed like a lady, she had waited for the master of the house to appear, and what good had it done her? Having no intention of apologising for the way she looked, ignoring the irate nobleman, she bent down and eased off her boots, placing them by the door. She then further astounded his lordship by going down on her knees and beginning to pick up the pieces of the broken figurine.

'Leave it,' he snapped. 'The servants will clean it up.'

'I made the mess so I will do it. I don't wish to put anyone to any trouble.'

'I said leave it. The servants are here for your convenience as well as mine.' When she took no notice he reached out and grasped her arm, his fingers biting into her flesh. There was a loud crack as Angelina slapped his hand away. Momentarily startled, he drew back. 'Why—you hot-headed little savage,' he barked. 'What the hell are you trying to do?'

His scowl bore into her as Angelina rubbed her smarting hand. 'That will teach you not to touch me,' she snapped, hotly irate. 'It's your own fault. Keep your hands to yourself in future.'

Alex's lean cheeks flexed tensely and his grey eyes narrowed. 'Do you have any idea how exasperating you are?' he gritted. 'And do you have to appear looking like a labourer?'

'I'm not afraid of hard work,' she snapped testily.

'I imagine you're not, but you will find that here you will do things differently.'

The pieces gathered up, Angelina got to her stockinged feet and placed them on the desk. 'I'm sorry I broke it,' she said, unaware of the streak of mud on her cheek as she faced him squarely, two fiercely indomitable wills meeting head on and each refusing to step aside to allow the other to pass. His face was as cold and hard as the stone from which his fine house was built. 'I didn't mean to. I suppose it was valuable.'

'Priceless.'

'If I had some money of my own I would offer to pay for it, but I don't.' Angelina recognised authority when she saw it. Everything about this illustrious lord bespoke power, control and command. The hard set of his darkly handsome face did not suggest much tolerance or forgiveness. 'No doubt you have already made up your mind where to bury me?'

'Not yet. But I dare say I will.' His voice was of a rich, deep timbre. He watched as she flexed her arm. 'Is anything wrong?'

'You hurt my arm,' she said crossly, her dark eyes narrowing and accusing.

'I apologise for that—if you will apologise for appearing like a field hand.' He waited, his grey eyes penetrating.

'I suppose so,' was all Angelina was prepared to relent.

Dressed in snug-fitting, calf-coloured trousers tucked into highly polished tan boots, and a fine white lawn shirt open at the throat, his body well honed and muscular, Angelina could see there was something purposeful and inaccessible about Alex Montgomery, and those grey eyes, which penetrated her own, were as cold and hard as newly forged steel. There was no warmth in them, no humour to soften those granite features.

She sensed his amazement that she had the effrontery to face him as an equal. Clearly this wasn't what he'd expected—and certainly not what she'd intended. She knew better than to be rude to a man in his own house, but after suffering the indignity of being spoken to so rudely and manhandled, she had mentally drawn the battle lines and moved her guns into position. They looked at each other hard, suspicion and mistrust on both sides.

His expression became suddenly thoughtful and he inspected her upturned face as if something puzzled him.

'Do you always subject people to such close scrutiny when you meet them for the first time?' she asked directly. 'I am not used to being looked at like that and find it extremely disagreeable. Is there something wrong with my face that makes you examine it so thoroughly?'

'When I look at you I think unaccountably of fairies and imps and things, and have half a mind to demand whether you have bewitched Uncle Henry and my servants—according to my uncle, every one of them seems to be under your spell.'

'I will not argue the point, but I assure you, Lord Montgomery, that it is not my intention to disrupt your household.'

With a look that betrayed a mild degree of surprise, he nodded. 'Thank you. I respect your frankness.' Thrusting his hands into his pockets, he walked to the window, standing with his back to her while he gazed out. His body was tense, his shoulders squared. 'I hope the servants are looking after you,' he said at length.

Angelina was uncomfortable, but she was relieved to hear civility in his tone. 'Yes—thank you,' she replied, imitating his politeness. 'Everyone is being very kind.'

'And you like the house?'

'Very much. But then, who wouldn't?' she said, warm in her admiration. 'Have you spoken to Uncle Henry since you arrived home?'

He turned and looked at her. 'Briefly.'

'And did he tell you anything about me?'

Alex nodded. 'He told me that when your mother died he did the Christian thing by making you his ward and giving you a home. He assures me you are a charming, delightful and re-markably intelligent young woman who, for the short time he has known you, has made him extremely happy. In short, you are an absolute treasure.'

Angelina was stung by the irony of his words. 'But you don't believe him.'

'Not if the past few minutes are anything to go by. I am more astute than my uncle. I prefer to reserve judgment.'

Lifting her chin proudly, Angelina met his gaze, not with defiance but a quiet resolve. 'You don't want me here, do you, Lord Montgomery?'

'I love and hold my uncle in the highest esteem, Miss Hamilton. I may not be happy about what he did, but whether I like it or not you are here now and a member of this family. As such, that is how you will be treated and how you will behave.'

'I realise that my presence in your house is an inconve-nience, but taking everything into account, you must see that I have been more inconvenienced than you.'

'In which case, since we have no choice in the matter, the obvious solution is that we should both try to make the best of things and be cordial to each other. Don't you agree?'

'Yes. I have no wish to upset Uncle Henry,' she said.

Absently she tucked a stray lock of silky hair behind her ear that had dared escape her tight braid. The unconscious gesture caused Alex to study her properly for the first time, and he was amazed by what he saw. Her hair was the colour of rich mahogany with highlights of red and gold, making him think of harvest corn, chestnuts and autumn fires. Parted at the center, it was drawn back and woven together in one long thick braid that reached her waist. Accustomed to seeing women with neatly arranged curls and ringlets, he found this style unusual, but strangely attractive on this young woman. He had the absurd desire to reach out and set her hair free and let it spill about her shoulders, convinced it would glow with the glorious vibrancy of autumn leaves.

Her eyes, surrounded by thick, curling sooty lashes, were captivating. At first they looked so dark to be almost black, but on closer inspection they were seen to be not black at all, but the colour of two glorious purple velvet-soft pansies. Her skin was flushed with warmth like that of a ripe peach, and she had an enigmatic mouth, ripe and full of wonderful promise. The daffodil-yellow gown she wore revealed a female form that was faultless, slim and strong, with long legs and curves in all the right places. With angular cheekbones her face was alluring, interesting, and overall there was an innocence and vulnerability about her that would put a practised seducer like him beyond the realm of her experience.

'You are not at all what I expected.'

'What did you expect?' she retorted sharply. 'A creature from the wilds who is half-savage, with brown skin and feathers in her hair?'

Alex smiled tightly. Nathan had said something along those lines. 'Heaven forbid! I certainly didn't expect to find someone with an interest in fine literature.'

'Education has reached America, you know. We are civilised.'

'Looking as you do just now, Miss Hamilton, I would say you have some way to go before you reach that status,' he said with an ironic curl of his lips. 'However, it's apparent to me that you are extremely clever.'

Angelina's eyes narrowed. She could feel her ire returning. 'Something tells me that it is not my interest in fine literature that you speak of,' she said, her smile deliberately cold and ungracious. 'It is plain to me that you are displeased about something

Alex crossed to his desk and perched his hip on the edge, crossing his arms with a casualness that aggravated Angelina's temper still further. His imperturbable gaze studied her stormy eyes. 'Miss Hamilton, when I read my uncle's letter informing me he had gone to America, everything about you displeased me at the time,' he told her firmly.

Angelina's temper flared at this open affront. 'I thought it might. And I sense your displeasure has increased since. Is it so very strange for people to look after relatives who find themselves destitute?'

'It is, when the parties concerned live on opposite sides of the world and there has been no contact between them for some time. I find it strange that after all these years, when not a word or a letter has passed between them, your mother should suddenly write to my uncle and beg him to make you his ward.'

'You're mistaken, Lord Montgomery,' Angelina answered, stung to the quick by his remark about her mother. 'My mother never begged for anything in her life. She wrote to Uncle Henry because he was her next of kin and she had no one else to turn to.'

Alex knew this not to be the case, but, having been warned by his uncle of the need for secrecy relating to this young woman's grandmother, he respected the request for silence.

'If you must know, I opposed it,' Angelina went on. 'I had no wish to leave America, but it was my mother's wish.'

'A woman with colossal aspirations where her daughter is concerned,' Alex said coldly. 'Do not think me ignorant of your situation in Boston, Miss Hamilton, and that your mother sent you to my uncle as a poor relation, seeking to save you from poverty.'

Alex caught the flare of anger his words about her mother brought to her face, but he also saw something that resembled pain and hurt in the depths of her eyes. For a split second her young face looked defenceless and exposed, and already he was beginning to regret his unjustifiable and unpardonable attack.

His cutting remark directed at her mother erupted inside Angelina like a volcano and she longed to lash out at him. Feeling the nightmare of the Indian attack closing around her again, she could see her mother's face as she lay on the ground after the knife had ripped into her, digging deep, and the rich, proud colour of her blood as it had poured from her wound to be soaked up by the dry earth.

'You cold-hearted, overbearing, arrogant beast. How dare you? You insult my mother, and I will not allow anyone to besmirch her memory. She was the kindest, gentlest of women ever to draw breath, but that is something a man as conceited and disgustingly rude as yourself would never understand.' Furiously she turned and marched to the door, her fists clenched by her sides.

For a split second a flicker of amused respect replaced Alex's anger as he gazed after the young American girl. 'Have you nothing else to say?'

She turned and glowered at him, feeling tears prick the backs of her eyes. Furiously she blinked them away. If she broke down and cried, he would have the mastery over her. She would not grant him that. 'Not to you. Might I suggest that in future you mind your own business and I will mind mine.'

Alex's black brows snapped together and his eyes narrowed, but his voice was carefully controlled when he spoke. 'You may suggest anything you like, but since you have raised the matter, you ought to know that I have full control over all my uncle's affairs.'

His words were insulting and their meaning cut Angelina like a knife. 'His business affairs, not his personal affairs,' Angelina corrected acidly. She should have withered beneath his icy glare, but she was too enraged to be intimidated by him. 'I should tell you that I have a streak to my nature that fiercely rebels against being ordered what to do.'

'I have a formidable temper myself,' he told her with icy calm.

'I do not come under the category of property, Lord Montgomery, and I am not asking you for anything. In the eyes of the law Uncle Henry is my legal guardian, and if you wish to challenge that then you are free to do so.'

'I have no intention of doing any such thing.' His words were like a whiplash, his eyes glacial. 'My uncle has taken you in and does not need to justify his actions to me or anyone else. What matters is that you are in this house under his guardianship and a member of this family, and because I care a great deal for his happiness, I will do nothing about it. But in time I suspect you will show your true colours without any help from me—so I advise you to take care, unless you want to be shipped back to America, lock, stock and barrel.'

Angelina glared at him, two bright spots of colour burning on her cheeks. She refused to look away, but there was little she could say in her defence. This man had already made up his mind about her, and anything she might say would be futile. He was convinced she was a clever, scheming opportunist out to rid his uncle of his last shilling, and nothing she said was going to change his mind.

'Have you nothing to say for yourself?'

'What's the point? There is no argument against a closed mind. You made up your mind about me before I set foot on English soil.'

Alex contemplated her with a half-smile. 'It may surprise you to learn that before I met you I was prepared to give you the benefit of the doubt.'

'And now?'

'That still applies. You accuse me of making up my mind about you before I met you. I accuse you of doing likewise. You also summed up your opinion of me,' Alex stated. 'From the moment you entered this house, no doubt you have listened to gossip from below stairs, but whatever you have heard, forget it. You don't know me.'

Angelina could not look away from him—in fact, unconsciously her feet took her slowly back to where he still perched on the edge of the desk, her rebellious eyes holding his. She stood close, her face on a level with his, her skirts brushing his tan boots.

'You're wrong. I may only have been in your presence a few minutes,' she countered, 'but I have made a very accurate assessment of your character.'

'Do you normally form an opinion of a person after so short a time?' he asked, trying to ignore the delectable attributes that stood just within his easy reach. Instantly, his whole body began to hum an ardent, familiar song that clashed with what he should be feeling.

'In your case it was not difficult,' she provided. 'You are rude, overbearing and dictatorial, and you have the manners of a barbarian.'

Alex arched his brows, faint amusement and a stirring of respect in the icy depths of his eyes. 'That bad?'

'Worse. You are cold and heartless and I cannot abide your superior male attitude—your insufferable arrogance and conceit.'

He looked at her with condescending amusement that in time she would come to detest. 'And you, madam, with a tongue on you that would put a viper to shame, can hardly be called a paragon of perfection.'

'Go to hell,' she blazed, which was most uncharacteristic of her. But at that moment she was sorely tempted to fling more than abuse at Alex Montgomery and inflict physical damage. No doubt this infuriating man was already telling himself that she was showing her 'true colours'. She cast a look of pure loathing at him, noting that her words had brought a satisfied smile to his arrogant mouth.

His dark brows rose and he gave her a lofty, superior look. 'I shall, but I shall go in my own way and in my own good time.'

'It cannot be too soon for me.'

Afraid that she was going to crack completely and make a fool of herself, Angelina raised her chin and turned. With all the dignity she could muster she picked up her boots and left the room, her slender hips swaying graciously. She didn't see the admiring light in Alex's eyes, or the indefinable smile lurking at the corner of his lips as he observed her less than dignified progress through the hall, for as she stormed towards the stairs she almost knocked over an elderly manservant who was carrying a silver platter.

The poor man halted in his progress and turned and watched her go halfway up the stairs, wondering what could have happened to wipe away her sweet expression and replace it with one of black thunder. His answer came when he glanced through the open door into the library and saw Lord Montgomery still perched on the edge of the desk. Shaking his head, he chuckled. His lordship was home, which explained everything.

Alex couldn't think of anyone, male or female, who would have stood up to him the way Angelina had just done, verbally attack him and walk away as regal as any queen. The girl had spirit, a fiery spirit that challenged him. Her arrogance was tantamount to disrespect, yet in spite of himself he admired her style. Nor was she afraid of him. That was the intriguing part about her.

He allowed himself to remember her face, an alluring face, captivating and expressive, he decided. Her chin was small and round, with an adorable, tiny little cleft in the centre. But it was her eyes he remembered most—enormous, liquid bright—the kind of eyes a man wanted to see looking up at him when he was about to make love.

Idly he picked up the books she had selected to read and left behind. On opening them he stared, so taken aback that he almost laughed out loud. Alex had a familiarity with the ways of the female sex, but nothing had prepared him for this.

Ornithology! Horses!

When all the women of his acquaintance read romantic poetry and cheap, insipid novelettes that had a deleterious effect on their impressionable minds, Angelina Hamilton preferred reading about birds and horses. He chuckled, shaking his head slowly in disbelief. The girl was a phenomenon.

Setting his jaw, with purposeful strides he left the library and climbed the stairs to her room, rapping sharply on the door.

Angelina opened it herself, glowering when she saw who it was.

'Well? What do you want?' she snapped, fully prepared for another angry confrontation. 'Have you come to tell me that the war is over and I've won?'

'No. In view of my former rudeness, I've come to make amends,' he told her, standing in the doorway in a misleading, indolent manner.

Angelina eyed him warily. 'Have you? You seem unsure.'

Alex raised his eyebrows quizzically. Without being invited to do so he stepped past her, as bold as may be, his eyes settling like a winter chill on her terrified maid. 'Leave us.'

Pauline looked nervously at Angelina, who nodded. 'It's all right, Pauline. I don't think Lord Montgomery intends to ravish me,' she said, her voice dripping sarcasm, 'since the only emotion I seem to rouse in him is a desire to strangle me. Not wishing to be hanged for my murder, I think we can safely assume he will keep his hands to himself.'

Alex's face was set in an almost smiling challenge. 'Don't be so certain. I am sorely tempted. I could break you in half like a twig if I so wished and to hell with the consequences.'

'Lord Montgomery,' Angelina retorted sharply, dark eyes locking on grey ones, 'if you plan another battle, you can leave right this minute.'

'Nothing so dramatic—merely a mild skirmish.'

Pauline gaped, amazed at her mistress's courage. No one ever spoke to Lord Montgomery in that tone. Bobbing a hurried curtsy she scuttled out.

'Well?' said Angelina, feeling strangely threatened now the closed door separated her from Pauline.

'You left your books,' he said, holding them out to her.

Disarmed, she was completely taken aback. 'Oh! Thank you,' Taking them from him, she placed them on a chair. 'Why did you dismiss Pauline?'

'I do not like my conversations being listened to by servants.'

'And are we going to have a conversation, Lord Montgomery? Do you mean to tell me that you sought me out in my room for a reason other than to bring me the books I selected from the library—which I could have collected myself?'

'Miss Hamilton, in common agreement, can we not strive to portray ourselves as being both gracious and mannerly for our uncle's sake?'

'A truce, you mean?'

'Something like that.'

At first she seemed to consider his offer, but then her expression changed and she was on the defensive. 'No. There will be no concessions. In the first place, I don't like you.'

Alex arched his eyebrows at her frank admission. 'And the second?'

'Until I have an apology from you.'

'An apology? What are you talking about?' he asked with infuriating calm.

'You insulted and degraded my mother. I cannot let it pass. If I were a man, I'd demand satisfaction and call you out. Believe me, I'm sorely tempted to do that anyway, but since your demise would cause Uncle Henry extreme distress, I suppose I shall just have to make do with an apology.'

Alex looked at her with a mixture of amusement and disbelief. The chit truly was incredible. 'You? Shoot me?'

'Yes. And I never miss my target.'

'Then, faced with determination such as this, you leave me with little choice. Very well. I apologise. It was wrong of me to say what I did.'

Angelina was astonished. She hadn't expected it would be that easy to extricate an apology from him. 'You apologise?'

'Of course. And consider yourself fortunate. Apologies don't come easily to me.'

'I gathered that.'

'You accept it, then?'

'Providing it isn't lukewarm and you mean it, I will,' Angelina replied stonily.

'Thank you.'

'Now you may leave,' she told him firmly, her smile deliberately cold and ungracious.

Alex calmly ignored her and looked about him for a moment, his eyes caught by Will's skilful carving of Mr Boone, which Angelina had placed on a table beside the bed. Every night since leaving Boston it was the last thing she looked at, and as she closed her eyes and went to sleep it made her feel less wretched and alone. With genuine interest Alex moved towards it, looking at it with admiration and the eye of a connoisseur.

'This is a fine, interesting piece of craftsmanship—lovingly carved. Yours, I presume?' he asked, looking at her.

'Of course it's mine,' she snapped, annoyed because he showed no inclination to leave. 'I haven't stolen it, if that's what you mean.'

'That was not what I meant. I was asking you if the dog was yours—a pet, perhaps.'

Angelina felt foolish for having misunderstood his meaning. 'Yes. A very dear friend of mine carved his likeness. He carves animals and birds and sells them to make a living—along with his beaver pelts,' she explained, captivated by Lord Montgomery's strong, lean fingers as they caressed the wooden object. 'He presented me with it before I left Boston.'

'Do you miss him?'

'Who?'

'Your friend.'

'Why—yes. Very much.'

'What was the name of your friend?'

'Will. Will Casper.'

'And your dog?'

'Mr Boone.'

A lazy smile spread over his face, which seemed softer now. 'So named after Daniel Boone, the intrepid pioneer.'

Angelina was pleasantly surprised to learn that he knew something of America's history. 'Yes. You've heard of him.'

Alex nodded. 'I'm a businessman. I make a point of keeping

abreast of world news. It proves advantageous where investments are concerned. And did your dog live up to his namesake?'

'Does. He's a brave little thing with a heart as big as a lion.'

'Is?' Alex's eyebrows snapped together as a sudden, decidedly
unpleasant thought occurred to him. 'You are not going to tell
me you brought him with you—that the animal is here, in this
house?'

Alex looked so horrified at the prospect of Mr Boone
capering through his stately rooms that Angelina's composure
slipped a notch closer to laughter. She bit her lower lip to still
the trembling as she caught his eyes. 'You needn't glower in
that ferocious fashion, my lord. You will be relieved when I tell
you that I left him in Boston with Will.'

His relief was evident. 'Thank the Lord for that. The last
thing I need right now is a dog disrupting the routine of things.'

Angelina made a pretence of looking offended. 'I will
have you know that Mr Boone is extremely well behaved and
never disgraces himself. Have you an aversion to dogs, Lord
Montgomery?'

'I keep several of my own at Arlington. But they are used
for hunting and well disciplined by their handlers. They are also
kept outside in kennels where they belong.'

'Yes, I expect they are,' Angelina replied, with a cheeky impudence that Alex found utterly exhilarating. The ghost of a
smile flickered across his face as his eyes locked on to hers in
silent, amused communication, and he was quite entranced by
the idea of sharing her humour.

He walked towards the fire where he stood, hands behind
his back, staring down at the glowing heat. 'How long did you
live in Boston?'

'About two years. We left Ohio when the Shawnee raided
our settlement. They—they killed everyone—including my
father,' she told him softly, 'and wounding my mother.'

Alex moved closer, looking down into the sensitive face
before him, but, unable to meet his gaze, she lowered her head.

'And you?' he asked, placing a finger gently under her chin

and tipping her face up to his, his eyes searching, probing, seeing something flicker in those dark, appealing depths: a secret grief, perhaps.

'As you can see, I was more fortunate. I am alive and I'm grateful.'

Alex saw her eyes register an anguish and horror he couldn't begin to comprehend, and observed the gallant struggle she made to bring herself under control.

There was silence, inhabited by the living presence of the fire. In spite of herself Angelina found her eyes captured and held by Lord Montgomery's silver gaze. Then, aware of Lord Montgomery's finger still poised beneath her chin, she suddenly recollected herself and recoiled with an instinctive fear that he might get too close.

'Lord Montgomery,' she said, her voice tight, 'I have known you long enough to realise that you didn't consider your manner towards me earlier as warranting an apology. Will you please come to the point and tell me the real reason for coming to my room? I am not so dim-witted as to believe it was your interest in my dog or my life before coming to England. I may have accepted your apology, but it doesn't change anything, does it? You still don't approve of me and think I'm out to hurt your uncle in some way.'

His eyes became as hard as granite. 'Contrary to what you may think, I sought you out because I could see that some form of atonement for my earlier behaviour was in order. However, since you are determined to harp on about it, I will remind you I am concerned about Uncle Henry's happiness and well being. As you will know, having spent the past few weeks in his company, he does not always enjoy the best of health.'

'That I do know, having seen how he is often plagued with rheumatic pains.'

'Correct. So naturally I was concerned when I returned to London after an absence of several weeks in the country and discovered he'd taken off for America without discussing the matter with me first.'

'I cannot for the life of me see why he should. Your uncle is of an age to act without your permission.'

As he rested his hands on his hips and looking down into her stormy eyes, Alex's own were so cold that Angelina was sure they could annihilate a man.

'My uncle is the finest, most generous man I have ever known, Miss Hamilton. What my opinions are concerning you has no bearing on the case, but because he and your mother were once close, and, as you correctly pointed out earlier, he is your next of kin, he will take his responsibilities where you are concerned seriously. If you hurt him in any way, I will personally make your life hell. Do you understand me?'

The look that passed between them crackled with hidden fire. Just for a moment Alex saw something savage and raw stir in the depths of Angelina's eyes, before they blazed with outrage.

'Perfectly,' she replied. With her fists clenched and her chin raised, she faced Alex like a raging hurricane, while he took a step back before the onslaught of her fury. 'Allow me to tell you a little about my background, Lord Montgomery. In Boston I was living with my mother in a two-roomed shack. Everything I owned I sold to pay for the doctor and her medicine. We had no money and the food we ate I provided. I do all manner of things a young lady ought not to do. I shoot, I fish, and I skin and gut whatever I kill. I dare say the properly reared young ladies of your acquaintance would be horrified and fall into a swoon at such behaviour and liken me to the savage you obviously think I am. I may seem gauche to you and lacking in social graces, but I am not ashamed of the way we lived.

'When your uncle came to Boston he was courtesy and kindness itself—and I give you my word that I shall not abuse his kindness. When my mother died it was a great comfort to me having him there. In the short time we have been together I have come to love him dearly and would sooner end my life than cause him pain. Despite what you believe, I haven't asked him for anything and I do not expect anything. I am simply grateful for a roof over my head wherever that happens to be. For this and his support at a time when I had nothing, I owe him much—much more than I can repay. Your uncle knows this and now you know it too, so if it's not a problem for him it needn't be a problem for you.'

Alex stared at the proud, tempestuous young woman in silent, icy composure. Her words reverberated round the room, ricocheting off the walls and hitting him with all the brutal impact of a battering ram, but it failed to pierce the armour of his wrath and not a flicker of emotion registered on his impassive features.

'That, Miss Hamilton, was quite an outburst. Have you finished?'

Pausing to take an infuriated breath, Angelina finally said, 'Far from it. You may have been born with blue blood in your veins and all the advantages that come with it, but you have a lot to learn. It isn't where a person comes from that matters. It's what a person is that counts. You are being vindictive without just cause, but if you want to carry on hating me then please do so. It does not matter one jot to me.'

Their minds and their eyes clashed in a battle of wills.

'I do not hate you.'

'No? Well, I hate you,' she told him, glaring at him wrathfully.

'I know you do,' he replied quietly. Not only had he heard, but also he sensed it. Cool and remote, Alex studied her for a moment, as though trying to discern something, and then crossed towards the door and went out.

Angelina stood looking blindly at the closed door for a long time, her heart palpitating with a raging fury. A whole array of confusing emotions washed over her—anger, humiliation, and a piercing, agonizing loneliness she had not felt since she was fifteen years old in Ohio.

Chapter Three

Henry and Alex were partaking of a glass of wine while they waited for Angelina to join them. Whenever Henry looked at his nephew, he was overwhelmed with pride.

At best, Alex was a fiercely private man, guarded and solitary, accountable to no one. At worst, he was a man with a wide streak of ruthlessness and an iron control that was almost chilling. To those who knew him he was clever, with an almost mystical ability to see what motivated others. To his business partners it was a gift beyond value, because it provided insight into the guarded ambitions of his adversaries. He could be cold, calculating and unemotional, which was how his rivals saw him.

'Angelina's a lovely young thing, don't you agree, Alex?'

Alex's look darkened. 'Lovely? She's certainly out of the ordinary. The girl's a hoyden. Good Lord, Uncle, what can you be thinking of? I've never seen you so taken with anyone as you are with this American girl.'

'You're quite right, but then I've never had a ward before, and so far I'm thoroughly enjoying the experience. Angelina's a delight. She's a thoroughly charming and engaging young woman with a remarkable intelligence. In the short time I've known her, I vow she's lopped ten years off my life.'

Alex's reply was a sardonic lift of his dark brows. 'You may find her charming, Uncle, but it is not the kind that passes for charm in the ladies of my acquaintance. Miss Hamilton's charm is more sinister and elusive than that. It is the kind that weaves spells and puts curses on people.'

An inexplicable smile traced its way across Henry's face. 'If that be the case, then take care she doesn't put a spell on you, dear boy.'

'I'm immune,' Alex said, bestowing the kind of lazy smile on his uncle that turned female hearts to water. 'Whatever she is, you're going to have your hands full.'

'Try and be more understanding towards her, Alex. Until she marries I am committed to her—and, as you know, I am not a man to shirk my duty. I've told you everything that I know of what happened to her in America—and the reasons why her grandmother's existence must be kept from her, so you will bear with her, won't you? I know how difficult you can be.'

Alex gave him a narrow look, deflecting his uncle's question by answering it with another. 'Did you tell her about me—listing all my transgressions?'

Henry chuckled, encouraged by his nephew's lack of argument. 'I did. I considered it wise to have her well prepared in every aspect of what her life would be like in England.'

'And?'

'When I told her I had all but despaired of seeing you suitably married, she asked me—with all the candid innocence of her youth—what was wrong with you.'

'Really.' Alex gave his uncle a mildly sardonic look. 'Evidently she regarded me as being way past the age of eligibility for marriage at twenty-eight.'

'No. I think she probably thought you were some fire-breathing monster with two horns and a tail. And when I told her you dealt with practically all my business affairs—'

'Let me guess,' Alex interrupted drolly. 'Did she by any chance ask if you trusted me?'

'She did.'

'I see,' he said drily, swearing that he'd not be bested by the dark-eyed witch.

'So you will try to curb your temper when you are together and be gentle with her, won't you?' Henry asked, casting his nephew an anxious look of appeal.

Alex hesitated for an endless moment and then nodded, a reluctant smile lurking at the corners of his mouth. 'Since I have no intention of laying a finger on her or being in her company for longer than I have to, I assure you, Uncle, that she will be perfectly safe from me. However, I feel I should warn you that I have already had a run-in with your ward; if that encounter is anything to go by, I cannot promise to be charm and graciousness personified where she is concerned. We may very well need a referee to keep us from murdering each other—which is where you will come in.'

Angelina swept into the dining room, intending to make a determined effort to be pleasant and agreeable to Lord Montgomery for Uncle Henry's sake. A chandelier suspended above the table filled the room with flickering light, reflecting on the large, ornate silver pieces set on the mahogany sideboard, next to where the two gentlemen stood drinking wine.

Breaking off his discussion with Alex, Henry placed his glass on the sideboard and came to meet her, his eyes twinkling in admiration. 'You look lovely, Angelina,' he said, taking her hand and drawing her towards his nephew. 'Alex tells me the two of you have already met.'

'Yes—and as you can see, Uncle...' she smiled with a hint of mischief dancing in her eyes '...I have survived the encounter without coming to grief.'

Henry lifted a brow to Angelina in a silent salute and smiled.

Angelina met Lord Montgomery's sardonically mocking gaze. With his eyes as intense as a hunting falcon's locked on hers, he moved forward, bowing his head with a studied degree of politeness, which to Angelina was a masterpiece of gracious arrogance.

Alex looked down at the tempestuous young woman in her

lilac gown. Her face, which arrested and compelled his eyes, was both delicate and vibrant, and her large amethyst eyes still stormy.

'Miss Hamilton was looking for something to read,' Alex told his uncle without taking his eyes from hers.

'Then I hope you found something to your liking, Angelina.'

'How could I not? There were so many interesting books to choose from. I had absolutely no idea that so much knowledge could exist in one place.'

'Alex must take the credit for that.'

'Yes, I thought he might,' she replied ironically.

Handing Angelina a glass of wine, Alex's lips curled with a hint of a smile. 'Miss Hamilton selected two illustrated editions—one on birds and the other on horses. Perhaps you prefer looking at pictures to reading, Miss Hamilton.'

Angelina's eyes narrowed when she took his meaning and bristled at the intended slight. 'I don't just look at the pictures, Lord Montgomery. Contrary to what you might think, I am not illiterate.'

Henry chuckled. 'Don't underestimate Angelina's intelligence, Alex. She reads anything you care to name and is conversant in French, Greek and Latin.'

'Perhaps if I had chosen Voltaire or Socrates you would have been more impressed. Usually I read for enlightenment, for knowledge, but yesterday I fancied something light. I cannot see why you should pour scorn on my choice of reading. It just so happens that I like birds and horses.'

'You speak French *and* Greek?' Alex asked incredulously, with surprise and doubt.

'You seem surprised,' said Angelina.

'I confess that I am. There are few ladies of my acquaintance who are familiar with the classics—and I am hard pressed to think of any one of them who is conversant in any language other than their own native English, and perhaps a smattering of French.'

Now it was Angelina's turn to be surprised. 'Then I can only assume that your experience with the female sex is somewhat limited, Lord Montgomery.'

A gleam of suppressed laughter lit Alex's eyes, and Angelina could only assume, correctly, that her remark about his inexperience with women had not been taken in the way she had intended.

'Angelina also plays an excellent game of chess,' Henry championed, giving Angelina a conspiratorial wink to remind her of all those times they had played together on board ship, when she had more often than not finished the victor. 'She can swim like a fish, outshoot most men, and handle a horse better than any female I've ever seen.'

Alex arched a sleek black brow in mock amusement when his gaze met Angelina's. 'I'm impressed! And to add to all these admirable attributes the cut and thrust of her tongue is sharper and deadlier than any rapier,' he drawled.

'I'm glad you've noticed,' Angelina replied with an impudent smile and a delicate lift to her brows, taking a sip of her wine.

Alex lost the battle to suppress his smile. The girl had spirit, he had to give her that. 'As you can see, Uncle, Miss Hamilton's opinion of me is far from favourable. Earlier she accused me of being rude, overbearing, dictatorial—and she told me that I have the manners of a barbarian.'

'And I fear I have to agree with her.'

'Really, Uncle! Where's your loyalty?' Alex demanded with mock severity.

'Forgive me, Alex. But that's a difficult dilemma.'

'I can't see why it should be.'

'I find my loyalties torn asunder. You see, they lie with you both. You are both family. Angelina is my ward—my cousin's daughter—and you are my nephew. Surely you can understand the pressure I am under.'

'Lord Montgomery is the other half of your family, Uncle Henry. Not mine,' Angelina pointed out forcefully.

'Noted for our obstinacy,' retorted Alex.

'Much good may it do you, my lord. I am no less obstinate, I assure you.' The smile Angelina turned on Henry was full of sweetness. 'It's a pity one can't be more selective with one's family as one can be with one's friends, don't you think?'

'I couldn't agree more, my dear. But I am going to ask you both to lower your swords as a favour to me—at least until after dinner so that we can do justice to Mrs Price's excellent cooking. It wouldn't do for all three of us to end up with indigestion, now, would it? However, I grant Alex can be a touch overbearing at times, Angelina.'

Angelina raised a sceptical brow, tempted to say that Lord Montgomery was a complete and total ass, but instead she said, 'Only a touch, Uncle Henry?'

'Well, perhaps a little more than a touch.'

Angelina caught Lord Montgomery's silver gaze that seemed to slice the air between them, warning her not to overstep the mark. She met his gaze calmly, with a defiant lift of her chin. 'And Lord Montgomery has no need of a sword, Uncle. He can accomplish as much with his eyes as he can with the point of a sword. I swear he could slay a man at twenty paces.'

'And you, my dear, have the unique distinction of putting his back up.'

Henry smiled indulgently and pulled out a chair for her at the table. Alex would sit opposite her and he would sit at the end—to act as referee if they were to continue sparring with each other. The air crackled and sparked between his nephew and his ward, and their looks and conversation were like daggers being hurled back and forth. It was better than he could have hoped for.

'But you must forgive Alex,' he continued. 'The ladies of his acquaintance are usually more languishing. He can be quite charming.'

Angelina favoured Lord Montgomery with a look of pure mockery as he took his seat across from her. 'Is that so?'

'Most ladies do find me charming and pleasant—and some actually enjoy my company.'

'And no doubt live to regret it,' she bit back.

With a mixture of languor and self-assurance, Alex started to relax and lounged back in his chair, absently fingering the stem of his wineglass as his gaze swept over her in an appraising, contemplative way.

His instinct detected untapped depths of passion in the alluring young woman across from him that sent silent signals instantly recognisable to a lusty, hot-blooded male like himself. The impact of these signals brought a smouldering glow to his eyes. So much innocence excited him, made him imagine those pleasures and sensations Miss Hamilton could never have experienced being aroused by him. The lazy, dazzling smile he bestowed on her transformed his face.

Angelina found herself staring at him, momentarily captivated by it, unaware of the lascivious thoughts that had induced it. It was the most wonderful smile she had ever seen and full of provocative charm. Oh, yes, she thought, feeling her heart do a little somersault, when he smiled like that and spoke in a soft-as-honey voice and looked at a woman from under those drooping lids, he could make a feral cat lie down and purr.

Angelina found hot colour washing her cheeks under his close scrutiny and she hated herself for that betrayal. Alex saw it and smiled infuriatingly. His strategy had worked. Little Angelina Hamilton was just like all the rest of her sex when it came to the matter of seduction. It would not be too difficult a task demolishing her pride and cold resentment and have her melting with desire in his arms, and the idea of conquering her appealed to his sardonic sense of humour—if that was what he had a mind to do, for he must remember that, for him, she was untouchable, being his uncle's ward.

'I'm sorry. Do I unsettle you, Miss Hamilton?' he asked with a slight lift to his sleek eyebrows.

'You don't unsettle me in the least.'

'Come now, you're blushing,' he taunted gently, being well schooled in the way women's minds worked.

'I am not.' Her unease was growing by the second, but she tried not to show it, attempting to maintain a façade of uninterest and indifference.

'Yes, you are. Your cheeks are as pink as those roses,' he

said, indicating the lovely bowl of deep blush-coloured roses on the table between them.

'Good gracious.' Angelina laughed. 'If that's the kind of melodramatic rubbish you engage in with the ladies of your acquaintance, I'm surprised they don't vomit.'

'I assure you they don't.'

'No—well—perhaps if they're all vacuous peahens unable to see further than your impeccable credentials, they wouldn't, would they?'

Alex was so astounded by her reply that he almost threw back his head and burst out laughing. 'No,' he replied his smile widening. 'They wouldn't dare. Now,' he said when a footman came in carrying platters of food, 'shall we accede to our uncle's request by lowering our weapons and agree to a truce while we eat?'

'Very well—but only while we eat,' she agreed. 'I've never tasted such wonderful food as Mrs Price turns out and have no intention of letting you spoil it. However,' she murmured, looking at him from beneath the thick fringe of her lashes, 'my sword may be sheathed, Lord Montgomery, but please remember that it is still there and every bit as sharp and lethal.'

Alex's eyes narrowed. 'I do not doubt that for one moment,' he replied—and, he thought with wry amusement, it will make the play between us all the more exciting.

Angelina bestowed a smile on him that was utterly devastating, and she was certain she glimpsed approval lurking in those inscrutable silver eyes.

A footman under the stern eye of Bramwell served the delicious meal. Angelina did full justice to the food and tried not to feel intimidated by Lord Montgomery when his eyes settled on her now and then, his lids hooded like those of a hawk. Just the cold pupils peered out from his closed face, but throughout the meal she could feel him tugging at her from across the table. It really was most unsettling.

From his vantage point at the head of the table Henry was more observant about what was passing between the two of them than either of them realised. He carefully noted the absorbed way Alex watched Angelina as she ate, recognising something in his expression that he hadn't seen in a long time, and he was utterly delighted and encouraged by it.

'You had a large complement of post while you were away, Uncle,' Alex commented while they waited for dessert to be served, tearing his gaze away from the tantalising creature sitting opposite. 'Was there anything of importance?'

'No, just the usual—most of it from Mowbray Park. Oh, and I've received a letter from Robert Boothroyd—Sir Robert is a very close friend of mine, Angelina, who resides in Cornwall,' he explained. 'As you know, Alex, I had planned to visit him before I went to America, but on receiving Lydia's letter it had to be postponed.'

Alex sensed his hesitation and threw him a questioning look. 'Is something wrong?'

'Robert has not been at all well. It's his heart, I'm afraid. He doesn't enjoy good health at the best of times, but this latest setback is causing both him and his family considerable concern. He has asked if I will go to Cornwall as soon as I am able—but of course I shall write and tell him it's impossible for me to leave London at this time. I couldn't possibly leave Angelina when she's only just arrived in England.'

'She could go and stay with Nathan and Verity at Hanover Square—when Verity returns from Surrey, that is. Failing that, she could go and stay with Aunt Patience at Richmond,' Alex suggested. 'Which she should do, anyway. It's most improper for her to be living alone in a house with two unmarried gentlemen.'

'Yes, I have considered that, but both Verity and Patience lead a hectic social life and Angelina would inevitably become drawn in. I would like to give her time to adjust—to settle into her new life gradually. I consider it too soon for her to go out into society just yet.'

Henry was not at all in agreement with Alex's solution, for he had no intention of removing Angelina from his nephew's immediate sphere. Before Lydia had died, he had promised her he would make the best possible match for her daughter, and he had known immediately who that would be. Angelina and Alex had much in common, both being wilful and spirited. Tragedy had touched them both at fifteen years old, and it was his hope that together they might find solace.

However, anyone listening to his ward and his nephew in verbal combat would say they were too much alike to ever come to a complete and harmonious understanding of one another. But Henry thought otherwise and was determined to bring them together. To achieve this it was important they spend some time alone away from London, and he had contrived for them to do just that.

'Of course,' he went on casually, taking a sip of his wine and deliberately avoiding his nephew's eyes and looking down at his dish as he began spooning his dessert, 'I suppose she could accompany you when you go to Arlington next week. And the country air will do her good.'

Alex's arm froze midway between his dish and his mouth as he was about to eat his strawberry soufflé. He stared at Henry as if he'd taken leave of his senses, returning the spoon to the dish with a resounding clatter. 'You are not seriously suggesting—'

'I couldn't possibly,' Angelina objected in growing alarm, appalled at what her uncle suggested.

'What in God's name would I do with Miss Hamilton at Arlington? Really, Uncle, it's quite impossible.'

'I don't see why.'

'I do. It's out of the question. Besides, it would be most improper for her to stay with me without a chaperon.'

Angelina glared at him. 'Don't worry, Lord Montgomery. The prospect is as distasteful to me as it is to you.' Looking with concern at Henry's downcast face, she hated being the reason that prevented him visiting his sick friend. 'But, Uncle Henry, of course you must go to Cornwall. Perhaps I could accompany you?' she asked hopefully, finding the prospect of being alone with his nephew absolutely horrifying.

'Thank you, my dear,' Henry replied with a smile, reaching out and patting her hand in a fond gesture. 'But I won't hear of it.'

Alex was suddenly contrite, knowing how fond his uncle was of Robert Boothroyd. 'I'm sorry, Uncle. Of course you must go. Miss Hamilton will accompany me to Arlington. To still the gossip, I shall ask Aunt Patience to come and stay. With her and a house full of servants, that should be more than ample to uphold the proprieties.'

'To protect me, you mean,' Angelina couldn't help retorting.

Having suddenly lost his appetite, Alex threw his napkin on to the table. He scowled darkly across the table at her and their eyes met and held, irresistible force colliding with immovable object. 'Let me assure you that you do not need protecting from me,' he said with scathing contempt. 'By nature I am not a violent man, but if you inconvenience me in any way or disobey me, you may have good reason to seek protection from me. Is that understood?'

Angelina merely glowered at him.

Henry seemed to be torn two ways, but in the end he gave in to their persuasion to go to Cornwall—a little too easily, Alex thought, giving his uncle a narrow, suspicious look. Henry would join them both at Arlington at a later date. 'And don't worry, Angelina,' he said when he saw the worried look in her eyes. 'You will like Arlington—and, if you find Alex's presence irksome, the house is so large that you can go for weeks at a time without bumping into one another.'

'That sounds appealing,' she responded, throwing Lord Montgomery a glance like a poison dart. 'And after your visit to Cornwall, are we to return to London?'

'Yes. It is important that we return to prepare for the Season in April. You will have to master all manner of accomplishments so we must allow ourselves enough time. I shall employ a tutor to instruct you in social protocol, conduct, polite conversation and that sort of thing. You must also have dancing lessons and arrangements will have to be made for a complete wardrobe—a responsibility I shall be more than happy to place in my dear sister's capable hands. We must see that you are well prepared when you make your curtsy. I am convinced you will be a tremendous success and will be inundated with suitors. Eventually you will make a perfect match.'

Angelina felt a terrible, unexplained dread mounting inside her. The whole idea of the Season terrified her. 'Uncle Henry, I know you think that what you are doing is in my best interests—and please don't think I'm not grateful because I am. I—I do so want to be worthy of you, to make you proud of me, but...'

'But what, my dear?'

'It's just that I have no interest in being paraded in front of society merely to acquire a suitable husband. Besides, I cannot see the point of going to all that bother and expense when I have no intention of marrying.'

Stunned into silence, both men looked at her.

'If it's all the same to you, I'm quite happy as I am. I don't want to be married. I'm never going to get married.'

Henry was troubled by the intensity of her statement. It was said with deep conviction, and more than a little pain. Recalling what Will had told him about rescuing her from the Shawnee, he wondered what had happened to her that she refused to speak of. Whatever it was, she hid it well, and he was certain it had something to do with her decision not to marry.

'Don't be alarmed, Angelina,' he said gently. 'It is not my intention to make you do anything you have an aversion to. You need time to adjust to things. Perhaps, after a few weeks spent at Arlington, you will come to see everything in a different light.'

'No, Uncle Henry, I won't,' she told him with a quiet firmness.

'I do not believe you realise the seriousness of what you are refusing,' Alex commented, listening with a great deal of interest to what was being said.

Angelina looked across at him calmly. 'What are you saying?'

'The point I am trying to make is that, as the ward of the Duke of Mowbray, when you fail to make an appearance when the Season starts people will want to know why. You will leave yourself wide open to a great deal of gossip and speculation.'

'I have little interest in what people think.'

'No, but my uncle has. There is more to this than you seem to be concerned about. There are standards to be upheld. Of course you must marry some time.'

'No. I meant what I said.'

'I applaud your honesty. Have you no desire for a family of your own—children? Is that not an incentive to marry?'

'Not to me.'

'Then what is it you want from life?' he asked, his steady gaze locking on to hers.

'I don't know,' she whispered, the sheer desperation and pain of the look she gave him making Alex forget all his hostility towards her. He was made uneasy by it. Something reached out and touched him in half-forgotten obscure places.

'It would seem, Alex,' said Henry, sensing the distress signals coming from Angelina and rallying to her rescue, 'that someone else is of the same opinion as yourself regarding the honourable institution of marriage.'

'On the contrary, Uncle. I've decided to marry after all.'

Henry looked at his nephew sharply, surprise registering in his eyes, and more than a pang of disappointment settling on his heart. 'Really? Now that is a surprise. You have been busy while I've been in America.'

'I imagine you are pleased that I have decided to marry and provide you with the heir you are constantly plaguing me about.'

'That depends on the lady you intend to marry. Who is she?'

'Lavinia Howard.'

'Lord Howard's eldest daughter?'

'Yes,' Alex replied, watching his uncle closely.

Henry nodded slowly as he digested the information. 'I see. Well, she is eminently suitable, I grant you, and her father has been hankering after a match between the two of you for long enough. She is a fine young woman of excellent character. Have you spoken to her father?'

'Nothing has been decided. I'm giving a small weekend house party at Arlington in two weeks' time and I have invited her along with her parents and a party of friends. If I am still of the same mind, I will speak to Lord Howard then.'

'His daughter will certainly preside over Arlington with grace and poise and has been trained to manage the demanding responsibilities of such a large house. However, it is evident to me that you are thinking with your head and not your heart, Alex. I see you are considering marriage to Miss Howard with the same kind of dispassion and practised precision you employ when dealing with your business transactions.'

Alex shrugged. 'Did you expect anything else? I am no more sentimental about marriage than anyone else. It's a contract like any other. Besides, considering my success in that area, the odds for our marriage being successful are highly favourable.'

'I think "excruciatingly boring" would be a more appropriate term to use. In this you are ill advised, Alex. Marriage is not a business transaction.'

Angelina met Lord Montgomery's gaze, amazed by his indifference to such an important matter. 'You are not in love with Miss Howard?'

Henry chuckled softly. 'Alex cast a blight on love a long time ago, my dear.'

'Why, those are my sentiments entirely, Lord Montgomery.'

'I'm glad we are agreed on one thing at least,' Alex responded.

For a moment they regarded one another in silence, finding it strange that they were in accord over something that to everyone else was the most important thing in their lives.

'Maybe we are. But I do feel that where something as important as marriage is concerned, then it is essential that the two people concerned love each other.'

Alex suddenly smiled. 'In my opinion, that is sentimental nonsense. Aren't you going to congratulate me on my forthcoming nuptials, Miss Hamilton?'

'No. You said yourself that as yet nothing has been decided. When it has and Miss Howard accepts your proposal of marriage, I feel the only sentiment I shall be able to offer will be my commiserations.'

The following morning Henry's widowed sister, Lady Patience Fortesque, arrived at Brook Street. She was eager to see her brother after his journey to America, and to meet his ward. Two years his junior, Patience resembled Henry in many ways. There was a fragile quality about her and she radiated a kindness and gentility that was immediately endearing to anyone who met her, but when she pleased she could be awe-inspiring.

Patience politely restrained herself from saying anything until Henry had finished telling her all about what had happened in America. The secret fears of what Angelina might have suffered at the hands of the Shawnee he kept to himself.

When he had completed his tale, he looked across at his sister who was calmly assessing what he had told her. 'Well, Patience? Am I a sentimental old fool? Was I behaving like a lovesick youth when I went tearing across the Atlantic the moment I received Lydia's letter? Should I have ignored it after all these years?'

'No, Henry,' Patience replied with gentle understanding. 'Lydia meant a great deal to you, I know that. Is Angelina aware how deeply you felt about her mother?'

'If you mean does she know I was in love with her, then the answer is no. Angelina is a remarkable young woman, Patience. When I first saw her and how proud she was, how resilient and brave after all she had been through, she stirred all my protective instincts. I find her such joy to be with. She is a rare jewel and with just a little polish she will outshine most of her sex. Lydia taught her well.'

'I am concerned about the matter of Angelina's grandmother. I know that since the death of her husband Lady Anne never comes to town. But there is the possibility that she will find out about her granddaughter coming to England when she makes her curtsy next year. It could be a major problem if she decides to see her.'

'I know, but we will deal with that *if* it arises.'

'What about Alex?'

The name seemed to hang in the air a moment before Henry replied. 'Ah—Alex!'

'Oh, dear! I take it from the tone of your voice that he does not welcome the intrusion of this American girl into his life.'

Henry chuckled. 'You've hit the nail right on the head. Battle lines were drawn and the artillery positioned the minute they set eyes on each other. Already they've had their first skirmish. Angelina refuses to be subdued and is unimpressed by both Alex and his title. At present I do not want her to go out into society—and nor does she wish to. She refuses to consider a Season, but I'm hoping that she can be persuaded. I feel some time spent in the country will be beneficial to her until she's had time to settle down—which is why I would like you to accompany her to Arlington.'

'Arlington? But why not to Mowbray Park?'

'Because I am to leave for Cornwall early next week to visit my good friend Robert Boothroyd. Besides,' he murmured, a mischievous twinkle in his eyes, which did not go unnoticed by his sister, 'Alex is to go to Arlington in a few days to check on the renovations he's having done to the house.'

Patience studied her brother carefully. 'Henry, are you matchmaking by any chance? If so, you must think very carefully and proceed with the utmost caution. Alex will not take kindly to your meddling.'

'Meddling?' Henry arched his brows in mock offence. 'I have no intention of meddling in anything. There is nothing I want more than for the two of them to wed,' he told her, taking her into his confidence. He needed his sister's unquestioning co-operation and willingness to comply with anything he suggested if he was to bring Alex and Angelina together.

Chapter Four

'Come here, my dear, and let me look at you,' said Patience with a gracious smile when Angelina entered. 'I've been so looking forward to meeting you.'

Angelina moved towards her and found herself enfolded in a sweet smelling embrace. 'I am happy to meet you, Lady Fortesque. Uncle Henry has told me so much about you that I feel I know you already.'

Patience stood back and smiled, approving of what she saw. Her features were delicate and pretty like Lydia's, but there was something untamed and quite unique about this lovely young woman.

'Your mother and I were close, Angelina. I was so distressed to hear of her death—and your father's, my dear. Come and sit by me, and please call me Aunt Patience. We are related, after all.'

At that moment the door opened and Alex strode in. He was dressed in riding clothes, his crop still clasped in his hand. Angelina noticed how fiercely elegant he was in his immaculate coat and polished brown boots, and the way his breeches fit his thighs like his coat fit the breadth of his shoulders, without a wrinkle—and, if they were inclined to do so, they wouldn't dare on so formidable an owner.

Closing the door and advancing into the room with ground-devouring strides, his cool gaze swept over the three occupants, pausing a little longer on Angelina before moving on to his aunt.

'Why, Alex, how lovely to see you,' said Patience, her face shining with adoration as she looked up at her handsome nephew.

Bending his tall frame, Alex lightly kissed her offered cheek, and as his head passed close to Angelina she caught the spicy aroma of his cologne mingled with leather and horses. As he was about to stand up straight he turned his head and looked at her, his eyes on a level with her own and no more than a foot away. Finding herself in such close proximity to him brought an indignant flush to her cheeks, which Alex observed and brought a slight smile to his lips, his silver eyes gleaming with knowing amusement.

Her contempt met him face to face until he straightened, looking down at her from his daunting height, seeing turbulent animosity burning in her dark eyes. She looked serene and almost coy, and yet he had the feeling that it was a charade, and that the environment forced upon her was too restricting for her ebullient nature. She made him feel alert and alive, and curiously stimulated.

'I really should scold you,' Patience went on, her eyes following her nephew as he strolled towards the fireplace, where he took up an infuriatingly arrogant stance beside Henry's chair, resting an arm on the marble mantelpiece and crossing one booted foot casually over the other, looking every inch the master of the house. 'You did promise to visit me at Richmond while Henry was away.'

'Forgive me, Aunt. I had pressing matters to take care of.'

'So I understand,' Patience replied with a note of reproof, having heard all about his affair with Amelia Fairhurst. 'I had hoped that with all your years of experience you would have learned to conduct your affairs with a little more discretion, Alex.'

'The pressing matters I spoke of were purely business, Aunt. And if you are referring to my friendship with Lady Amelia

Fairhurst, I assure you it was nothing more than a harmless flirtation and was blown out of all proportion. I did not think you paid any attention to gossip.'

'I don't, as a rule, and I'm certainly not going to become embroiled in your personal life. Next you will be telling me that you took pity on her and were trying to console her in her marital unhappiness. But what may seem amusing and harmless to you, dear boy, others may find offensive and insulting—which was the case with Lady Fairhurst's husband by all accounts, when he demanded satisfaction and challenged you to a duel.'

Chagrin and irritation flickered across Alex's face. 'And no doubt you heard that the old fool died of an apoplexy the night before. Amelia Fairhurst is a proficient flirt. You should know by now not to worry about my reputation, Aunt. You must know that most of what you hear is nothing but gossip and wishful exaggeration.'

'Are you telling us that you have been unfairly maligned, Lord Montgomery?' Angelina asked, gazing at him with an amazingly innocent smile on her lips, and an insolent light in her eyes. 'That what people say about you dishonouring every woman who is foolish enough to fall for your golden tongue is not true?'

Content to sit back and listen to the interchange in an amused silence, Henry met his sister's smiling, conspiratorial gaze, each admiring Angelina's courage for daring to speak out, while Alex favoured her with an icy stare that was meant to put her firmly in her place. But she merely held his gaze with open defiance, which told him that her proud nature knew nothing of compliance or submission.

'Not entirely,' he replied tersely, his jaw rigid. 'I see you have met our colonial cousin, Aunt.'

'Yes,' she said, smiling at Angelina and taking her hand in an affectionate clasp. 'I came just as soon as I received Henry's note telling me he had arrived back in London with Angelina.'

'And?'

'And what?'

'Is she all you expected her to be?'

'Yes, she is. Angelina is very much dear Lydia's daughter.'

'Tell me, Uncle Henry—was your nephew obnoxious as a boy, too?' Angelina asked boldly.

Her question earned her a broad smile of admiration from Henry. 'Why—I do believe he was.'

She frowned, feigning sympathy. 'How distressing for you all.'

'So distressing that both Uncle Henry and Aunt Patience have complained bitterly over the years and threatened to disown me,' Alex retaliated calmly, 'but as you see, Miss Hamilton, as a family we have a way of sticking together.'

Angelina sensed there was a hidden message for her in his words, which she prudently ignored. Looking at Patience, she smiled shyly. 'I can see Lord Montgomery's affairs both concern and embarrass you, Aunt Patience—so you must be relieved to know that he is considering marriage.'

'So Henry was telling me just before you came in. Is this true, Alex?'

'That is so, Aunt,' he replied, tapping his boot with his riding crop, sorely tempted to use it on the softest part of the chit's anatomy. 'I am considering it.'

'Lavinia Howard?'

'That is the young lady I have in mind.'

'A sensible choice. The title and position she will acquire if she marries you will delight her family—especially her mother,' she said with a faint trace of irony, 'for she has long been desiring a match between you. However, I'm glad to know you are thinking of settling down at last, Alex.'

'Thank you, Aunt,' he replied drily. His smile was sardonic. 'I shall endeavour to do my duty and produce an heir.'

'Nevertheless, it will hardly be a love match,' retorted his aunt with a note of disapproval in her tone.

'No, but I have a high regard for Lavinia.'

'Poor Miss Howard,' murmured Angelina. 'I doubt she

knows what a cold and cruel fate awaits her if she takes you
for a husband.'

Alex looked at her coldly. 'There are very few men who love
their wives, Miss Hamilton.'

'Or women who love their husbands, it would seem. If Miss
Howard will not be hurt by your indifference, she must be very
unhappy or very cold.'

'She is neither,' Alex countered.

'Henry tells me you are to give a small weekend party at Arlington to which she is invited,' Patience put in quickly in an
attempt to relieve the situation. 'I shall look forward to meeting
her again. In the meantime, I am so looking forward to getting
to know Angelina better—which is why I shall be staying here
until it is time for us to leave for Arlington next week.'

'You are?' Alex asked with some surprise.

'Of course. Angelina cannot remain in this house with you and
Henry alone. Her reputation would be beyond recall if it gets out.'

'Then the obvious solution to that is for you to take her to
Richmond. The park is lovely at this time of year. I'm sure the
air will be more conducive to Miss Hamilton's health and
temper than it is here in town.'

'There is nothing wrong with my health or my temper that
a distance away from you would not cure, my lord,' Angelina
countered.

The bright silver eyes considered Angelina without a hint
of expression, then with slow deliberation. Had it not been for
the coldness that came into them, his reply might have passed
as a flippant remark. 'Then I shall have to take that into consideration and adjust my affairs accordingly to assist you in
your cure, Miss Hamilton.'

Patience looked from Angelina to Alex crossly. 'Good
heavens! What is this nonsense? Why so formal? You must
address one another by your given names if you are to get on.'

Both Angelina and Alex disagreed. Formal address conveyed
neither affection nor intimacy, which suited them both.

'Come, now, what do you say?' Patience persisted.

Unwillingly, Alex conceded. 'Very well, Aunt.'

'Thank you. Now, in answer to your question, I did consider taking Angelina to Richmond, until Henry told me he is to visit Lord Boothroyd in Cornwall shortly. He has been away so long that I would like to spend some time with him before he goes. Besides, I would like to take Angelina shopping before we leave for Arlington. The clothes Henry had you fitted out with in Boston were adequate for the voyage, my dear, but I shall see you have some more day dresses for Arlington. When we return to London my dressmaker will fit you out for a whole new wardrobe. However, I shall ask her to call before we leave for Arlington and take your measurements so she can make a start.'

Alarm bells began ringing in Angelina's head and she could see the excited gleam of future arrangements in the older woman's eyes. 'Oh! But I—I explained to Uncle Henry that I—'

'Have no wish to be introduced into society.' Patience smiled. 'I know. Henry told me,' she said, glancing meaning-fully at her brother. 'Tell me, have you not considered having a Season just for the fun of it, Angelina?'

Angelina's expression became grave. 'It's a long time since I did anything for the fun of it, Aunt Patience.'

'Launching a young woman into society is a serious and ex-pensive business, Aunt,' Alex stated sternly. 'I dare say it can be "fun", but one must not forget that all that time and effort is taken for the sole purpose of procuring a husband.'

Angelina glared at him. 'I know that, which is precisely why I told you yesterday that it would be a waste of both time and money.'

'Well—whether you have a Season or not is immaterial, my dear,' said Patience lightly, attempting to defuse a situation that threatened to become explosive. 'As the ward of the Duke of Mowbray you cannot hide yourself away indefinitely. It is imperative that you have a fashionable wardrobe.'

'To pass her off in society, Aunt, she will need more than a fashionable wardrobe to be accepted,' Alex said curtly. 'She will also need instruction on manners and breeding, which, in my opinion, will take some considerable time.'

Patience studied her nephew's stony countenance with something akin to surprise. 'I disagree. Henry and I intend to employ a tutor to instruct her on all she needs to know. She is highly intelligent and cultured—which is more than can be said of some of the vain henwits who are turned out year after year for the Season, so it will take no time at all. What do you think, Angelina?'

Angelina knew Lord Montgomery was jeering at her, but refused to let him see how much the intended rudeness of his remark had hurt her. Glancing up at him, something in his look challenged her spirit and increased her courage in a surge of dislike. She managed to force her lips into a smile.

'I think that is an excellent idea, Aunt Patience. Perhaps your nephew would care to sit in on my lessons. Unfortunately, it may take him a good while longer since he has more to learn than I. He is a man of high birth but low manners.'

Alex's eyes narrowed and took on a most humorous glint, which Angelina took pains to ignore. She suddenly smiled radiantly, her soft lips parting to reveal her small, sparkling white teeth that dazzled her adversary. 'If you have an aversion to joining me at my lessons, you could take them by yourself,' she generously suggested, her expression serious but her dark eyes dancing with intended mischief, 'if you can find the time between your many amorous affairs and business commitments.'

Alex stared at her, caught somewhere between fury, astonishment and admiration for her defiant courage. It was the first time he had seen her really smile and the effect was startling. It started in her eyes, warming them, before drifting to her generous lips, stretching them, parting them, her teeth small, perfect and white. In danger of becoming entrapped by his baser instincts, he straightened abruptly from his stance by the fireplace and walked forward, ignoring Angelina as he glanced from his aunt to his uncle, who was enjoying himself immensely.

'Excuse me. I must go and change. I must also leave before

I relinquish my carefully held temper and do something to your ward that will embarrass you both—something I would not regret, I might add,' he snapped, clenching his crop between both his hands and leaving Angelina in no doubt what he would like to do with it.

When he reached the door he turned and looked back at Angelina, fixing her with a hard stare. 'If there is anything I can do to make your stay in this house more pleasant, please don't ask. I should hate to show discourtesy by refusing. But if you want to win my approval, you are going to have to change your attitude and make yourself more agreeable to me. That should be your first concern.'

Angelina's ire at his condescending superiority was almost more than she could contain, but she gazed at him with a cool hauteur that belied her agitation and managed to speak calmly. 'Why on earth should I want your approval? And as for my attitude, no one else finds it a problem. Perhaps it is your own attitude that is at fault.'

Alex glared at her before turning to leave. 'I'll see you all at dinner.'

'Of course, my lord,' Angelina quipped.

He swung round in the open doorway, his face glacial. 'My name is Alex. We agreed to dispense with formalities.'

'No. You did,' she replied, turning her head away, having told him she did not want the intimacy of addressing him by his given name.

When the door had closed behind him she relaxed, feeling as if a great weight had been lifted from her shoulders. Looking from Henry to Patience, who were watching her calmly, not in the least put out by the heated interchange between her and their nephew, a little impish smile tugged at her lips. 'Oh, dear. I don't think your nephew likes me very much, does he?'

For most of the journey to Arlington, Angelina stared out of the window, uncomfortable beneath Lord Montgomery's watchful gaze. He sat across from her next to a sleeping Patience, with his long legs stretched out in the luxurious conveyance, studying her imperturbably.

He had discarded his coat and his pristine white shirt and neckcloth contrasted sharply with his black hair and dark countenance. His body, a perfect harmony of form and strength, was like a work of Grecian art and most unsettling to Angelina's virgin heart. To rid herself of his studied gaze she closed her eyes, but even then the vision persisted and she could see and feel those piercing eyes boring holes into her. Unable to endure his scrutiny a moment longer, she snapped her eyes open and locked them on his.

'Well? Have you had an edifying look?' she demanded irately.

Quite unexpectedly he smiled, a white, buccaneer smile, and his eyes danced with devilish humour. 'You don't have to look so angry to find yourself the object of my attention. As a matter of fact I was admiring you.'

Unaccustomed as she was to any kind of compliment from him, the unfamiliar warmth in his tone brought heat creeping into her cheeks. In fact, she decided that she liked this softer side she was seeing even less than the one she was accustomed to. This other Alex Montgomery was beyond her sphere and she didn't know how to deal with him.

'If you think to use flattery as a new tactic to subdue me, it won't work.'

'I was merely thinking that when you aren't scowling you really are quite pretty.'

'And how many women have you said that to?' Angelina asked, raising her nose to a lofty elevation.

'Several. And it's always the truth.'

'Oh dear,' Patience said, fighting a sneeze, which brought her back to awareness. 'I do hope the two of you aren't going to argue again. If so, kindly wait until we reach Arlington. I don't think my nerves will stand it.'

Angelina was concerned about Patience, who had been suffering a chill for the past twenty-four hours. Unfortunately it seemed to be getting worse. Her eyes were bright and feverish, her nose streaming.

'I'm sorry, Aunt, we didn't mean to wake you. As soon as we reach the house you must go straight to bed. Lord Montgomery will send for the doctor.' Leaning forward, she tucked the rug over her aunt's knees.

Wiping her streaming eyes Patience looked too poorly to argue. 'I shall not be sorry to get to bed. I do hope I am in my old room, Alex, and away from the noise of the workmen.'

Reaching out, Alex gently touched his aunt's cheek with long caressing fingers, causing Angelina to stare in astonishment at the smiling, tender expression on his face, which was not in keeping with the man she knew.

'You are,' he said in reply to his aunt's question. 'As yet work hasn't started on the west wing. And Angelina is right. You must go to bed the instant we arrive.'

'Where have you put Angelina?'

'I hope you have accorded me the same consideration and I'm away from the noise too,' Angelina retorted quickly.

'The carpenters and masons do not work around the clock. They go home at night, so you will not be disturbed—unless you are in the habit of sleeping through the day,' Alex said with a hint of sarcasm.

Angelina threw him a wrathful look, but refrained from answering when Patience gave way to another fit of sneezing.

Nothing had prepared Angelina for the exquisite splendour that was Arlington Hall in the heart of the Hertfordshire countryside. She saw it from a distance sitting like a grand old lady on the crest of a hill, timeless and brooding, its elegant beauty expressing power and pride.

'Oh, my,' she breathed, with a growing sense of unreality. Her mother had told her about the grand houses the English nobility lived in, but never had she envisaged anything as lovely as this. Arlington Hall was certainly not a house of modest proportions. 'Why—it's beautiful. Is it very old?'

Alex smiled at the dazed expression of disbelief on her face, well satisfied with her reaction. 'I'm afraid it is,' he replied, folding his arms across his chest, preferring to watch a myriad of expressions on Angelina's face rather than the approaching house. 'Built during Queen Elizabeth's reign about two hundred and fifty years ago, the main structure survives relatively unaltered.'

'It must have taken years to build.'

'Actually, it rose at amazing speed.'

'And all those windows,' she murmured, watching as the evening sun caught the three stories of huge windows, lighting them up like a wall of flame, contrasting beautifully with the green and yellow tints and fiery shades of the finest, early autumn foliage.

'People were enthusiastic for enormous windows in those days. Glass was very expensive, so it became a status symbol. People used it in large quantities to show how rich they were.'

Angelina looked at Alex with large eyes, her animosity forgotten for the moment. 'Your ancestors must have been very rich.'

'They were. The first Earl of Arlington was a powerful politician and a trusted adviser of Queen Elizabeth.'

'And did Queen Elizabeth ever come to Arlington?'

'Frequently. She liked living at her subjects' expense. I'm having considerable alterations and improvements made just now—woodwork has to be renewed, rooms redecorated, and I'm having the modern convenience of running water installed. It's being done in stages and at the moment it's the east wing that's being renovated. Needless to say there's an army of workmen tramping all over the place so you'll just have to bear with it.'

'Is Uncle Henry's house anything like Arlington Hall?'

'No. Mowbray Park was built at a later time and is quite different. It was designed on a much larger scale and is very grand. But you'll see it for yourself before too long.'

'And will you inherit Mowbray Park one day?'

'Yes.'

She gave him a puzzled look. 'Then—who will live at Arlington?' It was a simple question, one she regretted asking when she saw his jaw tense and his eyes cloud over. 'Will you sell it? After all, you can't very well live here and at Mowbray Park.'

Alex hesitated, and for a moment Angelina thought she saw pain in his eyes. 'No, I don't suppose I can,' he answered quietly. 'But I will never sell Arlington. If I marry, I will pass it on to my heirs.'

Angelina shook her head and sighed with sympathy for their mutual plight. 'So you don't have any family either—apart from Aunt Patience and Uncle Henry. You say your mother's ancestors built Arlington Hall. Does she still live here?' she asked, recalling Uncle Henry telling her that Lord Montgomery's father was dead. Immediately she sensed his withdrawal. It was as if a veil had come over his features. Her eyes saw the changing expression on his face, a look that at once seemed to warn her not to pry and to shut her out.

Again Alex hesitated. When he replied to her question his tone was harsher than he intended. 'I would prefer it if you did not mention my mother to me, Angelina. I cannot imagine that she would interest you.'

'I—I just wondered—'

'Then don't,' he said coldly. 'My parents are both dead.'

There was so much finality and suppressed anger and bitterness in his voice that she refrained from asking any further questions.

The four bay mounts pulling the crested coach at last danced to a stop in front of the house and Alex got out, gallantly extending his hand to help his aunt and Angelina. Just for a moment Angelina's fingers touched his, and she felt as if the warm grasp of his hand scorched her own. The two following coaches carrying staff and baggage drew to a halt.

Scarlet-and-gold-liveried footmen appeared out of the house and descended on the coaches to strip them of the mountain of baggage. In a hurry to be inside the house, Patience went ahead of them. Alex turned to Angelina.

'Welcome to Arlington Hall.'

Side by side they climbed the steps and entered the house.

At a glance Angelina became aware of the rich trappings of the interior, the sumptuous carpets and wainscoted panelled walls and great beams crossing the ceiling. An ornately carved oak staircase opposite the entrance cantilevered up to the floors above. The butler, Jenkins, a lean dignified man with dark brown hair and rather austere features, stood aside as they entered, keeping a keen eye on the footmen to remind them of their duties as their eyes kept straying with frank approval to the young woman who stood beside the Earl. Angelina turned when Patience patted her arm.

'Forgive me, Angelina, but I really must go to my room. Mrs Morrisey, who is the housekeeper at Arlington Hall, will show you to your room,' she said, looking quite distressed and turning to a middle-aged woman who came towards them with a rustle of stiff black skirts. 'Go and settle in and refresh yourself before dinner.'

'Angelina, wait,' Alex commanded brusquely when she was about to follow Mrs Morrisey across the hall to the stairs.

Angelina's spine stiffened and she turned to him. Taking her arm he drew her aside. Gazing up at him through the thick fringe of her lashes, she met his piercing eyes. Inwardly she shivered, seeing something ruthless in that controlled, hard silver gaze. She stood perfectly still and tense, waiting for him to speak.

'I will see you at dinner?'

'If you don't mind, I think I will eat with Aunt Patience in her room,' she replied stiffly, averting her eyes.

'I do mind,' he told her quietly. 'Your opinion of me matters not at all, but I refuse to have the servants see my guest has an aversion to me. I would appreciate it if you would try to practise a little courtesy while you are in my house. Is that too much to ask of you?'

Angelina heaved a heavy sigh. It would be difficult to do as he asked, but she saw no reason why they should not at least be cordial to one another. 'No, of course not,' she conceded.

'Thank you. Dinner is at half past seven.'

Abruptly he turned and strode away, leaving Angelina to follow Mrs Morrisey up the stairs. The opulence and elegance of the blue and white room into which she was shown took her breath away.

'Oh, what a lovely room,' she enthused with delight.

'Lord Montgomery instructed me to have this particular one prepared for you because it offers such a splendid view of the garden. It also faces south and has an abundant supply of sunshine—especially during the summer months.'

'How considerate of Lord Montgomery,' Angelina replied, strangely touched to discover he had spared the time to think of her comfort.

Later, she joined Lord Montgomery in a small candlelit dining room off the main hall. Presenting a pleasing appearance, having donned one of the gowns Patience had purchased for her in London—a violet silk which complemented her figure and her eyes—she managed to maintain an outward show of calm, despite the tumult raging inside her.

Lord Montgomery was standing by the sideboard, pouring red wine into two glasses. Angelina was struck by his stern profile outlined against the golden glow of the candles. She saw a kind of beauty in it, but quickly dismissed the thought. It was totally out of keeping with her opinion of him. He turned when she entered and moved towards her, his narrow gaze sweeping over her with approval.

'I hope I'm not late. I went to look in on Aunt Patience.'

'How is she?' Alex handed her a glass of wine. Having lost all desire to quarrel with her tonight, he was relieved to hear she sounded more calm than aggressive.

'Sleeping—but she really does look quite poorly.'

'Then you will be relieved to know the doctor has seen her and has left some medication that should help relieve her discomfort. Is your room to your liking?' he asked, pulling out her chair at the damask-covered table decorated with orchids.

'Yes, thank you,' Angelina replied, slipping into it and taking a sip of wine, hoping the meal would be over quickly so she could escape.

'I'm glad you decided to join me for dinner,' Alex said, seating himself across from her. 'I hoped you would.'

'I could hardly ignore a royal command, could I?' Angelina replied, unable to resist taking a gentle stab at him, the impish curve to her lips softening the tartness of her reply.

His glance darted across the table. 'It was not a royal command.'

'No? That's how it sounded.'

Reining in his mounting irritation, Alex stirred impatiently. 'Angelina, don't be aggressive,' he told her quietly. 'I am in no mood for a quarrel.'

Angelina laughed shortly, a mischievous light twinkling in her eyes. 'Why, what kind of miracle is this! To what do we owe it?' When he shot her an annoying look she sighed in capitulation, though in the light of his previous animosity towards her during their brief acquaintance, she remained suspicious of this softening to his attitude. 'No. Neither am I,' she answered, smiling at an aloof-looking footman who was standing to attention like a soldier close to a large dresser containing platters of food.

'Good. Now that is settled, perhaps we can enjoy our dinner in peace.'

'I shall endeavour to do so.'

'As long as you don't upset my cook by not eating. Mrs Hall is very efficient—and, being a woman, she is extremely temperamental and takes it as a personal criticism if anyone refuses to eat.'

'What! Even you?' Her eyes sparked with laughter.

'Even me.' He smiled in response, spreading a napkin over his knees.

It was a simple, lovely meal, excellently cooked and served by the aloof footman who came and went. Alex talked amiably about Arlington Hall and the surrounding countryside, giving Angelina a brief insight of the people who lived and worked in and around the village of Arlington, just one mile from the hall.

'Do you often go to London?' she asked, wondering how

he could bear to leave such a lovely place for the hurly-burly of London.

'I have to take my seat in the House of Lords occasionally—more so at this present time with Europe in a state of turmoil and the war with the United States.' A faint smile touched his lips when he observed Angelina's expression of bewilderment, and realised that, coming from America, she would know very little about English politics.

'You are a politician?'

'No—at least not in the professional sense. It is simply that I, and all peers of the realm, have been trained to regard it as our right and duty to participate in governing the country. We enter Parliament as we do university and gentlemen's clubs—such as White's or Brooks's.'

Angelina was impressed. 'It all sounds very grand to me. And what do you debate in the House of Lords?'

'The issues at this time are many and varied—and of an extremely serious nature. Fortunately we have managed to stand against Napoleon, despite his attempts to throttle our trade. The present economic crisis is foremost in the debates, and the textile trade, which is getting worse. Following two bad harvests, there is general unrest in this country—especially in the north and the Midlands. And on top of all this comes the need to pay out gold to support the war in Portugal and Spain and our naval battle with America.'

'Dear me. What a muddle it all is. I wonder at you having time to leave London and come to Arlington.'

'I'm not required to spend all my time in the House of Lords, and much of my business can be taken care of here.' He went on to explain the basics of British politics and the English Court, telling her that King George III had lapsed into incurable madness and his son, the Prince of Wales, had been made Regent the previous year. 'There are times when I have to go to Carlton House and other haunts of the Prince Regent and the *beau monde*. But I must point out that political exigencies take me there, rather than personal tastes.'

'Uncle Henry told me that George III and his Queen set a standard of decorum and domestic virtue, but that their court was a very dull place to be—much different to that of their son.'

Alex smiled broadly. 'Uncle Henry was right. As soon as the old King was struck down with madness and fastened into his strait-waistcoat, the Prince of Wales took to wearing corsets and the ladies to shedding their petticoats. There are those who say the country is falling into a decline in moral standards—if not the onset of national decadence.'

'I was of the opinion that the English aristocracy has always been a profligate lot, who has indulged in loose living and has never ceased to do what it likes and cares only for its own whims. Why—I know you enjoy a certain reputation yourself, my lord,' she said softly, glancing across at him obliquely.

Alex looked at her sharply. 'Correction,' he defended curtly. 'I may have acquired a certain reputation, but I did not look for it and certainly do not enjoy it.'

Angelina shrugged, swallowing a juicy baby carrot. 'Whatever the case, it is no secret that you are something of a womaniser and that you keep a mistress—a notorious beauty by all accounts.'

Alex's gaze narrowed and slid to her seemingly innocent face. 'Really,' he said drily. 'You are well informed, Angelina. Did Uncle Henry tell you that too?'

Her eyes opened wide. 'Of course not. Uncle Henry is too much of a gentleman to indulge in tittle-tattle. But I do have ears—and servants talk. What's she like?' Angelina asked, popping another baby carrot into her mouth whilst lowering her eyes to hide their mischievous intent, secretly delighting in his discomfort.

Alex's jaw tensed and a flash of annoyance darkened his eyes. 'Who?'

Calmly Angelina met his gaze. 'Your mistress.' As he arrogantly raised one brow a dangerous glitter entered his eyes, which warned her that his temper was not far from surfacing.

'She's very sweet, as a matter of fact,' he drawled.

'Then instead of marrying Miss Howard, why not marry your mistress?'

'Gentlemen do not marry their mistresses, Angelina.'

'Why—I cannot for the life of me see why not. If a man considers a woman suitable to take to his bed, why not marry her?'

Alex's grey eyes observed her with ill-concealed displeasure from beneath dark brows. 'I think we will drop this particular subject. It is pointless and leading nowhere.'

Restraining the urge to giggle, Angelina shrugged flippantly. 'As you like.'

When he turned the conversation back round to his home, she listened with a good deal of interest, and mostly in silence when she realised just how much Arlington and its people meant to him. It brought to mind her own home and all she had left behind. Memory clouded her eyes and Alex seemed to sense her despondency.

'Tell me, are you homesick for America?' he asked suddenly, correctly guessing the cause of her dejected attitude.

Angelina raised her eyes and looked at him sharply. His question was unexpected. 'Very much,' she admitted, unsure whether she wanted his sympathy, but comforted by it nevertheless.

'And you miss Mr Boone and your friend Will, I suppose.'

'Yes, I do miss Will. He was a part of my life for a long time.'

'And now? What do you think he is doing?'

'Trapping beaver somewhere among the Great Lakes of North America, I suppose,' she murmured, unable to conceal the yearning she still felt for her homeland.

'What made your father go out west?'

'He was bitten by the bug that bit everyone else. The lure of the west changed him and eventually he became hungry to see it for himself.'

'He wasn't the only man lured by the Promised Land.'

'It was a dream shared by many. Thousands of men all seeking a better life, a different life, to raise their children—

all the time pushing further west in a valiant attempt to tame the land and carve themselves a niche. Hundreds perished in the migration, becoming victims of the elements or at the hands of the many tribes of hostile Indians.'

'And your mother? Did the lure of the west attract her also?'

'No, not really. She tried telling my father that homesteading was best left to those who know how to work the land, but Father was determined to go west.'

'And how did your father fare as a farmer?'

'Being unskilled in agriculture, he did not fare well. The weather became his mortal enemy—and then there were the Indian raids, when livestock would disappear overnight. Lack of money was a constant problem. The prosperity he'd dreamed of always eluded him. He possessed a grim determination to survive despite the odds stacked against him—but in the end he was defeated,' she finished quietly. 'The Shawnee saw to that.'

'Uncle Henry told me he was killed in an Indian raid, and that your mother was wounded,' Alex said gently.

The light in Angelina's eyes hardened. She seemed to withdraw into herself and her body tensed. 'Yes. Will looked after me and took me back to Boston with my mother—but I hate to remember. On the night of the raid I believe I faced the worst that could happen to me,' she whispered.

Having some comprehension and understanding of how desperate her plight must have been at that time, his own unhappy days as a child and the dreadful visions of his father's final moments returned to him vividly. Alex looked at her for a long moment, his eyes soft and filled with compassion. Whatever it was that had happened to her, she still saw her ghosts—just as he did. His voice when he spoke was kind, kinder than Angelina had ever heard him use in addressing her.

'Then we won't speak of it again. But if you truly believe you have faced the worst that can happen to you, nothing can really be that bad again.'

Angelina raised her pain-filled eyes to his, wanting so much to believe him. 'Do you really think so?'

He nodded. 'Yes, I do.'

The footman returned to serve them with a lemon pudding and they continued to eat in silence until he left them alone once more. Alex watched Angelina's unconscious grace as she ate. She looked so prim in her violet gown. Apart from her face and slender hands not an inch of flesh was exposed, and not a single hair escaped that severe plait.

In the soft light her face was like a cameo, all hollows and shadows. There was a purity about her, something so endearingly young and innocent that reminded him of a sparrow. He tried to envisage what she would look like if the little sparrow changed her plumage and became a swan, and the image that took shape in his mind was pleasing. Feeling compelled and at liberty to look his fill, he felt his heart contract, not having grasped the full reality of her beauty until that moment. She must have sensed his perusal because she suddenly raised her eyes, hot, embarrassed colour staining her cheeks as he met her gaze with a querying, uplifted brow.

'I would be obliged if you would please stop looking at me in that way. Your critical eye pares and inspects me as if I was a body on a dissecting slab.'

'Does it?' Alex murmured absently, continuing to look at her, at the soft fullness of her mouth and glorious eyes.

Her flush deepened. 'I have imperfections enough without you looking for more. Please stop it,' she demanded quietly. 'You are being rude.'

'Am I?' he said, his attention momentarily diverted from her fascinating face.

'Yes. And if you persist I shall be forced to leave the table.'

Her words brought a slow, teasing smile to his lips and his strongly marked brows were slightly raised, his eyes suddenly glowing with humour. 'I apologise. You cannot leave before you've finished your dinner. But I cannot help looking at you when you are sitting directly in my sights.'

Hot faced and perplexed, Angelina almost retorted that she was not a rabbit in the sights of his gun, but she halted herself in time. She had never known a man to be so provoking. She was suddenly shy of him. There was something in his eyes tonight that made her feel it was impossible to look at him. There was also something in his voice that brought so many new and conflicting themes in her heart and mind that she did not know how to speak to him.

The effect was a combination of fright and excitement and she must put an end to it. She was in danger of becoming hypnotised by that silken voice and those mesmerising grey eyes; the fact that he knew it, that he was deliberately using his charm to dismantle her determination to stand against him, infuriated her. As soon as she had finished her dessert she stood up.

'Please excuse me,' she said stiffly, making a display of folding her napkin in order to avoid his eyes. 'I want to look in on Aunt Patience before I go to bed.'

'Of course,' Alex replied, rising and slowly walking round the table to stand beside her. 'Would you like some coffee before you leave? Or perhaps you would like to stay a while longer and play a game of cards—or chess, maybe? Uncle Henry did say you play a pretty mean game.'

Meeting his gaze, Angelina felt her flesh grow warm. His nearness and the look in his eyes, which had grown darker and was far too bold to allow even a small measure of comfort, washed away any feeling of confidence. The impact of his closeness and potent masculine virility was making her feel altogether too vulnerable.

'No—thank you. Perhaps another night.'

'As you wish.' Alex's voice was as soft as silk. There were the uncertainties of innocence about her, telling him that the sudden panic in her eyes was not in the least feigned. He accompanied her to the door, opening it for her. 'I hope you sleep well. I must warn you that the old timbers creak and groan, so don't be alarmed if you hear anything untoward during the night. Tomorrow I will ask Mrs Morrisey to show you the house.'

Angelina felt a sudden quiver run through her as she slipped away from him, a sudden quickening within as if something came to life, something that had been asleep before. She went up the stairs in awed bewilderment, feeling his eyes burning holes into her back as she went.

Chapter Five

During her first few days at Arlington, Angelina contrived to keep out of Alex's way as much as possible. She became a familiar and welcome sight at the stables. From Trimble, the head groom, she learned that horses were Lord Montgomery's abiding passion. Possessing some prime horseflesh, he was immensely proud of his large stable. He was also an expert horseman, who adored his gun dogs and was passionately interested in every kind of field sport.

Arlington Hall was a complex maze of rooms and arched passageways leading into each other. A billiard room and a music salon led off from the long gallery, and the smaller rooms had been made into private sitting and dining rooms and libraries, ornate with Italian marble and Venetian glass chandeliers.

Around mid-morning she invariably found herself in the domestic quarters to partake of a cup of Mrs Hall's delicious chocolate. Her charm and friendly, open manner had precipitated the admiration and devotion of the entire army of servants.

Angelina had never seen so much food in her life as the amount that existed in Mrs Hall's kitchen. 'Are all the animals eaten at the Hall reared on the estate, Mrs Hall?'

'Why, yes—at least most of them. As you will have noticed,

Lord Montgomery likes good, plain food when he's at Arlington—none of your fancy French cooking smothered with rich sauces and the like, which he says he gets more than enough of when he's in town. He prefers a roast or a game pie any day of the week.'

'What? Rabbit and partridge?'

'Aye, that's right—although it's a while since I made a rabbit pie. I have to wait until the gamekeepers bring me some, you see. The woods round here abound with all kind of game. I dare say it's the same where you come from.'

'Oh, yes. Although shooting isn't a pastime as it is here in England. It's a way of life and often the only means of survival.' Suddenly Angelina was struck by an idea and her lips stretched in a wide smile. 'I shall get something to fill your pie, Mrs Hall,' she said, leaving the kitchen with a jaunty stride.

Mrs Hall smiled indulgently after her and did not take her seriously, but she would have been astounded if she could have seen Angelina fifteen minutes later, striding towards the woods with her rifle.

Alex was returning home after visiting Mr Cathcart, one of his tenant farmers, who was concerned about the large band of gypsies encamped on his land and the recent outbreak of serious poaching in the area. Many a rabbit or a pheasant found its way into a family's pot, but the offence was more serious when deer were killed on a large scale, the ill-gotten gains sold further afield.

Alex was riding across open country when he heard the report of a gun. Frowning, he reined in his horse sharply and looked in the direction of the woods. Recalling Mr Cathcart's grievance and determined to get to the bottom of it, he whipped Lancer, his horse, into a burst of speed and set off in the direction of the shot.

In the process of reloading her rifle in the hope of bagging another rabbit, Angelina paused, distracted by the thundering approach of horse's hooves. Horse and rider emerged out of the trees and came towards her, and, much in the manner she associated with him, Lord Montgomery swung off his still-prancing, powerful black horse. With long, purposeful strides he swooped down on her like Satan in his entire frightening wrath. Angelina beheld a countenance of such black, terrifying menace that she trembled, fear coiling in the pit of her stomach. Never had she encountered such cold, purposeful rage. He took in the dead rabbit on the ground, and, with a look of cold revulsion, his eyes raked over her, riveting on the rifle in her hands.

'What the devil are you doing?' he demanded. 'If you don't mind, I will take that.' He held out his hand for the rifle, but Angelina had no intention of parting with her precious possession. Once it had been her only means of protection against hostile predators—both human and animal—when she had made the long trek from Ohio to Boston, and also the means of supplying her and her mother with many a tasty dinner.

'Mind! But of course I mind,' she retorted, losing control of her temper. Recklessly and without thinking what she was actually doing, taking a step back she levelled it at Alex's chest.

Alex's face darkened even more. 'Give it to me,' he said in that infuriatingly same awful voice.

Undismayed Angelina glared at him without removing her hand on the well-worn grip.

'Angelina, I repeat, give it to me.'

'No, I won't,' she said, trying to ignore the fury her defiance ignited in his features.

'You little hell cat,' he said quietly, watching her closely. Almost gently he warned, 'Before you consider pulling the trigger, pause to consider if killing me is worth hanging for.'

Angelina didn't flinch. 'I actually think it would be worth it,' she hissed, but, seeming to realise the absurdity of her action, she slowly lowered the gun.

'I'll break that rifle over your backside if you so much as raise it again.'

Highly incensed by his threat, a feral light gleamed in the depths of Angelina's eyes. She was like a kitten showing its claws to a full-grown panther. 'You lay one finger on me,' she ground out in a low husky voice, 'and I'll scratch your eyes out. I swear I will.'

In the face of this dire threat Alex moved towards her and leaned forward deliberately until grey eyes stared into amethyst from little more than a foot apart. His eyes grew hard and flintlike, yet when it came his voice was soft and slow. 'You dare me?' Seeing flagging courage and alarm flare in those dark orbs close to his own, reaching out he plucked the rifle from Angelina's grasp before she knew what he was about. 'I have never been an abuser of women,' he said, speaking carefully and distinctly, 'but if you tempt me enough, I might change my mind. I become very unreasonable when I'm angry.'

Stepping back, he scrutinised the lightweight rifle, with its fine engraved patch box and ripple-grained stock. He recognized it as a Kentucky flintlock rifle, one of the most popular small firearms of the American frontier. It was also ideal for hunting and, Alex thought with annoyance, for use against marauding Indians and irate lords. 'Yours, is it?'

Rather than let him see she was afraid and refusing to be humbled, she raised her chin and assumed an air of remote indifference. 'Yes.'

'Now why doesn't that surprise me.' Before Angelina could protest he quickly unfastened the cowhorn powder flask from her waist, which, he would see when he looked at it at greater length later, was attractively engraved with designs of maps and ships. He looked down at the rabbit on the ground and then back at her. The blood he saw on her hands repelled him. 'What a bloodthirsty little wench you are,' he said in a savage underbreath. 'I imagine there are other things you enjoy as much as killing rabbits—like cock fighting and badger baiting,' he accused with scathing sarcasm.

'I don't,' she responded angrily, smarting beneath his hard gaze. He was looking at her like some irritating but harmless insect he wanted to crush beneath the heel of his expensive, glossy black boots. 'They are cruel sports. Such useless bloodletting utterly repels me. It's a different matter to kill in order to eat.'

'I do realise that things are different in America—'

'Good. Then you must realise that you hunt to kill.'

'And you are not squeamish?'

'I was taught not to be. It was a necessary part of my life.'

'Do you realise I could have you arrested for threatening me at gunpoint—and have you hanged for poaching with a firearm on my land?'

'Poaching? What do you mean? Considering I was going to take the rabbit to Mrs Hall to put in a pie for your dinner, my lord, I don't understand what it is you're complaining about.'

Alex stared at her, anger emanating from every pore. With deliberate cruelty he carefully enunciated each vicious word. 'I don't want you killing rabbits for me, or anything else for that matter. If it were not for the fact that you are a foreigner and can plead ignorance, it would be necessary to reprimand you very severely.' Turning to his horse, he fastened her rifle and powder flask to the saddle. 'Come, walk with me back to the house.' When Angelina made a move to do just that he looked down at the rabbit and then at her. 'Aren't you forgetting something? Now you've killed the wretched animal you might as well bring it with you.'

He frowned when Angelina bent to pick it up and suddenly produced a thin-bladed knife from the top of her boot. His silver eyes glittered and his mouth curled up at the corners, those sleek black brows snapping together. 'Don't you dare attempt to gut or skin it,' he hissed, his voice icy and vibrating with anger.

'Why? What will you do?' she taunted, glowering at him.

He met the angry daggers that came hurtling at him from that glower. 'I'm liable to choke you to death with my bare hands. We have servants to do that.' He paused, holding out his hand palm up. 'I'll take that too.'

Tempted to inflict the same treatment on him as she would have inflicted on the rabbit, reluctantly Angelina handed him the knife. To her consternation and fury, all of a sudden she felt infuriatingly close to tears. 'I can always get another.'

'I forbid it,' he snapped.

'My skinning technique is excellent.'

'I don't doubt that for one moment—which is why I've confiscated your knife.' He examined the weapon. 'A nasty weapon for a young woman. I'd rather see it locked away than one day find it stuck in my back.'

'If I wanted to dispose of you I would not stab you in the back. I would find some other means.'

'Oh?'

'I'd poison your food.'

'Would you indeed? In that case I shall have to be very careful what I eat when you're around. Now come along. You'd best take the rabbit to Mrs Hall.' Turning his back, he took the horse's bridle and walked away.

Angelina was absolutely furious when she saw he had an infuriatingly smug and supremely confident expression on his face, as if he had won that particular round. In fact, she was so incensed that she was tempted to fly after him to do physical violence. Casting her eyes down at the rabbit and picking it up by its hind legs, through a silvery blur of angry tears she glared at his back as he set off through the trees. 'Wait,' she called out. Alex turned and looked back at her. Clamping her mouth shut, she stalked towards him, thrusting the rabbit into his hands and feeling a tremendous surge of satisfaction when blood spattered his light grey riding breeches and marked his immaculate black coat and kid gloves.

'What an arrogant, conceited beast you are, Alex Montgomery,' she spat, so angry that she didn't notice that she'd addressed him by his Christian name. '*You* take the rabbit to Mrs Hall—and I hope that when you eat it it chokes you. I'm going for a walk.'

Brushing past him, she marched back down the path to the edge of the wood, and Alex won a private battle not to smile at her retreating, indignant figure.

* * *

After returning Lancer to the stables and handing the rabbit to one of the stable lads, instructing him to take it to Mrs Hall with Miss Hamilton's compliments, Alex returned to the house and locked Angelina's crude weapons in a cabinet in the gun room. Then, after changing his blood-spattered clothes, he went into his office and tried immersing himself in his work, but his concentration wavered and he found his eyes constantly straying to the windows, looking for Angelina's slender form returning to the house.

When his fury had finally diminished to a safe level after an hour or more, and there was still no sign of her, making sure she had not slipped into the house by a back entrance, he went to look for her.

He was thoughtful when he walked in the direction Angelina had taken when she'd left him. He could hardly believe that she had gone out into the woods to shoot rabbits, or that she had aimed the rifle at him, but with that wilful, fiery temperament of hers, he imagined she did do things spontaneously. Only Angelina would have done such a thing and then dared to confront him so magnificently.

A reluctant smile touched his lips when he remembered her standing valiantly against him. She had looked so heartbreakingly young, with those mutinous dark eyes flashing fire and the dead rabbit at her feet, seeing nothing wrong in what she'd done—and, to be fair to her, she could not be blamed. Obviously no one had told her it was a crime to shoot rabbits in England.

She had told him she'd killed the animal for him, and to his surprise he found himself chuckling. She was truly amazing. Of all the women in the world, not one of them would have offered him such a simple, primitive gift, and he had spoiled it for her. He had seen the hurt in her eyes, and it had wrung his heart. If he hadn't been so damned furious he would have given her the applause she deserved for the clean and accurate shot that had killed the rabbit outright.

He had long considered her the most infuriatingly exasperating woman he had ever met, believing her to be a scheming little opportunist, driven by nothing but her own ambition. It seemed he was wrong about her—very wrong—and he bore the heavy load of self-recrimination for the accusations he had heaped on her. His loyalty to his uncle had clouded his judgement, and it had been wrong of him to condemn her out of hand.

Angelina was sitting beside a brook, her arms hugging her knees to her chest. Her hurt and humiliating sickness had not lessened.

'I can see,' drawled a deep, amused voice, 'that with an expression like that on your face you must be thinking of me.'

Angelina's head swung round in surprise. Her eyes and brain recognised his presence, but her emotions were bemused by anger and damaged pride and were slow to follow. Alex had crept up on her with the stealth of an Indian, and was idly leaning against a large oak, his arms folded across his chest watching her. Angry at the intrusion, she let her scowl deepen.

'You're right. I was.'

'Don't tell me. You are plotting some new way to antagonise me or how best to murder me.'

'Yes. And with as much pain as possible. Why don't you go away and leave me alone? I don't want you anywhere near me. You are loathsome and I hate you.'

Unperturbed by her anger, Alex relinquished his stance by the tree and moved slowly towards her, an infuriating smile on his handsome mouth, his black hair curling attractively over his head and into his nape. 'Come now, you don't mean that.'

'Yes, I do. I never say anything I don't mean.' She glanced up at him towering over her, clutching her knees tighter. There was an uncompromising authority and arrogance in his bold look and set of his jaw that she didn't like. 'I told you to go away. Are you deaf?'

'No, and neither am I blind,' he answered, preoccupied with her cross little face and rosy mouth.

She looked at him sharply. 'What do you mean?'

'Only that you are lovely to look at—even when you are scowling.' He gazed down into her stormy eyes and proudly beautiful face. 'When I returned to the house I got to thinking about your unusual behaviour this afternoon.'

'Really? And what was your conclusion?' she scoffed, trying hard to ignore his compliment about her looks—if that's what it was, which she very much doubted.

'That you are hell bent on self-destruction or you are testing me.'

'It was neither.'

'No?' he replied in mock horror. 'Then this is more serious than I thought and needs further investigation.'

Lowering himself on to the grassy bank, he stretched out beside her. Bending his arm and propping his head on his hand, he lazily admired her profile as she continued to watch the water.

'Please go away. I know you dislike me as much as I dislike you.'

'You are mistaken. I don't dislike you,' he countered softly. Reaching out, he took the end of her plait in his fingers and began gently twisting it round his hand, idly contemplating its thickness, its softness.

'You don't? Then I can only assume that your opinion of me must be worse than I thought. You see, I always believe in first impressions, and your desire to offend me at the beginning of our acquaintance did nothing to endear you to me. So let us not pretend. In future we will strive to keep out of each other's way as much as possible.'

'We will?'

'Yes,' she answered, feeling the gentle tug on her hair. She turned slightly, and, seeing him twining her plait round his fingers, it dawned on her that he was far more interested in her at that moment than anything else. Considering what had happened between them earlier, she thought he seemed infuriatingly and disgustingly at ease. Casting him a sidelong glare, she yanked the plait out of his grasp. 'Please don't do that. Kindly leave my hair alone.'

Alex grinned leisurely as his perusal swept her face, watching as the crisp breeze flirted with tendrils of her hair, which had escaped their cruel confinement around her face. 'You have beautiful hair. It should not be restrained in a plait. You really ought to wear it loose.'

'I prefer to wear it like this,' she snapped, trying to ignore his virile body stretched beside her on the grass and the lean, hard muscles of his thighs flexing beneath the tight-fitting buckskin breeches that clung to him like a second skin.

Alex sighed. 'How can I defend myself when faced with so much determination and hostility?'

'You can't, so don't try. I'm sorry about what I did this afternoon,' she said, feeling the need to explain her actions to him.

'What—for threatening to shoot me or killing the rabbit?'

'Both—but I wouldn't have—shot you, I mean. Killing the rabbit was stupid, I realise that now, but—you see, I knew nothing about your laws governing poaching. Where I come from it is so very different. It's not because we are uncivilised, it's because some of us have to hunt to survive.'

'I know.'

'Do you?'

Alex nodded, his expression serious as he listened to her.

'That's how I was raised, you see—how it was for me and my mother when we left Ohio and returned to Massachusetts, and I can see nothing wrong with it. All I knew was hunting rabbits and wild turkeys and following fox. It was necessary. I make no apologies for that. However, I apologise if I offended you. When Mrs Hall told me your gamekeepers had not brought her any rabbits for some time, I thought I would oblige. Had I been told it was a criminal act to shoot rabbits, I would not have done it. Do you believe me?'

'Yes,' Alex replied, struggling to repress a smile, wanting to reach out and touch her fine-boned profile, tilted obstinately to betray her mutinous thoughts.

'And do you promise not to destroy my rifle? It once belonged to a frontiersman and Will gave it to me, you see.'

'I won't destroy it. I promise,' he answered, having some idea just how much that rifle meant to her. 'When I returned to the house I put it in the gunroom along with the rest. That is where it will remain. You may look at it whenever you wish, providing that's all you do—look.'

'Thank you. That rifle and I have travelled many miles together—and it saved my life on more than one occasion on the journey over the mountains. Without it the wolves or black bears would have made a meal out of me in no time.'

Alex stared at her, astounded. 'You shot bears and wolves?'

'Yes,' she replied, quite matter of fact, as if it were the most natural thing in the world to do. 'I had to. It was either them or me.'

'Good Lord!' Alex felt a stirring of admiration. He could not help but wonder at the grit of this young woman. She was truly remarkable. He had known no other like her, and the disturbing fact was that she seemed capable of disrupting his entire life, no matter what character she portrayed.

'So you can see why I've grown rather fond of it.' She glanced sideways at him. 'I suppose that, knowing all this about me, I've sunk even lower in your opinion.'

'Not at all. Quite the contrary, in fact. There isn't a man I know who would have the courage to go out and shoot a wild bear,' he replied, without a hint of mockery.

Angelina looked at him fully, probing the translucent depths of those clear grey eyes. 'I expect *you* would.'

'If I were confronted by one and I had a gun in my hand, yes, I would.'

She sighed. 'But it's not the sort of thing women do over here. You won't tell anyone, will you?'

Alex smiled, his eyes crinkling at the corners. 'Your secret is quite safe with me.'

'I can see I shall just have to try harder at being a lady.'

He grinned. 'You'll make it. Have you finished?'

She nodded.

'Then will you allow me to have my say?'

'If you must. But it will make no difference to how I feel.'

'And how do you feel, Angelina?' he asked softly.

'I will tell you.' She met his gaze coolly. 'I don't want anything from you. I don't belong here. I never will. I want to go home, back to America—but I can't go home. My mother saw to that when she made Uncle Henry my guardian.'

'You are right. Accept it. Your former life is over—permanently. And as much as you are against it, as the ward of the Duke of Mowbray you must face the fact that you will have to make your début into society.'

'I don't want a Season,' she cried explosively. 'I will not have you browbeating me into it.'

Her dark eyes sparkled with anger, and Alex thought what a waste it would be for her to hide herself away, but then, better that than having to endure half the hot young bloods in London targeting her. He decided not to pursue that subject for the time being. 'What is it that has made you feel you don't belong here?'

She shrugged. 'I don't know. I just feel it.'

'I thought you liked Arlington.'

'I do—but—but I would like to return to London,' she said suddenly.

Alex took a deep breath. 'No.'

'Why not? After what happened between us earlier, I'd have thought you would be glad to see the back of me.'

'Uncle Henry gave you into my care and authority. Until he returns from Cornwall this is where you will remain. Besides, there is no one in London to take care of you.' When she continued to glare at him mutinously his face hardened. 'And, of course, you know I'll come after you if you spirit yourself away,' he told her, knowing she was capable of anything, even running away.

Scrambling to her feet in a huff, Angelina was tempted to call him names that would have set his ears on fire, but, realising it would serve no purpose, she refrained from doing so.

'Do you have contempt for women in general, or just me? Is it cruelty that makes you so obnoxious towards me, or are you naturally so?'

'I don't mean to be obnoxious and nor do I hold you in contempt,' he countered, getting to his feet. 'A moment ago I asked you to let me have my say. Please oblige me by doing so.'

'Very well,' she said primly.

'First of all, I apologise for any offence I caused you when we first met in London. My affection and loyalty to my uncle clouded my judgement and it was wrong of me to upset you. Please forgive me,' he said with disconcerting sincerity. 'I was rude and boorish in my behaviour towards you and now I heartily beg your pardon.'

Angelina was astonished. She stared into those clear eyes, searching for mockery, the veiled contempt, but found neither. 'You were rude and insulting,' she agreed.

'I know. I also know you would not have flouted the law so blatantly had you known it is a criminal offence to go around shooting rabbits—or any other animal unlucky enough to find itself within your sights, for that matter. I should have realised you had not been told and not reacted so furiously. I do not ask you to like me, Angelina, I only beg you to grant me some of your time so that I might present my case. In so doing I am sure you will reverse your opinion of me.'

'I won't,' she said adamantly.

'Nevertheless, it would be poor spirited of you to deny me that.'

Angelina stared at him, her eyes wide with astonishment. To be responsible for an offence, punished for it, to feel shame and bitter remorse and then be forgiven and absolved, was a succession of events beyond her experience. Rendered almost speechless by his apology and change of attitude, she welcomed it and yet she was suspicious, wondering why he was suddenly bent on charming her. She found him easier to deal with when they were engaged in open warfare than when he was being agreeable.

'What are you saying?'

Sensing that she was wavering a little and that he was close to victory, Alex pressed home his advantage. 'Only that a truce would not go amiss between us. That is the obvious solution, don't you think?'

Not knowing how to react, suspecting a truce between them would be more dangerous to her than when they were enemies, she opened her mouth to object, but closed it quickly.

'Come. What do you say?' He moved closer, touched by the innocence in her large, liquid eyes. 'Why do you hesitate? Are you afraid of what might happen if we become too close?'

'Of course not,' she replied, with a confidence she was far from feeling. 'But a truce isn't friendship. It's only a halt in hostilities between enemies.'

Alex grinned. 'It's a start.'

'Perhaps it is, but I still don't trust you. And nothing will happen, so don't you dare think you can seduce me, because you'll be wasting your time.'

'Seduction is a time-honoured tradition in my family,' he told her, moving close like a hawk threatened to challenge. 'One that we're good at.' His wickedly smiling eyes captured hers and held them prisoner until she felt a warmth suffuse her cheeks.

Angelina took a step back. Her pride was taking a battering. He was deliberately manipulating her, forcing honesty into the battles between then. Oh, why did he have to look at her like that? The flush deepened in her cheeks. 'How many women have you said that to, Lord Montgomery?' she asked in an attempt to sound flippant in order to hide how she really felt.

A crooked smile accompanied his reply. 'Several. I am no saint. I enjoy the company of beautiful women, true, but is that such a crime? I would like to enjoy your company better, Angelina. I would like you to be more amiable towards me. I find you quite challenging.'

'Why? Because you want to bring me to heel, and when you have done so trample me under your foot?'

He arched a brow, amused. 'No, but I would like you to be less hostile towards me, less stubborn. Did anyone ever tell you that you have lovely eyes? You've got a lovely mouth as well.'

She looked away, staring fixedly at a point beyond the brook. 'Please don't say those things. I am not interested.'

'No?' Reaching out, he placed his forefinger gently on her cheek and turned her face back to his. He arched a questioning brow.

Angelina lifted her small chin and met his gaze unflinchingly, feeling his finger scorch her flesh. Firmly she removed it with her own. 'No. If it is your intention to gentle me, my lord, you will have to use brute force to subdue my rebellion rather than seducing me. Those are the only tactics I know.'

In spite of himself Alex threw back his head and exploded with laughter.

Wounded by his reaction, Angelina marched past him, yet her anger and resentment were considerably diminished. 'You brute. You're enjoying this, aren't you?'

'Every minute of it,' he confessed, laughing, his eyes dancing with merriment.

'Well, I don't know what you think you're doing, but I'm going back to the house.'

Alex matched her stride as they walked back across the park. Knowing exactly what he was doing and why, he smiled inwardly, enjoying the hunt and anticipating the kill with a good deal of pleasure.

Having no concept of his thoughts, after a moment Angelina turned and gave him a mischievous look.

'Tell me, Lord Montgomery—'

'Won't you call me Alex?'

After thinking it over for a moment, she smiled. 'Yes, all right,' she conceded to his immense surprise and satisfaction. 'Alex it is, then. Tell me,' she repeated, 'does all this belong to you?' Taking an energetic hop backwards better to see his face, she spread her arms wide to embrace the park and surrounding countryside.

'All of it,' he replied, utterly enchanted by her. Her dancing eyes and quick smile were sublime.

'So—if you wanted, you could grant permission to anyone who asked to shoot game on your land?'

The remnants of mirth still gleaming in his eyes, Alex shot her a warning look, seeing where her thoughts were travelling. 'Don't even think about it,' he growled.

Giving him an impish grin, with a laugh as clear as the purest water, Angelina left his side and skipped on ahead, releasing all her suppressed energy. Alex watched her go, her bright blue skirts dancing about her feet as she went, allowing him a tantalising glimpse of slim calves and ankles. He felt a surge of admiration. Her purity and the sweet wild essence of her shone like a rare jewel. She was innocence and youth, gentleness and laughter, a wood nymph surrounded by nature, and without warning he felt hot desire pulsating to life within him—not unexpected and certainly not unwelcome.

It was at dinner that same night when Angelina looked down at the succulent trout on her plate, then raised her eyes to the man sitting across from her in mock horror. 'What!' she exclaimed. 'No rabbit?'

Alex suppressed a grin. 'No. I've suddenly taken an aversion to that particular animal. I've instructed Mrs Hall to take it off the menu. Permanently.'

Angelina wasn't sorry. A softness entered her eyes and a haziness that suggested tears. Alex looked at her in disbelief, at a complete loss to know why his refusal to eat her rabbit should have brought her close to weeping.

'You're not going to tell me you're offended, are you?'

'No,' she whispered truthfully, humbled. 'I'm so sorry I killed the rabbit. I'll never shoot another as long as I live. I swear I won't.'

Alex stared at her. Those were not the words he had expected from her, but they were the ones he most wanted to hear. Somehow her regret for her foolish deed made him feel better. He grinned. 'Does that apply to fish, too?'

Angelina saw the humour lurking in his silver eyes and laughed. 'Oh, no. I'm good at fishing.'

'I'm glad to hear it. So am I. Now, eat your trout.'

Mrs Morrisey was busy supervising the housemaids as preparations for the weekend house party got under way. Angelina was not looking forward to it, finding the prospect of meeting strangers daunting. Aunt Patience was feeling much better and hopefully the doctor would permit her to leave her room by the weekend.

When Angelina left Alex to sit with their aunt after dinner each night, he had taken to accompanying her, where, under the ever-watchful eye of Aunt Patience, he would engage the young woman in cards or chess—and Uncle Henry had been right about her skill. At first he had doubted her talent, but he soon realised he had grossly underestimated her ability and that she was no novice.

They played in front of the fire, so engrossed in their game that they failed to notice Patience's expression of pure delight as she looked on from a roll-backed sofa, pretending to read a book. With a well-satisfied smile, she watched Alex as he relaxed in his high-backed chair with a decanter of brandy on the small carved table beside him. His eyes were fastened on the young woman across from him, and she strongly suspected his interest was not in the game.

While Angelina thought out her next move, the only sound in the room was the occasional crackle of the fire and the steady tick of the ormolu clock on the marble mantelpiece. Alex was fascinated by the way Angelina always vacated her chair and either perched on an embroidered footstool or knelt on the carpet, as she did now, as soon as they began to play. Her casual posture was not at all what he was used to among the proper ladies of his acquaintance, but he found it enchanting nevertheless. Sitting back on her heels and resting her elbows on the low chess table and cupping her face in her hands, her dark lashes curving against her cheek, she presented to him a captivating picture of bewitching innocence as she frowned in deep concentration over the board.

Every so often she would reach out and take a piece of pink Turkish delight, liberally sprinkled with powdered sugar, from a salver beside her and pop it into her mouth. Sipping at a glass of brandy, feeling the heat course down the back of his throat, Alex would watch from beneath half-lowered lids as she sucked the sugar from each sticky finger, her lips ripe, perfect, and so adorably kissable. It was almost impossible to believe that he could find such an ordinary act sublimely erotic, an act inflaming him beyond logic. As she was taking her time contemplating her next move, he looked down on the top of her head where the shining chestnut-coloured hair was drawn into an even parting, tempted to reach out and run his finger down the perfect line.

'Are you woolgathering or have you forgotten it's your move?' he said with a hint of gentle mockery.

Angelina shot him an indignant look. 'I am not woolgathering—whatever that means—and I know it's my move without you having to remind me. I just want to make quite certain that the move I make is the right one.'

'Who taught you to play?'

'My father. I used to beat him more often than not.'

'I am not your father, and you have not won yet, young lady. I have your knight.'

'And I have one of your bishops,' she countered.

'That makes no difference. It's the skill that matters. Now—are you going to move or not?' He flicked her lazy a grin. 'Of course, if you want to accept defeat, I'll accept your surrender.'

'I think not. The game is not over yet. And do you always talk as much as this when you play chess—or are you trying to put me off my game?'

'If you move your bishop, you will relieve my knight,' he suggested softly.

Angelina looked up, a deep furrow etched between her brows. 'Certainly not. If I were to do that, you would take great delight in capturing my queen,' she replied, giving his queen a scathing look where she lurked threateningly on the edge of the board ready to pounce.

Crossing one long leg over the other, Alex relaxed, content to wait until she was ready to make her move, fully prepared to wait all night if need be. He stared at her tight shoulders, at the taut, slim fingers moving her chess piece, each one exquisitely carved and depicting a character out of one or another of Shakespeare's plays. He watched her lift a finger to her lower lip and begin to nibble her nail in a characteristic gesture that made his blood run warm.

'That's a bad habit,' he chided softly.

She raised her eyes in surprise, the familiar, distant look of concentration in their dark depths. Her lips were slightly parted.

'What is?'

He smiled, looking down at her. 'Nail nibbling.'

'Oh—it helps me concentrate.' She flushed softly and quickly lowered her hand to her lap when his gaze lingered hot and hungry on her lips.

'Then try not to concentrate too hard, otherwise you will not have any nails left—and I will lose to you yet again.'

He sighed, beginning to enjoy himself as she took her time over her next strategic moves. It required every ounce of his self-control to concentrate on his own game. His pulse began to quicken as he dwelt on the graceful sweep of her neck and the mobile curve to her lips—so ripe, so soft, so kissable. Instantly his body began to hum a willing, familiar song and he wanted to toss the board and all those irritating little pieces aside and join her on the carpet right there in front of the fire and crush her against him.

'Check!' Angelina suddenly cried, cornering his black king with her white queen.

Alex grinned. 'Mate,' he responded, knocking his king over in final, willing defeat.

'That's two games to me to your one,' she told him.

The triumphant joy on her face was so startling, so captivating, that Alex was tempted to let her win every time. It would be well worth it to see her look like that. 'I admit defeat and consider myself well and truly trounced.'

'Will you not play another game to try to get even?'

Alex threw up his hands in mock despair. 'Alas, no. Don't you think I've been punished enough for one evening? We'll play again—perhaps tomorrow—and for your impudence I'm afraid I shall be forced to deal with you as you deserve,' he chuckled. He rose and went to his aunt, bending down and kissing her cheek. 'I will bid both you ladies goodnight and retire to my rooms to lick my wounds in private. As you know, Verity and Nathan will be arriving tomorrow—a day ahead of the other guests. I have business in St Albans in the morning so my secretary Hawkins and I will be away first thing. I should be back early afternoon.'

'Alex, wait,' said Angelina, scrambling to her feet and halting him as he was about to go out, remembering she had a request to make of him. With his hand on the door knob he turned and looked at her, waiting for her to speak.

'May I ride? You have so many fine horses in your stable. I've asked Trimble if I may ride one, but he told me to ask you first.'

'Of course. As long as you remain within the vicinity of the house you may. If you wish to ride further afield, a groom or myself must accompany you.'

'Why?'

'Because it is not done for young ladies to ride alone, that's why. There are also gypsies in the area, so I do not want you to venture too far.'

'Are they harmful?'

'As a rule, no. They have my permission to be on Arlington land just as they had from my predecessors—to come and go as they please, providing they behave themselves and abide by the law of the land while they are here. Unfortunately the gypsies encamped on the other side of the woods are strangers and therefore unpredictable. My bailiff has told them to move on. With luck they will have gone before the end of the week.'

Chapter Six

'I'm glad to see the two of you are getting on,' Patience said when Alex had gone.

'Yes, we are, but he never talks about himself. Despite his self-assurance, I sense a deep sadness in him, something frozen and withdrawn. He gives of himself sparingly. The only thing I know about him is that both his parents are dead.'

'Gerald, his father, is—but Margaret—his mother, is very much alive,' Patience told her with uncharacteristic bitterness. 'After the death of her husband, Margaret married a Spanish count and went to live in Spain.'

Angelina was surprised. 'Oh, I see. Did Alex not approve of this? Is this the reason why he refuses to speak of his mother?'

'There's much more to it than that.'

'And I should not ask,' Angelina murmured sagely. 'I'm sorry, Aunt. I don't mean to pry.'

Patience smiled. 'It's only natural that you are curious—and maybe I should tell you. Alex wouldn't want us discussing something that he considers to be a purely personal and private matter, but, if you know something of his background perhaps it will help you understand him a little better and not judge him too harshly.'

'I don't judge him at all. What was his father like?'

Angelina listened avidly as Patience told her how Alex's mother had married Gerald, Henry's younger brother. Pampered and spoiled, she'd had her sights set on Henry, but Henry—who was deeply in love with someone else—didn't want her. To spite him, Margaret married Gerald, who loved her to distraction. Being lamentably weak, Gerald was forced to endure her many affairs, which she flaunted shamelessly.

For some malicious reason of her own—which Patience suspected was because Alex bore such a striking resemblance to Henry—she had hidden nothing from Alex. He was young and impressionable and adored his father. Gerald began drinking heavily to blot out what Margaret was doing, until it became too much. One day when he was in his cups he shot himself. Alex was fifteen at the time and witnessed the whole dreadful business.

Angelina listened in horror, seeing her aunt's eyes cloud with pain and bitter memory.

'Because he sensed it could destroy him, Alex refused to submit to the anger and anguish that raged inside him. In Henry he found warmth and understanding. But no one has been capable of unlocking that closed compartment inside his mind where he keeps his pain. Margaret distorted his mind, inflicting mental injuries on her son no mother should. She fostered in him a loathing and terrible bitterness against the female sex. It will take an exceptional woman to succeed where all others have failed. Alex needs someone to love—and someone to love him unconditionally in return.'

Angelina felt a lump of constricting sorrow in her chest, deeply moved by what Patience had revealed to her, which went a long way to helping her understand Alex. She also realised that the same demons that chased her were chasing Alex, and that it was as hard for him to talk about what had happened to him as it was for her.

The following day saw a deterioration in the weather, with rain fluctuating from a drizzle to a torrential downpour. Disappointed at being unable to ride, Angelina's spirits drooped. Undecided about what to do with her time, she decided to take a bath.

Unthinkingly Pauline sighed. 'It'll be a relief when the workmen have finished their work and water pipes have been laid throughout the house. Then we won't have to haul water up from the kitchens any more. No doubt they'll be starting on the west wing soon now work on his lordship's apartments is complete.'

'Trust him to take care of his own comforts before anyone else's.' Recalling Alex telling her that he would be away today, interest kindled in Angelina's eyes as a sudden thought occurred to her, and when she turned to her maid they were feverishly gay. 'Oh, Pauline!' she said, laughing, scrambling off the window seat. 'I've just had a rather splendid idea.'

There was such a look of excitement on her face and a familiar gleam in her eyes that made Pauline suspicious. It was a look she was beginning to recognise, one that boded trouble.

Five minutes later, when Angelina presented herself at the door of Alex's rooms armed with a large pink towel and bathing lotions, Wyatt, Alex's valet, was so astounded that all he could do was gape at her with a look of palsied shock. Bestowing on him her most brilliant of smiles, using her softest voice and being her most charming self, she eventually managed to cajole him into letting her use his lordship's bath tub.

Carried along under some kind of compulsion in which his responses were suspended, shaking his head in disbelief at what he had permitted, knowing the full force of his master's wrath would descend on him if he were to find out about this, Wyatt went to spend half an hour or more in the domestic quarters.

Angelina let her gaze roam over Alex's apartments in wonder. Even if she hadn't known to whom these rooms belonged she would have guessed, for the familiar spicy scent of Alex's cologne hung like an invisible intoxicant in the air. Essentially masculine and fit for a king, the room in which she stood was tastefully decorated in dark green and gold, with walnut dressers and bureaus and a large bed on a shallow dais.

Placing her towel on a chair, her curiosity getting the better of her, she went and peeked into another room, seeing a large desk and leather chairs, the walls lined with books. It was a busy room, a working room, with everything neatly in place. Crossing to the room that Mr Wyatt had told her was his lordship's bathing chamber and adjoining dressing room, gingerly she pushed open the door. Blinking at the extravagance and unaccustomed luxury, she felt as if she had suddenly been transported to a magical cave beneath a tropical sea and that Neptune would appear at any minute.

The ceiling was white, the walls pastel blue, green and white tiles interspaced with sparkling mirrors. In the centre of the tiled floor strewn with soft rugs was an enormous bath of white marble and gold taps. This fabulous object—the very height of luxury—beckoned her, and, unable to resist it a moment longer, she immediately turned on the taps and added her perfumed lotions before stripping off her clothes and stepping in.

Having concluded his business in St Albans sooner than he had expected, Alex and Hawkins returned to Arlington Hall, sodden after their long ride. With no sign of his valet and in a hurry to get out of his damp clothes, Alex stripped the garments from the upper part of his body and unfastened the top buttons of his trousers before crossing to the bathing chamber, picking up a towel as he went. Something about the towel made him pause and look at it in puzzlement. Pink? All his towels were either green or gold. Unable to work out what a pink towel was doing in his room, he shrugged and began to rub his wet hair.

On opening the door a wave of moist, perfumed air hit him in the face. He stopped short, unable to believe the sight that met his eyes. An enormous cloud of fragrant steam was rising from the bath, and emerging from the steam was a head, a woman's head, crowned with a glorious wealth of chestnut- and copper-coloured curls. Stray tresses fell about her ears and clung to her nape in a saturated tangle, the rest of this adorable creature immersed in a mass of froth.

At first he was sorely tempted to ask her what the hell she thought she was doing in his tub, but it would have deprived him of the pleasure of watching her from his vantage point by the door. Until that moment he had never thought so much pleasure could be derived in simply watching a woman who was oblivious to being watched. The mere sight of her, with the soapy water lapping those twin orbs of femininity with infuriating, tantalising familiarity, was, for Alex, such a pleasurable experience that it made him ache.

It was the faint draught of cool air on her bare shoulders that alerted Angelina to the open door. With a gasp her head whipped round, and like a flame the powerful awareness of Alex's physical presence scorched through her. His unheralded appearance startled her to a sitting position, and Alex watched the soapy water sluicing off her satiny skin. The heat of his appreciative gaze ranged with deliberate slowness over her hair and face and down to her slender shoulders, pausing at length on the exposed, creamy swell of her breasts, leaving the frothy water to provide modest cover for the rest of her.

Alex's bold scrutiny caused Angelina's modesty to chafe. With her heart thumping in her breast and fighting to quell the shriek of panic that was rising in her throat, she cast a surreptitious glance about her. Her clothes lay in an untidy heap on the floor like a fallen barricade, and Alex was holding her towel.

Casually Alex relinquished his stance and, closing the door, moved further inside the room. Watching him, uncertain and silent, it was this action that caused panic and fear to course through Angelina. Suddenly she felt intimidated, vulnerable and alone. Memories she was unable to stifle paraded across her mind, and there was a haunting vision of her cowering, quivering and terrified beneath other eyes, with hysterical pleas tumbling from her trembling lips.

Having no concept of her thoughts, Alex crossed towards the bath where she cowered low in the water.

'Well, well,' he said, his voice low and mocking, his eyes

burning into hers, the atmosphere inside the bathing chamber hot and sultry. 'Not content with poaching in my woods and threatening me at gunpoint, you now have to add trespassing in my private rooms to your crimes. It's a good thing I returned early—but—on second thoughts—perhaps I should have waited a while longer. Had I done so, your curiosity about my rooms might have extended to my bed.'

Angelina felt the colour drain from her face. Alex loomed large and menacing, his awesome presence filling the bathing chamber. With his hair a cluster of shining black moist curls, all she could do was stare with a bemused intensity. Compulsively and with a will of their own, her eyes travelled over his broad chest spread with a dark mat of hair, down over the hard leanness of his flat stomach, the pink of her cheeks returning when she saw a trail of black hair start beneath his navel and disappear into his trousers, where a bulge strained against the material.

Alex was watching her closely; her continued regard of that most private part of his anatomy increased the heat in his loins and he felt his tumescence grow. Good Lord, he thought. To his horror he realised his body was reacting to her without the least encouragement on her part.

With a jolt of mortification Angelina tore her eyes away when she realized that she was staring. She looked up at him in desperate appeal, terrified that her blatant intrusion into his private rooms and audacity to make use of his bath would have aroused his wrath to such a degree that it would bring some terrible dark vengeance down on her. She watched him with the terrified eye of a mouse watching a stalking cat.

'I—I didn't hear you come in,' she whispered, disturbed by the scorching heat of his perusal, and quite put out that he had been silently watching her and had made no effort to alert her to his presence. 'You should have made your presence known to me.'

'What! And deprive myself of the pleasure of watching you?' he murmured softly, desperately wanting her to look at him as she had a moment ago. 'If you don't get out this instant, you cannot depend on my ability to exercise restraint.'

'Why—what will you do?'

'Join you,' he said, casually lowering his hand to the few remaining buttons securing his trousers.

Horror registered in her eyes when she realised he intended removing that last vestige of decency and joining her in the bath, which was disgustingly large enough to accommodate the two of them. 'Please, Alex. Pass me my towel, I beg of you. I'll get out.'

Without revealing any more of her lovely form than was exposed to him already, she held out her hand, dripping water on to the floor. Alex saw it was trembling. Raising his eyes, he studied her as if he were truly trying to understand her. His gaze moved over her pale face, searching her dark eyes and discovering something in their agonised depths that brought a puzzled frown to his brow. Just when Angelina thought her time was up and no angel of deliverance would come to her aid, and that he would either scoop her out of the water or climb in with her, he handed her the towel and turned abruptly, actually scowling.

'Get dressed,' he ordered succinctly. 'I'll wait in the other room.'

His command penetrated Angelina's paralysed thoughts, and, when he had gone, she climbed out of the bath immediately, shaking in every limb. After drying herself and struggling into her clothes, she unpinned her hair from its fastening and shook it loose so that it cascaded just past her waist. Emerging from the bathroom into the lion's den, she drew a deep breath as she tried to steady her nerves. Having thrown on a shirt, Alex stood with his back to her looking out of the window, his whole body tensed into a rigid line, as if he fought some private battle within himself.

Sensing her presence, he turned, his jaw set. She was oblivious to the sight she presented to him. The pure, sweet bliss of having her close spurred his heart. She was too damned lovely to be true. Her cheeks were still rosy from her bath, and her hair—all the wonderful shades of autumn he'd imagined it to be—formed a torrent of brilliant silk tresses, with adorable damp tendrils clinging and curling around her face. The very sight of her here in his rooms wrenched his vitals in a painful knot, and the urge to go to her and pull her into his arms savaged his restraint. If she knew the full force of that emotion he held in check, she would tremble and seek the sanctuary of her room.

In a calm voice that nevertheless carried an unmistakable threat of command, he said, 'Come here.'

With the width of the room between them, clutching her towel and lotion bottles to her, Angelina could almost believe she was crossing an immeasurable abyss. As she slowly moved towards him, Alex's towering height increasing. Halfway there she paused.

Alex raised one black devil's eyebrow. 'Closer. That's not far enough.'

He looked like a dark, invincible god, forbidding, intimidating, and yet strangely compelling. When she stood close his hand reached out and touched her tumbling hair, taking one curling tress and winding it gently round his finger.

'You have beautiful hair, Angelina. It's a sin to restrain it the way you do.'

Frantically she began to think of things she could say, but all she could do was stare at him in mute appeal. Alex's suppressed energy and desire seemed to burn in that warm, elegant room, where all reality had been suspended. Angelina felt weak, unable to find the antagonism amid her confusion.

'You should not be here.'

'I know,' she whispered, finding her voice at last. Her pulse quickened when he stepped nearer. Feeling the bold look of his hungry gaze she trembled and instinctively took a step back, her only thought being to avoid any contact with him. 'I—I was not expecting to see you back so soon.'

'Evidently. I concluded my business in half the time and returned early—and it's as well that I did. The last thing I expected was to find you making use of my bathtub. I shall have a few choice words to say to Wyatt.'

Angelina's eyes flew to his, alarmed that he would vent his wrath on poor Wyatt when the fault was all hers. 'Oh, no. Please don't be angry with him. I am entirely to blame.'

'I believe you,' Alex replied drily, thrusting his hands into his pockets to keep from reaching out and dragging her into his arms.

'I—I didn't mean to intrude, but—I—'

'You wanted to sample my bathing chamber.'

'Yes.'

'Then don't you think it would have been common courtesy to ask me first? Why didn't you?'

'Because I didn't find out until this morning that you had one. Besides, you would have refused,' she said softly.

'On the contrary. I would gladly have given you my permission,' Alex said, finding that with the light from the window washing over her she was like a radiant sunburst and looked adorable.

Surprise etched Angelina's lovely features and her misty eyes widened. 'You would?'

'Yes,' he answered reasonably. 'Does that surprise you?'

'Yes, it does.'

'Why?'

'Because I—I don't understand you,' she murmured hesitantly. 'I never know what to expect from you. At the beginning you were hostile towards me. You were my judge, jury and executioner all wrapped into one.' Her luminescent eyes were large and desperate with confusion. 'And now—these last few days—you—you—'

'I told you not three days ago that I was wrong in my assessment of both you and your mother and I apologised. But you know, Angelina,' he said softly, seeing his reflection in the dark centres of her eyes, 'I seriously think you enjoy baiting me, and nobody does it as well as you. But shall I tell you what I think when I look at you now?'

'I—if you like,' Angelina said, trying to answer lightly, but her voice was low and husky.

'I see an extremely beautiful young woman with shining hair

all the wonderful shades of autumn and the smile of an angel.'
His heavy-lidded gaze dropped to the inviting fullness of her
mouth, lingering there.

Angelina stepped back a little, but an answering quiver that
was a combination of fright and excitement was tingling up her
spine. 'Please don't look at me like that,' she whispered.

'Then I think you'd better go.'

Alex's desire for Angelina was hard driven, but he couldn't
overstep the mark. But then, he thought, dwelling on a suspicion that had been forming in his mind since before he'd left
London, would his uncle mind all that much if he made
advances towards Angelina? Wasn't that what that wily old man
had in mind when he'd insisted on her accompanying him to
Arlington while he removed himself to Cornwall?

Clutching her towel and bottles to her chest, Angelina
crossed the room and opened the door, only to find it slam shut
when Alex came up behind her with the sure-footed skill of a
panther. She stood there, frozen, anchored between his strong
arms, the sleeves of his shirt rolled back to reveal their power.
Unable to turn, she could feel his closeness, the muscular
hardness of him, the vibrant heat of his body pressed close
against her back and his warm breath on her hair.

She trembled when he drew the heavy tresses to one side,
feeling defeat, afraid, when she felt his mouth on the soft warm
flesh on the back of her neck. On a gasp she sucked in her
breath when he parted his lips and touched her skin with the
fiery tip of his tongue. Her heart was pounding, and for a
moment she knew a feeling of sheer terror when his voice
spoke very quietly into her ear. 'I want you,' he murmured
hoarsely. To his surprise she didn't fight him; in fact, as his lips
began a slow, erotic seduction over her flesh, she didn't seem
to know what he was doing to her.

'Please—don't do this,' she whispered, her heart thundering in her ears.

'Why? Don't fight me, Angel. What are you afraid of?'

You, her mind screamed. *You, and what you might do to me.*

'You are as much a victim of the overwhelming forces at work between us as I,' he murmured, his lips continuing their tender assault on her neck, the scent and living heat of her invading all his senses. 'You and I are one. The simple truth can no longer be denied.'

Lowering her head, a small knot in the wood of the door became the focal point of Angelina's concentration, a misshapen image tugging at the heart of her memory, conjuring indistinct, cloudy visions in her mind and blending them with a confused jumble of events that took her back to another time, another place, when other hands had touched her, when she had wanted to flee, but had been unable to escape the filthy, groping fingers. She fought a welter of unwelcome emotions that threatened to drag her down to a new depth of despair.

But she was not immune to Alex standing behind her, of the hard rack of his chest pressed against her back, making her feel things she had never felt before, things that were alien to her that she didn't want to feel. An alarming, treacherous warmth was creeping through her body, a melting sensation unlike anything she had known. She wanted to relax back against him, to feel his arms close around her, but because she could still feel those powerful emotions that seemed to have been drawn into her heart and soul from that night when she thought her life had ended, she could not bring herself to make that move.

With desire crashing over him in tidal waves, Alex looked down at Angelina's bent head, his lips brushing her shining hair. Slipping an arm about her waist he drew her tight against him, feeling a shimmering tremor in her slender body.

For a moment Angelina leaned into him, let his arm hold her, let him prevail in his hunger, his desire—but she didn't want it. Her confusion, her passion and her pain rose to a pinnacle as she stood trembling against him. To be this close to him felt like suffocating. She didn't think she could survive it. Terrified of making an overestimation of her ability to carry out the course she had chosen for herself, somehow she managed to place her trembling fingers on the doorknob and turn it.

'This is mistake,' she whispered, knowing that if she allowed some tenderness now between them she would be lost. 'I told you on the day we met that I do not want to be close to any man in the way you imply—and that includes you.'

Twisting herself out of his embrace, she opened the door and then she was gone, her feet driven by panic away from the east wing. Let him rant and rail, let him insult and chastise her to his heart's content—anything. Just let him never look at her as he had just then, or touch her with such tender intimacy. She would not let herself be at the mercy of a man like Alex Montgomery, who radiated sensual hunger in every glance, every move and every touch, but she could not deny that something had passed between them that would change their relationship for ever.

On reaching her room, she was struck by a desperate, impelling urge to get out of the house. In an act of rebellion and to bring some semblance of order back to her confused and troubled mind, she strode into the closet and rummaged in her trunk, finally finding what she was looking for—her old breeches and shirt. Removing her dress, she pulled them on, tucking the trouser legs inside her new pair of dark brown leather riding boots and lacing them up—incongruous against her shabby garb. After hastily plaiting her hair, she left the house by a back entrance without seeing a soul until she reached the stables.

When Angelina had left him, Alex stood in the centre of his room in deep reflection. Angrily he attacked his sentimental thoughts until they cowered in meek submission, but they refused to lie down. His attraction to Angelina was disquieting—in fact, it was damned annoying. If he wanted an affair or diversion of any kind, he had a string of some of the most beautiful women in the country to choose from—so why should he feel this insanely wild attraction for an eighteen-year-old girl who had hardly left the schoolroom?

He tried to put her from his mind, but failed miserably in his effort. The sweet fragrance of her perfume lingered everywhere, drifting through his senses, and the throbbing hunger began anew. He cursed with silent frustration, seized by a strong desire to go after her and cauterise his need by holding her close and clamping his lips on hers.

Instead he went into his study and attempted immersing himself in his work. Sitting at his desk, he set himself the task of going over the household accounts, subtracting and multiplying and adding long columns of figures. Under normal circumstances this was a simple matter for his keen, mathematical mind, but, slowly, a face with a pert, dimpled chin, a lovely and expressive mouth with soft, full lips, cheeks as flushed as a ripe peach, and thickly fringed amethyst, velvety eyes crept unbidden into his mind—teasing him, tantalising him, laughing, beckoning him—fearing him.

At this thought Alex leaned his head back against the chair and set down his quill, giving in to his reluctant musings. Fear! Having marked Angelina's unexpected vulnerability when she'd cowered beneath the water, he now realised that that was what he'd seen in her eyes, but failed to recognize, when he'd threatened to join her in her bath. Then he remembered the words she had spoken before she'd left him and the pain in her voice—that she did not want to be close to any man, including him.

Why? He was both puzzled and curious. What had happened to her? Did it all stem from the time the Indians had attacked her home? Had they attacked her? Was the cause of her determination to close her heart and mind on marriage, on men, something to do with the relationship that had existed between her parents—or something else of an entirely different nature that she dared not reveal to anyone?

He directed his gaze to the window and his eye was caught by a mounted rider galloping across the park at breakneck pace. Frowning, he stood up, straining his eyes through the slightly distorted diamond panes better to recognise the person—which he did. Immediately. He was unable to believe his own eyes, as his gaze became impaled on the figure on the horse.

It was Angelina.

In the space of a heartbeat, fury had replaced Alex's calm composure. He was furious that Angelina worried him with her recklessness, furious that she was able to evoke any kind of emotion in him at all. Clenching his fists, he stood and watched her. Crouched low over her horse's neck with her face almost buried in the dancing mane, she rode as no lady should, in breeches and astride. There was simplicity and confidence as she soared over a hedge, at one with her mount, its tail floating behind like a bright defiant banner.

Her mount!

Alex's face was almost comical in its expression of disbelief when his eyes shifted from the breeches-clad girl to the horse. It was Forest Shadow, a high-spirited, excitable sorrel stallion he'd purchased two months ago at Newmarket to introduce into his hunters. Forest Shadow presented a challenge to even the most accomplished rider, who would be hard pressed to keep the high-stepping animal under control. White with rage, he felt his body go rigid.

'Of all the brazen, outrageous females,' he said in a savage underbreath. When she had shot the rabbit, he would have sworn he was incapable of feeling more furious than he had then, but the rage that exploded inside him at that moment surmounted even that.

Turning quickly, he strode to the door, jerking it open, the stallion bearing its young rider already a diminishing speck in the distance. How dare she ride out of the park alone after he'd forbidden her not to, and how dare she take that horse out of the stable when there wasn't a lad employed by him who was willing to ride out on the animal? On the other hand, he thought with increasing fury as his long legs descended the stairs in leaping strides, that defiant, conniving, dark-eyed witch would dare anything.

Jenkins waylaid Alex in the hall. He shot him an impatient look. 'What is it?' he demanded brusquely.

'I was just coming to inform you that Sir Nathan Beresford

and his wife Lady Verity arrived a few minutes ago, my lord. They are with Lady Fortesque in her room.'

'Thank you, Jenkins,' Alex replied. Brushing past the butler he stalked towards the door. 'I have an urgent matter to attend to at the stables. Apologise for my absence and tell them I will be along directly.'

On reaching the stables he cornered one of the lads. 'Who gave Miss Hamilton permission to ride Forest Shadow?' he demanded.

'I don't know, milord. She just appeared—saying she was going to ride him. We thought you must have told her she could. She wasn't afraid to ride him, milord.'

'No, I don't imagine for one minute that she was,' he seethed.

'Miss Hamilton's good with the horses. Seems to have taken a special fancy to the Shadow—and the Shadow to Miss Hamilton. She understands him. She seems to have a natural communication with him.'

'Indeed!'

'Yes, milord. At first, though, when she mounted him, we thought he was going to throw her, but the oddest thing was that when she talked to him—quiet like, into his ear—he seemed to know what she wanted him to do and settled down.'

'And didn't anyone think to go with her?'

'Yes, milord. But she refused the offer of a groom. Will you be wanting Lancer saddled?' the lad asked, hoping not, having just finished rubbing the stallion down and giving him his feed after returning from St Albans with his lordship. He considered it prudent to keep to himself the stir the young American miss had created by appearing at the stables in breeches—breeches that had seen better days, by the look of them—and of how she had grasped a handful of the Shadow's mane and leapt on to his back with the casual grace of a well-trained acrobat.

'No,' Alex snapped, striding out of the stables like a raging hurricane. He could see no point in riding all over the estate looking for the pesky wench when he knew damn well that she'd come back of her own accord anyway, and when she did he'd teach her obedience if he had to beat it into her.

Walking quickly back to the house, Alex knew a wrath that was beyond anything he had ever felt in his life. That was the moment he encountered Nathan, who had left Verity chatting to her mother and come to look for him. After greeting each other Nathan fell into step beside him.

'Patience tells me your uncle is in Cornwall,' said Nathan.

'He's visiting a sick friend.'

'Convenient, don't you think,' he remarked, observing his friend thoughtfully, 'leaving you and Patience to care for Miss Hamilton?'

'Absolutely,' Alex growled.

Nathan sensed that Alex was definitely put out about something, and he suspected the cause of it might be about to appear out of the woods on which Alex's eyes were fixed. Rather than wait for an explanation, he plunged straight in.

'At the risk of intruding into your thoughts, Alex, might I ask why you are wearing such a formidable frown? Your thoughts appear to be damnably unpleasant—in fact, you look fit to commit murder.'

'I am,' Alex ground out.

Nathan smiled. 'So you have not found the peace at Arlington you sought when you left London.'

'Peace? I cannot envisage any peace with someone like the American chit around. Never did I realise that when I quit London for Arlington—where peace and quiet has reigned supreme for centuries—that it would lead to such frustration and aggravation. But then I never could have imagined a girl quite like Angelina Hamilton either.'

'I think this business with your uncle's ward is preying too much on your mind.'

'I seldom think of her—if it can be avoided.' Which was true—but impossible. It seemed that whenever he thought of Angelina his thoughts became angrily chaotic. She was like some dancing, irrepressible shadow imbedded in his mind.

Nathan gave him a laughing, sidelong look. 'So you would have me think. But I did notice before you left London that your conversations were often sprinkled with varied references to Miss Hamilton.'

Alex threw him a black look. 'Really?' he growled with a hint of mockery. 'I didn't realise you were being so observant, Nathan—but since you are, you will have noticed that the only references I have made to that pesky wench have been unfavourable.'

'And nothing has changed now you have got to know her a little better?' he inquired.

'No—in fact, they have taken a turn for the worse.'

'Patience told me you were beginning to get on rather well.'

'We were, until she decided to take one of my best stallions for a ride to God knows where—without an escort or my permission.'

'Which one?'

'Forest Shadow.'

Nathan's blue eyes widened with astonishment. 'What? You mean that magnificent sorrel you bought at Newmarket recently?'

'The same.'

'Good Lord. He's a peppery beast at the best of times. Much too powerful for a young woman to handle.'

'One thing I have learned about Miss Hamilton, Nathan, is that she is no ordinary young woman—as you will discover very soon. She is also more trouble than I need right now.'

'Shouldn't you go after her?'

'No. The pesky young whelp is only happy when she's courting danger and annoying me. If she chooses to test her skills against that restless, high-stepping beast, then so be it.'

Nathan's chuckling merriment could not be restrained and he laughed out loud. 'Pesky she may be, Alex, but Patience tells me she has been blessed with the most incredible looks. Considering your reputation as a rake of the first order, you cannot have failed to notice.'

Alex's frown was formidable. 'It depends on one's taste—which is something we never did agree upon. The girl is a menace and has wreaked havoc in my life from the day I met her. She is everything I expected—a savage—and temperamental. She brings out the worst and everything that is alien to my nature. She also has the infuriating ability to rouse all that is evil in me, and she has a tongue that would flay the skin off a man's back better than any cat.' Yes, he thought, everything about her annoyed him, everything except her courage, which was a quality he could not help but admire.

'Perhaps if you were not so hard on her—if you tried to be more understanding towards her—you might find her more amenable,' Nathan said, blithely ignoring the simmering rage emanating from his friend. 'Give way a little. Try a softer, more gentle approach. Smooth her feathers and you'll soon have her purring like a kitten. I'm sure if you do you'll discover a more docile and agreeable young woman.'

Alex stopped and looked at his friend as though he'd taken leave of his senses. 'God in heaven, Nathan! There is nothing docile or agreeable about her. She has no respect for authority—and the only feline she resembles is a hellcat. That girl's the biggest stumbling block my temper has ever known. Try a softer approach, you say! The only softness about her I would like to make contact with right now would be laying the flat of my hand firmly on her derrière. The girl needs a sound thrashing that will leave her unable to sit down for a month. I will not be defied and dictated to in my own home by an eighteen-year-old chit of a girl.'

'Or anywhere else for that matter,' chuckled Nathan. It was clear that, where Angelina Hamilton was concerned, Alex's patience was wearing thin and he was in no mood to negotiate a better relationship with her.

Alex's mouth tightened. 'Her defiance cannot be overlooked. She resolved to be difficult from the start. With each day that dawns I wonder what kind of uproar she will cause next. The other day she went shooting rabbits for my dinner, and this very morning I caught her making use of my bathing chamber—and now the brazen wench has ridden off on a high-spirited, excitable horse without my permission.'

Nathan's brows shot up in astonishment. 'Do you mean to say she actually shot a rabbit?'

'She did,' Alex replied icily, 'and she very nearly shot me in the process.'

Stupefied, Nathan stared at him, thoroughly amused. It was unbelievable that Alex, who always had absolute control over his emotions, who treated women with a combination of indifference, amused tolerance and indulgence, could have been driven to such an uncharacteristic outburst of feelings by an eighteen-year-old girl.

'Miss Hamilton has a way with her, I've been told. Your uncle is enslaved, and she has your entire staff eating out of her delectable hands. According to Patience, every one of the grooms down to the youngest stable lad are all in love with her. She's even managed to charm old Jenkins. God help you if she uses it on you, Alex. You may well be lost. There will be no escape—and I very much doubt you will wish to.'

Alex glared at him. 'Don't count on it.'

Nathan directed his gaze towards the house, knowing there would be no reasoning with his friend until he had severely chastised Miss Hamilton. 'I am already feeling sorry for Miss Hamilton. The look on your face tells me you are going for blood, no less.'

'You're right,' Alex replied, lengthening his stride. 'And after the run-ins we've had in the past, she doesn't have very much left to lose.'

Having ridden further than she intended on the brave, fast horse, Angelina found herself enveloped in a shadowy world of muted sounds, where damp and decay rose from the undergrowth and assailed her nostrils, and squirrels skittered in the upper branches of the trees. Without the sun a bitter chill had fallen on this twilight world.

A feeling of unreality crept over her and she shuddered, glad when she saw an opening in the trees ahead where sunlight slanted through. Riding towards the light, she reined in beneath a canopy of oaks. The scent of wood smoke hung heavy in the air. Experiencing a prickling sensation at the nape of her neck and an eerie, familiar feeling, her head snapped up like an animal scenting danger.

She had emerged into some sort of encampment with an assortment of brightly painted caravans and carts, all of which had a shabby appearance. Dogs roamed and several piebald ponies grazed nearby. Men, women and children prowled about furtively in their garishly coloured attire, and some older people sat around a fire where ribbons of smoke spiralled upwards out of the embers.

Angelina knew instinctively that these people were the gypsies Alex had told her about, the gypsies he had told to move on. She sensed that every eye had become fixed on her. Two men with gold rings in their ears and brightly coloured scarves tied loosely around their necks rose from where they were sitting on the wooden steps of the caravan nearest to her. She swallowed nervously as they stood quite still, watching her.

They looked foreign—their skin swarthy and their hair hanging loose, lank and shiny black. Distrust and resentment lurked in their fathomless, totally unrevealing dark eyes. Her heart almost ceased to beat when her eyes were drawn to a knife sheathed at one of the men's waists, and when she met his gaze she felt a sudden chill, as if a shadow had passed in front of the sun, robbing her of its warmth.

No one made any attempt to speak to her, but the air was charged with an ugly tension, menace bristling all around her, the very silence an enemy. She shuddered, feeling extremely vulnerable and afraid. Through a veil of confusion and fear, what she now saw was a scene from her past. She glimpsed the dark, shadowy images creeping with stealth out of the locked doors of her mind, and she was sure they were catching up with her. All her deepest, darkest nightmares lay among the ghosts these gypsies resurrected, and with her emotions heightened to fever pitch, she feared she was about to be attacked again.

Whirling Forest Shadow about, she kicked him into a gallop. Trembling with fear she was borne homeward, unaware as Forest Shadow's iron-shod hooves struck the cobbles in the stable yard with ringing tones that her low state was about to be brought even lower.

Chapter Seven

Angelina's distress on coming face to face with the gypsies had lessened a little when she entered the house, but the threat they posed to her peace of mind was not forgotten.

Hoping to reach her room without encountering anyone, she was disappointed to find Jenkins waiting for her in the hall. When he saw her his body froze and he seemed to lose control of his expression as his gaze swept over her attire. His thick eyebrows rose up his forehead, and Angelina was sure she saw a little smile tug at the corners to the stern line of his mouth. But apart from this he was too respectful to show any other reaction. When he spoke, his voice was perfectly calm and controlled.

'Lord Montgomery has asked to see you the minute you return from your ride, Miss Hamilton.'

Angelina's stomach plummeted to the bottom of her boots with dismay. 'I'll go up and change first. I can't possibly face Lord Montgomery looking like a ragamuffin.'

At that moment a door across the hall was flung open and Alex materialised. 'Angelina.'

Her head shot round. 'Yes.'

'A word, if you please.'

Angelina bristled, not caring for the tone of his voice. 'And if I don't please?'

'Then I shall say what I have to say right here.'

'But—I was just—'

'I'm waiting.'

Angelina could see that Alex was furious. The glacial look in his silver eyes and the stern set of his features sent shivers down her spine. There was certainly nothing soft or lover-like in his tone, as there had been when she had left him in his rooms earlier. On a sigh she frowned. Casting a weary glance at Jenkins, she saw sympathy in his eyes.

'Oh, dear, Jenkins,' she breathed softly, 'I think I'm for it.'

'Chin up, Miss Hamilton, and you'll be all right,' he murmured, with his back to his ill-tempered master and with all the skill of a ventriloquist, for Angelina was certain his lips never moved.

She doubted the conviction of Jenkins's words as she turned and walked across the hall. There was not a single trace of reason in Alex's expression, only an undeniable aura of restrained fury gathering pace inside him, waiting to be unleashed on her.

He stood at the door to the sitting room like a soldier on sentry duty, waiting for her to pass—which she did, tilting her chin in a haughty manner.

Just through the doorway Angelina stopped. The ominous thud of the door behind her was too much for her lacerated nerves. Turning to face him, she was vaguely aware of two people seated at the opposite end of the long room, but she and Alex might as well have been alone—in fact, they should be, and she was angry that he had not chosen to chastise her in private. Her blood froze at the anger burning in his eyes. He had savaged her emotions once already today and it would seem he was about to do it again, but instead of seducing her into submission, she strongly suspected that this time he was about to go to the other extreme.

With her hands thrust deep into the pockets of her breeches, in a state of grinding tension, for what seemed an eternity she stood perfectly still, glaring at him mutinously, watching as his mercurial mood took a turn for the worst. As his eyes raked over her they opened wide, his sleek black eyebrows climbing higher and higher. Slowly he began walking round her, and she could only surmise that he was contemplating her shapeless flannel shirt and deerskin trousers. She thought to escape and her eyes shot to the door. He saw her intention.

'Don't try it,' he said, his silken voice almost turning Angelina's blood to ice as he continued to walk round her.

Alex kept his mercurial gaze levelled on her, a nerve jerking at the side of his rigid jaw. Undaunted, she lifted her chin with a small but stubborn toss of her head. It was a gesture of open defiance. Stopping in front of her, he moved closer, the silver eyes boring down into hers. When he could finally bring himself to speak his voice was ice cold.

'I have hired scullery maids better garbed than you. I do not know the meaning of this, Angelina, but you have a propensity to wilfully defy me at every turn. How dare you take a horse out of my stable without my permission and without the animal being approved by me first? Nor you did not take just any horse, but Forest Shadow, the most dangerous horse in my stable.'

'Were you worried about my welfare?'

'Don't flatter yourself,' he growled, demolishing the sudden flickering of hope he saw in her eyes. 'Forest Shadow is also my most valuable horse.' This was not entirely true. Forest Shadow was his most prized horse, but he'd been worried as hell about her on that powerful beast. However, he would not give her the satisfaction of telling her so.

'You need not have worried,' she said, with infuriating calm and no hint of an apology for taking the horse without his permission. 'I took good care of him. I do ride extremely well, you know.'

'So my uncle went to great pains to point out before he went to Cornwall,' Alex mocked. 'I have no doubt that he did not exaggerate about the excellence of your prowess. But until I have seen your *exceptional* skills for myself, the stables are out of bounds. Is that clear?' he seethed, his blistering gaze sliding over her face.

Angelina's reply was to glower at him.

'And another thing I want you to remember, I consider stallions to be unsuitable mounts for females to ride.'

'Why—you conceited, pig-headed beast,' she gasped. 'I am just as capable of riding stallions as any man.'

'Be that as it may, but not at Arlington. Now, you will go to your room and remove those outrageous clothes and appear dressed in normal attire. I will see you before me in precisely ten minutes. Is that understood?'

Angelina glowered at him with stubborn, unyielding pride, her chin pert, her hands balled into tight fists by her sides, sorely tempted to tell him to go to hell. 'Who do you think you are? I will wear what I please and do what I please.'

With his hands fixed firmly on his hips, Alex thrust his face close to hers, his eyes glittering with a fire that burned her raw and his eyebrows drawn close, giving him an air of fiendish intensity. 'I know who I am, Angelina. What bothers me is who you are. While you live in this house—*my* house—and until my uncle returns from Cornwall, you are under my care. You will do well to remember that and the sooner you accept it the better it will be for us all. You will be accountable to me for your actions. Is that understood?'

Angelina didn't even recoil from the blazing violence as she took the full force of his volcanic rage. Fury rose up like flames licking inside her, her face as uncompromisingly challenging as his. 'You can go to hell, Alex Montgomery, and the sooner the better. I own no man my superior—and least of all you. Ever since I left Ohio I have never been accountable to anyone for my actions. I do not intend to start now.'

'Yes, you will. Someone should have taught you some sense and beat that wilful pride out of you years ago,' he said, anger pouring through his veins like acid, his fury making him carelessly cruel. 'I am not daunted by your defiance.'

'You wouldn't be daunted by a pit of rattlesnakes,' she spat. In her fury Angelina forgot the man and woman watching them with astonishment and a good deal of interest from across the room.

Nathan and Verity found it hard to believe that Alex, a man so self-assured and masterful when in the presence of some of the most powerful men in England, had been stripped of his composure and was being baited with such boldness by an eighteen-year-old girl. They were taken aback by the quite unexpected heated altercation between these two. They were such a combustible combination, and it was evident that Angelina, who looked magnificent, glorious and indestructible as she faced the master of Arlington despite the shabbiness of her garb, had a will every bit as strong and stubborn as Alex's own.

'Go to your room,' Alex gritted. 'I will not have you behaving in this disgraceful manner in front of my friends and relatives.'

'Friends!' she scoffed, breathing hard. 'You don't have friends—you have subjects who bow and scrape at your feet. Tell me, does everyone always march to your orders?'

'Always.'

'Not me, Alex Montgomery,' Angelina flung back. 'I shall match you stride for stride and be damned to your orders.'

'You little baggage. If you continue to flout my authority and do anything else to inconvenience my staff or myself while you live in my house, I will personally make your life a living hell. Is that understood?'

'Why—what will you do? Beat me?' she scoffed.

'Out of respect for your sex, I will curb my temptation to resort to physical violence. But if you brazenly defy me one more time, do not depend on my ability to exercise similar restraint. More of this and you will find yourself on your knees begging my forgiveness. You are outrageous, outspoken, as obstinate as a thousand mules and your manners are deplorable—and look at you. You don't even look like a female and you certainly don't act like one. You will make a laughing stock of us all if you continue in this disgraceful manner. It is unacceptable. If you think you can go traipsing around my estate dressed like a gypsy, then you would do well to think again. I know females younger than you who are married—but who in God's name would marry you looking as you do, like a savage?'

Mentally adding his words to the list of insults thrown at her by him over the past weeks, like a cat Angelina slowly moved towards him, a feral gleam lighting up her eyes as she faced him in blinding anger, so close that she could feel his hot breath on her face.

'How easily that word trips off your tongue, my lord,' she seethed, each word clearly enunciated, 'and how ready you are to insult me. How do you know what a savage looks like? Have you ever seen one—a true savage, an uncivilised being marked by brutality and deprivation—in this privileged, cocooned world of genteel drawing rooms you inhabit? I do all manner of unladylike things you disapprove of, don't I? And if being outspoken, outrageous and unfeminine makes me a savage in your eyes then you are right. I am a savage.'

There was something close to murder in Alex's blazing eyes. As she turned from him, pushed beyond reason he reached out and grasped her shoulder, his fingers biting into her like knives. Like lightning and acting purely on instinct, Angelina flung her head round like an enraged lioness and violently thrust his hand away, accidentally catching his flesh with her nail. The unexpected action stunned Alex into momentary inaction, then he regained his senses and quickly took a step back.

'You witch,' he said in a savage snarl, white faced with fury, all his former admiration for her beauty, her strength of mind and courage instantly demolished as spots of bright red blood began to seep out of the small puncture mark on his skin. 'If you were a man, I'd run you through for that.'

'If I were a man, I'd have done the same to you the instant we met. Don't you ever touch me again,' she hissed through her teeth, standing with her legs braced and her fists clenched by her sides. Transfigured with fury, rigid with accumulated pride and rebelliousness, she dominated the situation as much as he. Her eyes were shining assertively, alive with the hidden mysteries of a rare jewel, her breasts rising and falling with suppressed fury as she struggled with the furious sensation burning through her veins. 'I killed the last man who dared do that. Is it not enough that you insult and degrade me without laying your hands on me? Keep them to yourself and perhaps we'll get on better.'

'That won't be difficult.'

'You are a loathsome, overbearing, despicable monster, Alex Montgomery—'

'I think I have the picture,' he drawled.

'Good. Then I needn't go on—but how I wish I'd never come here. I wish I'd never come to England and met you. I want to be free of you. I didn't want any of this. I didn't ask for it. It was thrust on me against my will.' She breathed as if she couldn't inhale enough air. 'Don't you understand that I hate you?'

Alex looked at the proud beauty that was glaring at him like an enraged angel of retribution and realized that she was on the brink of tears. He felt a twinge of conscience, which he quickly thrust away. 'I know you do,' he said coldly. 'And you will hate me a good deal more before I'm through. Now go to your room. I said ten minutes. It's now eight. Go and change—and if you disobey me, by God I shall come and remove those infernal breeches myself and render a certain part of your anatomy incapable of sitting down for a week. Is that clear?'

Angelina glared at him, her vow to murder this illustrious nobleman renewing itself in her mind. She would like to rend his heart to pieces. She would like to do so much damage to this mocking, sardonic man that it would prove irreparable. She would like to see him on his knees begging her for her favours, to grovel, and then she would spurn him. Turning from him, she walked away.

Alex watched the door close behind her, standing perfectly still, unable to believe the tempestuous, brave young woman who had stood and faced his wrath. His anger gave way to a reluctant admiration at her magnificent show of courage in admitting that she had once killed a man. He was stunned and deeply troubled by her confession, which, in her fury, she hadn't seemed to realise she had made. Remembering her stormy eyes shining with unshed tears, he felt a consuming, unquenchable need to know more about her past—but for the present he was determined not to let what he considered to be a childish act of defiance pass.

With Nathan and Verity sitting quietly in the background, Alex's fury had been reduced to a dangerous calm as he watched the door. He sat and waited, his jaw hardened with resolve, mentally crossing off the minutes and the seconds as Angelina's time ran out, his fingers tapping on the arm of the chair in a clear indication of his impatience. When her eight minutes were up he rose.

'Damned wench,' he muttered. He reached for the doorknob at the same moment that it swung open and Angelina swept in, dressed in her daffodil yellow gown. Tipping her head, she met his eyes with a smile of pure innocence—unchastened and unrepentant.

'Dear me, Alex. You do look vexed. You should be careful. It really is not good for anyone to get so worked up.' She smiled demurely and walked past him, with no trace of her previous anger or the mental exhaustion that had engulfed her when she had entered her room following his severe chastisement. She had seriously considered defying him and not returning to the sitting room, but the overriding fear that she would have to deal with his wrath once more put paid to such meanderings of the mind. She knew that Alex Montgomery was a force to be reckoned with, and that when he had told her he would come to her room and remove her clothes himself it had been no idle threat. But she had loathed him with each discarded garment for making her do it.

'Aren't you going to introduce me to your guests?' she asked, trying to crush the apprehension that was stirring restlessly inside her on being introduced to the tall, fair-haired gentleman and Aunt Patience's daughter.

Alex was rendered speechless. How was it he'd started out as the conqueror and ended up feeling like the vanquished? Neither threat nor punishment would oblige Angelina Hamilton to bow to a higher authority. At that moment he wanted to stride across the room, take hold of that impudent madam, and shake her. His eyes met Nathan's in a 'now do you understand' way. Nathan was visibly and infuriatingly amused.

Eager to be introduced to the tantalising young American girl who had turned his friend's world upside down and inside out in the matter of just a few short weeks, Nathan came towards her. As he reached for her hand, his handsome, boyish face broke into a brilliant, reassuring smile and his blue eyes twinkled with delight.

'Your servant, Miss Hamilton,' he said, bending over and pressing a gallant kiss on the back of her hand. 'And may I say I am truly delighted to meet you at last—having heard all about you from Alex,' he said meaningfully, casting his friend a mocking, lopsided grin.

'I'm sure you have—and nothing pleasant, I'll wager,' Angelina quipped brightly without looking at Alex. She liked Nathan Beresford at once, and for the life of her she could not understand how such a charming and amiable man could possibly be the friend of her antagonist. 'But please—you must call me Angelina. Everyone does.'

'Thank you—and you must call me Nathan—and this is Verity, my wife,' he said, taking Verity's hand and drawing her forward. 'No doubt her dear mama, Lady Fortesque, has told you all about her and how she keeps us all on the straight and narrow,' he said on a teasing note, casting his wife a fond look.

Angelina looked at him obliquely. Aware that Alex was hovering behind her like a dark threatening thunder cloud, her smile did not falter. 'An unenviable task, if I may say,' she replied softly, leaving no one in any doubt that she was referring to Alex.

She looked at the slender young woman dressed in a fashionable high-waisted gown of emerald green and smiled, wishing she had paid more attention to her own appearance instead of dragging on the first dress her hands had come into contact with. Verity was a pretty brunette, with a delicately arched nose and winged brows over friendly blue eyes. Her hair was gathered in glossy curls about her ears, a braided coil sitting prettily at her crown.

'I'm so glad to meet you at last, Angelina,' Verity said, her tone warm with obvious sincerity. 'I must welcome you to the family. Mama has been singing your praises for the past hour— telling me how patient and considerate you've been to her during her illness. I really must thank you. I had no idea she was so ill, otherwise I would have come to Arlington sooner.'

'She has been quite poorly, but as you will have seen for yourself she is a good deal better and hopes to grace us with her presence at dinner this evening.'

'I must offer you my deep apologies, Angelina. Alex should not have subjected you to that rude display of ill temper earlier,' Verity said, throwing her cousin a glance of severe displeasure. 'He can be so overbearing at times.'

'My sentiments exactly,' Angelina agreed, feeling a fresh surge of anger against Alex for chastising her in front of these two, which he must have known would humiliate her. Her confrontation with Alex had been so distressing and unsettling to her peace of mind however, she remained silent, wanting to put the unpleasant incident behind her.

Alex had no intention of letting her off the hook lightly. He moved to take a dominant, indolent stance by the fireplace, one arm braced on the mantelpiece. His jaw was set hard, his eyes intense as he slanted a look at Angelina.

'By taking Forest Shadow out of the stables without my permission, what else did you expect from me? To ask if you'd had a pleasant ride?' he asked, the ghost of an ironic smile suddenly touching his mouth as his manner began to soften towards her at last. 'I am a reasonable man, Angelina, and I am perfectly willing to allow you as much freedom as you wish, but that does not mean for you to act brazenly and irresponsibly—and taking the Shadow was an exceedingly irresponsible act on your part.'

'Pay no attention to my ill-tempered cousin,' Verity said, casting Alex a slightly imperious though smiling look in an attempt to ward off further argument. 'I must express my admiration for your courage. You have my profound sympathy for what you must have endured—having to put up with him at Arlington all alone whilst Mama has been indisposed. It cannot have been easy for you.'

'No—but I've found myself in far worse situations than trying to keep on the right side of an irate lord.'

Verity laughed, a pleasant, warm sound, which went a long way to relieving the tension in the quiet room. 'Come and sit by me and we will have a quiet gossip together without being overheard by these tiresome men. I'm sure they'll have plenty to converse about without us. I want to hear all about America. There is a breath of adventure and excitement about it I find fascinating. We hear such varied and colourful tales that I would simply adore to go there myself.'

'You would?' Nathan remarked, somewhat astonished. 'First I've heard of it.'

'That's because you can see no further than Europe and what's happening in France, my love,' his wife said with sudden playfulness, which was so much a part of her charming nature. 'My husband's interest in politics exceeds everything else, Angelina. Whenever France and that upstart Napoleon are mentioned, he immediately becomes embroiled in a serious debate. I'm afraid that the Duke of Wellington and the progress of the war in the Peninsula eclipses all else.'

'As it does in all who are politically minded,' Nathan stated.

With a deep sigh Verity gave Angelina a long suffering 'now do you see what I mean' look. 'My dear husband eats, sleeps and breathes politics. You really should consider being a Member of Parliament, Nathan, and then you could air your views openly in the House of Commons—where, hopefully, you would wear yourself out in debate and be happy to come home to me. We could then converse on more agreeable matters that interest us both.'

Taking Angelina's hand, Verity moved away from them and drew her down beside her on a sofa. 'I'm so glad we're going to be friends, Angelina.'

'So am I. When I returned to Boston from Ohio I had so much to do and so many responsibilities. I had no true female friends.'

Verity saw a strange brooding look darken the brilliant eyes. 'Then we shall rectify that as soon as you return to London,' she said gently. 'We shall go shopping together and drive daily through the park—and there will be parties to attend and the theatre. We shall have such fun together. Although I must warn you that London in winter can be a cold and dreary place, so I shall steal you from Uncle Henry. You must come to Hanover Square and stay with us.'

'I would like that.'

'I was truly sorry to hear of your mother's recent death, Angelina. Pray accept my deepest sympathies.'

'Thank you. Uncle Henry has been very kind to me. I am so looking forward to seeing Mowbray Park. While I'm there I hope to persuade Uncle Henry to take me to Kent so that I might see where my mother lived.'

Verity merely smiled and nodded, taken aback by what she said, wondering if Uncle Henry and Alex knew what she intended. Like everyone else, Verity was aware that Angelina's maternal grandmother was still alive. She had no idea why Uncle Henry wanted it kept from his young ward, and her natural curiosity had been roused, but, not being the sort of man to indulge in subterfuge without good reason, she would respect his wishes and remain silent on the matter.

Angelina was unaware when Alex left the room and returned after just a few minutes' absence. She would have been surprised and angry to learn that he had gone directly to her room, startling a bemused Pauline, who watched in rigid, terrified silence as he strode into the dressing room and snatched Angelina's discarded trousers and shirt off the floor where she had left them in a heap. Alex thrust the garments into her arms.

'Drinkwater, the gardener, is burning some rubbish in the kitchen gardens. Take them and burn them before your mistress returns,' he ordered.

When he returned, Angelina caught the smug, self-satisfied look he threw her way but thought nothing of it just then. It would be some time before she missed her breeches and shirt, and when she did they would have ceased to matter.

Sleep, chased by a thousand images, eluded Angelina. Dark shadows darted eerily into the corners of the room, transforming them into secret places hiding a hundred ghosts. Scrambling out of bed, she went to the window. Suddenly a brilliant cobalt blue streak of lightning flashed in a sudden spurt of brilliance across the sky, quickly followed by a rolling rumble of thunder. Rain began lashing at the glass panes and the wind rose to a fierce pitch, bending and twisting the trees in the garden so that they resembled grotesque, tortured beings, their huge shadows moving on the ground like furtive, creeping—what? Indians? Gypsies?

They were like the fairytale monsters of her childhood that had waited somewhere beyond the bed in the dark. Something terrifying pierced the raw centre of her soul, tearing open old wounds and clawing at her with savage, dirty fingers. Quickly she ran back to bed and buried her head beneath the covers, telling herself not to be silly and forcing herself to concentrate on sleep, willing the past to go away. But it refused. It whispered in the air about her, creeping closer still. A branch was beating on the window like the rhythmic beat of a drum, growing stronger and stronger as the wind increased in strength.

Eventually she fell into a fitful sleep invaded by hideous memories and her nightmare returned for the first time since she had left Boston. Cold and shivering, suddenly she was fifteen again and her terrors engulfed her—cold and implacable, real. A mist swirled around her, cloying, choking. The figure of the Shawnee materialised out of the shadows, out of the dark, and she was screaming and struggling with this creature who had killed her father and injured her mother, who was now trying to kill her. She was clawing at the face, watching bright red blood spurt from where her fingernails had raked his skin. She had to kill him—but where was the knife? Oh, dear God. Where was the knife? She must find the knife.

After sharing a few late-hour brandies in front of the fire with Nathan when the ladies had retired, Alex bade him goodnight. Walking past Angelina's room, he paused, straining his ears, hearing faint sounds coming from within. Believing the noise he'd heard to be the night storm, he was about to move on, but the sound came again. Someone was crying, whimpering, he was certain of it. Remembering how pale and anxious Angelina had been before going to bed, he became concerned. Unable to quell his curiosity or stem the need to comfort her, he went inside.

Closing the door behind him, he stood for a moment as his eyes adjusted to the gloom. Angelina's broken crying and muttering came from the bed. Wondering what could have happened to bring her to such wretchedness, he went to her, thankful when the moon chose that moment to appear from behind the clouds and to wash the bed in its silver glow. Looking down at her, the state of the tumbled bedclothes told him she had been thrashing about for some time. Perspiration glistened on her forehead and she was flinging her head from side to side, her fingers clawing at the covers and hitting out at some imaginary object.

'Angelina,' Alex murmured in alarm, about to reach out and gather the distressed girl in his arms. But he stopped when suddenly her eyes snapped open and she stared in abject terror at the dark figure bending over her, a figure looming larger that life.

With a strangled cry, like lightning she scrambled out from

beneath the covers and huddled at the head of the bed like a terrified animal, clutching her nightdress about her knees, visibly trembling. Her eyes, black and enormous, burned with the fever of unspeakable agony.

'Get away,' she hissed. 'Don't touch me.'

Alex could see she was in extreme distress, confused and disorientated. 'Angelina—it's me—Alex,' he murmured gently, longing to reach out and take her in his arms and soothe her as he would a frightened child who was having a bad dream. But he could see her nerves were stretched tight, and that any sudden strain might cause them to break and fling her into a state of hysteria. 'I'm not going to hurt you.'

Looking at him for a long moment, every nerve vibrating, his voice slowly penetrated the inner sanctum of her mind. 'Alex?' she whispered. 'Oh, Alex.' Quite suddenly her features crumpled. She closed her eyes and shuddered violently, clasping her arms tight around her chest and beginning to rock back and forth as if in some terrible grief.

'Angelina—don't. Please don't.' The painful, unfamiliar constriction in Alex's chest made his hand tremble slightly as he reached out for her, but she jerked away, screwing her eyes tight shut, as if to blot out some intolerable sight, hitting out at him wildly, as though she imagined herself to be in the grip of an enemy.

'Don't. Please don't touch me.' Her voice was a hollow whisper. She began to cry silently, huge tears spilling over her lashes and coursing down her cheeks, her eyes begging him not to come near. 'Don't. Don't,' she repeated. 'Please…' She backed away against the head of the bed, unable to go any further.

It was an agony for Alex to watch her anguish, raised from the vast reservoir of despair threatening to drown her. He was unable to know how to deal with her. He couldn't leave her like this, because if he did he felt he would be failing her. Nor could he go for help without raising eyebrows about what he was doing in her room at this hour of the night.

Lighting the taper beside her bed, he looked at her pathetic huddled figure illuminated by its glow, weeping silently, wretchedly, shrouded in a thick curtain of long silken hair. The forlorn droop of her head went straight to his heart. Caught totally unprepared by her fierce display of emotion, he felt reason and control swept away. Sitting on the edge of the bed, with aching tenderness he reached out and took firm hold of her, pulling her close and fastening his arms around her like a vice.

At first she resisted and struggled, lashing out at his re-straining grip, but then she grew still and grimly endured his touch. Through the material of her nightdress Alex could feel the alert tension of all her body. Her tears had ceased and her breathing was rapid. The warmth of the room wrapped itself around them so that it seemed that they were alone in a world without substance or reality.

'It's all right, Angelina. I'm not going to hurt you,' Alex breathed, his lips against her hair on the top of her head. 'I don't know what has frightened you and I am not going to leave you until you are all right. Try to relax.'

As if awakening from a deep trance, Angelina began to do just that. The storm of tears had ceased, and with its passing some of her tension had been washed away. Having dealt with tragedy and adversity for three years, she was too weak to fight Alex when he was being kind and understanding—and besides, he felt so warm and strong, his arms comforting and his voice soothing. His mere presence gave her a sense of security and safety. Alex was both surprised and touched when she nestled closer and turned her face into his chest. It was as if she wanted to hide herself in his embrace.

'Tell me, Angelina,' he said at length, 'have you experienced anything like this before?'

She nodded.

'And this nightmare you keep having, is it always the same one?'

'Yes,' she mumbled.

Releasing his hold, Alex turned her face up to his, stroking her hair from her damp face. 'What happened to you in Ohio, Angelina?' he asked, cradling her face in his hands and tracing her cheekbones with his thumbs. 'What are you afraid of?'

Fresh tears collected in her eyes and spilled hot moisture over his fingers. He brushed them away gently, feeling her give a convulsive shudder. 'Don't. Please don't,' she whispered, feebly trying to push him away to evade his touch, but Alex was having none of that now he had succeeded in subduing her and drew her firmly against him, placing her head on his chest once more and stroking her hair.

'Tell me about Ohio, Angelina,' he asked again. 'What happened to you there on the night the Indians came?'

White faced, she shuddered. 'No. I will not tell you,' she answered in a voice that was a raw whisper, her whole body rigid with anger in his arms—whether anger against himself for asking or her memories Alex didn't know, but to his relief she made no attempt to remove herself. 'Don't ever ask me, because I won't tell you. I try never to think about it.'

'But you do, don't you? And I can see that it pains you.'

'Yes—yes, it pains me,' she said in a torrent of anguished words, gulping on her sobs and pressing her face to his chest in an attempt to shut out the memory. Drawing a deep, quivering breath she tried to still her trembling limbs, trying to gain control of her rioting emotions. 'Damn you for mentioning it. Damn you, Alex Montgomery. It was vile and ugly—and I don't want to remember.'

'I can see that,' he said softly. 'But whatever happened to you, Angelina, you cannot go on carrying it around inside you like this. Have you never spoken of it to anyone?'

She shook her head fiercely.

'Perhaps talking about it will finally exorcise it from your mind.'

'It won't. It won't, I tell you.' No, she thought, not after keeping it to herself for so long. It would be like sharing her soul. Pride and shame had prevented her from speaking openly—even to Will. But Alex! No. Never to Alex.

Not wishing to cause her further distress, Alex decided not to press her on the matter just then. 'What was it that brought this on?' he asked, gentling his voice. 'Was it because I upset you earlier—or the storm?'

'No,' she mumbled through her sobs. 'Neither. It was the gypsies.'

Alex frowned. 'The gypsies?'

She nodded against him. 'I saw them when I was riding. I came upon their encampment on the other side of the woods.'

Alex stiffened and held her away from him, forcing her to look at him. 'Angelina, did they hurt you?'

She shook her head. 'I thought they were going to attack me. Seeing them—they—they reminded me—'

'Of the Shawnee,' Alex finished for her, understanding how the swarthy-skinned gypsies, with their dark eyes and black hair, would resemble the red-skinned Indians of America. Silently he cursed the gypsies and his bailiff for failing to get rid of them as he had ordered him to do. First thing in the morning he would ride out to their encampment and order them to move on himself.

He pulled Angelina back into his embrace and, his strong arms tightened about her. With her face pressed into the curve of his shoulder she seemed so small, so utterly female, warm, fragile and vulnerable. His heart ached with the fear of what the Shawnee might have done to her. Not even in his mind could he bring himself to voice his suspicions, but they were there, thrusting through his brain like knives. He couldn't say it. He couldn't even think it. The thought of Angelina knowing a moment's terror was too agonising for him to deal with.

Murmuring soothing words of comfort, he held her tightly, tenderly, as she wept, soaking his shirt front with her warm tears; racking sobs that shook her slender body with such violence that Alex was afraid they would tear her apart. They remained like that until her sobbing turned to quiet whimpering, and finally she grew silent and still.

'Do you feel better now?' he asked.

She raised her face to his, giving him a teary smile. 'I'm sorry. It—it's just that I didn't think it would happen again after I left America.'

'These things have a habit of recurring when you least expect them.'

Angelina felt the strength of his arms and the warmth of his masculine body. Slowly the fear began to recede, but she made no effort to free herself from that tight circle of arms—and Alex had no intention of letting her go while she was content to remain there. She could feel the hard muscles of his broad chest and smell his maleness and the spicy scent of his cologne. A tautness began in her breast, a delicious ache that was like a languorous, honeyed warmth.

As he sensed the change in her Alex's arms slackened. His senses were invaded by the smell of her. It was the soft fragrance of her hair—the sweet scent of roses mingled with a musky female scent—that made his body burn. Curling his long masculine fingers round her chin, he tilted her face up to his. She was calmer now, her eyes large, black and soft, her eyelashes moist and glistening. Gently he brushed the remaining tears from her cheeks, his fingers infinitely gentle.

It seemed a lifetime passed as they gazed at each other. In that lifetime each lived through a range of deep, tender emotions new to them both, exquisite emotions that neither of them could put into words. As though in slow motion, unable to resist the temptation Angelina's mouth offered, slowly Alex's own moved inexorably closer. His gaze was gentle and compelling, when, in a sweet, mesmeric sensation, his mouth found hers. Angelina melted into him. The kiss was long and lingeringly slow.

Raising his head, Alex gazed down at her in wonder. Her magnificent eyes were naked and defenceless. 'My God, Angel,' he whispered, his voice hoarse, 'you are so sweet. The next time you disobey me, instead of lashing you into submission with threats of physical punishment, in future I can see I shall have to change my tactics.'

'Oh?'

'All I have to do is kiss you into compliance.'

Angelina was full of remorse and regret for that unpleasant incident earlier. 'I did behave badly, didn't I?' she whispered, her words filled with shame and a hundred other things Alex could not identify. 'I'm so sorry I hit out at you, Alex.' A knot of tenderness swelled in his chest as he watched her take his hand in both her own and press her trembling lips gently to the place where she had accidentally caught it with her nail. 'I should not have scratched you—I didn't mean to. It was unforgivable of me.'

Deeply touched, he smiled down at the incredibly desirable young woman who was setting his body on fire with her innocent gesture. Her beautiful profile was solemn. 'You may feel free to scratch me whenever you wish, providing you kiss it better afterwards.'

'It was wrong of me to take Forest Shadow without your permission. I know that now.'

Alex sighed, placing a kiss lightly on the soft curve of her cheek. 'Yes, it was. I was almost driven out of my mind when I discovered you'd taken him. He is barely broke to the saddle and still a bit wild and hard to handle—even for me.'

Angelina's heart jumped with elation. 'So you were concerned about me?'

'I told you. I was out of my mind with worry. That was why I was so angry.'

His expression was touching, his words so sincere, that Angelina forced down a lump forming in her throat. 'I—I didn't mean what I said.'

'What didn't you mean?' he murmured, nibbling her ear.

'When I said I hated you. I don't.'

'I know,' he answered, gently drawing the curtain of hair from her face and draping it over her shoulder.

'You do?'

His eyes fastened on her lips once more. 'Your lips have just told me so.'

With her heart pounding turbulently Angelina saw his eyes translucent in the ghostly candlelight, his lean features starkly etched. 'Oh?'

'Another kiss I would have, Angel—to confirm what your lips first told me,' he murmured.

She shook her head in feeble protest. The insistent pressure of his body, those feral eyes glittering with power and primeval hunger, washed away any measure of comfort she might have left. A strange, alien feeling fluttered within her breast and she was halted for a brief passage of time when she found her lips entrapped with his once more, and though they were soft and tender, they burned with a fire that scorched her. Closing her eyes, she yielded to it, melting against him.

Alex tasted the sweet, honeyed softness of her mouth, finding himself once more at the mercy of his emotions, when reason and intelligence were powerless. Savouring each intoxicating pleasure he gloried in her innocence, her purity, painfully aware of the trembling weakness in her scantily clad body pressed against his own.

Alex's conscience, which he had assumed was long since dead, chose that moment to resurrect itself. Expelling a ragged breath and out of sheer self-preservation, he flung himself away, raking fingers of angry self-disgust through his hair as he fought to reassemble his senses and bring his desire under control. Devil take it, he cursed silently as he fought to tame his body's fierce, frustrating urges, what the hell was happening to him? He was using Angelina as he would one of his sexually experienced mistresses. But she was not like them. She was uncompromised and untainted. Compared to them, she was a gullible child.

Kissed and caressed into almost unconscious sensibility, a moment passed before Angelina realised something was wrong, that there was an unexpected lull in their kiss. She opened her eyes in a daze of suspended yearning, newly awakened passion glowing in the velvety depths of her eyes. 'Alex?' she murmured, reaching out and lightly touching his bare forearm, feeling empty and unable to understand why he had stopped kissing her.

Turning his head, he looked at her, his gaze smouldering, his breathing ragged, the throbbing ache in his loins reminding him how much he wanted to make love to her, how close he had come to taking her. With her hair tumbling around her in a glorious silken mass, she lay like a beautiful, pagan goddess among the ruins of her bed. He stilled her fingers tracing up his arm. It was a provocative movement and she was too innocent and inexperienced to be aware of the devastating effect it was having on his already ravaged self-control. Riven with guilt, he raised her hand to his lips and pressed them to the soft centre of her palm.

'We must stop now, Angel, before things go too far for us to draw back.' His voice was tight. He was unable to believe this innocent temptress had surrendered in his arms, returning his passion with such intoxicating sweetness that had almost shattered his self-control. Unwittingly he had released the raw sensuousness he had known all along lurked beneath her veneer of prim respectability.

Alex wanted Angelina more than he'd wanted anything in his life…more than he could believe possible. The weeks of being around her, of self-denial and frustration, the tension and explosive emotions her nearness elicited by her stubborn refusal to be dominated, had been hell. Like a siren in Greek mythology whose singing was believed to lure sailors to destruction on the rocks, Angelina's weeping had lured him into her room, and her vulnerability had finally broken all bounds of his restraint.

'This shouldn't have happened. It was a mistake. When my uncle left you in my charge I agreed to take care of you until he returns. I will not break that agreement by seducing you. Not only would I be failing in my duty to my uncle if I did that—but I would also despise myself. I should not be here alone with you,' he said, getting off the bed.

Angelina drew the covers around her. 'Thank you for coming, Alex,' she whispered, reason beginning to return.

'I heard you crying. I couldn't walk by your room. Will you be all right?' His face, like an ancient warrior prince, was set in determined lines.

She nodded, wanting to conceal how deeply she was affected by what had just happened between them. 'Yes.'

He reached out and let his fingers lightly brush her cheek, then he turned. Her eyes followed him out of the room. Not until then did her mind come together from the far reaches of her senses where it had fled the instant Alex had taken her in his arms, and realise the full impact of what she had done. She, Angelina Hamilton, the woman who had been so sure in what she wanted, who had vowed never to yield to a man's embrace, had almost brazenly given herself to the one man she had every reason to despise.

Chapter Eight

As Pauline was about to pull back the curtains Angelina grimaced, in no condition to endure the brightness of daylight, feeling as tired and ill as she did.

'Please don't pull the curtains back, Pauline. My head aches so.'

Pauline stopped when she observed her mistress's pale face in the dim light. Her wan face and puffy eyes surrounded by mauve shadows bore mute evidence of her sleepless night.

'Oh, Miss Angelina, you do look poorly. You stay right where you are. I'll go down to the kitchen and have Mrs Hall make you up a breakfast tray.'

Angelina's eyelids, feeling like lead weights, closed, and when she opened them again it was to find Verity beside the bed. Trying to clear the fog from her mind, she struggled to sit up, but Verity put out a hand and pressed her back into the pillows.

'Don't get up,' she said softly. 'You're not well.'

Angelina sighed, unresisting, amazed at how weak she felt. 'It's nothing, Verity. Truly. I'm just tired, that's all.'

'Does your head still ache?'

'No—at least not like it did earlier. I'll get up shortly. Alex's guests are arriving today.'

'You're not to think about getting up. With rest you'll be as right as rain in no time.'

Alex's head snapped up and alarm brought him to his feet when Verity told him that Angelina was indisposed. His face taut, his eyes narrowed, he sharply demanded to know what was wrong with her, his reaction causing everyone round the table to look at him in amazement.

Ever since he had left Angelina's room in the early hours, Alex had tried not to think of her and to concentrate on the arrival of his guests, but now he became consumed with anxiety and unable to think of anything other than Angelina.

After a full night's sleep Angelina awakened, feeling much better. Wrapping herself in a warm cloak, she ventured outside to walk in the deserted gardens. Reluctant to bump into any of Alex's guests, she left the house by one of the many passageways.

The air was cold, the heavy clouds loitering overhead heralding more rain. From the terrace she was about to descend a flight of steps when quite unexpectedly she came face to face with Alex. She was aware of the elegant presence of the woman by his side, but in that moment of meeting there was no room in her vision, her heart or her mind for anyone else but Alex.

As surprised by her appearance as Angelina was by his, a world of feelings flashed for an instant across Alex's set features when their eyes locked, but it was the expression of immense concern she saw that touched Angelina the most, replaced at once by one of polite inquiry.

Tenderness welled in her heart as she remembered how he had comforted her in her moment of need, and she remembered how desolate she had felt when he'd left her.

'Angelina,' he said with polite formality, giving no indication how her pale features and the mauve shadows beneath her eyes wrenched his heart. He stood beside Lavinia Howard with all the tenderness of a lover, but his eyes never once left Angelina's. 'You are recovered, I hope?'

'Thank you, yes. I am much better. Feeling the need for some fresh air, I thought I'd take a turn around the garden before it comes on to rain.'

Alex turned to the haughty woman by his side. 'Lavinia, allow me to introduce Angelina Hamilton—my uncle…the Duke of Mowbray's ward. She is staying at Arlington until he returns from Cornwall, where he's visiting a friend.'

Lavinia's austere gaze settled on Angelina in a cool and exacting way. Impersonally her eyes raked her from head to foot in a single withering glance. She had heard all about the Duke of Mowbray's ward—gossip travelled like a forest fire among the *ton*—and it was rumoured that this untutored American girl was nothing but a poor relation and had no social credentials to recommend her. Nevertheless, having sensed that she might have a rival for Alex, she resented the American girl's presence here at Arlington. With a practised smile she looked at Angelina.

'Why, Miss Hamilton, how delighted I am that you are able to join us at last. How do you like Arlington?'

Protected from the cold by an immaculately cut, full-length dark green coat with a black fur trim, Miss Howard was a striking looking woman, secure in her own strength and sure of her own incomparable worth. Sadly, Lavinia Howard's appearance at Arlington on Alex's arm had stepped in to shatter Angelina's newfound happiness. Angelina smiled, seemingly oblivious to Lavinia's animosity, and because it was so elegantly done, and because Alex was looking at Angelina, he appeared not to notice.

'I like it very well,' Angelina said in reply to Lavinia's question. 'It is so very different from my own home.'

'You are American, I believe,' Lavinia said, her tone lightly contemptuous. She touched a perfumed handkerchief to her nostrils and sniffed delicately, as if Angelina carried a bad smell. Angelina felt her hackles rise and a faint surge of anger momentarily diverted her thoughts from her own disappointment at seeing her with Alex, her kid-gloved hand placed in a possessive manner on his arm.

'Yes—although my parents were from England,' Angelina informed her, in full possession of herself, the hard light of battle gleaming in her eyes. She had taken an instant dislike to Lavinia Howard and had no intention of letting the woman bait her. She pulled the hood of her cloak over her head to protect her from the cold, the fur trim brushing her cheeks and framing her exquisite face in the most charming manner. 'If you will excuse me, I will continue on my walk. It is far too cold to be standing about.'

Smiling frostily, Lavinia stepped aside to let her pass. 'Shall we have the pleasure of your company at dinner this evening, Miss Hamilton?'

'Yes, you will,' Angelina answered, having no intention of hiding herself away in her room any longer. She had decided that she would show all the Lavinia Howards of fashionable London society what being an American girl was all about.

'Verity, I have decided not to hide myself away any longer,' Angelina announced when Verity came to her room later. 'I shall have some fun for a change.'

Verity was pleasantly astounded, though cautious, as she asked, 'And a Season?'

'That too.'

'Oh, Angelina, I am absolutely delighted—and I know Mama will be over the moon. As for Uncle Henry—well—it is what he wants, for you to become a proper lady and take your place in society, which was what your mother wanted too.'

'I know, although I am certain I shall encounter many difficulties.'

'You are bound to—and you cannot be blamed if you get it wrong occasionally, for you cannot assume a way of life utterly foreign to you overnight. But you are clever and will learn quickly. I have not known you very long, but I do know you have the strength of character that will survive in any kind of society.

'And now,' she said, holding Angelina at arm's length, 'we

have the important task of making sure you look your best for dinner this evening. I swear you will not recognise yourself by the time I have finished.'

The forty or so guests assembled in the hall were about to go into dinner. With Lavinia by his side Alex was talking to Lord Asquith, an old friend, who was bemoaning his poor harvest, but when Angelina appeared on the stairs he heard not a word. For the first time in his life Alex was rendered speechless as his eyes fastened on the young woman wearing a high-waisted white gauze dress flecked with gold descending the stairs. Her lustrous hair was drawn from her face with a thin strand of white ribbon, leaving the heavy tresses to tumble freely down her back to her waist. Angelina possessed the grace and beauty of a Grecian goddess and the regal bearing of a queen. Her presence reacted on everyone assembled like a rare sunburst.

In a shifting blur of people, of colour and flashing jewels that moved beneath her eyes, Angelina saw Alex. Magnificent in an olive green coat and white breeches, he was striding towards the stairs to meet her. Angelina's gaze went to the woman he had left standing, and she saw a face ice cold, the eyes glowering up at her. Steeling herself, she looked non-chalantly away.

When she reached the bottom step Alex took her hand. There was a twinkle in his eyes, and a slow, appreciative smile worked its way across his face as his eyes leisurely roamed over her body. The unspoken compliment made her blood run warm.

'You look entrancing,' he said in a quiet voice. 'I'm delighted you were able to join us—if tardily.'

'I'm sorry. Am I late?' The look she gave him was one of unadulterated innocence.

'You know you are. What were you trying to do? Hold out to make a grand entrance?'

'What? Me? Really, Alex—you know me better than that,' she murmured quietly, meaningfully.

He glanced down at her with a hooded gaze. 'Do I?'

She smiled impishly. 'No one knows me better,' she breathed.

'Minx,' he replied. 'Come and meet my guests before you say something that might embarrass us both.'

'You, my lord? Embarrassed? Never.'

Blind to the satisfied, conspiratorial smiles Patience and Verity exchanged, Alex's manner was that of pride as he calmly presented Angelina to his house guests—a polite, friendly gathering, and some of the more sedate members of London's *haut monde*.

Lavinia, who cleverly contrived to place herself on Alex's right-hand side at the end of the long dining table, gave Angelina a cool glance and then directed all her attention on their host.

Seated at the head of the table, Alex found his eyes drawn to Angelina like a magnet, where she sat halfway down the table, sandwiched between Nathan and Lord Asquith. She lit up the room simply by being present. Looking for unease on her face, he found nothing but calm and the soft glow of light in her velvet-dark eyes. Despite her inexperience in social repartee, she was extremely popular. She became lively, amiable, a laughing, beautiful young woman in possession of a natural wit and intelligence.

The following morning found a large complement of guests out for the ride into Arlington village. The stable yard was a hive of colourful activity, the atmosphere jovial and relaxed as people mounted Alex's splendid horses—some having brought their own, all champing at their bits, eager for the ride.

Looking extremely fetching in a ruby-red riding dress, with a matching hat cocked at an impudent angle atop bunches of delectable ringlets that bounced delightfully when she moved her head, Angelina appeared among them. With his noble head leaning over the stable door, Forest Shadow whickered on seeing her, stretching out its nose and shaking its mane vigorously.

'Poor thing,' she whispered, removing her glove and rubbing

his velvety nose affectionately. 'What an infuriating tyrant your master is. How awful for you having to stay behind while all your friends ride out without you.'

At that moment Alex appeared by her side. 'Tyrant I may be, lady, but that horse is staying here.' Taking her elbow, he propelled her away towards a snowy white mare Trimble was holding. 'Let me introduce you to Sheba. Sheba is to be your mount for today.' He scowled when he saw her cast a regretful glance over her shoulder at Forest Shadow. 'Forget it, Angelina,' he said firmly, taking the reins from Trimble and leading Sheba to a quiet corner of the yard.

Angelina followed, looking at Alex admiringly, thinking how attractive he was, with his darkly handsome face and the breeze lightly ruffling his shiny black hair. He was resplendent in an impeccably tailored dark-brown riding coat. His gleaming white neckcloth was perfectly tied, and snug-fitting buckskin breeches disappeared into highly polished tan riding boots. But there was still an aggressive virility about him, an uncompromising authority and infuriating arrogance that was not to her liking.

When he brought the horse to a halt he turned, the heat of his gaze travelling the full length of her in a slow, appreciative perusal, before making a leisurely inspection of her face upturned to his.

'I'm pleased to see you are appropriately dressed for the ride.'

'Why—did you think I wouldn't be?' she asked, smiling provocatively at him out of the corners of her eyes.

'Thank God you didn't decide to wear those disgusting breeches. I half-expected you to turn up in them just to antagonise me,' he remarked, curious as to whether her maid had told her he'd ordered her to burn them—and knowing how she would react when she realised he had. Her reply told him she hadn't.

'Why, Alex! As if I would,' she gasped, feigning innocence, but inwardly goaded by the mocking amusement in his eyes. Then her cheeks dimpled as her lips suddenly curved in a vengeful smile. 'Although I must confess that I did consider it.

However, to save you from embarrassment and disgrace, not to mention the scandal it would cause, I decided against it.'

'Then I suppose I must be thankful for small mercies,' Alex jibed lightly. 'Now—give me your opinion of Sheba.'

'I'll be able to do that better when I've ridden her.' The mare rubbed her head against her, her soft dark eyes alive with intelligence. Angelina wrinkled her nose at the saddle with distaste, having forgotten she would be required to ride side-saddle. 'How on earth can anyone be expected to communicate with the horse on that contraption—let alone stay on! I shall probably become unseated at the first obstacle and break my neck—which I am sure will fill your lordship with morbid delight,' she retorted tartly.

Alex grinned. 'Heaven forbid! All the other ladies seem to manage it. You do ride side-saddle, I hope?'

'Not since I was a girl—and I didn't like it then. I love to ride, but this stupid saddle will take all the pleasure out of it. Still…' she sighed out loud '…it's a serious handicap, I confess, but because I have no wish to drive you to murderous fury today by insisting that the saddle be changed, I suppose I have no alternative but to get used to it.'

'Very sensible. I'm happy that you are beginning to see things my way,' Alex said with a wicked grin.

'Don't count on it.'

'If you're afraid to ride Sheba side-saddle—if it's more than you can handle—simply say so,' he suggested generously, a lazy, challenging, taunting smile tugging at his firm lips.

Angelina merely glowered at him, affronted that he should dare suggest such a thing.

'No lady rides like I saw you riding Forest Shadow the other day. Had anyone seen you, you would be ostracised from society before you've had a chance to enter it.'

Running her hand over Sheba's glossy flank, Angelina tossed her head, indifferent to his words. 'That doesn't concern me in the slightest.'

'No,' he chuckled, 'I did not imagine for one moment that it would.'

'Does Sheba have any peculiarities that I should know about before I risk life and limb?'

Alex lifted one eyebrow lazily. 'She's as docile as a lamb.'

'Not too docile, I hope. Although, should the horse balk, I shall be straight over her head.' She scowled at Alex. 'If I am, no doubt you will blame my poor horsemanship and not the saddle. I know that it would please you enormously if I were to make a spectacle of myself, my lord, but I am determined not to gratify your wish to see me take an undignified tumble—so come, help me into this monstrous instrument of torture before I change my mind and retire to one of the carriages.'

Placing his hands on her waist, Alex lifted her effortlessly into the offending saddle, watching as she hooked one knee around the pommel and placed her foot in the stirrup before settling her skirts. 'Take her out into the park and have a trot round. Get used to her before we set off.'

Taking the reins as Sheba moved restlessly, Angelina controlled the horse effortlessly and slanted Alex a querying glance. 'I don't see Miss Howard here. Shouldn't you go and find her and ensure she is properly mounted?'

'Lavinia isn't riding. She dislikes horses and has no fondness for riding. She is to follow on in one of the curricles with some of the other ladies. We'll meet up with them at the Wild Boar in the village.'

Angelina smiled inwardly, secretly suspecting this was because Miss Howard was an indifferent horsewoman and had no wish to be shown up, but she prudently kept her suspicion to herself.

Alex's expression suddenly became serious. 'There is one thing I should mention before we depart, Angelina. We won't be riding to Arlington directly and will more than likely pass the place on the other side of the woods where you encountered the gypsies.'

Angelina paled, her eyes locked on his.

'Don't be alarmed,' he told her gently. 'They moved on yesterday so you are in no danger of confronting them again.'

She nodded, her relief evident, glad that they had gone and were no longer a threat to her peace of mind. But how long would it be before something else came along to remind her?

When the party set off a biting wind had risen. Out in the park whips cracked and they were off at full gallop down the hill towards the lake. Angelina was happy that Sheba turned out to be a spirited little horse, certainly less docile than she had first thought. Several hounds bounded on ahead. Followed by a sea of horses—Alex and Nathan out in front setting the route—they poured over the land with a fluidity reminiscent of a river in full flow.

After a time they slowed their horses to a leisurely walk. Turning in his saddle, Alex looked back at Angelina, reining in his horse to wait for her to draw level.

'My compliments, Angelina. I know few men who ride as well as you,' he told her, falling in beside her. 'I am certain that the huntress Diana could not rival you.'

'That is a compliment indeed—coming from you.' The genuine warmth and admiration in his voice and in his eyes flooded her heart with joy.

'Is Sheba to your liking?'

'She most certainly is, but she does not perform as well as Forest Shadow. She's an ambler in comparison—but we get on well enough.' She laughed, leaning forward and stroking Sheba's neck when she saw the mare prick her ears back, as if aware of what she was saying. 'She's a beautiful horse.'

'I'm glad you like her. She's yours.'

Angelina stared at him, almost speechless with pleasure. 'Mine? Oh, Alex. No one has ever given me such a wonderful gift. I can't possibly accept it.'

'Yes, you can—unless you wish to offend me.'

She smiled a little shyly. 'I wouldn't dare. I don't know what to say.'

'Thank you will do.' He'd decided to make her a gift of the horse days ago, but because of her disobedience over Forest

Shadow and the arrival of his guests, somehow he'd never got around to it.

'Thank you. But what will happen to her when I return to London? Will I have to leave her here?'

'You can take her with you if you like.'

'Really? Oh, that would be wonderful.'

Alex studied her in silence for a moment before saying, 'You're a strange young woman, Angelina Hamilton. Has there been no young man in your life? Before you came to England.'

Angelina sighed, a wistfulness entering her eyes. 'There was once,' she confessed, remembering Stuart Thackery, her childhood sweetheart.

'Tell me about him?'

'There's nothing to tell really.'

'Was he handsome?'

'Oh, yes—very. To my romantic imagination he was Apollo and Lancelot all rolled into one—a thousand times more wonderful than all the knights of King Arthur's Round Table. No legendary hero could compare.'

Alex found himself resenting and thinking jealously of that young man. 'He sounds like the answer to every maiden's prayer. And what happened to this prince among men?' he asked carelessly, unaware how deeply his cruel sarcasm hurt Angelina.

The question seemed to discomfit her. As if stalling for time she looked straight ahead, fighting a sudden mistiness in her eyes. She waited a moment before answering, and when she did her voice was low, almost a whisper. 'He—he was killed by the Shawnee.' Suddenly she urged her horse on.

Alex cursed his thoughtlessness. With a heavy guilt and his words eating away at him, he rode after her, catching Sheba's rein and bringing her to a halt. Angelina's expression was so wretched that it drove a piercing pain through his heart. At that moment he wanted all the other riders to disappear into thin air so he could drag her from her horse on to his own and kiss away her pain. She averted her eyes, looking anywhere but at him.

'Angelina, I apologise for my thoughtlessness.' Leaning across, he tipped her chin. 'Look at me and tell me you forgive my insensitive, thoughtless blunder.'

Her face broke in a teary smile and she looked directly into his eyes, seeing they were soft and yearning as they rested on her. 'Of course I do. How could you know anything about Stuart when I've never mentioned him? Along with many other things, I have several reasons for not wanting to talk about him.'

'I think there are a lot of things you don't speak of. Maybe you should. Quite often when one talks of what is troubling them, it helps relieve inner pain.'

'I can't. I will not confide in you or anyone else to share my misery.'

Alex looked into the moist depths of her eyes for a lengthy moment before nodding slowly, hesitant to press her further on an issue that clearly caused her extreme distress. 'I won't mention it again. Now, dry your eyes and we'll join the others.' Taking a handkerchief from his pocket, he handed it to her, realising how far they had lagged behind the rest when he looked ahead. 'We are in danger of being left behind and becoming the subject of a good deal of senseless gossip and conjecture.'

Angelina wiped her eyes and handed the handkerchief back to him.

'Are you ready to ride on?'

She nodded, a faint smile on her lips.

'Good girl,' he murmured, angry with himself for hurting her, and grateful to her for accepting his apology so graciously.

It was a merry group that arrived back at Arlington in the late afternoon. Everyone dispersed to their respective rooms to make themselves presentable for dinner. Jenkins approached Alex, slightly agitated.

'There is someone to see you, my lord.'

'Who is it?'

'A gentleman by the name of Mr Monkton. He arrived just

a few minutes ago and has been shown into the library. He has come from Spain.'

Alex's face hardened, his gaze shifting from the butler's face to the closed library door. Angelina saw his jaw clench and his hands ball into tight fists as, in frigid silence, he strode towards the library and went inside. Her instinct told her that Mr Monkton's arrival boded ill.

She was proved right. Her aunt's expression was grim as they went in to dinner.

'Alex's mother has died, Angelina—some kind of seizure, I believe. Her death followed that of her husband, who died of his wounds following a military engagement in July.'

Not having known Alex's mother, Angelina had no feelings on the matter, her only concern being how Alex was affected by this news. 'Have you seen Alex?'

'Yes—an hour ago.'

'How has he taken it?'

'Very much as I expected he would. He is unmoved, coldly indifferent and without any emotion. I told you Margaret had a zest for hurting people—especially Alex. The damage that woman did to him makes me furious.' She sighed, distressed by all that had happened. 'I don't know why Alex's attitude should upset me, but it does.'

Throughout dinner Alex presided over the meal with his usual calm composure. He was politely courteous and attentive to his guests, giving no hint of his feelings.

Afterwards, guests found their way up to the long gallery, where they gathered in intimate little groups to amuse themselves. Angelina heard Alex excuse himself to Lavinia, telling her he was to join a group of gentlemen to play a game of billiards.

It was to the music room that Angelina was drawn, but not before she had observed Alex walk the length of the long gallery, bypassing the billiard room, and disappear through a door that led to the east wing. In the music room Patience was already ensconced on a sofa. The older woman's face brightened when she saw her and she patted the space beside her invitingly.

'Sit by me, Angelina. Miss Asquith is about to play for us on the pianoforte.'

Angelina excused herself on the pretext that she was to fetch her fan. Reaching Alex's suite of rooms, she knocked gently on the door she knew opened into a small anteroom that led into his office, without the visitor having to pass through his bedroom. When there was no response, she opened it and stepped inside, moving slowly towards the open study door.

Having removed his coat and rolled up his shirt sleeves, Alex was standing by the window, a drink in his hand. Angelina's heart twisted with remorse when she saw the pain etched on his unguarded face. He sensed her presence his shoulders stiffened and he turned, his expression stony and preoccupied.

'If you want me to go away, I will, Alex. You only have to say.' She was relieved when she saw his granite features relax a little.

'No—please stay.'

Angelina moved towards him, feeling momentarily at a loss to know what to say, how to comfort this suffering man.

'What made you seek me out?'

'I saw you leave. I was worried…'

His sudden sweeping smile was disarming and confounded her. 'What better way to lure you into my chamber.'

She gasped, thinking how absolutely unpredictable he was. 'I thought you were upset—because of the news Mr Monkton brought you…'

His smile faded abruptly and his expression became guarded, his eyes as brittle and cold as glass. Moving away from her towards the fire, he braced his foot on the brass fender. Leaning his shoulder against the mantelpiece, he folded his arms over his chest and looked at her coldly. 'So, you know about that?'

'Yes. Aunt Patience told me.'

'What did she tell you? How much?' he demanded tightly.

Drawing a long breath, Angelina knew she had come too far to stop now. 'That your mother has died and—'

'How my father shot himself?'

She did not lower her gaze. 'Yes. That too. Alex, what happened is no secret. Aunt Patience did not betray a confidence. When I came to see you, I hoped that you would have had time to come to terms with the news and I—thought—'

'What? That now my fury has abated I would be crying into my cups?' His lips twisted with irony. 'If you thought that, you do not know me.'

'No. I don't think I do,' she said quietly, refusing to back away from this hard, cynical man. 'Does anyone?'

'No. That's the way I like it. Angelina, I appreciate your concern, but do not involve yourself in something you know nothing about. I'm dealing with this in my own way. I don't need your help.'

Angelina stiffened, but she managed to keep the hurt out of her voice. 'That's all right. You don't have to accept it. I don't mind.' She looked towards the door and turned away. 'I'm sorry. I shouldn't have come.'

Alex reached out and placed a restraining hand on her arm. 'Stay. I admire you for having the courage to seek me out at this time. But as you see, you were correct in assuming I've had time to come to terms with the news Mr Monkton brought me. I never loved my mother—I loved neither her inconstancy nor her heartlessness.'

Angelina looked at his proud, lean face, moved by the pain that edged his voice. 'And you are still tortured by what she did to you, I can see that.'

'That woman inspired me with nothing but disgust and loathing. As long as I live I shall never forget that day when I watched my father kill himself—the horror-sickening shock, the feeling of helplessness, the overwhelming despair, betrayal—and the hatred I felt when I realized that my mother alone was responsible. My father was weak—some might have called him spineless—and my mother, who considered male superiority a myth, mocked him for it. She should never have married him. It was Uncle Henry she wanted—but he—' Aware of who it was he was talking to Alex suddenly stopped and looked at Angelina. 'I'm sorry. I shouldn't be telling you this.'

'I think you were about to say that Uncle Henry wouldn't marry her because he was in love with someone else. Is that not so?'

He nodded slowly, meeting her candid gaze, wondering just how much Angelina knew about the feelings Uncle Henry cherished for her mother to this day. 'Yes.'

'Did your father do nothing to stand up to her?'

'His continual submissiveness to her amoral behaviour was something I was never able to understand. It infuriated me when he tried to make excuses for her. I wanted him to berate her, to stand up for himself. She humiliated him, spurned and shamed him before his friends, flaunting her lovers in front of him—and instead of teaching her a lesson, my father sought oblivion in drink before shooting himself.'

'And you still carry your hurt and bitterness around your neck like a millstone.'

Alex's smile was one of cynicism. 'Does it show all that much?'

'Sometimes.'

'There are some things, Angelina, that cannot easily be put aside. You, more than any other person I know, should understand that.' He stopped his pacing and looked down at her. 'You said you came because you were worried. About me?'

She nodded.

'So, you came—even though you knew I might send you away.'

'I anticipated that—and I must confess to feeling how Daniel must have felt when he entered the lion's den.'

'Were you not afraid of my anger?'

'I don't fear you, Alex,' she replied, calmly looking into his clear eyes. 'You should know that by now. Among the many emotions you must be feeling I knew you would be angry and hurt, but seeing you at dinner, so composed, so…'

'Anaesthetised,' Alex suggested wryly when she hesitated for want of an appropriate word.

'If you like.'

Alex's gaze searched her face with something like wonder in his silver eyes. There were depths to Angelina that every other woman he knew lacked, and she never ceased to amaze him. 'You confound me—do you know that? You try my patience like no other, you shoot rabbits like a barbarian and ride a horse like a gypsy, and yet what an amazingly sensitive, perceptive, wise little thing you've become, Angelina Hamilton.'

'If I were wise, I would have come to terms with everything that happened to me in Ohio and put it behind me, but I can't. That is still a millstone around my neck I have to bear. I, too, was fifteen when I saw my father die—brutally—so I know how you must have felt when you witnessed your father's suicide. I also saw my mother run to his side only to be brought down by an Indian's knife thrust into her back. I laid their ghosts to rest before I came to England. Perhaps you will be able to do the same now you know your mother is dead.'

Alex picked up a decanter from his desk to replenish his glass. Finding it devoid of liquor, he uttered a soft curse and strode towards the door to his bedroom. Holding it open with his arm, he indicated that she follow. 'Come, you already know your way around my apartment,' he grinned. 'Will you join me in a glass of wine?'

Seeing her hesitate, he said, 'You can't leave. You came to comfort me in my hour of need. Remember? I'm still in need.' He smiled lazily when she jerked her head in alarm. 'Why—you're not afraid to enter my bedroom, are you, Angelina?' he murmured with a sardonic tilt to his dark brows, his eyes compelling, flashing with that particularly silver light that was a herald to trouble.

Angelina was amazed at his ability to push his worries into the background so effortlessly. 'Yes—no, of course not.'

'You were brave enough to enter it on a previous occasion as I recall. Remember?'

His voice held a quiet challenge, and when she saw he would not take no for an answer, she relented. 'Well—perhaps just for a minute. I told Aunt Patience I was going to my room to fetch my fan. I also told her I would not be long,' she said, throwing him a meaningful glance.

'I'm sure Aunt Patience will not mind if you don't return immediately. Before I left, I observed her settling down in the music room to listen to Miss Asquith perform on the pianoforte. She may not even notice your absence,' he said, standing aside to let her sweep past. 'Welcome to my parlour.'

'Said the spider to the fly,' Angelina couldn't help retorting drily.

Alex grinned. 'In no way do you resemble a fly, Angelina. You are far too nimble and sensible to become entrapped in any kind of web—especially one of my weaving.'

Chapter Nine

'Allow me to congratulate you.' A lazy, devastating smile passed over Alex's features, his eyes doing a slow sweep of her body so that Angelina could almost feel him disrobing her. 'It appears the engaging young girl I first knew has become a gorgeous young woman of exotic beauty. In the space of twenty-four hours you have endeared yourself to every one of my guests—especially the gentlemen. No doubt when you return to London you will slay the lot of them.'

'Alex, please don't exaggerate.' Angelina moved closer to the fire to hide her confusion, aware of the magnetic charm he was exuding, and beginning to wish she had left when she had said what she had come to say.

'I don't. You will bowl them over and down they will fall like skittles. No doubt they will all turn poets overnight to express their love for this bright new star in their heaven.'

'Really?' She smiled, her eyes slanted and quietly teasing, feeling a treacherous warmth seep through her. 'And will you pen one yourself, my lord?'

He grinned. 'Haven't you broken enough hearts among my guests without wanting mine? So, tell me. What is your opinion of Miss Howard?'

Angelina was completely taken aback by the question and

her head snapped up. 'We are not acquainted—but—she seems—quite nice,' she answered hesitantly.

'Liar,' Alex said, amused at the way she tried to equivocate. 'You cannot stand her.'

Angelina's cheeks flamed. 'Then if you know my opinion, why did you ask me?' she retorted crossly. Not for a moment did it enter her head to deny it. She moved to step past him in the direction of the door, but his hand shot out, capturing her elbow.

'You're not leaving.'

'I think I must.'

'No, you're not. You are going to stay here and have a glass of wine with me.' Striding to a small carved table, he poured two glasses of red wine and handed one to her. She took it reluctantly.

'You are neglecting your guests, Alex. Don't you think it's time you returned to them?'

'No—not when I find myself in such enchanting company.'

'Why did you invite all these people if all you want to do is escape?' The answer dawned in her eyes when a slow smile curved his firm lips. 'Oh—I'm sorry. I forgot. It was to assess Miss Howard as a possible wife without appearing too obvious. Am I right?'

'Absolutely.' He chuckled. 'But it isn't difficult. Lavinia is the kind of woman any man would enjoy having as his wife. She is accomplished in many things and will preside over Arlington Hall and Mowbray Park with grace and poise. She will not be daunted by the many duties she will find thrust upon her, and she is also sophisticated and clever.'

'And cold and dispassionate and difficult to please,' Angelina concluded drily. 'I wish you joy in her. Good luck, Alex. You will certainly need it. But if I did not know any different, I would think it is a woman who has just applied for the position as your housekeeper you speak of—not the woman you intend making your wife. All of a sudden I am beginning to feel pity for Miss Howard. You seem to have considered marriage to her with the same dispassionate reasoning that marks everything you do in life.'

Alex disregarded the sardonic edge to her voice and cocked a sleek black brow at her, his eyes shining with suppressed humour. 'Jealous?'

Angelina looked at him, her eyes steady and her expression serious. 'No, Alex. I am not jealous. I have no reason to be. Besides, jealousy is an emotion I have never experienced in my life.'

Alex was immediately contrite and wished he'd never asked the stupid question. 'I know, Angel,' he said softly, reaching out and lightly touching her cheek. 'I'm sorry. So, you are of the same opinion as Uncle Henry and Aunt Patience. You don't think I should marry Miss Howard either.'

'It's just that I have no wish to see you made unhappy,' she answered quietly, reaching up and placing her glass of untouched wine on the mantelpiece.

Alex was moved by the sincerity of her words and a constricting knot of tenderness formed in his throat. 'And if I marry Lavinia, you think I will be?'

'Undoubtedly.'

For a moment Alex considered her in thoughtful silence. 'I'm touched. I didn't realise you cared.'

'I do care, Alex—otherwise I wouldn't be here. Miss Howard is cold and hard, and when she's fifty she'll look just like her mother.'

Unable to contain his mirth, Alex was laughing now with real amusement, his teeth flashing white from between his parted lips.

'Good Lord, I do believe you're right,' he said, composing his features once more. 'And is there a danger that I'll become like Lord Howard?'

'No—you're not in the least like Lord Howard. He never opens his mouth unless Lady Howard gives him permission to do so.'

'Nevertheless, Lavinia does have some good points.'

'I know. I feel like a pincushion already,' Angelina told him, her lips curving with humour. She looked at him a little quizzically. 'Do you realise that whenever you mention marriage to Miss Howard, you become tight lipped and your expression goes all serious—in fact, you become positively grim?'

Alex's mouth grew hard and he looked annoyed by her question, but he answered it. 'No. As a matter of fact I don't.'

'Well, you do. And there,' she accused, 'you're doing it again. Have you given her reason to believe you care for her? Have you kissed her?' Her head cocked slightly on one side as she looked at him, knowing she shouldn't ask so personal a question, but unable to stem her female curiosity.

His eyebrows shot up in sardonic amusement. 'Your question is impertinent, but, to appease your curiosity, the answer is yes.'

'Oh.' Angelina was unprepared for the rush of disappointment she felt, and was surprised by it, for why she should care whether he had kissed Miss Howard or not bemused her.

Alex's smile was merciless. 'Are you wondering how you compare?'

Two high spots of angry colour mounted Angelina's cheeks. 'Of course I'm not—and please don't be crude, Alex. You must forgive me if I appear stupid—but I am confused, you see. By you. I never know quite what to expect. Will you tell me why you kissed me when you came to my room? A man of your experience—you knew exactly what you were doing. I'm not used to that sort of thing, you see. I don't go around kissing people.'

'I hope not.' His lips quirked with wry amusement at her naïvety, and then, raking his fingers through his hair, he sighed, no longer in any mood for the light banter that had laced their conversation so far. 'I'm sorry, Angel. I never meant for it to happen. It was wrong of me to take advantage of you. You must forget it happened.'

But I can't, Angelina almost shouted at him. That's the trouble. The memory of that night lingered far too strongly for her to discount its effect on her. 'So,' she said, 'your intentions weren't honourable when you entered my room and took advantage of me in my weakened state.'

She tried to sound light and flippant when she spoke, but

somehow it didn't sound like that to Alex. When he heard the tell-tale catch of hurt in her voice, it was so touching and tragic that he was moved in spite of himself. In a blinding flash it dawned on him that she might expect him to say he loved her, and if so he must put a crushing end to it before she had time to nurture the idea.

'I entered your room because I heard you were distressed. I wanted to comfort you—and it should have stopped at that. In time you will learn that kissing does not bring commitment. Understand this, Angelina. For a moment I may have lost my head, but I am not going to make any undying declarations of love. I don't need any woman—and I don't need the added guilt and responsibility of a naïve eighteen-year-old girl. The ritualistic proposal that usually follows such encounters will not come from me.'

His words sounded so final, so insulting, that Angelina felt as though she had been slapped. An icy numbness crept over her body, shattering all her tender feelings for him. Deeply regretting the impulse that had brought her to his rooms to offer words of comfort, she now realised she should have stayed away, for he did not deserve either sympathy or understanding from her. She expelled her breath in a rush of tempestuous fury as the fragile unity they had shared moments ago was shattered and the battle that constantly simmered beneath the surface between them was resumed.

'How dare you mock my feelings. What a callous, self-opinionated, loathsome blackguard you are.'

He arched an eyebrow, his tone one of irony when he spoke. 'Yes, I am all those things. What did you expect—some infallible being?'

'No, not that. How excruciatingly naïve you must find me. Just to set the record straight, my lord, I do not expect a proposal. It never entered my head.'

'It didn't?' He seemed genuinely surprised.

'Why, you conceited ass,' she flared. 'Cast your mind back to my arrival at your house in London. I told you then that I have no intention of marrying—nor will I become any man's light-of-love, fawned over today and forgotten tomorrow. I meant it then and I mean it now. Matrimony is not for me. I will not sacrifice myself on that particular altar for any man.

'But should I change my mind, my lord,' she seethed, planting her hands firmly on either side of her tiny waist and thrusting her angry face closer to his, her eyes sparking with ire, 'if you were the last man on earth I would never marry you. I find the whole idea of us forming any kind of relationship quite ludicrous.'

'I agree,' Alex snapped rudely, his cold, threatening gaze impaling Angelina to the spot as he moved closer to where she stood. 'You, my pet, would make an exceedingly poor wife.'

'And you, my lord, would make an exceedingly poor husband,' Angelina countered furiously, humiliated to the core of her being by his unkindness. 'However, one thing has changed since last we spoke. I have told Verity that I will concede to everyone's wish and be introduced into society at the next Season.'

'What! With all the glitz and ostentation?' He smiled wryly. 'God help all those unsuspecting males when you descend on them. But do you realise that when you make your début you will be making yourself available to every unattached male in the country?'

'That does not mean to say I have to accept any of them. I value my freedom and independence too highly to give it up.'

Alex's face could have been carved from a block of granite. 'So, unlike others of your sex, you harbour no ambition to snare a wealthy husband.'

'Material wealth does not interest me. But if I did marry, I would marry the meanest pauper if I loved him and he returned that love. But what of you? Don't any of the ladies of your acquaintance fall in love with you? Oh, I'm sorry,' she exclaimed heatedly, glowering at the man before her and tossing her head back haughtily, the curls on either side of her face doing a frenzied dance. 'What a stupid thing to ask you of all people, when half the female population in England must have been in love with Alex Montgomery at one time or another. But what do they love about you, Alex? Your wealth? Your title? What you can give them? Don't any of them love you for just yourself? Oh, I pity you. What a lonely, bitter old man you will be in years to come.'

Alex's jaw hardened. 'I told you I do not need any woman's love. I certainly do not want it. If my mother taught me anything at all, it is that love is more destroying than hate.'

'That is not true. Love is what is essential to make a marriage work. Money has no place when it comes to happiness.'

'That is the kind of sentimental drivel spoken only by romantic young girls and idiots,' Alex uttered with biting scorn.

'Which is precisely what I am.'

'And is only for the naïve,' he mocked cruelly.

'Then I am also naïve.'

'I know that, too.'

'Oh, my, Alex,' Angelina remarked, her tone heavily laced with sarcasm. 'Your notion of love is nothing more substantial than mere indulgence. The only kind you seem to know about is the kind made between the sheets. You really are so insecure and disenchanted with life that I find myself feeling almost sorry for you.'

He fixed his cold eyes on her. 'Don't. Men in my position must marry to beget an heir, and after fulfilling that requirement—'

'Don't tell me. They are then free to enjoy their mistresses,' she flung at him derisively, her fiery, angry spirit giving her a radiance that reminded Alex of all the female attributes that stood just within his reach, a radiance that was drawing him towards her with increasing power. 'What a degenerate blackguard you are, Alex Montgomery, with mistresses strewn all over London town. That's what you like, isn't it? Pedigree ladies who look good. Ladies who don't make you feel too much. But where is the decency in that, pray? Have you no conscience—no sense of honour?'

'Apparently not,' he answered, torn between anger, amusement and desire as he looked down at her proud beauty. 'I will not change the way I live my life, and I make no apologies for it either. But I do not recall you complaining when I kissed you,' he said on a softer note, moving closer, his gaze devouring her face.

Suddenly the walls seemed to close in on them, making each aware of the closeness of the other, of the warmth, the intimacy. The pull of Alex's eyes was far harder for Angelina to resist at that moment than the frantic beat of her heart.

'Don't you dare touch me,' she warned, unable to move towards the door because he blocked her way. 'I swear that if your hand comes anywhere near me I'll shred it to the bone, you vile, despicable knave.'

His laugh was merciless, his eyes unrelenting. 'I'll risk it.'

She was about to spring past him, but iron-thewed arms went around her with stunning force and drew her against a broad, hard chest. 'Get off me. How dare you?' she objected furiously, struggling against him. His face was so close that she had no difficulty defining every detail, and the lazy smile awoke disturbing memories. 'Let me go. Must I remind you of my virtue—and that you are almost a married man?'

'A fact that weighs more heavily on your mind than it does on mine, Angel,' he murmured, chuckling softly. 'Damn it all, your virtue is the greatest stumbling block I have ever encountered. Were you not my uncle's ward, I would have demolished it long since.'

'Please let me go, Alex,' she whispered, overcome with an irrational fear, primitive and instinctive. Never had he looked so tall, so powerful, so coldly frightening as he did at that moment. She saw the burning light in his eyes, and deep within her she felt the answering stirring of longing she'd felt when he'd held her in his arms once before and kissed her. 'Do you forget so soon your promise not to repeat what happened between us the other night?'

'I have a hankering to repeat the offence—especially when I look at you,' he said huskily, turning the full force of his gaze on the young woman he was reluctant to let go. His conscience was making a damned nuisance of itself again and telling him he should end what he had started, but his body was sending out messages of a different kind.

Because Angelina was not the kind of sophisticated, worldly woman he usually made love to it made her more alluring, more desirable. She was nothing like the glamorous, experienced women who knew how to please him, women who were mercenary and hell-bent on self-gratification, whose beds he sought only to leave the moment his ardour was spent.

Reading the sudden glow in his eyes, Angelina was alarmed. 'Please don't—you can't do this to me.'

Deaf to her pleas, Alex's arms tightened, his gaze focusing on her lips. 'But I can. I am a degenerate bastard,' he said, calmly repeating the accusation she had flung at him earlier, 'with no moral principles, honour or conscience, so I can do anything I please.'

'Not with me.' He was so close that Angelina could feel the heat of him. 'Release me,' she ordered, infuriated by his obvious intention to weaken her resolve.

'Not a chance,' Alex whispered, as touched by her fear as he was by her innocence and inexperience. This time there was no burst of conscience as he gazed at those soft pink lips quivering close to his own. 'What I want, Angelina, is the same thing I want every time I look at you.' All he could think of was shattering her demureness and reserve and laying bare the woman of passion. His mouth covered hers, and, forcing her lips apart, he began kissing her with fervency, determined to make her respond.

Angelina's determination not to yield was as strong as his determination to make her. She knew that he wanted her full co-operation, and that if she gave it, it would be more damaging to her pride than anything else. Tears gathered under her eyelids and the world seemed to tilt around her and retreat. She fought the weakness, not wanting to be completely at his mercy, but her body was already beginning to respond with a gross miscalculation of her will. She wasn't made of stone. She was flesh and blood, and her blood was on fire.

The moment she leaned into him and opened her mouth in response, Alex's arms tightened round her. With the swell of her breasts pressed against his chest, he kissed her deep, drawing her tongue into his mouth and caressing it with his own. The sheer wonder of it sent exhilarating sensations darting and tingling to the far extremities of Angelina's body.

Knowing he must stop before he went too far, raising his head, his eyes hooded and dark with passion, Alex looked down into her upturned face. 'Good Lord, Angelina! What have you done to me? What might you do to me if I let you?' he whispered hoarsely, standing there with her in his arms in an agony of lust, wondering how someone as innocent, as pure and devoid of guile as she, could drive him half-mad with desire. Slowly he released her and stepped back.

Still trapped in the throes of passion, Angelina felt a tightening in her throat as she met his gaze. His eyes were hooded and moody, and his frown made a deep furrow over the bridge of his nose. Why? Why did he look like that?

'Alex—what is it? What is wrong? Is—is it like the last time—and you regret kissing me?'

'Yes. It was a mistake—my mistake,' he said, his voice strained. 'You must have cast a spell on me, for I do not seem to have the strength or the inclination to resist you. However, deflowering a properly reared virgin—and one who happens to be my uncle's ward—violates even my code of honour where women are concerned, no matter how degenerate you consider me to be.'

Picking up his coat, he thrust his arms into the sleeves and straightened his cravat. 'I'm sorry, Angelina. I take full blame for what happened.' He glanced towards the door. 'I think you'd better go while you still can.'

In the tearing, agonising hurt that enfolded her, Angelina was ashamed at how easy it had been for him, following all her harsh words, to expose the proof of her vulnerability. Tears blinded her vision. Lowering her head, she moved towards the door, silently weeping for her lack of will and with a fear of her feelings for Alex she seemed unable to control.

As Alex watched her go, he wasn't to know that what had just passed between them had been the second most humbling event of her young life. Her head was bent forward, her steps slow, and he thought he saw her shoulders shake. She looked so young, so small and vulnerable, he felt disgusted with himself and his conscience wrenched. Unable to watch her leave after she had sought him out to offer words of comfort, he was about to go after her, but at that moment her head lifted and she squared her shoulders. She turned once more. He stiffened, feeling reluctant admiration for her stubborn, unyielding refusal to cower before him.

In her fury and ravaged pride, looking like an enraged angel of retribution, Angelina dashed away her tears and looked once more at the granite profile of the man who had just kissed her into mindless oblivion, whose face had taken on a judicial look.

'You conceited, supremely amoral beast. How dare you take liberties with me and then try placating me with a lame attempt at an apology? Weren't you satisfied with the humiliation you inflicted on me two nights ago without doing that? I'll never forgive you for what you've just done, Alex. Ever. If you ever touch me again…' she told him with a quiet firmness, 'I will fight you with my dying breath.'

Her words scorched Alex's soul with its fierce, despairing passion. 'You won't fight me, Angel. I know you. I know how you feel.'

'No, you don't,' she cried, her cheeks and eyes blazing hot, fists tightly clenched as she struggled to contain her rioting emotions. 'No one knows how or what I feel. No one. When you asked my opinion of Miss Howard, I told you she was heartless and cold. The same applies to you, Alex. Should you decide to make her your wife, I wish you joy with her. You deserve each other.'

Alex was disgusted with himself, disgusted and contrite. Angelina was right. He was cold and callous for ridiculing her, for mocking her feelings. His passion for her was torn asunder by guilt. It had to end. In the past hard logic and cold reason had always conquered his lust—with Angelina it was different. He had to purge her out of his mind before he was completely beaten and went insane—and if she continued living in the same house he would lose the battle. He was in danger of losing his heart to her, and he would not permit that. The stakes were too high.

He had no choice but to send her away.

When the last of the guests had left, in thoughtful and determined mood Alex joined Patience, Verity and Nathan in the sitting room.

'I have come to the decision that it would be best for all concerned if Angelina returned to London with you,' he stated without preamble.

Three pairs of eyes became glued to him. 'What?' they uttered, simultaneously.

'You will have to go with her, of course, Aunt. She can stay with either you at Richmond or Nathan and Verity in Hanover Square for the time being. It really doesn't matter which. Notify Bramwell at my house in Brook Street, and when Uncle Henry returns from Cornwall he'll naturally know not to come to Arlington. He'll understand why I had to do this.'

'Will he!' Verity exclaimed, not at all pleased with what her cousin had decided. 'Well, we don't.'

'It is time she went, Verity—she—she's too much of a disruption.'

Verity gasped, unable to believe what she was hearing. 'That's an excuse and quite ridiculous, Alex, and you know it. The only disruptions Angelina has caused are inside you. Angelina is a nuisance only in upsetting the precarious balance of your temper.' Alex threw her a withering look, but she was not deterred. 'Goodness. You can't send her away. She's just beginning to settle down. Have you any idea how much Arlington has come to mean to her?'

'She can visit. She'll settle down just as well in London. I don't want her here,' Alex said with icy finality.

Wearily Patience sighed, determined to fight for Angelina. 'Please don't do this to her. Do not forget so soon that when Henry brought her to England she had lost everything. You are familiar with death and the loss of a parent, Alex—or have you forgotten that?' Patience reminded him.

Her words hit their target with such force Alex tensed, his jaw tightened and his hands clenched. Patience pressed her advantage, but she knew as she spoke that Alex's mind was made up and nothing would change it. 'Angelina is still very young, Alex, and she has come to love and trust us, to see us as her family. Try to remember how it was for you when you found yourself alone. You were in the same situation as Angelina. Please do not make her feel unwanted by sending her away.'

Alex could not be swayed. 'My mind is made up. She goes to London.' His gaze slid to his cousin, sitting ramrod straight beside her mother. Verity was incensed and he knew it. 'What's on your mind, Verity?' he demanded. 'I can see you're in high dudgeon about this.'

Verity's eyes snapped to his. 'Yes, I am.'

'I know.' His eyes appealed to Nathan, who had moved away to take a natural stance by the window. 'Nathan, can you not exert your husbandly influence and persuade your wife to guard her tongue?'

Nathan smiled wryly. 'I'm afraid not, Alex. She's too much like you in that,' he reminded him.

'Not entirely,' Verity objected, shooting her husband a look of annoyance.

'Well, perhaps not quite,' Nathan conceded.

Verity rose to face Alex, and they stood in the centre of the room, their gazes clashing—cousins, with the same unyielding Montgomery blood in their veins. 'I always thought you took your responsibilities seriously.'

'I do.'

'No, you don't,' she contradicted angrily, as she prepared to do battle on Angelina's behalf with the hardened cynic. 'Uncle Henry placed Angelina in your care, and after just three weeks you've had enough and have decided to pack her off back to London. You're heartless, Alex. Do you know that?'

He grimaced. 'I have been accused of being so on occasion.'

'And unjust.'

Glaring down at her from his superior height, Alex's eyes turned to shards of ice. 'You go too far, Verity.'

'It's about time someone did. I am extremely tired of watching everyone pussyfoot around you in fear of offending or annoying you. It's little enough to ask you to let Angelina stay at Arlington until Uncle Henry returns from Cornwall.'

Alex was quickly beginning to lose his temper. 'No. Angelina goes to London,' he said flatly. 'Verity, whatever you may think of me, I am no fool—and I know Uncle Henry better than he thinks. However, I never thought I would see the day when he would play Cupid. Do you think I don't know why he went to Cornwall, leaving Angelina in my care—that I cannot see what you are all trying to do that you have some idiotic romantic notion of bringing us together? Can you deny it?'

Confronted with the truth, with guilt written all over her face, Verity didn't reply, but she had the grace to look contrite and some of the anger drained from her face

'It won't work, Verity. Forget it. You too, Aunt Patience,' Alex said on a gentler note when he addressed his aunt. 'I know you are capable of setting a town alight when you put your heads together—and Uncle Henry is an interfering old rogue. He has played an important role in my life, and the gratitude and love I feel for him is immeasurable. But I will not marry Angelina out of mere sentimentality. I know both you and my uncle mean well, Aunt. But you don't always know what's best for me. I will not be influenced or manipulated by anyone over this.'

In a desperate attempt to soothe the situation before it

erupted into open warfare, Patience stepped in. 'You are right. Henry is an old rogue, but his interference—if that is what it is—is kindly meant. He is of the opinion that the best way of restoring your zest for life is to revive your appetite for love.'

'Good God, Aunt Patience!' Alex expostulated, astounded to hear his aunt utter such drivel. 'To hear such talk from you I can only assume there must be a decline in your reading standards. I have repeatedly condemned such trivial and uninstructive reading flooding the market and always thought you above such rubbish. Contrary to what my uncle thinks there is nothing wrong with my "zest for life". And as for reviving my "appetite for love"—how can something be revived that was never there in the first place?'

Patience refused to let go of the argument. 'But Angelina is a rare treasure, Alex. Any man would be proud to have her as his wife.'

'I agree. But not me. You seem to have forgotten that I am on the brink of offering for Lavinia Howard.'

'You are?'

'I am considering it. But whatever I decide, I am not marrying Angelina and that is final.'

After pinning all their hopes on a union between them, Alex's harsh words doused all Patience's and Verity's expectations. Alex ignored their despondency, knowing he'd dashed their scheme, but it had needed saying.

'Take Angelina to London,' he went on. 'Give her a Season and find her a husband—which shouldn't be difficult, given the fact that every male I invited to Arlington this weekend went away singing her praises and all more than halfway to being in love with her.'

'Have you forgotten that Angelina has stressed time and again that she has no intention of marrying?' Patience reminded him.

'No. But I recall her saying that she did not want a Season, either—and she changed her mind pretty quickly about that. She'll change her mind about marriage soon enough when she gets to London and has every rake in town sniffing after her. Uncle Henry won't have long to wait before he has her off her hands,' he said unkindly.

'Alex! Do not speak like that. Why are you deliberately trying to be cruel?' Patience reproached harshly. 'I know you aren't as unfeeling as you sound. And who's going to tell her?'

'I'll save you all the trouble,' came a quiet voice from the doorway.

Every eye turned towards the door to see Angelina standing there, unable to believe what she had heard—Alex was sending her away.

Her world tilted crazily. There was no room in her sights for anyone except Alex. She beheld the faint widening of his eyes as they turned on her, but his expression was as inscrutable as a marble mask. She found it difficult to endure his gaze, but she did, his words sounding inside her head like a death knell.

Displaying a calm she did not feel, as she crossed the room she managed with a painful effort to dominate her disappointment and accept the slap fate had dealt her. She must blot from her mind the events of last night, the exquisite sweetness of Alex's kiss. Jerking her mind from such weakening thoughts her eyes encompassed the other three, having decided not to make an uncomfortable scene.

'Would you mind if I spoke to Alex alone?'

With a pained expression Patience moved to her side and gently squeezed her hand. 'Of course not, my dear. I think it's as well that you do,' she said, bestowing on her nephew a cross, disapproving look.

'Angelina, I am so sorry,' Verity said, looking extremely concerned.

She managed a faint smile. 'It's all right, Verity. Truly. I always knew I would have to leave some time.'

When they were alone, Alex raised one brow in arrogant inquiry, knowing she had heard his remark and unprepared to refute it—which was no consolation for Angelina. Why did he adopt this cold, remote, almost hostile attitude to her? Was it possible he was ashamed of the way he had behaved towards her, or was his hunger for her so great that he couldn't bear to be close to her? She hoped it was the latter, but the way he was looking at her made her discount it. Her eyes met his proudly.

'So! You really think that, do you, Alex? That as soon as the rakes and fops in London begin paying me attention and whispering sweet nonsense in my ear, I am so silly and weak that I will be unable to resist them and reverse my decision not to wed?'

'Why not?' His mouth curled with irony. 'You were eager enough to yield to me when I held you in my arms.'

His cutting tone and the injustice of his words increased Angelina's anger. But it was the way he retained his arrogant superiority that was hard for her to take. 'I don't know why you are being deliberately cruel to me, Alex, but as I recall, you gave me little choice. I did not invite you to kiss me. In fact, if you will cast your mind back, you will recall that I begged you not to.'

'I admit that I behaved in a manner for which I am ashamed and regretful,' he said, his voice curt, thinking when he looked at her how hard it was going to be sending her away.

'You? Ashamed? Are you quite sure you know the meaning of the word?' she scoffed. Drawing herself up proudly, she showed him that she too could be hard and cold. He would never know how much he had hurt her. 'And if Uncle Henry really wanted me off his hands, he would not have encumbered himself with me in the first place. He is warm and generous— unlike you, a man whose heart is encased in ice.'

Angelina expected the words she flung at him to get a reaction, but, except for a glacial hardening of his eyes and a muscle that began to twitch in his jaw, there was none.

'Do you mind telling why you are dismissing me as though I were an untouchable?' she asked. She knew the answer, but wanted to hear him say it. 'What have I done that makes you treat me so despicably?'

Everything, Alex thought wretchedly. She was too much of a threat to his sanity. He couldn't live in the same house with her any longer if he was to have any peace. Everywhere he turned she seemed to be there, ready to ensnare him, and when she was absent his need to see her made him seek her out. He was furious with himself for feeling like this—for wanting her. He'd never realised that sexual desire for her would become a complication. Better that she was away from him altogether, before she disrupted his whole life.

'Nothing,' he said. 'At least, not intentionally. You will stay with Aunt Patience until Uncle Henry gets back from Cornwall. Now you have decided to be launched into society, you can begin preparing for it. According to Verity it's time consuming, so you cannot begin too soon.'

Angelina could hear the absolute finality in his voice that told her it would be futile to argue. 'Then there is nothing more to be said. I thank you for your hospitality, Alex,' she said with the polite cordiality of one of his guests who had just departed. 'I have enjoyed my stay at Arlington, and I am now ready to return to London.' Her words were of resignation, not defiance.

Suddenly Alex looked at her with unexpected softness. Surprised by the change in his expression, she opened her mouth to speak, but he stopped her and, taking a deep breath, continued, 'You have to go, Angelina. You must. I want you to go. There are some things you cannot understand.'

Angelina's face was a pale, emotionless mask as she turned from him and crossed to the door. Her heart and mind felt empty, and she was chilled to the marrow, and even now, when she was desperate with the thought of leaving him, she had to ask herself why it should hurt so much, and to question what was in her heart.

Chapter Ten

It was decided that Angelina would stay with Nathan and Verity in Hanover Square, and that Patience would delay returning to her own home at Richmond for the time being. Angelina became firmly fixed under Aunt Patience's wing as the elderly lady arranged her vast wardrobe for her début, employing modistes who enjoyed her own and Verity's patronage.

There followed many long weeks of intensive instruction in perfecting the intricate steps of the minuet and the quadrille—a dance, like the waltz, which was considered 'fast' by some and only danced at informal affairs and in private. She learned how to curtsy without wobbling, deportment, and how to utilise her femininity by learning the art of the correct use of the fan—how to hold it, how to close it—which almost drove her to distraction.

To alleviate the tedium they often drove through Hyde Park, which was a rendezvous for fashion and beauty, with splendid, shining carriages and high-stepping horses. Angelina was a new distraction, drawing the admiring, hopeful eyes of several dashing young males displaying their prowess on high-spirited horses. Under the watchful eye of Nathan, she was introduced to several, promising to dance with each and every one of them at her début ball.

Under Verity and Patience's instruction, Angelina blossomed into an extremely attractive and desirable young woman, who was refreshingly unselfconscious of her beauty. The furore she was causing delighted them, and they were secure in Angelina's certain victory before the Season got under way. Before too long she would have London at her feet.

There were few people in the elevated circles of society who hadn't heard of the Duke of Mowbray's American ward, and all the unattached males clamoured to be introduced. It was not just her beauty that drew them to her, or the mystery of her American background and the fact that she had, until recently, been staying at the home of London's most notorious and sought-after rake, Lord Montgomery, but also the huge dowry the Duke of Mowbray would be certain to settle on her.

On Henry's return to London, Patience told him everything that had transpired at Arlington and the reason why they had returned to London earlier than intended. Henry was disappointed and yet unperturbed to learn that Alex had made it plain that marriage to Angelina was out of the question. From what he knew of their highly volatile relationship, he suspected that Alex was sorely missing Angelina and when Patience told him Alex was to come to London two weeks hence—stressing he had to attend important business meetings—Henry's instinct told him that it was an excuse to see Angelina again.

In the beginning it had been Henry's intention to throw the two of them together, but now he would do exactly the opposite. In an act of pure mischief he whisked Angelina off to Mowbray Park for Christmas.

When Angelina wasn't in London waiting to receive him, Alex knew a disappointment and fury that was beyond anything he had ever felt in his life. Despite his belief to the contrary, when she had left Arlington he had found it no easy matter thrusting her out of his mind. He threw himself into his work, but it was Angelina he saw in his mind, Angelina who stole his thoughts away from important matters at hand.

When she'd been with him he'd had difficulty keeping his eyes off her, and at times he'd been unable to keep his hands off her. And now she was gone he couldn't keep his mind off her. Who was she with? What was she doing? Were suitors already lining up, waiting for the Season to begin so they could offer for her? He could hardly contain his jealousy at the thought of any other man touching her.

Cursing himself for behaving like a love-smitten youth, he tried to divert his irrational thoughts away from her, but it became an internal battle—one he began to lose a little more with each passing day. He couldn't eat, he couldn't sleep, and he spent most of the night pouring brandy down his throat and pacing up and down his room so that he almost wore a path in the carpet. That was when the need to see her became paramount to all else.

But that was before he arrived in London and read his uncle's letter informing him that he had taken Angelina, Nathan, Verity and Aunt Patience to Mowbray Park for Christmas. Alex knew a fury like he'd never known. He knew that this was his wily old uncle's way of trying to manipulate him. Not for one moment did he consider going after them. He'd meant what he'd said to Aunt Patience, that he would not be coerced or lured into marriage. But on returning to Arlington and finding no peace without Angelina, he reached the most momentous decision of his life—he would return to London in time for Angelina's début ball.

On the day itself, with her thoughts on what lay ahead and the many difficulties she may encounter during the evening, Angelina stood while Pauline fastened her in her ball gown, feeling extremely nervous now the moment had arrived. When she was pulling on her gloves Verity, resplendent in pale blue satin, came to tell her that Uncle Henry had arrived.

'My dear Angelina. You look wonderful,' she enthused.

Beholding her reflection in the mirror, Angelina knew Verity was not exaggerating. Her fashionable, high-waisted gown of white satin, with an overskirt of white tulle, was intricately embroidered and decorated with seed pearls. The sleeves were elbow length, with a flow of delicate Brussels lace caressing her forearms. The French hairdresser had skilfully entwined a slender necklace of diamonds through the heavy curls at her crown so that, every time she moved, her head glittered and sparkled.

Henry watched her descend the stairs, his expression one of admiration and calm. Taking her hand, wonderingly he shook his head. 'You look enchanting. How I wish your dear mother could see you now. She would be so proud—as I shall be when I walk into Romney House with the most beautiful débutante in the whole of London on my arm,' he said, not mentioning the unexpected guest who would be making his appearance at the ball later.

The streets in Piccadilly were congested with carriages depositing the cream of London society outside the open doors of Romney House. Inside, footmen in powdered wigs and crimson-and-gold livery lined the stairs up to the ballroom. The head footman announced the Duke of Mowbray and his party in a stentorian voice, and there was much fluttering of fans, bobbing of curtsies and bowing of elegant heads. Guests were arriving all the time—débutantes in gorgeous pale-coloured gowns accompanied by their chaperons, and young men dressed in black, with brightly coloured waistcoats and pristine white cravats.

They were greeted by Lord and Lady Romney in the foyer and then climbed the stairs to the grand ballroom, with its highly polished parquet floor, Venetian mirrors and crystal chandeliers, to be announced again. Between the long French windows opening on to a balcony were huge urns on pedestals, bursting with a profusion of flowers, and elegant gilt chairs were placed at intervals along the walls.

Angelina was dazzled and confused by this impeccable *ton-*

ish company, recognising several faces from her drives through the park and visits to private drawing rooms. She felt a sudden shyness combined with a curious reluctance to join these distinguished, sophisticated members of society—this gay, rakish and exclusive set who graced 'The Regent's Clique'. Looking like a vision from heaven, she entered the ballroom on Henry's arm.

Every influential head turned to the new arrivals and conversation became hushed as eyes strained to have a look at the Duke of Mowbray's American ward.

Henry gently squeezed Angelina's hand in the crook of his arm, sensing her nervousness. 'Don't be nervous, my dear. Within half an hour your card will be full. But make sure you save a dance for me. This is going to be the most enjoyable evening I've had in a long time.'

Within minutes there was a near riot to see who could get to her for the first dance. Laughter and frivolity surrounded her, and she found herself responding to it automatically. The first two dances of the evening went to young men she recalled meeting in the park, one of them a dashing and flamboyant young lord called Duncan Aylard.

'I'm delighted to see you again, Miss Hamilton,' he said with a sardonic grin as he swept her a deep bow. 'You haven't forgotten me, I hope—or that you promised me a dance.'

'No.' She laughed, warming to his natural charm and easy manner. 'I do remember you, Lord Aylard—and, yes, I shall be delighted to save a dance for you.'

His grin was impudent as he subjected her to a long, lingering gaze. 'And the next and the one after—and perhaps you will permit me to take you into supper later.'

'More than two dances would be quite improper and commented upon,' she chided teasingly, amused and flattered by his persistent manner, 'and I have arranged to have supper with my uncle. Do you forget that this is my début, Lord Aylard, and I have my reputation to uphold?'

'I would not dream of doing anything to damage that—so I

shall have to be content with two…waltzes,' he insisted with a grin, preferring the darting flurry of the waltz to the minuet. The waltz was considered by some to denote a general decline in moral standards, but Lord Aylard thoroughly approved of the dance and would not consider partnering the staggeringly beautiful Miss Hamilton in any other.

He proved to be a superb dancer and Angelina happily abandoned herself to his encircling arm as he twirled her about the floor. Unashamedly he flirted and flattered her and made her laugh, but their entertaining conversation came to an end when someone caught his attention. He stiffened. 'Good Lord! Did you know he was to attend the ball? I had no idea he was back in London.'

'Who?'

'Lord Montgomery.'

Angelina felt her heart slam into her ribs. She froze for an instant, her thoughts scattered. She could feel Alex's presence with every fibre of her being, and, despite the shock of seeing him again after so long, an increasing comforting warmth suffused her. A strange sensation of security, of knowing he was close at hand, pleased her. But the memory of their parting, of the pain and the hurt he had caused her, was still present.

Over the heads of the crowd Angelina saw him standing with Nathan, even more powerfully masculine and attractive than she remembered. For a second their eyes met, then he looked away, seemingly without interest. Praying Lord Aylard had not taken note of her discomposure, she studied Alex surreptitiously.

His commanding presence was awesome, drawing the eye of everyone in the room. A group of people moved to speak to him, and she noticed how everyone was hanging on his every word, doe-eyed young débutantes gazing at him dreamily, and that there was a tension about the group that seemed to begin and end with him.

When he had arrived a short while ago with Nathan, Alex had paused in the action of kissing the hand of an acquaintance's wife and quickly glanced up to see Angelina taking to the floor with young Aylard. Nothing had prepared him for his first sight of her after months of absence. His heart wrenched when he looked on her unforgettable face—so poised, so beautiful that he ached to hold her.

Never had he seen her look so provocatively lovely, so regal, glamorous and bewitching—and he wanted her to belong to him entirely, to take her in his arms and send her persistent suitors packing. He was not noted for his patience. His yearning was like an obsession in his blood.

His gaze shifted to Aylard, who was looking down at her upturned face like a hungry fox looking into a hen coop. Of all the males in London, why did she have to draw the attention of Aylard—a young man with the potential to earn a reputation to rival his own? He could not bear to see other men vying with each other with infuriating persistence to dance with her, coveting her, to watch the admiration and appreciation in their eyes as they followed and devoured her every move. He guessed their thoughts were not so very different from his own, and he despised them for it. For the first time in his life he experienced an acute feeling of irrepressible jealousy that twisted his gut and caught him completely off guard.

The dance over, Lord Aylard escorted Angelina back to her uncle. Unfortunately he couldn't do that without passing Lord Montgomery. Good manners dictated that he stop and offer polite words of greeting, which he did, bowing with a grand, sweeping gesture.

'Lord Montgomery, it's good to see you again.'

Alex did not deem to pay Aylard the same homage. Looking the younger man over with a haughtily cocked brow, he nodded, his eyes cold and ungracious. 'Likewise.'

Angelina stood by Lord Aylard's side and looked at Alex. After a parting of five months, it was like coming face to face with a stranger. That well-remembered silver gaze slid from Lord Aylard to her. She had not forgotten how brilliant and clear his eyes were—how cold they could be.

'Hello, Alex,' she said quietly. 'I had no idea you were in London.'

Smiling pleasantly, Lord Aylard turned to look at Angelina. 'If you will excuse me, I will leave you now. Should you find you have another dance free, I shall be more than happy to oblige.' Passing his appreciative eyes over her exquisite features, he was unheedful of Alex's face hardening as he witnessed the perusal.

'I don't think so,' Alex said stonily, the cold grey eyes considering the other without a hint of expression, then with slow deliberation. 'Miss Hamilton's dance card is full. However, should any over-eager young swain on her card have the misfortune to fall over in their rush to get to her and break a leg, I shall oblige.'

Uncertainty flickered across Lord Aylard's face, cutting through his easy, friendly demeanour. Angelina felt her ire rising at Alex's deliberate rudeness, having no reason to think it stemmed from jealously.

'Why, Alex! Since when did you care a fig for my reputation?' she flared.

Before Alex could reply, Lord Aylard gave Angelina a brief nod of farewell, and left the ballroom in search of strong liquid sustenance, feeling unusually put out.

Angelina watched him go and then turned to Alex, incensed. 'You beast. How could you be so rude to Lord Aylard?'

He cocked a brow and regarded her with a tolerantly amused smile. 'Was I?'

'Inexcusably so and you know it. He has done nothing wrong and did not deserve such a cruel set-down. I will not tolerate your interference in matters that are none of your concern. And should one of my partners have the misfortune to fall and break a leg, there are others already waiting to oblige.'

Alex grinned in the face of her rage, meeting her stormy eyes. 'Then take my advice and choose your partners with more care. Aylard's a veritable tulip who floats around the edges of the Carlton House set. The man's a rake of the first order.'

'Which you should know all about, Alex,' Angelina was quick to remind him, 'having the reputation of a rake yourself.'

'Be that as it may, but I may not be around to save you the next time.'

'I sincerely hope not.'

Alex noted that the angry exchange was not going unnoticed by those close by. 'Do you mind not looking at me as if you are about to run me through, my pet? Do not make a spectacle and try smiling. People are staring at us.' His voice was soft, though his smile was knowingly reproachful.

Angelina forced her face into more subdued lines, but when she spoke her voice shook with quiet fury. 'How dare you call me your pet after the way you treated me at Arlington? I am not your pet and people can stare all they like. Excuse me. I'm going to find Uncle Henry.' Turning on her heel, with her head held high and two angry red flags of colour burning her cheeks, she stalked away, longing to bring that arrogant, insufferable man down a peg.

Chuckling softly and watching Angelina's retreating figure with admiration, Nathan moved to his side. 'My word, Alex. Methinks the lady is extremely vexed. Her aversion to you will not easily be appeased—and who can blame her, considering the way you sent her away from Arlington.

Alex watched the tempestuous beauty rejoin his uncle and Aunt Patience. Her beauty fed his gaze, stirring a sweet, hungering ache deep inside that could not easily be put aside with anything less than what he desired.

'With a little tender persuasion I am certain I can overcome that problem. However, I can see that, despite all the teachings in etiquette she has received since I last saw her, her spirit remains intact.'

'Would you have it any other way?'

Alex shook his head. 'I intend to marry her, Nathan, to gentle her, to make her complaisant to my demands, but God help me if I do anything to change what is inside her. She is quite unique.'

Nathan was astounded by his declaration. 'So, the renowned libertine and despoiler of women has decided to call it a day and settle down to domestic bliss. Have a care, Alex. Angelina has a strong will, and it's a courageous woman who will pit her will against yours.'

'In that, as in everything else, I intend to have the upper hand. She'll soon come to realise that.' He spoke with supreme confidence. Lounging back against a pillar, his arms across his chest, a dangerous light entered his narrowed eyes and a smile tempted his lips.

Nathan saw that look, and if he'd had to tell Angelina what it foretold, his explanation would have angered her far more than she already was. Alex looked exactly like a marauder who was about to invade a particularly challenging and desirable country and claim it for his own—and refused to be deterred by any fight from the opposition.

Now Alex had made up his mind that he was going to marry Angelina, he began to enjoy the ball and was in fine spirits for the rest of the evening—enjoying it all the more when Aunt Patience suddenly complained of feeling unwell. After making her excuses to Lord and Lady Romney, Alex saw her out to her carriage—Uncle Henry too, for he was so overly concerned about the onset of his sister's sudden weakness that he refused to allow her to go home alone. Of course, he made Alex promise to remain with Verity and make quite certain that Angelina was properly chaperoned and to see her home.

Alex wasn't fooled and knew *exactly* why his aunt had suddenly decided to feel unwell. He was convinced that she was perfectly well and that her sudden weakness was nothing more than part of the scheme concocted by her and Uncle Henry to throw Angelina in his path. He chuckled with humour. This time he wasn't complaining. He was content to follow the course his uncle had been plotting from the beginning.

He found Angelina in conversation with Verity, looking quite bemused by what she was telling her. She looked at Alex anxiously when he appeared by their side.

'Verity tells me that Aunt Patience has been taken ill,' she said, her eyes filled with concern. 'Perhaps we should all leave.'

Alex smiled imperturbably. 'I am sure Verity has told you that her dear mama has nothing more serious than a headache, which I strongly suspect is feeling much better already. Don't you agree, Verity?' he queried with humour, giving his cousin a look that clearly stated that he fully understood the situation.

Verity flushed with embarrassment at being caught out. 'Yes, I'm sure you are right—as always, Alex,' she replied drily.

Alex turned his attention to Angelina, and there was something subtle in the way his expression changed that made her uneasy.

'Uncle Henry has left you in my very capable hands, Angelina—to make quite sure you enjoy what is left of the evening and are returned home unmolested.'

'I find it hard to believe that Uncle Henry would trust you to protect and uphold my virtue. It's rather like a wolf being left in charge of a flock of sheep,' she quipped.

Alex's answer was a slow, impudent grin. 'My uncle's skill with weapons is as sharp as it was thirty years ago, and I do not doubt for one minute that he would take up arms against me should I fail in my duty.'

Angelina regarded him sceptically. 'And I can dance with whom I like?'

'Providing I approve of your choice of partner,' he prevaricated.

'I do not need you to check out my dancing partners, Alex. I am not a child.'

'That's the first sensible thing I've heard you say all evening. I agree with you absolutely.'

His remark and taunting grin brought a bright hue creeping into Angelina's cheeks, and made her realise the folly in baiting him.

'I believe this next dance should have been Uncle Henry's,'

he said, slipping a hand beneath her arm to escort her onto the floor as the orchestra struck up the next waltz. 'Come. I would have this dance before you are swept away by yet another devoted, over-zealous swain.'

'My feet ache. I think I prefer to sit this one out,' Angelina said, resisting by pulling back.

'No, you won't. I insist,' he said, tightening his hold on her elbow.

Without more ado he headed towards the dance floor. A group of young bloods with flirtatious grins standing on the periphery raised their glasses in a salute as Angelina drew level, and Alex fumed when he saw her acknowledge their homage with one of her bright, generous smiles.

'Do you have to smile at every man you come into contact with?' he seethed between his teeth.

'Why not?' she replied, her look one of complete innocence. 'I was only being polite.'

'Forward to the point of being fast is how I would describe it. You smile and flutter your lashes like an accomplished flirt.'

'As I understand it, flirting is an accepted, highly desirable mode of social behaviour,' Angelina argued quietly.

Angelina abandoned her waist to his encircling arm. It was as steady and firm as a rock. Alex was a superb dancer. As he whirled her into the dance she seemed to soar with the melody. It was as if they were one being, their movements perfectly in tune.

'My uncle informs me that the evening has been a resounding success for you,' Alex remarked at length.

'That depends upon what you mean by a resounding success. For myself I am enjoying every moment of it. What brought you to London, Alex? Business?

His hooded eyes captured hers. 'That was one of the reasons.'

'I'm surprised you decided to attend a ball with nothing more interesting to amuse you that a host of silly débutantes.'

'Don't be. The company at White's tonight was exceedingly dull. I came here to please Aunt Patience and Uncle Henry—and to see you.' She stared up at him, searching his eyes for the truth behind his words. 'I am quite serious,' he assured her softly in answer to her unspoken question. 'You look enchanting, by the way.'

'Thank you. Did Uncle Henry know you were coming to London?'

'Yes. I wrote and told him several days ago.'

'Then why didn't he tell me?'

'My uncle moves in mysterious and devious ways. Perhaps you should ask him—and while you're about it, ask him why he whisked you off to Mowbray Park on the eve of my coming to London before Christmas.'

Angelina gasped, her eyes opening wide. 'You mean Uncle Henry knew you were coming and didn't wait to see you?'

'Exactly.'

'But why?'

'You'll have to ask him,' he replied drily, twirling her round. Making a quick sweep of the room, Alex was not unaware of the attention they created. 'We've become something of a curiosity among the gossips, my pet,' he said softly, his palm firm against the small of her back, his breath warm and smelling pleasantly of brandy on her cheek. 'Nathan tells me you have become extremely popular—the darling of the debutantes, I heard someone comment at White's earlier.'

'I'm glad of the opportunity to show them I'm not a red-skinned savage with feathers in my hair,' Angelina responded, laughing merrily with a light-hearted toss of her head.

'Don't get carried away, Angelina,' Alex murmured with a note of caution, smiling nevertheless. 'It's true there have been rumours drifting about town about the Duke of Mowbray's American ward for some time now, and most people who have not had the opportunity of seeing you have dealt with a wild, rather plain young woman who wears buckskins and her hair in a pigtail. Nothing has prepared them for how you look tonight.' His eyes rested warmly on her face. 'You dance divinely, by the way.'

'So every one of my partners has told me.'

'Saucy minx,' he murmured, smiling.

'And you dance better than most.'

'Praise indeed,' he quipped, sweeping her into another dizzying whirl.

Content to let the music carry them along they fell silent, unaware of the passing moments. Angelina stared up at Alex's achingly handsome face and into his bold, hypnotic eyes, lost in her own thoughts, before she realised that his gaze had dropped to her lips and his arm tightened around her waist, drawing her against the hard rack of his chest.

'Have you missed me, Angel?' he asked.

'Yes—a little,' she confessed awkwardly, feeling his warm breath fan her cheek. In truth, she had missed him more than she could have imagined.

'Only a little?' Alex watched the reaction to his question play across her expressive face, correctly interpreting it.

'I thought you were still angry with me.'

'Why? Should I be?'

'I don't know. I was so confused when I left Arlington. We both said things—'

'Forget them. Everyone says things they don't always mean in the heat of the moment—and as I recall,' he murmured, a spark of laughter in his eyes, 'the temperature was definitely heated on the occasions when I kissed you.'

Angelina's cheeks burned and her heart began to throb in deep, aching beats. The reminder of his kiss, his touch, had been branded on her memory with a clarity that set her body aflame. She raised her eyes to his, seeing them darken and his expression gentle.

'You, my pet, are blushing.'

'Any female would blush when you say the things you do and look at them like that. Please stop it, Alex. People are watching.'

'Then let's go somewhere more private.'

Before Angelina knew what he was about, he'd waltzed her through the glass doors and out on to the deserted balcony. His arm slipped about her waist and tightened, bringing her full against his hardened frame.

'Alex,' she protested, 'this is most improper.'

'To hell with proprieties. I will not stand by and watch every male in London ogle you.'

'Why, Alex—are you jealous, by any chance?'

With his lips close to her cheek his voice was husky and warm, his eyes devouring her with a ravenous hunger. 'I am jealous of your every word, thought and feeling that is not about me. I want you. It is my dearest wish to make you mine. Don't waste yourself on the likes of that young cockscomb Aylard. They're not worth it.'

Trying to ignore what she saw in his eyes, his lips hovering just above her own, Angelina tried to still her rapidly beating heart. 'And what of you, Alex?' she asked, breathing heavily. 'Are you worth it? You say you want me. If I were to yield myself to you, would you honour me?'

'Until death,' he breathed, brushing the round softness of her cheek with his burning lips, one of his hands sliding beneath her hair, his fingers caressing her nape. 'Since you left Arlington you have been for ever in my thoughts, plaguing me, torturing me. Dear Lord, Angelina. You sorely test my restraint. Don't you know how much of a temptation you are to me?'

Her mind reeling over the shock of what he was saying, Angelina could only stare at him as a torrent of emotions overwhelmed her.

'I want you, Angel,' he murmured, raising his hand and tracing the gentle curve of her cheek with his fingertip. 'There is a chemistry between us—has been from the start.'

She shook her head in an attempt to regain her sanity. 'What I am afraid of is how many other women you share your chemistry with, Alex.'

'You listen to the gossips too much.'

'It's difficult not to where you are concerned.'

'What if I were to tell you that I need you?'

'I would say you don't. You collect things. Women in particular.'

A look of exasperation crossed his face. 'Angelina, stop it. All that is over.'

'No, it isn't. You're a rake.'

'I'll reform. Does my reputation worry you?'

'Not in the slightest.'

Alex grinned suddenly, lifting an impudent brow. 'There is a saying that reformed rakes make the best husbands.'

'They do?'

'Yes.'

'Who said it?'

'I did.'

Suddenly, something he'd said snapped Angelina's eyes to his. 'Why did you say that?'

'What?'

She swallowed. 'About husbands.'

'Because, princess, I want to marry you—to make you my wife.'

Understanding dawned with his meaningful gaze. In the deafening silence that engulfed them, neither of them moved. Angelina breathed at last, staring at him in confused shock as she understood the truth of what he was asking of her.

'I want to marry you,' he repeated, watching her closely.

The entire colour drained from her face and her body became tense. Raising her clenched fist to her mouth, she pulled away from him, seeking to be alone so she could think clearly.

After a moment Alex came slowly towards her. 'Angelina, look at me.'

Reluctantly she raised her eyes to his and looked at him in desperate appeal. What Alex saw in their innermost depths— a confusion of anger, pain and fear—almost took his breath.

'Angelina, what is it?'

'I cannot believe that you want this. I have certainly not encouraged it.'

'Unconsciously you have encouraged it every time we have been together. Have you any objections to me as a husband?'

'All I know is that I don't want to marry anyone. You know that. Besides, what sort of marriage would it be when you treat love lightly?'

Placing his hand under her chin, he tilted her face to his, wanting more than anything else to eradicate the reluctance oozing out of her.

'You are wrong. I confess that I know nothing about the kind of love you speak of, but what I do know is that when you left Arlington you were never far from my deepest thoughts. You suit me better than any other woman I have known or am likely to. You anger, amuse, delight and frustrate me to the point where I don't know whether to throttle you or make love to you. You test my patience and my sanity beyond the limits of my endurance. And yet, despite all this, I still want you for my wife. I've had mistresses, yes—but it is to *you* that I offer marriage. No other woman has been able to get that close. So, what do you say? Will you do me the honour of accepting my proposal—and become my wife?'

Angelina looked directly into his face just above her own, feeling herself respond to the dark intimacy in his voice. His expression was gentle, understanding, soft as she had never before seen it. And there, plain for her to see, was the sincerity of his words.

'Have you spoken to Uncle Henry about your intentions?'

'Not yet, but for us to marry is his dearest wish. Uncle Henry is as crafty as an old fox and it has been his intention to bring us together from the start.'

Her lips trembled into a little smile. 'Yes, I can see that there has been a real conspiracy going on—and that Uncle Henry has been aided and abetted by Aunt Patience and Verity.'

'I was determined not to be lured or coerced into marriage by anyone—which was one of the reasons why I sent you away from Arlington and why I did not follow you to Mowbray Park, which, I might add, was part of Uncle Henry's plan.'

Confusion clouded Angelina's eyes. 'But—how? Surely if he wanted to draw us together, the last thing he should have done was take me away from London when you were expected.'

'One thing I learned from an early age is that there is always method in our uncle's thinking, my sweet. When he saw his little scheme had failed to bring us together at Arlington, he decided on a different approach—that absence inclines to deepen the affection.'

'And did it?'

Alex grinned, having no wish to deny the truth. 'I confess it did. For once in his life that cunning old man got it right.'

'And when did you realise you wanted to marry me?'

'When I came to London, expecting to see you, only to find Uncle Henry had whisked you away. I missed you like hell when you were no longer there, but my pride refused to capitulate to Uncle Henry's scheming. But things have changed, so don't disappoint everyone by refusing my suit. Uncle Henry will be mortified.'

'I wouldn't intentionally do anything to hurt Uncle Henry. I love him dearly and would sooner die than cause him pain. I am grateful for all he has done for me. At a time when I had nothing he gave me a home and his protection.'

'I gave you my protection too when you needed it at Arlington,' Alex reminded her with an impudent grin.

'Now you're trying to make me feel beholden to you.'

'That's because the more indebted you feel towards me, the more compliant you will feel when you consider your answer to my proposal. If you refuse me, another suitor will take my place tomorrow or the next day.'

'I don't have to marry any of them.'

'I shall try to persuade you to consider my suit. Since you have just listed my many shortcomings, allow me to convince you of my merits. As you know, I come from a long line of noble forebears, and I have titles and wealth envied by many—which I would like to share with you. I am not unattractive to look at—at least, so I've been told,' he said with an arrogant quirk to his lips, 'and which you can determine for yourself.'

Angelina looked at him obliquely, a smile tugging at the corners of her mouth. 'You're passable, I suppose.'

He grinned. 'Come now, Angelina. Admit it. You find me more than passable.'

'If I do, I see no sense in giving you a bigger head than you have already by telling you so. If you desire compliments from me, then you are going to have to work extremely hard to get them.'

'I intend to.' He laughed, unable to stem his mirth. 'Now, where did I get to? As I was saying—we know each other well enough and share common interests as well as family. Furthermore,' he murmured, his eyes rapturous, 'we have a shared passion. I know you are not indifferent to me. So don't fight me, my sweet. Face the truth of what I've said.'

'I thought you had decided to live your life in unemotional objectivity. Marriage to me will bring you a wealth of strife.'

'I don't doubt that every day you will pit your will against mine—but do not forget that, in a conflict of wills, man has force on his side. I am certain that you will flout my wishes and drive me to distraction with your disobedience, but it will be stimulating. You and I will never be bored.'

'Nevertheless, it is arrogant of you to assume I might prefer you to any of my other suitors.'

One dark eyebrow rose in a measuring look. 'I won't change my mind. I know exactly what I want.'

'You're so sure of yourself, aren't you, Alex? I hate it when you are.'

'I know you do. But that is something you will have to learn to live with. Will you accept my proposal?'

After he had treated her so badly at Arlington, Angelina was reluctant to make any kind of commitment to him. Besides, his conceited assumption that she would accept without demur tempted her to decline his suit out of hand. But then, she thought with quiet mischief, might it not be both interesting and satisfying to keep this arrogant lord dangling for her favours?

'Marriage is important and serious and not something to be undertaken lightly—especially for me,' she said, facing him squarely. 'Forgive me, Alex, but I'm reluctant to commit myself to you or anyone else just now. Everyone has gone to a great deal of trouble in making me a débutante and I want to savour the opportunity to enjoy the Season. I would also like to take the opportunity to look over other eligible suitors before I settle on a husband.' She smiled up at him obliquely. 'But don't be too despondent, Alex. I promise to consider your proposal— along with any other I may receive.'

Alex sensed victory slipping away and, momentarily thwarted, his expression hardened. 'I'm not noted for my patience, Angelina—as you well know.' Cupping her chin in his hand, he gently kissed her lips before raising his head and looking at her with that all-absorbing attention Angelina had come to know. 'The die is cast, Angel. You will be mine in the end.'

For the rest of the evening, without a qualm Angelina happily used all her untapped ability at flirtation. She smiled happily at the gentlemen who flocked around her, allowing first one and then another to lead her into the dance, clinging on to their arms and hanging on to their every word. Alex stood watching from the sidelines, his face a veneer of bland sophistication, while inside he was seething. With the wisdom born of years of experience with the female sex, he knew what Angelina was playing at, and no matter what game she played, he did not doubt his own ability to lure her into marriage to him.

Henry's expression was one of calm speculation as he regarded Alex. He quirked a brow in amused inquiry, waiting for him to speak.

Alex looked directly into his uncle's eyes, his expression unreadable, neither warm nor cold. 'I believe I have to ask your permission to marry Angelina?' he asked, having no intention of beating about the bush.

Henry beamed, scarcely able to conceal the rush of joyous satisfaction. His plans had advanced even further than he had hoped. Here he was, offering for her like an impatient, love-sick swain on the eve of her début, rushing in before the competition got a foot in the door.

'As her guardian it is the correct thing for you to ask me. I was wondering how long it would take you to get round to it.'

'My compliments to you, Uncle. You and Aunt Patience from the beginning have planned this very carefully. You can congratulate yourselves on the outcome.

'I am so glad you have come to realise what a dear, sweet girl Angelina is.'

'I would not describe Angelina as sweet,' Alex replied, his tone impervious, irritated because his uncle looked like he was enjoying his predicament enormously. 'It has taken me five months to appreciate that that high-minded little madam is the most exasperating female I have known in my entire life. She is also the woman I want for my wife.'

'Pardon me, Alex, but I have to say that you do not look in the least like a man in the full flush of love.'

'I am not.'

'After weeks spent brooding on your regret for sending Angelina away from Arlington, during her absence I realise how anxious you have been to see her again—and the more disagreeable and difficult you have become.'

'I am not disagreeable.' Alex's patience was being strained.

'If you say so,' Henry said, smiling, the taut expression on his nephew's face belying his words. 'Tell me, Alex, why do you want to marry Angelina? Have you come to care for her?'

'Of course I care for her—more than I have ever cared for any other woman, which is why I want her to be my wife,' Alex replied, annoyed when he saw his uncle's victorious smile widen on hearing his confession. 'I want to marry her as soon as it can be arranged.'

'That will not be appropriate. You will marry her after a decent interval of courtship, Alex, and not before.'

Alex stared at him in frigid silence, unable to believe all his carefully thought-out plans were about to be demolished. The last thing he had expected from his uncle, after all his machinations to bring himself and Angelina together, was opposition. The two men looked at each other, both stubborn and tenacious, both unyielding, but this time one of them would have to retract, and it had to be Alex.

'How long?' he asked tautly.

'July.'

'July?' Alex exploded with disgust. 'Do you mean I have to endure weeks of letting the *ton* gawp at her and other suitors call on her before I can make her my wife? Good Lord, Uncle! July is three months away. I can't wait that long.'

'You'll have to, Alex. You will just have to curb your impatience—and your lust,' Henry told him with a mocking grin, knowing that his nephew was caught in something he had not bargained on, something he could not control and could not be easily cooled. When he saw his nephew's impervious expression begin to waver, his eyes became amused. 'Besides, you haven't asked her yet so how do you know she will accept your suit?'

'I have asked her—and—she's thinking about it.'

'Has it not occurred to you that she might very well turn you down?'

'No. If she does, I am confident she can be persuaded,' Alex replied, with a steely determination that he would succeed in doing just that. He had some knowledge and experience of Angelina, and he knew he could seduce her into insensibility in a matter of moments.

Henry saw the tell-tale gleam in his nephew's eyes and knew exactly along which path his thoughts were travelling. 'Angelina is not one of your mistresses to be tumbled and then tossed aside, Alex,' he admonished sternly. 'She is innocent and guileless and unused to the irresponsible ways of men. She must be treated with the respect she deserves. Where women are concerned you are quite ruthless. The world and its neighbours know you are no saint—that you have nothing to boast about in your dealings with the female sex—but all that must change if you are to marry Angelina. Your reputation for profligacy must be a thing of the past.' His chuckle was rich and deep as he quirked a brow. 'Who knows—perhaps you might be redeemed by a good marriage?'

'Maybe I will, if I'm allowed to get on with it,' Alex replied with a low grunt of derision. 'I can see I can get no sympathy from you.'

'You're correct—you won't. I know your pride has taken a hammering over this, that you have tried to fight your feelings for her but to no avail. But that will mend. You will have to dispose of your current mistress, you understand.'

'I've already eliminated that problem.'

'I'm glad to hear it. Considering Angelina's aversion to marriage, I insist that you woo her first, Alex—gently. We must observe *all* proprieties. If you go rushing in with your usual impatience, you'll be bound to intimidate her. Let people see you together before you announce your betrothal. When it's announced, I have no doubt it will be received with dismay among the ladies of society and relief among the bachelors, glad that you are out of the way at last and they no longer have to compete.'

Alex stared into those grey eyes so like his own and struggled to contain his exasperation with this wily old uncle of his, whose expression was a combination of infuriating satisfaction and sublime innocence. 'I have the distinct impression that you are both for me and against me on this, Uncle,' he said, watching an inexplicable smile trace its way across the older man's face.

'Am I? Explain what you mean, dear boy.'

'From all that confusion I can draw no argument,' Alex conceded.

'Fine. Now that's out of the way, I think a toast is in order,' Henry said, getting to his feet and pouring them each a large brandy and handing one to Alex, already thinking what wonderful great-nephews and great-nieces they would produce to continue the illustrious Montgomery line. 'I am delighted things have turned out this way. I could not be happier.'

'Good,' Alex said, suddenly thinking that his uncle looked ten years younger. He tossed his brandy back before fixing him with a hard stare, humour tugging at the corner of his mouth. 'Now we have established that Angelina is to be my wife, there is just one small matter we need to discuss.'

'And what is that, pray?'

'Her dowry.'

Alex had the satisfaction of watching his uncle almost choke on his brandy. 'Dowry?'

'Dowry,' Alex repeated, a wicked, calculating gleam lighting his eyes. 'You must have thought about it. It is usual for a bride to bring a dowry to her husband on marriage, and, as her guardian, that is for you to take care of.'

'But of course—and I did say it would be generous. But—'

'Don't think you're going to escape settling a dowry on her because she is marrying your nephew,' Alex warned, scarcely able to conceal his mirth when he sensed his uncle was about to try to evade the issue. 'Now,' he said, handing him his empty glass and settling comfortably into a chair as he prepared himself for a long and interesting discussion on the issue of his future wife's dowry, 'pour me another splash of brandy and we will sit and discuss how generous you are going to be.'

Chapter Eleven

After Angelina's first ball the house in Hanover Square was deluged with callers, and there followed an intense round of social functions. Escorted to all the stylish gatherings by family members, there were regular visits to a play at the theatre at Covent Garden or Drury Lane, or the opera at the King's Theatre in the Haymarket. Occasionally they visited the gardens at Marylebone where they drank tea, or visited the Pleasure Gardens at Ranelagh.

Like a bird set free Angelina was surprised to find herself revelling in the fun of it, and most of all she was happy because Alex was nearly always present, attentive, considerate—conspicuously so—and she knew this was to frighten off prospective suitors, which quietly amused her. His proposal was never mentioned between them, but his eyes were ever watchful, showing nothing of his frustration as he watched her suitors come and go. Aylard was the most persistent, and Alex was sure she encouraged that young coxcomb merely to put his back up.

But this period was not all fun and games—Angelina went through a great deal of deliberation and heart searching, before deciding that, for better or worse, she would become Alex's wife. She could hardly believe how deep her feelings were running, and the joy coursing through her body melted the very core of her heart. She loved Alex. She knew that now, and that perfect certainty filled her heart and stilled any anxiety she might otherwise have had.

The feeling was so strong there was no room for anything else. Ever since their first meeting they had moved towards this end, and now there was no doubt in her heart. Nothing could change it. Nothing could touch it—neither now nor in the future. She gave him her answer to his proposal when they were walking in the garden at his house in Brook Street.

An unbearable sense of joy leaped in Alex's heart. The yielding softness in her eyes, the gentle flush that bespoke her untainted innocence and youth, brought faint stirrings of an emotion he thought long since dead. Reaching out, he cupped her chin in his fingers, tilting her face to his and softly placing his lips on hers.

'Thank you,' he murmured. 'If at times I have seemed brutal in my behaviour, it is because I found it difficult coming to terms with how I feel about you. But, Angel, what I want you to know is that I shall never force you into anything. I want you to accept me of your own free will.'

His words gave Angelina reason to hope. 'Do you promise?'

'I never say anything I don't mean.' He smiled suddenly, a warm gleam entering his eyes. 'I think I can still see a shadow of doubt in those glorious eyes of yours, which I intend to eradicate. You have just become betrothed to me and I intend sealing the bond by kissing you senseless.'

'You wouldn't.'

'Watch me.' He let his eyes drop once more to her lips, moist, soft, beckoning his own. 'I am afraid, Angel, that we need to reach a better understanding before we commit ourselves at the altar. I want to make quite sure I am not bringing a frigid, unwilling bride to my bed. You have no idea what I will do to you when we have said our vows, my pet,' he warned hoarsely. 'I cannot look at you without wanting you.'

Lowering his head, he placed his lips on the soft curve of her cheek, moving gently, exquisitely, assaulting her defences, his eyelids lowered in anticipation of what was to come, so he did not see the fear cloud her eyes, could have no idea of the cold tremor of dread that passed through her at the mention of his bed and what he would expect of her when she was in it. Angelina told herself that he could have no idea what he was threatening, that she must trust him, and when his lips claimed her own she told herself that she would do just that.

Everyone was delighted at the way things had turned out.

'Now, where will the happy event take place?' asked Patience, already mentally making out the invitation list, who to include and who not to.

'We'll be married at St George's Church here in Hanover Square,' Alex stated. 'It will be more convenient than Arlington for most of the guests, who tend to remain in town after the end of the Season anyway. We shall be wed as soon as the banns have been called for the ritual three weeks—the week after, in fact.'

'A month? But that's too soon,' Patience gasped. 'Alex, you cannot possibly mean that.'

'I do.'

'But—why—there's so much to do—not to mention Angelina's bridal gown. A guest list has to be drawn up before the wedding invitations can be sent out, and there are the menu and the flowers to be taken care of. Oh, really, Alex! It's obvious you have never been married, otherwise you would know it is virtually impossible to arrange a wedding on a scale that befits the ward of the Duke of Mowbray in four weeks. And do not forget that we have bridesmaids to find and dresses to be made.'

'I don't see why that should be a problem. There are children in abundance on your husband's side of the family to choose from. And then there are the two Asquith girls.'

'I still think a little more time is needed,' Patience said.

'My dear aunt,' Alex said, not in the slightest perturbed by his aunt's objections. 'You and Verity are two of the most competent and capable women I know. I have every confidence that you will be able to arrange the bridesmaids, the food and the flowers in time.'

'But we can't possibly.'

Alex grinned, casually propping one booted foot on the opposite knee and gently stroking the palm of Angelina's hand with his thumb in the folds of her skirt, knowing how susceptible she was to his caress when he heard her breath catch in her throat and saw a pink hue mantle her cheeks. 'Yes, you can. Four weeks,' he insisted implacably, trying to maintain his straining patience and his own escalating pulse rate caused by the closeness of the adorable young woman by his side. 'A long delay seems pointless. You must approach my secretary. He will assist you in the preparations and knows how to go about getting things done.'

'Very well,' Patience conceded, knowing her nephew's mind was made up and there was no point arguing.

When the betrothal the Duke of Mowbray's ward to the Earl of Arlington was officially announced in the *Post*, it was received with considerable surprise, although, since the Earl of Arlington's attentiveness towards the American girl at all the stylish gatherings had been duly noted, word was already getting out that she had won the heart of London's most eligible bachelor.

When Lavinia Howard was told, furious and humiliated to the core, she discreetly removed herself to the Howard ancestral home in the country.

When Angelina walked slowly down the aisle with her hand resting on the Duke of Mowbray's arm in the candlelit church and bearing a spray of white lilies, all the radiance in the world was shining from her large amethyst eyes, which were drawn irresistibly to the man who was waiting for her at the front of the church, overwhelming in stature, his ebony hair smoothly brushed and gleaming. His plum-coloured coat, dove grey trousers hugging his long legs, matching silk waistcoat and crisp white cravat were simple but impeccably cut.

Unable to contain his desire to look upon Angelina, Alex turned. The vision of almost ethereal loveliness he beheld, her face as serene as the Madonna's, her body slender, breakable, snatched his breath away. Something like terror moved through his heart. Dear Lord, he prayed, make me cherish and protect her all the days of my life, and give her the joy and happiness she deserves. With Nathan by his side he stepped out and took his place in front of the priest, waiting for her in watchful silence.

Angelina's eyes were irresistibly drawn to him, clinging to him, and she met his gaze over the distance without a tremor, surprised to find she felt perfectly calm, her mind wiped clean of everything but the moment. She was unaware of all the eyes focused upon her, the many faces belonging to people of social prominence on either side of her a blur. There was a faint smile on Alex's firm lips, and her heart warmed as if it felt his touch.

When Angelina reached him, she looked up into his piercing grey eyes, and the gentle yielding he saw in those liquid depths almost sent him to his knees. Still smiling, he took her hand, his long fingers closing firmly over hers. She responded to his smile—in that moment of complete accord, her marriage to Alex seemed right. Together, side by side, they faced the priest to speak their marriage vows, unaware of Patience and Verity dabbing away their tears of happiness and Henry looking proudly on.

When at last they were pronounced man and wife, Alex bent his head and gently kissed his bride on the lips, unable to believe this wonderful creature belonged to him at last.

The wedding breakfast was a truly opulent and impressive affair, with course after course of exquisite, mouth-watering dishes served with all the pomp and splendour expected at the Earl of Arlington's table.

Alex leaned close to his wife, the sweet, elusive fragrance of her setting his senses alive. 'What are you thinking?' he asked quietly.

She turned and looked at him, her face lively and bright. 'Oh—about all this—our wedding. I never believed it possible that this could happen.' A cloud crossed her eyes and a note of regret entered her voice. 'My only regret is that my parents are not with us.'

Alex squeezed her hand comfortingly under the table. 'They are not far away. I am certain that they are watching you from that mysterious place where we all go to one day.'

'Do you really think so?'

'Yes. Perhaps our children will produce their likeness,' he said softly, his eyes gleaming into hers, lazy and seductive, feeling a driving surge of desire at the sultriness of her soft mouth and the liquid depths of her eyes.

Angelina stared at him, unaware that she had paled. 'Children?' A lump of nameless emotion constricted her throat. Alex's casual reference to any future offspring they might produce reminded her of what would come later.

'At least half a dozen,' Alex replied, laughter rumbling in his chest. 'But you have to promise me one thing.'

'What is that?'

He stretched his arm possessively across the back of her chair without taking his eyes off her, slowly running his fingers along the back of her neck. 'At least one of them must look like you.'

She smiled, enjoying his caress. 'I'll do my best.'

Later, when the orchestra struck up and began to play the first dance—a waltz—Alex proudly led his wife into the centre of the floor and took her in his arms. Gazing down into her upturned face, he whirled her around to the delight of everyone, their bodies falling gracefully into the rhythm of the music.

They were the only couple dancing, the others being content to watch and admire. The desire that leapt between the groom and his beautiful bride was like nothing they had witnessed before. They watched transfixed as Alex's long fingers splayed across the small of his bride's back. All the while he was looking at her, and she at him, as if there was no one else present, and everyone was bewitched by the mystery that seemed to lie behind the highly charged communication of their eyes.

The revelry at its height, few people noticed when they slipped away. Angelina was halfway up the stairs when the full impact of what was about to happen hit her. Panic engulfed her, but she managed to cling to her composure with strength and fortitude as if it were a shield with which she could protect herself from Alex.

Pauline was waiting to remove her wedding finery. The girl was noticeably quiet as she proceeded with the ritual, which Angelina welcomed. After slipping the white satin nightdress over her mistress's head and letting it fall in a swirl about her feet, in numb silence Angelina watched as she snuffed out the candles, leaving just one burning close to the bed, its covers turned down. Pauline went out, leaving Angelina to her fate.

For what seemed an eternity she stood perfectly still, trembling with apprehension. Her eyes fixed on the connecting door, she saw a sliver of light beneath it, and a shadow passing to and fro. When at last it opened her heart slammed into her ribs. She took a step back as though to escape.

From the doorway Alex was looking at her in a way he had never looked at her before. He was implacably calm, but now he positively emanated a ruthless determination. Taking refuge inside herself seemed to Angelina the safest, most natural thing to do, and with revulsion and denial starting to heave in her chest, she felt herself shrinking back into the person she thought she would never be again.

Nothing Alex could say or do could make her climb into that bed with him, feeling as she did at that moment. Her decision made, there was a sour feel to her mouth and her throat was dry. She watched him close the door and move slowly further into the room, his robe falling open to the waist, revealing his firm, well-muscled chest covered with a mat of dark hair.

He paused, his eyes devouring her as she stood so very still close to the bed. Her nightdress gleamed, outlining the womanly shape of her: the soft swell of her breasts, her tiny waist, rounded hips and long, slender legs. In that strange pattern of candlelight she looked almost ethereal.

Suddenly he paused, and Angelina knew it must be the tortured expression and the way she was looking at him with numb paralysis that had brought him to a halt.

'Angelina? Is anything the matter?'

'Alex—I—I want to talk to you,' she said, shrinking at the presumptuously possessive gaze he swept over her, her self-control teetering very close to the edge.

'To talk is not what I have in mind,' he gently mocked.

Swallowing nervously, she saw in his eyes a need that would not be denied. 'Please don't look at me like that.' Her voice was scarcely above a whisper.

'How am I looking at you?' he asked cautiously. A hard line settled disquietingly between his black brows. 'A man is entitled to look at his wife any way he chooses.'

'Not when she doesn't want him to,' she whispered, her words ragged, his look prompting her to seek the protection of her robe. Thrusting her arms into the sleeves, she wrapped it around her with a protective tightness.

'Angelina, what is this?' Alex asked with an ominous quietness. 'I am not a monster ready to spring at you.' Not having expected to encounter resistance, Alex was both puzzled and annoyed by her behaviour. He sensed that all was not well with her, that the past had reasserted itself, and in the hope of finding out what it was, he made a supreme effort to overcome his impatience. 'Why don't you tell me what is wrong?' he asked quietly.

Angelina turned from him and moved away from his threatening presence to stand by the window, gripping the sill. Her eyes burned and her throat ached, as if her heart was being pushed up into her mouth, but she was determined not to cry. Alex came up behind her, his fingers closing around her shoulders, feeling a shudder pass through her entire body at his touch.

'Angelina,' he asked gently. 'Are you so frightened of letting me make love to you?'

Shrugging herself out of his grip as if it scorched her flesh, she moved to the centre of the room, averting her eyes.

Her silence chafed, and when Alex spoke his voice was edged with anger. 'If you are thinking of what happened to you in Ohio, I ask you to forget it. It is in the past. You must put it behind you.'

Her eyes darted to his and flamed. 'Is it?' she said fiercely. 'The ugliness of what happened is still between us. My memory is still clear. No matter how hard I try, I cannot forget.'

'Angelina, listen to me. I don't know what happened to you and I swore I would put no pressure on you to tell me, hoping that you would eventually. Lacerating yourself with memories will only deepen the pain, so don't you think it would be easier and sensible to tell me your secret so its power will be less potent? The past will always be with you. It is almost impossible to forget. But you must put it behind you. I know it hurts to hear that, but you're young and it's the only way.'

'But I can't,' she cried, 'and nor can I speak of it.'

'Good Lord, Angelina!' he said, raising his voice in exasperation. 'You behave as if you have some terminal disease.'

His eyes taunted her and Angelina felt the heat rise to her cheeks. 'That's how it feels—to me.'

Alex moved closer but she backed away.

'Don't come near me, Alex. I don't want this.' All the blood drained out of her face, leaving it ashen.

Alex's firm jaw tensed and his fists clenched. 'Do you mind telling me what has got in to you? His eyes were penetrating, searching, and he was no longer able to stem the question that had been uppermost in his mind ever since he had found her in the grip of her nightmare. He tried to prepare himself for the answer she might give him, dreading it with every fibre of his being. 'Angelina, did those savages rape you?'

Looking down in abject misery, she shook her head. 'No.'

The word was spoken so softly that Alex almost didn't hear it, but when he saw her lips form the word relief and thankfulness tore through him. 'Thank God,' he murmured, exhaling long and deep.

'But they might as well have. They have taken away my sense of worth, and I loathe myself with all the passion of my being.'

When at last she looked up it was as though a mask had dropped over her exquisite face, leaving it remote and expressionless. Her eyes were lifeless and dull, as if something inside her had died. Never before had Alex seen her like this. He was tempted to ignore what she was telling him and draw her into his arms, but a sixth sense warned him not to move too close.

'Have you been hurt so badly that you recoil from the touch of another human being—from me?'

'No. Please don't think that.' She wanted to tell him that she loved him, and that whatever he did to her she would bear the pain of it to make him happy. But it wasn't the pain that worried her. It was something else, something dark and insidious she could not put a name to.

'Then forgive me if I appear stupid,' Alex ground out, trying hard to fight his feeling of inadequacy and his inability to break through the invisible barrier she had erected around herself. Raking his fingers impatiently through his hair, he began pacing up and down. When he had walked into her room he hadn't known what to expect—but rejection? Never. Suddenly he came towards her and stopped, hands on hips, his elbows bowed outward.

'I admit to being confused, for whenever I have kissed you you have raised no objection and returned my kisses with an ardour equal to my own.' He fell silent, for he remembered that at those times he had been tender, gentle with her. 'Angelina, you knew what to expect when you agreed to become my wife.'

'Yes—I did. For some time my subconscious has been urging me to face the things I am afraid of, to question my weakness, and until the ball tonight I had every intention of being a dutiful wife. I thought I could, but—'

'Then what happened?'

'I don't know. I only know the closer it came to retiring, my fear increased. It's not you, Alex. It's me.' She drew a long shuddering breath, drawing from an inner strength the courage she needed for what she was about to ask him. 'Please—will you agree to wait—give me time?'

Apart from a tightening of the lines around his mouth his face was expressionless. 'You do realise that what you ask is highly irregular?'

'Yes.'

'And if I refuse to do as you ask?' His voice was dangerously quiet.

Her soft mouth trembled as she stared like an animal wounded unto death into those fiery silver eyes that rested on her. 'Alex, I am begging you. You must. I'm not ready. I thought I was, but I'm not. You would not force me to submit to you?'

One black brow rose as he gave her a long, cool look. 'I find your choice of word distasteful, Angelina. When I eventually take my wife to bed, I hope she does not find it necessary to prepare herself mentally before she will let me touch her. I do not expect her to yield or surrender to my will or authority— to subject herself to me as if it is some form of punishment for wrongdoing.'

To Alex at that moment Angelina looked both beautiful and tragic. Not wishing to drive her to the precipice of hysteria, cursing silently he turned away in angry frustration. For the first time in his life he found himself confronted by a wall he could not breach. 'Before God, Angelina, I will not force you. I want to make love to you, not fight you.'

'All I am asking is for you to give me a little time—a delay, that is all.'

Alex moved closer, anger ripping through him when she visibly shrank from him. With a quivering finger he pointed to the bed. 'Either you get into that bed with me now, or I shall walk through that door—and it will remain between us until *you* decide to come to *me*. But I will not allow it to remain between us for ever.' He regarded her with a terrifying firmness. 'The choice is yours.'

The temptation to give in, to cast herself into his arms, was so powerful to be almost irresistible. She needed him so much, his warmth, his strength. Yet fear restrained her on the very verge of yielding and it chilled her heart. Naked pain slashed across her face and she looked at him, not knowing what to say. In the end, she lowered her eyes and shook her head. 'I'm sorry, Alex,' she whispered.

His fury erupted and his eyes flashed a dangerous steely silver as he made as if to go to her, but checked himself. 'When you have the courage to become my wife in every sense, you know where I am. Out of consideration for your anxiety and fear and my ignorance as to what did happen to you in that accursed land, I will make concessions and agree to wait. But be warned. My patience is not inexhaustible. You cannot evade the issue indefinitely.'

Crossing the room in long swift strides, he opened the door, where he paused and turned back to her. 'To keep your memories of that time in Ohio is not good. It's like running away, and whatever you run away from will always come to find you.'

'Is that what happened to you when you saw your father kill himself?'

'Yes, so I do understand some of what you are going through. Has it never occurred to you that a thing feared and dreaded is better done and put behind you—that to combat a fear one must meet it head on?'

She shook her head, wanting to believe his assurances and surrender to hope. But she had lived so long with pain and grief that she was unable to do so just then.

Angelina's suffering was so near the surface, it was plain for Alex to see. Unable to be so dismissive about what had happened to her, something moved in the region of his heart. His expression softened as he looked at her with aching gentleness. 'I will not give up, Angelina. Whatever it was those savages did to you and your family—that made you feel inadequate as a woman—I know they did not break you. I believe the image of what happened is more vivid because you have made it so.'

'Do you hate me?' she whispered brokenly.

'I hate this demon that's consuming you. Fight it, Angelina. Beat it.'

'I can't.'

'Yes, you can. Let me love you. Do not forget that I have felt the way you surrender in my arms—that you return my kisses with equal passion. Whatever I set out to do I achieve, and a woman whose desire for me is as great as mine is for her will not defeat me. I want you, Angelina, and I mean to have you—but on terms that are agreeable to us both. Will you promise me to think about this seriously and accustom yourself to marriage?'

'Yes, of course I do.'

'Thank you. Having no wish to bring ridicule to me or my name, I must insist that this sorry state of affairs remains between ourselves.'

'Of course it will. I would not embarrass you by speaking of it to anyone,' she replied. He had always said he didn't give a damn to what people thought of him, but he did after all.

He nodded and left her then, closing the door firmly behind him. That was the moment when Angelina knew the true meaning of heartbreak.

Back in the splendour of his lonely room, intending to drown himself in drink, Alex poured himself a generous brandy and tossed the fiery liquid back, immediately pouring himself another, knowing he would get no sleep that night. With the woman—his wife—he wanted more than any other in his bed just behind the door, he intended getting well and truly foxed to stop himself thinking about her, to keep his mind from riveting upon the way she had looked today as his bride.

He paced the carpet, and with each footstep he swore violently under his breath, and each time he turned he threw a virulent look at the closed connecting door. He found it incredible that he—the future Duke of Mowbray, courted for his favour by men and women alike, a man who with cold logic could override his emotions whenever he wished, should find himself in this intolerable situation. Good Lord, this was his wedding night and his wife had denied him her bed—and what was worse, much worse, was the fact that he had allowed her to do it.

The weather was fair, the sun adding warmth to the day when Alex and Angelina returned to Arlington. Their marriage was the cause of much celebration in the surrounding districts. It was a time for gaiety and dancing, when villagers, tenant farmers and their families, servants and lords and ladies alike joined in the merrymaking. Angelina was happy to be back at Arlington, to reacquaint herself with the staff; however, it soon became obvious to them all that things weren't as they should be between the Earl and his new wife.

Feelings between Angelina and Alex were strained and tension ran high. At first they tried being amiable to each other, but they were both guarded, and it was impossible to sustain empty pleasantries indefinitely. In public they put on a cheerful front, seeming to be loving and agreeable, but in private it was a different matter. All Angelina's attempts to engage her husband in amicable conversation yielded nothing but cold, uninterested responses.

Alex went about his work with his usual single-minded determination and efficiency, but he had withdrawn from Angelina as if those tender, happy moments they had shared in the weeks prior to their wedding had never been. He became a stranger to her, cold and unapproachable.

After three weeks the situation became intolerable. Each avoided the other, and when they did meet, usually at dinner, Alex was so imperiously polite that Angelina wanted to hit him. The Alex she had come to know and love was no longer there in the new role he had created for himself.

One morning, after taking her early morning ride, she was returning to her suite of rooms in the east wing adjoining her husband's when, passing his door, she halted her steps when she saw his valet and a servant carrying a large trunk out on to the landing. Slowly she moved inside, looking at them in alarm.

'Where are you going with that? Is my husband going somewhere?'

'Your husband, madam, is leaving for London,' came a cold voice from behind her.

Angelina spun round with disbelieving eyes when Alex emerged from his dressing room, fastening his waistcoat. His valet and the servant made a hasty retreat on to the landing, closing the door behind them.

'London! Oh, I see,' she said quietly, feeling her heart almost grind to a halt when she looked at his hard, handsome face, seeing that his mercurial mood she had been living with since their marriage had taken a bewildering turn for the worse. 'Am I to go with you?'

'No,' he replied, trying not to notice how ravishing and invigorated she looked after her ride, dressed in her scarlet riding clothes, her cheeks adorably pink and her eyes sparkling. Fastening a gold pin in his cravat, he strode past her without giving her so much as a glance, disappearing into his office. 'You are to remain at Arlington,' he said to her through the open door. 'No doubt you will find plenty to occupy your time.' He emerged, carrying official papers and correspondence and thrusting them into a large leather bag on the bed, his long fingers threading the straps through buckles to secure it.

Angelina stood watching him in tearful silence, hurt and disappointment tearing her in two. 'May I ask why you have suddenly decided to go away?'

His face was unyielding and impassive, with no sign of the passionate, sensual side to his nature, and when he turned his gaze on her she felt the full blast of his contempt. 'I would have thought that was obvious.'

Angelina's cheeks burned from the cruelty of the remark, and she was swamped with guilt. In silent, helpless protest she stared into his icy, metallic eyes, feeling as if something had shattered inside her. He was dismissing her as someone he considered unworthy to be his wife. He wanted to leave her—to be rid of her. She could feel it. And why shouldn't he, something inside her cried accusingly, when he had saddled himself with a wife who had spurned him on their wedding night? Any other man would have got rid of her before now, or forced her to comply.

'When will you be back?' she asked, clutching her riding crop with her gloved hands in front of her, wishing she hadn't asked when she beheld the cold glitter of his eyes and the rigid hardness of his jaw.

Taking his jacket from a chair and thrusting his arms into the sleeves, he met her gaze directly. 'I can't say. I have important business matters to take care of. My stewards will see that things run smoothly at Arlington while I am away.'

'You're always busy, Alex. You do too much.'

His eyes snapped to hers, his mouth curving into a humourless half-smile. 'Meaning?'

'That I—I see so little of you,' she murmured hesitantly, desperate for him not to go, thinking wildly of some way to reach him.

'Are you complaining?'

She became flustered, cautious. 'No, of course not. Can't your business transactions be taken care of here?'

'I can only do that in London. It may have escaped your notice, Angelina, but owing to the war in both Europe and America, there is an economic crisis. If I am not in London to discuss matters at first hand with my business managers and bankers, the implications could prove disastrous. I also think it would be best if we were apart for a while.'

Angelina flinched. 'I see.' She stared at him as he strode around the room, picking things up and throwing them on to the bed for his valet to pack into bags, fighting to control the mistiness that suddenly affected her vision. She drew a shaking breath. 'Alex. Are—are you leaving me?' she asked quietly, overwhelmed with emotions and the fear that this might be so.

He stiffened, and when he turned and looked at her she could almost feel the effort he was exerting to keep his temper under control. 'What in God's name gives you that idea?'

'I—I thought that because—we—don't—'

'What? Sleep together? You are quite wrong,' he snapped. 'I renounced my freedom for you. You belong to me as I belong to you. I do not admit defeat so easily. There will be no separation between us, no matter how much you desire it.'

'But I don't,' she cried.

'I meant what I said. I have important business commitments that need my personal attention, and I shall return to Arlington as soon as they are settled—in which time I hope you will give serious thought to what we discussed before we left London.'

'I will. Alex, I am not doing this to hurt you. The fault is entirely mine—I accept that, and you can't possibly blame me more that I blame myself.'

He gazed down into her pain-shadowed eyes, fighting the simultaneous impulse to shake her for her stubborn refusal to be a proper wife to him, and the stronger urge to clasp her to him, carry her to bed and lose himself in her. She was very lovely, this obstinate young woman he had married. So lovely, in fact, that he would forgive her the past three weeks and the insult she had offered him night after night with her firmly closed bedroom door, and postpone going to London if tonight she would come to him willingly.

'I'm not blaming you.'

'Going away won't solve anything.'

'For me it will.' He strode back into his office.

'That seems like an easy way out of a difficult situation,' she said, following him, standing in the doorway whilst he collected the documents from the top of his desk and began thrusting them in drawers.

'It is not easy. I have to do something to quench the fury of not being able to make love to my wife,' Alex retaliated coldly.

He was going away because, having become hopelessly entangled in his desire, he couldn't help himself. Every night he fought against it to go to her. He thought he was stronger, but she had bewitched him. He was obsessed by her and if he didn't put some distance between them he was afraid of what he might do—that he would force himself on her and she would hate him for ever more, and they would set about destroying each other like mortal enemies. Emerging from his office, he stopped what he was doing and came to stand before her, his awesome presence filling the room, his face austere, his voice calm and authoritative.

'I do not think you realise what this enforced abstinence is doing to me, Angelina. It is both unacceptable and intolerable. Like every other man, I have needs.'

'And these needs you speak of are the kind that you go to London to satisfy? How excruciatingly naïve and stupid you must find me, Alex,' she said scathingly

Alex's eyes narrowed dangerously as he fixed her with a piercing stare. 'Are you accusing me of seeking my pleasure elsewhere?'

'What else am I to think?'

'I agree. There are numerous beds in London with willing occupants.'

'And when I recall your reputation as being London's most infamous libertine, no doubt you are familiar with every one of them.' she accused coldly, two high spots of indignation highlighting the flush on her cheeks.

'Some of them,' he admitted. 'And I shall not fail to avail myself of one of them if I so wish. I feel more like a man considering holy orders than someone who has recently married. Do you expect me to live the life of a monk?'

The threatening quality of his behaviour sparked Angelina's anger. She suddenly felt weary before this display of selfish rage on the part of her frustrated husband. How could he ignore all she had told him—her sufferings and fears, her grief? None of that interested him. The only thing he cared about was sating his lust. She had to summon all her patience to stop herself bursting out in fury.

'My, you are feeling sorry for yourself, aren't you, Alex?' she said, her words heavily laden with sarcasm. 'There are other worthier ways of finding forgetfulness for yourself than in the women who will willingly fall into your arms. You are being quite unreasonable.'

'Don't push me, Angelina,' he snapped coldly, his eyes glittering like shards of ice, his tone promising terrible consequences. 'By denying me your bed you have already reached your limit. In my present "unreasonable" mood, nothing would give me greater pleasure than to throw you on to that bed and spend the rest of the day showing you what is expected of a wife and how attentive a husband I can be. The very thought of you, the sight of you here in my room, having you close, wrenches my insides in a painful knot and begs to release the desire you have aroused in me. I have been patient long enough. I shall give you ample time to come to terms and prepare yourself for what I shall expect of you when I return.'

'Which is?'

'I don't think I need to spell it out. Do not forget that you are bound by your word and I expect you to fulfil the vows you made to me in church.'

'I intend to—'

'So, I am to live in hope, am I?' he cut in with bitter irony.

'Yes, of course. But how dare you remind me of what I promised when you are considering breaking your own?' Angelina went on recklessly, the colour heightening on her cheeks as she glared at him with bitter accusation, heedless of his mounting rage.

'Am I not being driven to it my own wife? Are you still afraid of the prospect of lying with me?'

'I—I don't know,' she answered truthfully.

'If you would allow me, I think I could remedy that.'

He was standing so close and was looking at her so intently, that Angelina's eyes moved involuntarily to his mouth. On impulse she backed away. 'Don't, Alex.'

His arms reached out and caught her, bringing her slamming against his chest. She gasped, thinking he was going to kiss her when his head lowered slightly, but he continued to look at her with a humourless smile, his warm breath fanning her lips.

'Don't threaten me, Angelina. It is not in my nature to rape an unprepared innocent. But you are my wife—and, by God, when I return from London you will be my wife in truth. My patience is at an end. There will be no more childishness.'

'If you bully me, it will avail you nothing.'

'I advise you to think very carefully if you intend continuing with this charade, because if you do you will regret it, I promise you. I will decide which course our future will take, and I do not intend spending our lives together sleeping apart. Do I make myself clear?'

'Perfectly,' she answered, flinching from the sharpness of his tone, hearing determination in every word.

'Good,' he said, releasing her as abruptly as he had taken hold of her. 'I'm glad we understand each other.'

'No, Alex,' she flared, her face scorching. 'I understand you but you do not understand me. Your own conduct where I am concerned cannot be faulted, I suppose? Has it not occurred to you that I would have found it easier to adjust to my new, awesome position as your wife if, since coming to Arlington, you had not been so ill tempered and treated me with callous indifference? You are manipulative, stubborn and extremely selfish. Let me remind you that as your wife I am equal in all things—not your possession or your chattel, to be told what I will and will not do.'

Alex gave her a long, speculative look. 'Will you not?'

'No,' she snapped, throwing back her head and raising her chin mutinously. He was playing the role of a husband whose honour has been smirched a little too well. 'And it is really too much for you to start laying down rules in this lordly fashion. If you insist on being disagreeable, I suggest you make haste and leave for London—and do not feel that you have to hurry back.' With that she turned and walked across the room so he wouldn't see her tears of humiliation.

Not until her hand touched the handle did his cold, ominous voice slice across the chasm that separated them. 'Angelina!'

Despite herself she stiffened and half-turned back to him,

eyeing him suspiciously as she waited for him to speak, recognising that the stern set of his face and the thin line of his
lips did not suggest much tolerance. He came to stand in front
of her, and when his eyes peered into hers, she could sense the
menace behind them.

'I meant what I said. I do not see why I should have to go to
the inconvenience of travelling to London to avail myself of a
mistress when I have a wife who shares my money and my
name living under the same roof. When I return, you will not
deny me. Is that understood?'

Bravely she tried to smile, hoping her voice wouldn't break
and trying to hold on to her shattered pride. He made his
feelings plain in the one inimical glance. 'What you mean is
that I must learn my place. Yes, I understand you perfectly.'
Feeling her control collapsing, she went out, hot tears burning
her eyes, the lump in her throat almost choking her.

Alex watched her go, tempted to go after her, but he
remained motionless. Having made her understand what he
expected of her when he returned from London, he was certain
she would give it serious thought and obey him. The idea that
he would allow her to go on as they were, living together but
sleeping apart, was unthinkable.

When Alex had left for London, never had Angelina felt so
bereft. Her conscience smote her and she was sick with dread
that he might have returned to the arms of one of his former
mistresses—and she had sent him there. She tried telling
herself that he would not do that to her, but her tortured
imaginings almost drove her crazy.

What had she done? Alex was the most precious thing in her
life. Without him it meant nothing. Alex might not love her, but
he liked her enough to want her, to want to make their marriage
work. He could not be faulted. After one whole week of self-
condemnation and missing him so much it was driving her to
distraction, she told Pauline to pack her trunk and arrange for
the carriage to take her to London.

Chapter Twelve

The streets were congested when Angelina arrived in London. During an enforced halt her attention wandered to the carriage next to her own, an open barouche, its occupant an elderly lady. She was conversing with a gentleman on horseback whom Angelina recognised as Duncan Aylard—graceful and indolent and decked out in the very height of fashion. On seeing her, he nudged his horse closer to her carriage and, true to form, proceeded to charm and flatter her before turning to the lady in the carriage and introducing them.

Lady Broadhurst, a kindly widow, was in London to attend Lord and Lady Unsworth's party that evening and was to return to Kent tomorrow. Eager to chat, she said how pleased she was to meet Lady Anne Adams's granddaughter and how disappointed Lady Anne had been when she had been unable to attend the wedding, due to a recent accident.

Lady Broadhurst's words drifted off somewhere into the bright afternoon sunshine. Angelina could hear her, but her words made no sense. She felt her face drain of colour and her body felt ice cold in this dreamlike world that had come upon her so suddenly. Giving no sign of the blow Lady Broadhurst's words had dealt her, she cleared her throat painfully and continued to make polite conversation, gleaning as much as she could about her grandmother—the woman she had always believed was dead—before moving on.

Travelling to Brook Street Angelina could feel only anger. Everything her mother and Uncle Henry had told her about her grandparents being dead had been a lie, and what hurt more than anything else was that Alex had colluded with them. He knew—had known all along—and he hadn't told her. It was wicked and cruel, deceitful and underhanded. When the coach stopped outside the house and a footman opened the door, her rage was contained in a deadly calm.

Fully prepared for a confrontation, Angelina marched past Bramwell and made her way to Alex's study. Not bothering to knock, she walked straight in, halting in the doorway. Having removed his jacket, her husband was seated at his desk. As she looked up his body became rigid, but then very calmly and deliberately he pushed back his chair and stood up. His jaw was set with implacable determination, and he seemed to emanate the restrained, unyielding authority Angelina had come to know and dread. But she felt no fear as he moved towards where she stood, undeterred by the deadly menace she saw in his eyes.

'Angelina, what are you doing here?'

'If I had any hope that you might be pleased to see me, your question has told me you are not,' she said tightly.

'That is beside the point. How dare you disobey me?'

Angelina glared her defiance, refusing to lower her eyes beneath that terrible silver gaze. 'Disobey you? What are you talking about?'

'I specifically told you to remain at Arlington until I returned—and yet, not one week after my departure, here you are. Well? I am waiting. What is it that is so important you wish to speak to me about?'

Angelina's eyes locked on his. There was no warmth in her fine-textured skin and her eyes were like shards of frosted glass beneath the long sweep of her lashes as she spoke, enunciating each word. 'Why was I told that my grandmother was dead?'

Stunned as much from the icy tone of her voice as the words, it took Alex a moment to react. At last he said cautiously, 'Who told you?'

'That is not important. It is true, I take it?'

They faced one another, the truth standing between them like an open door.

'Yes, it's true.' Alex said in a calm, flat voice, leaning his hips on the edge of his desk and folding his arms across his chest, closely watching the irate young woman in front of him.

'I knew it,' she hissed, her anger beginning to mount. 'Of all the treacherous, deceitful—'

'Angelina,' he interrupted with irritating calm. 'Please remember that I was not the one who told you your grandmother was dead.'

'Nevertheless, you were a party to it,' she argued, standing her ground, determined to have the satisfaction of hearing his explanation, disappointment and betrayal spinning inside her. 'I trusted you. I expected better from you than that.'

'If you must know, I was against it. I have always been of the opinion that you should be told the truth, but I promised Uncle Henry that I would abide by his wishes.'

'Why?' she demanded, her voice shaking with angry emotion. 'Why did you keep it from me? What is so terrible about my grandmother being alive that Uncle Henry has made you pledge not to reveal to me?'

'You must ask Uncle Henry.'

'I am asking you,' she fumed. 'You knew, Alex—and yet you let me go on believing my grandmother was dead, that I had no family of my own. How could you? How could you of all people deceive me like this? It was unspeakably cruel.'

Alex relinquished his perch and moved towards her. Despite her haughty stance and the fact that her eyes were hurling knives at him, he sensed that she was deeply hurt by what she had learned about her grandmother, and rightly so.

'I can neither defend nor condemn Uncle Henry's actions for keeping it from you. I agree that you should have been told, but then again, Uncle Henry had no choice but to respect your mother's wishes.'

'Why did my mother tell me my grandmother was dead?' she persisted. 'Why did she want to keep it from me? What happened to make her reject her own mother? And why did she make Uncle Henry my guardian instead of my grandmother?'

'You ask questions that I am not at liberty to answer.'

Angelina moved to stand close to him, looking deep into his eyes as she steeled herself to ask the question that had lain dormant since Uncle Henry had made her his ward, knowing that if she disturbed it there was every possibility that it would crucify her.

'Will you tell me something, Alex?'

'That depends on what it is.'

'Was Uncle Henry the reason why my mother married my father and went with him to America? Was that the reason for the rift between her and my grandparents?'

Alex's heart wrenched at the way she was looking at him, recognising her attempt to control her fear on being told the truth. 'I can neither confirm nor deny what you ask. That is something you must take up with Uncle Henry. What I will say is that his guilt has been torturing him. He's been tempted to tell you about your grandmother many times—especially before the wedding, when he knew how much you wanted kin of your own to see you married. But he promised your mother he wouldn't. He begged her to make amends and write to your grandmother, but she told him it was too late. It came as a cruel blow to your mother when your grandfather wrote and told her he was severing all ties between them, that he had no daughter. After that as far as she was concerned she had no mother, you no grandmother, and that was the way she wanted it to remain.'

'Well, I am not my mother and I think that it's up to me to decide whether or not I want to see my grandmother.'

Alex frowned when he saw a thoughtful, determined gleam implant itself in his wife's eyes. He had long since learned to be wary of such a look. 'Angelina, you are not thinking of going to see her?' His voice held a quiet warning.

Angelina regarded her husband with disturbing calmness. 'Yes. I have every right to see her if I want to.'

'You are not going anywhere while you are thinking irrationally.'

'Don't try and stop me, Alex. Perhaps she will be more forthcoming about what really happened all those years ago,' she flung at him bitterly.

'To have a granddaughter turn up on her doorstep…a granddaughter whose existence she would have known nothing about until you were made the Duke of Mowbray's ward and she saw your name splashed all over the newspapers—in all probability the shock may cause the poor woman to suffer a seizure.'

'If she knows who I am, then why hasn't she tried to contact me?'

To Alex at that moment, Angelina looked so unbearably beautiful, young and vulnerable, facing him so courageously in this outrageous defiance, that if the situation weren't so serious, he would have smiled. 'Hasn't it entered that stubborn head of yours that she might not want to? Just as your mother chose to keep it from you that your grandmother was alive, she too may have her reasons for remaining silent. Perhaps you should respect that.'

'But I can't,' Angelina cried, trying to control the wrenching anguish in her chest when she recalled Lady Broadhurst's words—that it would have given Lady Anne such joy to see her granddaughter wed. To Angelina, this implied that her grandmother would be happy to see her granddaughter. Her face became intensely passionate in her determination. 'I'm going to see her at once.'

Alex was adamant. 'Don't be ridiculous. You are not going to Kent until you have spoken to Uncle Henry. Perhaps when he's explained everything, you will understand.'

'My grandmother will explain it all to me.'

'Angelina, you are going nowhere.' His voice was implacable and as cold as steel.

She stared at him with growing anger. 'Yes, I am.'

'No, you are not. Remember that no one but myself has the

ordering of my coaches. This is my house and my servants and you are my wife. I do not choose to risk the life and limb of man or beast in some harebrained scheme of yours to go tearing off to Kent at this hour of the day. So, in case you have some crazy idea of doing just that, I shall instruct the driver to block any such move.'

Her eyes dashed fiery venom over him. 'You wouldn't.'

'Try me.'

'Are you forbidding me to go?'

'Most definitely—until you have spoken to Uncle Henry.'

'But it could be weeks before I see him.'

'Why the hurry?'

'My grandmother is ill and I wish to see her,' she answered, turning towards the door.

'Then I will write to Uncle Henry and ask him to return to London. Or, if you prefer and to save time, we could journey to Mowbray Park together.'

'That will take too long. I shall walk to Kent if I have to,' she flared furiously, turning back to him.

Her wilful defiance ignited a blaze of fury on her husband's hard features. 'Angelina! You are going nowhere. Now, let that be enough.' Turning from her, he went back to his desk, his manner telling her the matter was closed. 'I have been invited to an important party at Lord and Lady Unsworth's house on the Strand tonight. Now you are here, you might as well accompany me. Who knows—you might even enjoy yourself. We mustn't stay too late. I have an important appointment at nine o'clock in the morning.'

'Blast you, Alex Montgomery. Go by yourself. I am in no mood for partying.'

'Angelina!'

About to open the door, she spun round, her anger in no way diminished. 'What?'

'Just one thing piques my curiosity. How did you find out about your grandmother? How do you know she is ill?'

'Lady Broadhurst told me. She is my grandmother's neighbour.'

He looked at her with narrowed, questioning eyes. 'I didn't know you were acquainted with Lady Broadhurst. When did you meet?'

'When I was on my way here. There was a snarl up in the traffic and Lord Aylard—' She stopped...too late. A cold, sinking fear gripped her and she groaned inwardly, wishing she could cut out her tongue for mentioning Lord Aylard's name, for it never failed to ignite Alex's wrath. Alex advanced on her with the predatory grace of a stalking Indian. His threatening manner almost made Angelina back away, but with the door behind her she was forced to remain where she was. He loomed over her, his eyes gleaming oddly. 'So, you have been speaking to Aylard.' His voice was ominously quiet.

'I happened to see him when the coach was stopped. He was speaking to Lady Broadhurst and he introduced us.'

'I see.' One black eyebrow went up as he bent a long, cool look at her.

Angelina watched her husband turn away as the demon jealousy that took hold of him whenever Lord Aylard's name was mentioned in connection with his wife began to relax its grip.

'Go to your room. Since you have no wish to accompany me tonight, I will see you in the morning.'

Not until he was alone did Alex frown and cast a puzzled glance at the closed door. He recalled the intense feeling of joy that had shot through him when he had raised his eyes and seen Angelina, hoping her reason for following him to London was because she had been missing him, only to have his hopes dashed when she had challenged him about her grandmother. But then, he mused, lounging back in his chair, when she had left Arlington she had not known about her grandmother—and so, what had brought her to London?

Angelina realised that the answer to her dilemma was staring her in the face. Unsworth! She distinctly recalled Lady Broadhurst telling her that she was to attend their party and that she was to leave for Kent in the morning. Angelina was certain the good lady could be persuaded to let her accompany her. Alex had an engagement at nine o'clock so he wouldn't discover she was missing until she was halfway to Tonbridge.

Unfortunately, by the time she sent Pauline to inform her husband that she would go with him to the party, he had already left. He was to dine at his club with friends and go on to the party later. Angelina had no alternative but to order one of the carriages to take her. At first the driver was reluctant to comply, having been ordered by his lordship not to take his wife out of London under any circumstances, but when told she was going to join her husband, he agreed.

It was late when Angelina arrived at the house along the Strand to attend the party—a truly magnificent affair, with only the cream of London society invited. The large ballroom was filled to capacity, a festive air prevailing. Standing alone at the top of the steps leading down to the ballroom, she looked about her, seeing several familiar faces, but not that of Lady Broadhurst. Lady Unsworth came to welcome her.

'Good evening, Lady Montgomery. How nice of you to honour us with your company. I'm so delighted you were able to attend our party after all.'

'My husband has arrived?'

'Just a few minutes ago.'

From where he stood conversing with a group of friends, like everyone else Alex was aware of a distraction. Absently his eyes did a quick sweep of the ballroom. He saw Lady Unsworth descending the stairs with one of her female guests, but paid scant attention, then something in the way the woman moved and the rich vibrancy of her hair brought his eyes snapping back.

'I say, Alex,' said Lord Asquith beside him. 'Isn't that your wife?'

Alex stared at Angelina, whose whole presence seemed to blaze across the ballroom at him, eliminating all else. His whole manner was calm and composed, while inside he was seething. How dare she embarrass him like this by arriving late and unescorted? But as he kept her within his sights he could not deny that, clad in the deepest pink chiffon gown with a scooped neckline, lower than any he had seen her wear before, her neck and shoulders and the soft swell of her breasts aglow, she looked sensational.

Angelina watched the tall, daunting, devastatingly handsome man, attired in an exquisitely tailored claret jacket and pristine white cravat, cut a pathway through the throng with a feeling of impending disaster.

Lady Unsworth was full of smiles as she received him with lighthearted repartee, but Alex, impatient to have Angelina to himself and take her to task, bowed his head respectfully as he excused himself.

Beneath his icy calm, such was the force of his fury that Angelina flinched. His long fingers closed on her elbow like a vice as he walked with her towards the dance floor, where the orchestra was striking up the next waltz.

'You needn't hold my arm so tightly, Alex. I'm not going to run away.'

'Shut up,' he seethed, increasing the pressure on her elbow.

When he took her in his arms his face was so close to hers that she could see the ice-cold satanic glitter in his eyes. He didn't speak, and to Angelina his silence was both unbearable and insulting.

'Why did you drag me out here if you can find nothing to say to me?' she said at length.

'I can find plenty to say. It's knowing where to begin.'

Angelina smiled, a trace of irony on her lips. 'Why, Alex, I never thought to see you lost for words.'

'Does your rebelliousness know no bounds?' he ground out, incensed, keeping his voice low so as not to be overheard by others. 'What the devil are you trying to do? See how far you can provoke me?'

'What? More than I have already, you mean?'

'Don't be flippant and smile, damn it,' he said through

gritted teeth when she glowered up at him. 'We are the object of every pair of eyes in this ballroom. Rumours are already being bandied about that there is a rift between us.'

Angelina's eyes opened wide with genuine astonishment, and she experienced a sharp pang of regret. 'Alex, is this true? But that's ridiculous.'

'Is it?'

'Well—maybe you have yourself to blame for that,' she said quietly.

His eyes impaled hers. 'What the devil are you talking about?'

'Perhaps you shouldn't have returned to London alone so soon after our marriage. That alone must have fuelled the rumours.'

'Your own actions tonight won't have helped matters. Was it your intention to make me a laughing stock—to embarrass and publicly humiliate me by coming to the party alone?'

'No, Alex. I wouldn't do that. And anyway, I didn't think you cared a hoot for what people think of you.'

'I don't,' he said, aware of the lingering and lascivious looks from raffish young bloods that Angelina was inviting by sporting an outrageous décolletage. His eyes were like shards of ice as they insolently dropped to the daring display of her creamy expanse of bosom—giving no indication how his hands ached to touch and feel that soft skin next to his own, a desire so great that it was driving him insane. 'What I do mind is my wife making a public exhibition of herself by choosing to wear a gown that I consider indecent in its exposure. It gives me no satisfaction to see other men coveting you.'

The insult brought Angelina's head snapping back and her eyes flying to his in anger. 'On the contrary, Alex. I think I am very *à la mode*. And if the glances I am receiving from some of the other gentlemen are an indication of how I look, then I would say that you are alone in your opinion. I expose no more than any other woman here tonight and you know it,' she flared, surprised how quickly she had overcome her own unease when she had donned the gown. 'Just because I haven't chosen to wear a gown so revealing before now is entirely my own affair.'

The modest cut of her gowns had not gone unnoticed by Alex, and, sensing her reluctance to expose herself—as other women delighted in doing—had something to do with her past, he had tactfully not mentioned it. 'Then why did you choose to do so tonight?'

'For no other reason than that I thought the gown would look nice on me.' His blunt criticism of her beautiful gown caught her between hurt and the urge to kick him in the shin.

When Alex saw the disappointment in her eyes, her pursed lips and angry frown, some of his imperious expression began to waver. 'What made you decide to come to the party?'

'I simply wanted to sample a little enjoyment myself, that is all. Unfortunately, by the time I decided, you'd already left for your club. I did not think you would mind if I came alone— and I foolishly believed you would be pleased to see me,' she said quietly, pulling back an inch, her eyes unwavering as she met his gaze. 'I also thought you would like my dress.'

'I would like it a lot more if there was more of it,' he said drily.

'If you insist on being disagreeable for the entire evening, Alex, when the dance has finished I suggest you return to your friends and let me reacquaint myself with some of the ladies I recognised when I came in.'

His arm tightened around her, drawing her closer to his chest. 'Not a chance,' he said, his lips close to her ear. 'Until it is time for us to leave you will remain cleaved to my side.' His mood softened. It felt good to hold her again, to have her close, to smell the elusive scent of her flesh. A slow, lazy smile spread across his features as he gazed down at her alluring face, and when he spoke his voice was low and seductive.

'I am pleased that you decided to come, Angel, and, despite the fact that it displays your charms with a wantonness I and every other man present find hard to resist, I do like your gown.'

Her eyes widened until they were huge amethyst orbs. 'You do?' He nodded slowly. 'I've never worn anything quite like it, and I confess to feeling a trifle awkward and over-exposed.'

Alex was determined to continue the seduction. He dropped his eyes, bold and admiring, taking another look at those tantalising orbs swelling out of the bodice of her gown and feeling his blood run hot. 'Think yourself lucky that you are in the middle of a dance floor with an audience, my love. It is the only thing that keeps you safe from me—but not for long.' He grinned, aware of her unease. 'So, am I to understand that you are no longer angry with me for deceiving you about your grandmother?'

Her face became grave. 'Yes. I apologise for what I said to you earlier. It was wrong of me to take it out on you. I know none of it is your fault, and that you were bound by your word to Uncle Henry.'

'Angelina…when are you going to tell me why you came to London?'

She looked up at him. His eyes were intense. 'You mean I haven't?'

He shook his head, holding her gaze, waiting for her to tell him.

In panic her eyes darted away from his. 'I didn't like it at Arlington on my own,' she confessed. 'I was upset when you left so abruptly. You were so angry. I wanted to settle the argument between us.'

'You did?'

'Yes.'

'How?'

'By saying I'm sorry.'

'You are?' Alex looked down at her dubiously, noticing the soft light in her eyes.

Angelina nodded. 'Yes.'

'What a chaste little thing you are,' he murmured.

Her flush was one of pure innocence. 'I—I know I must appear that way to you and I—I told you I was—'

'A virgin, I know. But it's curable. It is my dearest wish to have done with it. I want to show you how to love in the tenderest way I can. Whatever happened to you in the past, I will make you forget—and I know you will be an avid pupil.'

* * *

True to his word, Alex did not leave his wife's side for a moment, but all the while Angelina's eyes searched the throng for Lady Broadhurst. Her inattention did not go unnoticed by her husband. His brows drew together with displeasure.

'Your attention seems to be wandering, my love. If you are looking for Aylard, he has just arrived—and by the look of him he's disgustingly foxed and making a damn fool of himself.'

'As a matter of fact I wasn't looking for Lord Aylard. I have seen him and he does look rather worse for wear,' she remarked, observing the man in question amidst a circle of his friends, each and every one of them flushed and whooping with unrestrained merriment. She was unable to resist a little smile when she saw Lord Aylard sway slightly as he leaned forward to plant a huge kiss on Lady Unsworth's cheek.

'Then who is it your eyes are searching for?'

'If you must know, I am looking for Lady Broadhurst. She happened to mention that she would be here tonight.'

Alex threw her a look of annoyance. 'This must stop, Angelina,' he said harshly. 'Nothing can be achieved by it. There must be no more questions about your grandmother until you see Uncle Henry. Is that understood?'

Though Angelina's chin was tilted a notch too high for comfort, to Alex's relief she remained silent, but as he turned away to speak to a gentleman on a political matter, so engrossed did he become in the issue that he was unaware of the moment his wife left his side when she saw Lady Broadhurst at the bottom of the stairs saying goodbye to their hosts.

Lady Broadhurst told Angelina that she would be delighted to share her coach with her. It would make the journey to Kent more pleasurable having someone to talk to.

Her mission accomplished, Angelina uttered a sigh of relief—which was not without trepidation. Alex would be absolutely furious when he found her gone, but she refused to think about that just now lest it weakened her resolve.

Suddenly a satin-garbed gentleman appeared by her side

and seized her attention, astounded at his good fortune to find the adorable Angelina Montgomery at the party—without her husband lurking behind her like some damned guard on sentry duty.

Positively glowing with robust health and champagne, his face almost as red as a cock's comb, he made a sweeping bow, swaying in the process and almost falling over. 'My dear Countess! You are simply ravishing,' he complimented enthusiastically, making small effort to subdue the admiration that shone in his mischievous blue eyes.

Unable to resist Lord Aylard's ebullient mood, Angelina laughed. 'Why, Lord Aylard! You have arrived at last, I see. And here was I thinking you were avoiding me.'

'Not you, sweet Angelina. Never that. 'Tis your glowering, pompous husband I avoid. Where is he, by the way?' He looked over her shoulder, as if expecting to find him lurking behind her back.

'He's talking to an acquaintance.'

'Remiss of him to let you out of his sight.'

'Alex doesn't watch over me every minute of the day.'

'Seems like that to me. Whenever he and I meet, I swear he would like nothing better than to slay me on the spot.'

Angelina was suddenly surrounded by a boisterous pack of Lord Aylard's friends. A footman passing by with a tray of brimming champagne glasses was accosted and divested of his load amidst a rousing burst of laughter.

'Come, Countess.' Lord Aylard grinned as he attempted to extricate a glass of champagne from one of his friends. 'I'm having a high old time. You must have a glass of champagne with me to celebrate my good fortune at the tables this evening.'

'No, thank you. And I think you are awash with it already,' Angelina commented, looking for a way through the throng of surrounding males, confident she could manage to fend them off without making a scene. 'You must excuse me.'

Lord Aylard was persistent. In no hurry to let her go he took her arm and looked deep into her eyes, having to blink to try and keep his own in focus. His face was lethargic and sleepy looking now he had stopped grinning for the moment. 'I think you are wonderful. Do you know that every man in this room is madly in love with you?'

Gerald Buckley, one of his more sober friends, seeing Angelina throw him a look of helpless appeal, came to her aid. 'Steady on, old man. You'll end up making an ass of yourself. As you can see, Countess, my friend isn't himself right now. Since his luck at the tables tonight he's imbibed too much.'

Angelina gave him a smile of tolerant understanding as Lord Aylard waved him away dismissively.

'Go away, Gerald,' he snorted. 'The Countess and I are going to dance. You do want to dance with me, don't you Countess?'

'No—really…' Angelina laughed, resisting his arms, which seemed to be all over the place. 'If I dance with you in your present state, I fear we are both in danger of ending up in a heap on the floor—and then where will my dignity be? You have drunk far too many glasses of champagne.'

'That's because I am celebrating my colossal win at tables.'

'I know. Why, your face is almost the same colour as your waistcoat.'

Lord Aylard looked down at his flamboyant scarlet-and-gold waistcoat with pride, puffing out his chest. 'It is rather splendid, isn't it?'

'It—certainly catches the eye.'

He grinned. 'Gerald here doesn't like it,' he said, turning his back on his friend, who was hovering close in case Angelina should have need of his protection. 'Says it's much too brash—but I think it's rather elegant.'

'You certainly have distinctive taste. Now, please excuse me. I simply must return to my husband.'

'I have a plan,' Lord Aylard said, catching her arm and half-lowering his eyelid in a conspiratorial wink. 'Why don't you ditch that devilishly handsome husband of yours and run off with me?'

'I wouldn't dare. I value my life too much.'

'You are absolutely divine. Have I told you?'

'You do have a habit of repeating yourself.' Had it been anyone else behaving so outrageously, Angelina's sensitivity would have been offended, but she liked Lord Aylard too much to be cross with him.

He swayed, and it was no straight line he walked before he plonked himself down into a chair. Angelina gave a couple of quick little steps to avoid his hand as it reached out for her, but catching her heel in the train of her skirt, she tripped and lost her balance, unable to prevent herself from falling in an undignified heap in Lord Aylard's lap.

'Good Lord!' he exclaimed, his arm snaking round Angelina's waist. 'You are incredible, Countess. You really should run away with me, you know.'

'I think not,' Alex said.

Everyone, not least Angelina, was suddenly aware of a tall male presence. Alex had moved across the room with such speed and the silence of a panther that no one had seen him come. At a stroke amusement fled from the florid faces. Angelina froze. Her eyes were wide open, her expression incredulous. Their eyes met, Alex's glacial, his mouth drawn into a ruthless, forbidding line.

He glared down at Aylard. 'You, sir, forget yourself.' His voice was like steel. Tempted to commit murder, he restrained himself, but it was an effort.

Lord Aylard's friends stood back with the wary disbelief of the innocent and uninvolved. Quickly Angelina sprang up from Lord Aylard's lap, but he remained sprawled out in the chair, his senses and his body too anaesthetised by champagne to be concerned by the threatening menace emanating from the formidable Earl of Arlington. Making no attempt to rise, he grinned inanely up at Alex—seeing double.

'Hello, Montgomery. Would you care to join us for a glass of champagne—or is it to be pistols at dawn?'

Alex subjected him to a look of severe distaste and chilling contempt. 'You're drunk, Aylard, and not worth the shot.' His eyes sliced to his wife. 'If you are ready, Angelina, we will say goodnight to our hosts.'

With a mask of feral rage, on reaching the house Alex marched Angelina into her bedchamber. His eyes sliced to Pauline. 'You may go to bed. Your mistress will not be needing you tonight.'

After Pauline had wordlessly made a hasty retreat, Angelina waited for the onslaught of her husband's fury. She deeply regretted the unfortunate incident that had occurred. Alex was a proud man and she had foolishly made him an object of public ridicule. It would be no simple matter placating him.

Drawing a quick breath, she tried to swallow her mounting alarm by saying, 'Really, Alex. If you are going to be difficult, might I suggest you go to bed.'

His look cut through her. The anger and rage were gone from him. What there was instead was ice. 'I intend to. With you. But I have a matter to settle with you first, lady.'

'I thought you might.'

'Damn it,' he snapped, raking his fingers through his hair and pacing the room with angry, frustrated strides. 'Are you so simple that you didn't know what you were doing? Have you forgotten so soon that you are a lady and my wife? The incident with Aylard would not have happened if you had done as you were told and stayed with me.'

'And how could I know that?' she flared. 'I am not some trained pet to do as it's told. You were engaged in conversation with someone else—and I saw someone I wished to speak to, so I left.'

'And when I next saw you you were cavorting with Aylard on his knee. How dare you play and flirt with that man so shamelessly?' he accused, his anger making him unreasonable, for he had seen her trying to distance herself from Aylard before she had tripped and overbalanced into his lap. 'I will not stand by and watch you parade and flaunt yourself brazenly before Aylard and his friends as though it pleases you to make me a laughing stock.'

Angelina gasped. 'Alex! That's not fair. I think you forget yourself.'

'Oh, no, lady. It's you who forget yourself. It's you who plays the strumpet with Aylard.'

Stung by his insult Angelina clenched her fists by her sides and her cheeks flamed. 'I object to that. How dare you say that to me? I tripped and accidentally fell on to his knee. And I am not a strumpet.'

'Then why were you behaving like one?'

'Oh, you mule-headed oaf. I was not. You make too much of it. Lord Aylard was—'

'Drunk out of his skull,' Alex shouted, throwing his arms in the air in exasperation.

'And are you always so very civilised and proper?' she mocked.

'My own behaviour is not the issue.'

'Had it been anyone else's lap I'd fallen into, you wouldn't have turned a hair. The mere presence of Lord Aylard at the party was cause enough to tweak your nose. When will it penetrate that thick skull of yours that you have nothing to be jealous of? He accosted me when I had been speaking to an acquaintance.'

Alex stopped pacing the carpet, his eyes snapping to hers. 'What acquaintance?'

Realising her mistake too late, Angelina remained silent. Her husband's brows knit together.

'What's this?' he seethed savagely, moving closer, his eyes, refusing to relinquish their hold on hers, a terrifying gleam visible and deadly in their depths. 'More secrets? Don't dig the hole deeper for yourself, Angelina. What is needed in this marriage is less secrets—not more.'

'What do you mean by that?'

'You went to speak to Lady Broadhurst, didn't you?'

Angelina raised her chin, trying to look scornful and proud, despite the trembling in her limbs. 'Yes, I did.'

'Dear Lord. My patience as a husband is fast running out.'

'Then perhaps you shouldn't have married me in the first place. Perhaps I chose the wrong husband,' she flared daringly.

Alex's eyes narrowed and he moved closer still, so close that Angelina could feel his hot breath fanning her face. 'If you had chosen anyone else, lady, one thing you can be sure of is that he would not have been as considerate as I have been. He would not have spent his wedding night alone and the subsequent four weeks. Now, get your clothes off and get into bed,' he ordered coldly, his eyes looking directly into hers, leaving her in no doubt as to his meaning and intention. 'This is one night I will not sleep alone.'

'Whose bed, my lord?' Angelina asked, as he was about to go to his own rooms to undress. With her elbows akimbo and her fingers drumming on her hips, her manner mocked him. It bore the submissive tones one might expect of a chattel. 'Shall I get into my own bed to await your pleasure, or yours?'

Alex ignored her overstated humility. An almost lecherous smile tempted his lips as his eyes swept her bed. 'Which bed do you prefer?'

'Neither.'

'Angelina,' he said softly. The warning in his narrowed eyes and in his voice was unmistakable.

For a moment she shrank from him, her tender eyes darkening in fear. But then her soft lips tightened and her chin came up proudly. 'Very well, then. Considering I've never seen your bed—let it be my own.'

'The fact that you have never seen my bed is not my fault. Now get undressed. I'll be back in a minute,' he said, striding to the connecting door and opening it, his long fingers forcefully unfastening his cravat as he went.

'And what if I have no desire to sleep with you, Alex?' Angelina persisted, knowing she was provoking his anger to dangerous heights, but she would do anything to stave off the moment when she would have no choice but to get into that huge bed with her husband in his present mood. 'I would remind you of the promise you made.'

Without warning he exploded. Slamming the door, he bore down on her relentlessly. Grabbing her by the shoulders, he gripped her with a violence that ripped the breath from her lungs as his fingers bruised her flesh.

'Until you tell me what happened to you in Ohio, you will not mention that time to me again. If you do—so help me God I swear you will regret it,' he said, speaking through clenched teeth. His fingers did not relinquish their brutal grip as he thrust his enraged face close to hers. His eyes were narrowed, the silver orbs burning ruthlessly down into her own, his anger surmounted by growing passion. 'I am heartily sick of it. I will not stand aside and watch you sacrifice our whole future because you cannot bring yourself to speak of it or forget. I refuse to let you go on moping, of seeing it haunt you. I'm damned if I will allow this situation to continue.'

He thrust her from him roughly. 'Take off those bloody clothes and prepare yourself—and let there be no tears, no virginal platitudes, no outraged modesty or cries of shame. Love me or hate me, Angelina, I will have my own way—especially in my bedroom. Whether you consider it a duty or a pleasure—one way or another it will be done. If you do not remove your clothes, I shall personally remove them myself.'

Her chest heaving, her cheeks aflame, Angelina glared at him. 'You wouldn't dare.'

His dark brows rose. 'Try me. You have precisely the time it takes me to remove my own to find out.'

Chapter Thirteen

When Alex strode back into the room two minutes later in a maroon velvet robe and saw her still fully clothed, her eyes blazing defiantly, his own were a fierce white hot heat. Slowly he moved towards her.

'Perhaps I did not make myself clear before.'

'You made yourself perfectly clear, my lord.'

'Well?'

'It is simply that since you took it upon yourself to dismiss my maid, I cannot reach to unfasten the buttons down the back of my dress.'

'Then allow me.'

Angelina turned her back, standing perfectly still while his fingers quickly released the row of innumerable tiny buttons from their loops.

'I can tell you have done this before,' she commented drily.

'Correct.' Task complete, he stood back.

Turning to face him, Angelina kept her eyes fixed on his, taking strength from her anger. Slipping her gown off her shoulders, she pushed it down over her petticoat and stepped out of it, kicking it to one side and making no attempt to go any further.

Hands on hips, Alex quirked a questioning brow. 'Do you

prefer to remove the rest yourself, or would you like me to oblige.'

Angelina struck a mountain of stubbornness as great as his, and with one glorious movement she drew her petticoat over her head and flung it on to the floor. Although no word passed her lips, the look in her eyes as she silently met his gaze was one of pure mutiny.

'I will die before I let you touch me,' she hissed.

A crooked smile accompanied his reply. 'Then die, lady, because I am not leaving. Pray continue.'

'Go to hell,' she breathed, the flush of anger deepening over the delicate softness of her cheeks, knowing that without her clothes she would have no protection against those probing eyes.

Her gaze was scornful, as challenging as his own. But Alex was determined. When he moved closer Angelina did not flinch as his fingers gently shoved the thin straps off her shoulders and down her arms, slowly peeling the bodice down and exposing her pert, soft young breasts.

With outraged modesty she had an urge to cover herself with her arms, but with a superhuman effort she managed to conquer her fear and refrain from doing so. As she held his gaze her anger overrode the shock of finding herself almost naked. She allowed his hands to do what she had vowed she would never let happen to her again—to touch her bare flesh, to cup the gentle swell of her breast—and Alex, suspecting what was going through her mind, thanked God for her spirit, for it had given her what she needed to exorcise her fear of what inevitably must happen between them.

Compassion flashed across his features as he caught a fleeting glimpse of the naked pain in the translucent depths of her eyes, and at the sight the demon anger relaxed its grip on him at last. But then his jaw tightened. For some obscure reason he wanted her to maintain her anger, for it would help sustain her over the coming moments until her desire was aroused, and to do that he must remain firm.

It was a difficult moment for Angelina. She wanted to keep an air of cold disdain, to face her husband in calm defiance, but her mauled pride and aching memory of the past assailed her senses. Momentarily a rush of tears blinded her, and she was furious with herself that she should display such weakness. When she saw his gaze resting on her with something akin to pity, it was too much for her to bear. It came to her mind that the time had come to consummate their marriage, and desperately she sought to delay that moment.

'Alex, let me go.'

'Not a chance.'

An iron-thewed arm snaked around her waist and his mouth swooped down on to hers. Like a tigress Angelina struggled violently against him, but she was no match against the power of his arms, imbued with even greater strength by the charged passion overwhelming him. When his lips left hers she breathed deeply, feeling the rising pleasure, the kindling of desire that threatened to smother her reason. Suddenly it was all too much. She shook her head, drawing back in his arms.

'Don't. Please don't,' she begged. 'Please don't make me.'

'Why not?' Alex murmured, dragging his lips down the slender curve of her neck. 'Are you as cold as you would have me think?'

She tried to shove away from him, but his arms tightened around her. 'Oh, no, my angel, my little tease. You have flouted my authority and tormented my senses for long enough. Now I have you—now your reckoning is upon you.'

Angelina arched her back as he held her, pressing her body close to his, his lips caressing and burning her bare skin like fire as he lowered his head to her breasts. To Angelina he seemed larger, more powerful than she had ever seen him, and, strain as she did, she couldn't break free.

Suddenly some protective barriers snapped inside Alex and he scooped her up into his arms.

Angelina's breath came in heated spasms. 'Please don't. Oh, please. I loathe you—I hate you.'

Her words came on a breath and without conviction. Alex's

grin was almost fiendish. 'I know, my pet, and you can hate and loathe me to your heart's content—in bed.'

Suddenly she felt the downy softness of the bed beneath her back. In desperation she resumed her struggle, but somehow Alex managed to tear away what remained of her garments and strip off his robe.

She gasped, her eyes widening at the sight of her husband towering over her, his body eternally masculine and primeval in its naked power. Her shocked reaction to his nakedness brought a smile to his lips and a low chuckled sounded in the back of his throat.

'So, my love, I have your full attention now.'

In an attempt to cover her own nakedness she reached for the covers, but he tore them from her grasp and snatched her to him, his eyes capturing hers, challenging.

'No, Angel,' he said, his eyes telling her there would be no denial as there had been in the past. He would not be turned away with this craving hunger eating away at the pit of his belly. 'There will be no more barriers between us. I will look at my wife, as is my right. Now and always.'

The softness in his tone and the tender, compelling light in his eyes reassured and calmed her. Fighting him was futile. Besides, physical resistance would be useless against his un-swerving seduction. She waited for the screaming denial to come from that dark corner of her mind she had kept locked for so long, determined to ban its intrusion. But there was nothing, only a strange, empty silence. She lowered her hands that had risen to push Alex away, one of them covering part of the flesh from her naval to her groin whilst the other reached up and brushed her fingertips against his warm, sensual lips with a tenderness that astounded him, her eyes silently telling him that she had no thought of holding back or refusing him.

'Then look, Alex,' she said softly, 'and tell me what you see.'

His lean, handsome features were starkly etched above her.

As she watched his eyes course down the supple curves of her body, over the proud swell of her breasts and narrow waist, to the beckoning curves and soft, secret hollows and shadows of her hips, she tried not to remember the agony of the last time her body had been laid bare for other eyes to look at, when, in shame and humiliation, she had wanted to die. But this time it was Alex looking at her, not a stranger but her husband, and she loved him with all her heart and soul.

Angelina's voluptuous bloom of womanhood evoked in Alex a strong stirring of desire. He could not believe how much he wanted her, that the body his own had so fiercely craved for so long lay alongside him. His hand reached out and gently traced the outline of her hip, his fingers moving over her slender waist and on to her breast, cupping its fullness.

'Have you any idea how lovely you are, Angel—how adorable, or how much I want you?' he murmured huskily. Her hair had come loose from its pins in the struggle and lay in luxuriant, tangled disarray around her head like a vibrant halo. Alex's eyes were hungry and dark with passion, and, unable to resist her a moment longer, he leaned over, covering her mouth with his own, snatching her breath away, teasing her lips when they opened to his. Her lips were warm, eager and sweet as sweet could be.

Slowly his hand slipped about her waist as he drew her body against his so that they were touching full length, while he kissed her in a passionate frenzy, amazed and intrigued by the mixture of innocence, boldness and fear which fired this woman. At first he had intended to take her swiftly, but now he had no such haste in mind. One thing he was sure of—he would not stop until he had achieved what he intended and sealed their vows securely in a physical knot of passion. Nothing short of an earthquake would prevent him making love to her now he'd started. He would make her body sing with rapture before he was done.

Angelina could not believe the pain of ecstasy increasing within her. Where his hand had gone before, so his lips followed. He would have gone further still, but a straight silver scar running from just below her waist to her groin caught his eye. Her arm had concealed it earlier, which was the reason why he had not seen it.

Momentarily he paused. His whole being silently screamed when he saw the evidence of what he knew those savages had done to her, the pain they must have put her through. Please God, let that be all they had done to her, that, despite telling him her virtue was still intact, she had not been violated. He clenched his eyes until the screaming had stopped, feeling her hands as they sought him, wondering why his caresses had stopped—and then she knew. He brought his face on a level with her own, his expression hard, his eyes filled with an intensity and something else that she could not define.

'Alex—please don't look like that.'

'Did those savages do that to you?'

She nodded, her eyes bright with unshed tears, her face tormented.

Alex scooped her into his arms, cradling her head in the hollow of his shoulder, burying his face in her tumbling, sweet scented hair and feeling a deep surge of compassion and grieving. 'God above, how you must have suffered—how they must have hurt you. Little wonder you hated being touched.'

Angelina raised her head and looked at him. 'Don't. Please don't make me remember—not now. You told me you could make me forget, Alex. Please try. Kiss me,' she murmured, her lips close to his own.

Alex needed no prompting as he captured her mouth in an all-consuming kiss, rousing her sensations and persuading her heart to beat in a frantic rhythm. His hands stroked downwards over the curve of her hips and then upwards along the velvet softness inside her thighs. She gasped, reflexively tensing her muscles and clamping her legs together. Alex felt her resistance and groaned.

'Angelina, please, my love,' he said huskily, his face taut with restraint. 'Trust me. Relax, my darling.'

Above her Angelina could see his face was hard, his eyes dark with passion, and yet there was so much tenderness in their depths that her heart ached. But it was the desperate need she heard in his voice that made her respond.

His blood spilling through his veins like molten lava, Alex rose above her and lowered his hips between her thighs, seeing fear and sudden panic in her wide eyes when she felt the probing, burning heat of his maleness intruding into her delicate softness.

'I'm sorry, Angel,' he whispered, his hands moving behind her and raising her hips. 'I'm going to hurt you.'

With a faint sob Angelina wrapped her arms around his neck, pressing her face against the base of his throat when she felt the unrelenting pressure against her tight, resisting flesh, feeling his rigid hardness inch its way into her soft warmth. Her body jerked and she gasped when he breached the barrier and buried himself deep inside her, a burning pain exploding in her loins. She clung to him, digging her nails into his back, but he seemed not to notice.

Waiting for the pain of his intrusion to subside, Alex found her lips and kissed her with a long, leisurely thoroughness that soon turned her pain into a hungering, throbbing ache. He filled her fully, touching all of her. It was incredible, and as she slowly began to move as he moved, beauty and something wonderful began to happen to her body.

Fury of a moment ago had become raw hunger, her fears burnt beneath the scorching heat of their mutual desires as they were merged into one being, husband and wife, wrapped in the absolute bliss of their union. The awakened fires, the bittersweet ache of desire so long restrained, overwhelmed them both. They were two beings fused together in a spinning eddy of passion. And then ecstasy as they came closer still, and Angelina felt his seed erupt, spilling into her, their lives merging. She gasped and cried out, unable to stop the words that sprung naturally to her lips as she was torn into a thousand shimmering pieces.

'I love you.' Whether Alex heard or not she had no way of knowing.

Holding her close with his lips against hers, he waited until the flame that had ignited them both subsided and they relaxed. Sated, a fine film of perspiration glistening on his body, his hair damp, his breathing deep, he moved his weight from her and pulled her into his arms as he came down from the unparalleled heights of passion she had just sent him to. In all his years of amorous liaisons, not once had he ever come close to the shattering ecstasy he'd just experienced. His wife was innocence and wantonness, passionate and sweet.

Angelina sighed and melted into her husband's embrace, unable to believe that she could feel such joyous elation quivering inside. She was overjoyed that she had been able to give Alex what he had desired and sought from her since making her his wife, and her only regret was that she had made him wait so long—that she had denied them both the pleasure they were able to give each other. If only she had known it could be like this. Now she did, Alex would find her an eager, willing wife.

'Are you still angry with me?' she whispered, her dark eyes awash with tears of happiness, lingering passion and innocence.

Alex reached out and gently smoothed her tumbled locks from her face, tracing his finger down the soft curve of her cheek. He gazed at her with something akin to awe and reverence, feeling humbled by her beauty and her unselfish ardour and uninhibited giving of herself.

'On the contrary, Angel. How do you feel?' he asked, his voice gentle, his gaze so tender that Angelina's heart contracted.

'Like your wife,' she murmured, placing her lips gently on his chest.

'Then why do you weep?'

'It's happiness that makes me weep,' she reassured him. 'Happiness and freedom—and the final shattering of a door I have kept locked and bolted in my mind for far too long. Oh, Alex,' she said, trailing her arm over his lean waist and sighing against him, reflecting on their love-making, 'thank you for being so understanding and patient with me. But now I know what I've been missing I wish you hadn't.'

'So do I, sweetheart. So do I,' he chuckled softly.

'You could have forced me.'

'I could. But I was not willing to gamble with so precious a prize. I had no wish for you to hate me for ever more. But you were well worth the wait.'

'And did you wait?' she whispered, feeling uncomfortable as she asked the question, but she had to know.

Alex frowned, lowering his head better to see her face. 'What do you mean, Angelina? What are you asking?'

Suddenly she wished she hadn't spoken. 'Oh, it—it doesn't matter. Forget I asked.'

Taking her shoulders, Alex forced her to look at him. 'Yes, it does matter,' he said quietly. 'You wouldn't have asked otherwise. So ask me.'

'When you left Arlington—you—you led me to believe that you—you were coming to London to—'

'Avail myself of a mistress,' he finished for her. Drawing her into his arms, he silently cursed, loathing himself for causing her pain. 'No, my love. I've been an idiot. I was angry when I left Arlington and I wanted to punish you for refusing me your bed. Since I returned to London my mind has been too full with thoughts of you to think about seeking another woman to relieve my lusts. I know I implied that I would and that was a mistake. My regret is that I hurt you. Condemn me for saying it if you must, but I can be pardoned for not doing so. Besides, you're the one I want. No other.'

A warmness stole over Angelina, bringing a smile to her lips. 'I'm glad. Thank you, Alex.'

'My pleasure,' he murmured, smiling tenderly into her upturned face and bending his head to caress her lips lightly with his own. When his mouth left hers his hooded eyes smouldered with renewed desire as they moved with leisured thoroughness over her delicately hued curves, his loins already hardening in demanding response to her nearness. 'Now, speaking of pleasure...'

Angelina's mouth curved in a sublime smile while her eyes grew dark and sultry. The heat of his gaze set her blood on fire and set her heart racing with sweet anticipation. 'Yes?'

'There's more,' he told her, nuzzling her ear.

Her eyes opened wide. 'There is?'

'I'm afraid so. I don't think I can blame Aylard for coveting you, Angel. What man could be indifferent to a woman like you? I find myself completely enamoured with this beautiful sprite that came into my life with such panache. There is something about you that makes a man commit the wildest follies. Oh, Angel, my sweet. You have the power to make my life hell. One must either love you to distraction or strangle you.'

Drawing back from his lips, which were about to descend upon hers once more, Angelina eyed him closely. 'And what would you choose, Alex? You haven't strangled me yet—so can I assume you—?'

Realising the folly of his words and what she was about to ask him, Alex placed a finger on her lips, silencing her. 'Not now, Angel. There is much, much more I have to teach you in the way of pleasing me.'

Angelina was hurt by his reply, but did not show it. 'Then teach me,' she murmured, her sensual lips quirking in a half-smile, a rosy blush covering her soft cheeks. 'It would seem I have some catching up to do, so I think we should begin my lessons right away.'

Alex's happiness shattered the moment he read Angelina's note. Incapable of any kind of rational thought, what he felt at that moment was raw, red-hot anger. As he prepared to leave for Kent, his volcanic anger grew, and it wasn't until he left London that it began to abate and he realised that he may have been too hard and insensitive to her desire to see her grandmother.

On a sigh and a whimsical smile tugging at the corners of his mouth, he admitted the truth of it. At twenty-nine years old and more women than it was decent to confess to, he had fallen victim to a beautiful, courageous, nineteen-year-old innocent,

who was in possession of an undesirable streak of fiery rebellion, who constantly taunted, mocked and incurred his displeasure at every turn. He felt his body tense as the unfamiliar
emotion drove into him like a physical force, becoming aware
that his reticence had been eroded by that stifling, most destructive of all emotions, making the paradox of his passions and
conflicting needs difficult to control.

Despite everything, he was now in no doubt that he loved
Angelina, that what they had together was real and transcended
anything else. It filled him with a sense of wonder, want and
hunger—an ultimate love that can only be understood by the
two people involved.

When Lady Broadhurst had left, Angelina waited for the
housekeeper to tell Lady Anne of her arrival. The house was
quiet, its walls exuding something of the old days that was
stable and unchanging. The sound of her mother's laughter
drifted through her mind, while the face of her father passed
ghostlike through her memory. Tears pricked her eyes and
sadness claimed her heart. They had been happy as a family,
which was nothing now but a vacant shadow in her memory.

Her gaze came to rest on a picture over the mantelpiece. It
was of a young woman in a blue gown, her hair arranged in exquisite curls around a heart-shaped face. Her smile was enigmatic, and the warm intensity of her eyes gazed back at her with
eyes that were extraordinarily alive.

It was her mother.

Angelina's heart wrenched, her gaze clinging to that achingly
familiar face, as if, by dint of will, she could hold on to remem-
brances of her life in Ohio with her mother and father before the
Shawnee had come. The woman she saw in the picture was a
woman she had never known. It touched her deeply.

When she was admitted to her grandmother's room, there
was a lump in Angelina's throat and tears pricked the backs of
her eyes as she moved slowly towards a small, frail old lady.
There was a calm serenity about her features. She was dressed

in a beribboned pale pink robe covering her nightdress and a blanket was tucked around her legs.

Angelina could only stand and look at the woman on the sofa, all the questions dammed up in her mouth. Sensing her discomfort, Lady Anne, who had absorbed every detail of this lovely young woman, smiled reassuringly and stretched out her hand, indicating that Angelina should sit in the chair close by her.

'So, you are my granddaughter,' she said softly. 'You are so like your mother. You have her eyes.'

'Yes,' Angelina replied, sitting down. 'Although I have my father's colouring. I am sorry that I come here as a stranger.'

'You are not a stranger to me, my dear. And it is not natural for those who are so close to be strangers to each other. But I have an unfair advantage. You see, I have known of your existence since your arrival in England. The papers have been full of the Duke of Mowbray's beautiful young American ward— Angelina Hamilton. Of course, I realised you had to be Lydia's daughter—and that my lovely Lydia must have died and placed you in the care of her cousin, Henry Montgomery. I also read about your recent marriage to the Earl of Arlington—which was very grand, by all accounts.'

'My only regret is that you weren't there to share it with me. It would have made my wedding complete. Why didn't you write to me?'

'Because I suspected your mother would have told you I was dead. Am I right?' she asked, arching a quizzical brow.

Angelina bowed her head as a deep sadness crept over her. 'Yes.'

'I did not know how you would feel if I wrote to you, that perhaps you would bear some resentment.'

'Of course I wouldn't. It wasn't until yesterday that I discovered you were not dead after all.'

'How did you find out that I wasn't?'

'I met Lady Broadhurst. I was shocked when she told me.'

'And you came directly,' Lady Anne murmured, touched by Angelina's eagerness to meet her.

'Lady Broadhurst was returning to Kent and she very kindly let me accompany her.'

'I see. And your husband? He did not come with you?'

'No.'

'He does know you're here?'

'Oh, yes. I—I left him a note.'

'A note? Dear me. From what I know of him, I believe the Earl of Arlington is renowned for his formidable temper. Was it wise to leave London without telling him?'

'No, not really. Alex does have the devil's own temper, and I know he will be absolutely livid. But I couldn't wait to meet you—and I was so concerned when Lady Broadhurst told me about your accident that I wanted to come at once. How are you feeling now?'

'Much better. My legs don't always do what they should, but I make a point of going downstairs during the afternoon and coming back upstairs after dinner.'

'I'm so glad I came. I knew that if I didn't leave with Lady Broadhurst, it might have been weeks—or even months— before Alex allowed me to come.'

'Am I to understand that he does not approve of you visiting me?'

'No—I mean—yes. But not until I had written to you and spoken to Uncle Henry first.'

Lady Anne looked at her intently. 'I can understand that. So, should we expect a visit from your husband?'

'It's very likely. In any case, he'll have to come to fetch me home.'

Lady Anne smiled, a smile so amazingly young and mischievous that Angelina was astonished, and she saw in her eyes a restless vitality that had been her mother's. 'Then I shall look forward to meeting him—and we must prepare ourselves as best we can to placate him. I—believe he bears a strong resemblance to his uncle.'

'They are very alike. Poor Alex. I led him a merry dance when I first came to England—America was so very different and to him I was just an awkward, ill-bred girl from the back-woods. I'm grateful to Aunt Patience and her daughter Verity, who helped and supported me enormously.'

'Patience is my niece, but we haven't seen one another for years,' Lady Anne replied with a note of regret. 'You would have found out about me in time, you know. This house and everything else I own will be yours one day.'

This had not even entered Angelina's head and the knowledge of it astounded her. 'Will it? But—but I didn't—oh, Grandmother!' she gasped, horrified that her grandmother might think she had come to stake her claim on her inheritance. 'Please don't think I came because of that.'

She smiled and patted her hand. 'I don't think you came for anything other than to see a sad and lonely old lady.'

Angelina suddenly realized how she had addressed the older woman—that she had called her 'Grandmother'. It was only a word and it had tripped off her tongue naturally, but there was a world of feeling in it, and Angelina sensed that there was a need in them both for some of the familiarity and warmth of kinship. 'Are you really sad and lonely?'

'I missed your mother so much when she married your father and went to live in America—more so when Jonathan, your grandfather, died.'

'What went wrong between you and my mother? Why did you never write to her?'

'In the beginning I wrote to her many times, but—but the letters were never posted,' she confessed. 'Your grandfather was not an easy man to get on with—and Lydia was not of a sub-missive nature. Things happened that were extremely upsetting at the time and are not easy to explain. They are wounds best not reopened, my dear,' she said quietly, and there was something in the tone of her voice and the expression in her eyes that told Angelina not to question further. 'Tell me—was she happy?'

'Yes, she was.'

'And—and was Henry with her at the end?'

'Yes.'

'I'm glad,' Lady Anne said after a prolonged silence. 'Now I know that my darling Lydia would have died happy.' Smiling at Angelina and taking her hand, she held it affectionately. 'There is so much I want to tell you about Lydia as a child, Angelina. You will stay with me for a few days, won't you?'

'If I may. I will leave you to rest now, Grandmother. I can see you're tiring.' After placing a gentle kiss on the old woman's cheek, she moved to the door.

'Angelina?'

She turned and looked back. Their eyes met with an intensity that was far beyond words.

'I'm so glad you came.'

Angelina smiled. 'So am I. Now we have met we shall not lose each other.'

The following afternoon when Angelina entered her mother's old room, the first thing that she became aware of was the familiar, subtle smell of jasmine. In that room she felt close to her mother and she loved her in death as she had in life, with a pure and filial love devoid of selfish need. Lovingly she touched the silver-backed mirror and hairbrush on the dressing table, seeing that strands of her mother's hair still clung to the bristles. Unable to stem the tears and the tide of grief, she lay prostrate on the bed, too wretched to move.

When she arose at last, all cried out, she sat on the window seat, drawing her knees up to her chin and wrapping her arms round her legs as she gazed out over the well-kept garden to the green meadows and woods beyond. Everything was serene and dappled with sunshine, and she wondered how many times her mother had sat on the same seat, looking out as she did now, and what her dreams had been.

This was how Alex found her.

When he came in, Angelina stared at him, feeling her heart give a joyful leap. Gradually life began to flow back into her body. Placing her feet on the floor she stood up, watching him nervously as she waited for him to speak.

His face was inscrutable, and after a long moment he said, 'Darling, come here.'

His arms were open, and like a sleepwalker Angelina's legs moved to obey his summons, but, unable to wait, Alex met her halfway and pulled her against him, wrapping his arms around her. Angelina was startled. She had expected cold rage, for him to chastise her for disobeying him, not this. Never had she known a man who was so perplexing.

'You're not angry with me for coming here without asking you?' She tilted her head and stared into his fathomless silver gaze while his soft voice caressed her.

'It was not my intention to come in here and berate you, my love. I know this was your mother's room, and I am not so insensitive that I don't know what you must be going through. There are things to be said—matters to be settled between us—but they can wait until later.'

'Have you seen my grandmother?'

'Yes. We talked.'

'What about?'

His lips quirked in a wry smile. 'You,' he said, reaching up and tracing the curve of her cheek with his fingertips. 'She told me you were up here. When you didn't come down I didn't think you would mind if I came to find you.'

'No, I don't mind,' Angelina murmured. 'I'm glad you've come, Alex. Can—can I stay with my grandmother for a while?'

'If that's what you want.'

'And will you stay with me?'

He smiled down into her upturned face, his arms tightening about her slender body, feeling her breasts pressed against his chest and unable to suppress the exquisite sensation that passed through him. 'Try to stop me.'

Angelina gave him a wayward smile. 'After disappearing the way I did, you appear remarkably calm, my lord.'

'I wasn't, and for a man who has neither eaten nor slept since you took off from London like that, it's nothing short of a miracle that I am now. After reading your note, if I could have got to you within the hour I would happily have murdered you. You can thank your lucky stars you had a head start.' Taking her hand, he sat down on the window seat, pulling her down beside him. 'We'll stay here three or four days and then go on to Mowbray Park. Feel free to come and see your grandmother whenever you wish, but don't stay too long, my love, because I really don't think I can do without you. And I would not want my wife to forget about me altogether when she is away from home.'

'I could never forget you,' she whispered after a moment, an aching lump beginning to swell in her throat. Without looking at him she raised his hand and solemnly placed her lips against his fingers. 'I love you, Alex. I love you as much as it is possible for a woman to love a man. I have loved you for so long, ever since you caught me taking a bath in your tub and you told me that you wanted me. And when I had my nightmare and you heard me crying, when you kissed me it sealed what I felt for you in my heart.' Raising her eyes, she looked at him, and the gentle yielding and the love in their melting dark depths defeated him. 'I hope you don't mind.'

'Mind?' The heartrending tenderness of her words sent a jolting tremor down Alex's spine. With a groan he snatched her into his arms, crushing her to him, and with a raw ache in his voice he said, 'Bless you, my darling. I don't deserve you.' Combing the hair from her face with his fingers, he tilted her head and kissed her lips tenderly, all the love that had been accumulating over the months he had known her contained in that kiss. 'I love you,' he murmured, his breath warm against her lips. 'Though I would have been the last to admit it, I think I loved you even before that day I found you making use of my bathtub.'

Catching her breath, Angelina raised her brows in amazement, silently questioning, hoping.

'I have come to realise just how much you mean to me,' he

went on. 'When I sent you away from Arlington all those months ago, I went dead inside. You spoke the truth that night when you sought me out in my room. You accused me of being insecure and disenchanted with life. I remember how cruelly I mocked you for saying it, but you were right. I told you I did not need any woman's love—that I did not want it. But I can see now that I was wrong. I want your love, Angelina. All of it.

'So you see, my darling, you have caught me in the tenderest trap of all.' On a sigh and a whimsical smile tugging at the corners of his mouth, he admitted the truth of it. 'What we have transcends all else. You are a rare being, Angelina Hamilton, and I love you.'

'Montgomery,' she corrected with a teasing smile. 'My name is Montgomery now.' She kissed him gently. 'Thank you, Alex. That's the nicest, most wonderful thing you've ever said to me. I hope you mean it, because now that you've said it, I couldn't bear it if you didn't.'

'I'll never lie to you,' he promised quietly, and she believed him.

Chapter Fourteen

After dinner—during which Lady Anne gave them an insight into her daughter's life as she had been growing up, which Angelina listened to avidly—when they retired for the night Angelina knelt in front of the fire in the room she was to share with Alex. Clad in only her nightshift, she waited in a state of nervous anticipation for him to emerge from the dressing room.

When he appeared, attired in his robe, his face was inscrutable. Sensing he had something on his mind, she reached up and took his hand.

'What is it, Alex?'

He sat beside her, one leg propped up and an arm resting lightly on top of it, thinking how sensational she looked kneeling in front of him, with the glow from the fire shining on her, warming the amber and gold lights in her hair.

'Earlier I said that there were things to be said, matters to be settled between us.'

'I know. But does it have to be now?'

'I'm afraid so.' Slipping his arm about her shoulders, he could feel her soft flesh beneath the thin material of her nightshift. He was eager to take her to bed and make love to her, but that must wait. They had to talk. The one remaining barrier that stood between them had to be demolished.

'Do you miss America very much, Angelina?'

'I miss Boston and my friends.' Her eyes softened as she gazed into the glowing embers of the fire, thinking poignantly of Will. 'They were people who were like me, ordinary and poor, but they were blessed with a special kind of happiness most English people will never know. They will never have kicked off their shoes to wade in the rivers to fish, to swim in those same crystal-clear waters, to ride the high mountains and low meadows, through forests, with nothing to depend on but your senses, the horse beneath you, and your rifle.'

'You make it sound wonderful, but I suspect it is anything but to those who aren't born to it,' he murmured, watching her with pride.

'It was wonderful to me. But now I am here and I have you. That is compensation enough.'

'I would like to see it one day.'

'You would?' Hope abounded in her heart.

'When the war between our countries is over, I'll take you back for a visit. Would that please you?'

Her eyes lit up joyously. 'Oh, yes. And shall we go to Boston?'

He laughed, planting a kiss on her shoulder. 'Anything my lady desires.'

'Oh, Alex. That would be wonderful.'

'On one condition.'

'Oh?'

'You will introduce me to your Will and Mr Boone.'

She kissed him. 'Done. Now, what do you want to say to me that is so important it must take precedence over you taking me to bed?'

Taking her chin between his long fingers, Alex forced her to look at him, the expression in his eyes suddenly grave. 'It's about secrets,' he said quietly.

'Secrets?' Angelina looked bemused, but then light dawned on her. 'No, Alex. Don't spoil it. Don't bring that up now. It doesn't matter any more.'

'It does matter,' he said with gentle firmness. 'Didn't your parents tell you that a trouble shared is a trouble halved—that two can bear a cross more easily than one?'

'Yes, but I don't want to go over it. Can't you understand that?'

Alex noticed a marked change in her mood. Despite the indications that she was likely to fly into a temper, his conscience and his need to shatter that final door in her mind forced him to press on. 'You may not want to tell me, Angelina, but can't you see that *I*, as your husband, need to know. Not knowing what happened to you is torturing me.'

Angelina's heart almost broke as she stared at him. It had never occurred to her that what had happened to her would affect him so deeply.

'All I want to do is to keep from losing my mind. To speak of it will be like reliving it.'

Angelina worried Alex with her last statement and the supplicant way in which she looked at him. It was like a frightened child pleading for help. He decided to push on. 'I will not let the matter rest until you tell me, Angelina.'

'I appreciate your worry about me, but you mustn't,' she said vehemently. Tears were forming in her eyes. 'I want to forget it.'

'It can't be done. It will always be there.'

'It isn't your problem.'

'Yes, it is. It became my problem when you married me. Share it with me, Angelina.'

Conscious of his scrutiny, suddenly agitated she got to her feet. 'How can you be so sure that telling you will make me feel better—that it will resolve everything?'

'I'm not saying that. But it will make me feel a damn sight better,' he said, standing up.

With tears spilling over her lashes, Angelina looked at him long and hard before turning away, wrapping her arms around her waist as if to contain the horrors behind that locked door in her mind. Hysteria threatened her, and she put her hands on either side of her head, as if to relieve her over-burdened mind. No matter how she tried to push the memories from her, they returned, lapping inside her mind like an ascending sea. Still she hesitated, but she was beginning to realise that it was important for Alex to know. In the end she turned to confront him, and a flicker of sanity lit the chaos of her thoughts.

'I know you are right, Alex but—but—Oh, God…'

When Alex saw the tears and the fear steal into her eyes, he suddenly pulled her to him and held her very tight. Gently he brushed the hair from her face. Her lovely, luminous eyes were saturated when at last she drew back and looked at him, but, knowing what he was asking of her, she covered her face with her hands.

'I can't tell you the things they did to me.'

Alex removed her hands. 'Yes, you can.'

Shaking her head, she was gasping for breath, and Alex could only guess at the torment the Shawnee had inflicted on her, and he loathed himself for adding to it by forcing it out of her. As she turned away from him her thoughts were in chaos, her eyes registering horror as she realised that the door, kept closed and locked at such great cost for so long, was wide open, and she was about to let the horrors spill forth. Very slowly she took hold of her emotions, rigidly controlling herself as she turned once more to face him.

'You are right. I should tell you everything. I owe you that, at least.' She held his eyes a moment, and then her gaze slid away. Drawing a deep breath, she let it out harshly. 'It's difficult to know where to begin.'

Alex settled himself into a chair, crossing his legs, watching her calmly, his heart going out to her. 'When the Shawnee came would be as good a place as any,' he suggested quietly. 'It is clear the people and your parents living in the settlement were unprepared for the attack.'

'There is only so much people can do to prepare themselves for an attack on the scale the Shawnee launched on us that night.'

She paused, and, although Alex appeared calm, he waited in a state of nervous tension for her to go on, relieved when she did, but she wasn't looking at him, she was looking into the flames, as if the images of the past were marching with each dancing flame.

'I was asleep—it was the middle of the night. That's when they always came, furtively, usually to steal our livestock—but that night they came to kill and burn.' She wrapped her arms around her body and hugged herself as she remembered. 'Our cabin was away from the settlement, across the river. The settlement was on fire and I went to wake my parents, but they were already up and dressed. They told me to get dressed and stay in my room until it was safe to come out. Safe!'

Wringing her hands in front of her, she turned away and hugged herself again. She turned towards him, her brows knitting together. Watching her, Alex clenched his hands into fists, having to struggle to stop himself going to her and cradling her in his arms. Her voice tore through him, her face was ravaged, but he couldn't make it easier for her. He had to let her go on.

'I did as they bade me. I stood at my window and watched a lone Indian ride towards the cabin—and my father...' She faltered and began gnawing at her bottom lip. 'My—my father went out to him, and—and the Indian...'

'Did the Indian kill your father, Angelina?' Alex asked gently.

Tears sprang to her eyes and she nodded, swallowing hard and looking down at her hands. 'My father was a gentle man— not forceful or violent, and he—he never even raised his gun when the Indian swooped on him and split his head in two like he would an apple. Mother ran out of the cabin to help him and—and the Indian stabbed her in the back. She fell beside my father and I thought she was dead too.'

Her pain and anguish tore at Alex. Her body shook violently. He reached out his hand to comfort, to make the telling easier for her, but she jerked away.

'No, Alex. Don't touch me,' she cried in her wretchedness. 'If you do, I won't be able to tell you the rest of it—and I must. I hid in my room, in a corner, hoping the Indian wouldn't find me. But he did. When I heard him come in I was so frightened

I thought I would die. I wanted to. I prayed for God to let me—but he didn't hear me. When the Indian saw me he—he dragged me out of the corner—and I fought him, Alex. I tried to get away from him, but he wouldn't let me,' she said, her words pouring out of her with such unmistakable pain. 'He was too strong for me, too big. And then he rolled me in a blanket and he—he hit me. Everything went black, and the next thing I knew I was in an encampment and it was still dark.'

She fell to her knees in front of her husband, reaching out and gripping his hands, as if she needed something to hold on to, as if by doing so some of his strength would pass to her, giving her added courage for what would come next.

'I was in a tepee and there were a lot of Indians. They—they ripped away my clothes—until—until—' she swallowed, her dark eyes huge, her voice barely above a whisper '—I didn't have any on at all. That was when one of them cut me with his knife—but I didn't feel the pain at first—not until later.'

Having seen the wound with his own eyes, Alex's face became taut and grim, his grip on her hands tightening, but she wasn't aware of it.

'I didn't know what they wanted, what they were doing—when they—when they— Oh, Alex—they—they touched me,' she cried brokenly and with so much wretchedness that his heart wrenched. 'They hurt me so much—and I was so ashamed and humiliated. I cried and begged them not to do it—but they wouldn't listen. Then they tied me up and left me alone while they went to drink the liquor they had taken from the settlement. I was bleeding so much, and I prayed to God to let me bleed to death so they couldn't hurt me any more.'

Something black and formless began to uncurl inside Alex. He had known something terrible had happened to her, thinking in his ignorance that it might be the manner in which her mother and father had been struck down before her eyes—that it might have been her mother who had been violated that haunted her—but not this. Never this. How alone she must have felt, how terrified. The full reality of what had happened to her came to him in that silent moment. But they hadn't raped her, thank God. But they might as well have raped her, for that's how it must have felt to an innocent, fifteen-year-old girl on the brink of womanhood.

As the full implication of what she was telling him began to sink in, he saw the truth at last, along with all the horror locked away inside her since that night. It made what had happened to him when he had been fifteen years old—when he had seen his own father blow out his brains—pale into insignificance. There was small wonder she had been afraid of being touched.

'Eventually the Indian who had captured me came back,' she went on, her voice controlled as she looked at a space beyond Alex. 'When he severed my bonds I scrambled away from him. But I slipped and fell to my knees. He clamped his hands around my throat and I thought he was going to strangle me. When he finally let me go he threw me down on to the blankets where I lay choking, gasping for breath. Somehow I managed to struggle to my knees but he grabbed hold of me, hauling and bruising me, shoving me back down.'

She fell silent, bowing her head over Alex's hands still gripping her own until she was able to go on. 'The Indian grabbed my arm and pulled me towards him. He fondled me, Alex, and tried to cover me with his vile body—laughing at me when I tried to wriggle free. I screamed, but my screams brought only laughter from the Indians outside.' With her head still bowed, silent tears of misery rolled down her cheeks onto Alex's hands. 'In desperation I fought him, but I was overpowered by his size and strength. He pinned my arms above my head and my terrified impulse was to submit to whatever it was he wanted to do to me, anything to stop him hurting me, but I knew that beyond that point something terrible awaited me—something vile and sinful.

'When the Indian released my arms and wedged a knee between my thighs, fearing I was about to be cast down into hell—I knew there could be no yielding. He had taken everything from me that I loved. I would not let him have more. I wasn't sure what he would do to me that he hadn't already done, but something inside my head told me there was more. That was when I reached out onto the ground and retrieved the knife he'd used to sever my bonds. It was all over in the blink of an eye—just as he was about to—to—violate me…' she whispered, avoiding Alex's eyes, unable to go on. Sitting back on her heels, she shuddered violently and covered her face with her hands.

Alex raised her up off her knees and dragged her to his chest, cradling her on his lap and wrapping his arms around her tightly, as if he would never let her go. 'You killed him,' he stated quietly.

She nodded, sobbing out her wretchedness. 'Do you hate me?'

'Hate you? Never that, my love. Don't you remember when I berated you for taking Forest Shadow from his stable, how you told me then that you had once killed a man for daring to lay his hands on you the way I did that day?'

Angelina gasped. 'Did I? I don't remember.'

'You were angry, and rightly so.'

'Then why do I feel so ashamed?' she wept.

'Don't. You brave, brave girl. What you did was for your own preservation. You cannot be blamed.'

Angelina's head shot back, and Alex was surprised at the pure cold hatred etched in every line of her lovely face as she remembered the look on the Shawnee's face, how, for a split second, he had seemed mesmerised by the very poise with which she held the knife, waiting for the inevitable thrust.

'What I remember is how I felt, Alex. At the time I was glad—glad the Indian was dead. Glad that I had killed him. I found it strange that I was no longer trembling. I raised my hand and stabbed at his heart and felt nothing when the blade sank into his flesh. He looked at me with surprise. Mercifully he uttered no sound as his whole weight fell on top of me. I shoved him off. Sitting up, I threw the knife on to the blankets, and for a short time I knew no pain, no fear. But it soon passed when I realised what I had done.

'I was glad he was dead, but I could not believe that I had killed him. Until then I had never raised a hand against another human being, but at that moment it felt no different to when I shot a rabbit or speared a fish in the river. Besides, I thought, it was no better than he deserved for killing my mother and father and abusing me. In that moment I forgot my parents' teachings—that it was a mortal sin to take a life, even in defence of one's own. All I could feel at that moment was an enormous relief.'

Tenderly Alex wiped away the strands of hair clinging to her wet face and tucked them behind her ears. 'What you did was no more than an act of personal survival—something anyone quick thinking and courageous would have done, faced with the same situation. How did you escape?'

'Will found me. He'd seen the Indian ride away with me from the settlement and followed. He cut his way into the tepee and helped me to escape. By that time the Shawnee were too drunk to notice. Will took me back to the settlement where he had left my mother. I couldn't believe she was still alive. After that we made our way back East, but for weeks afterwards we lived in fear that the Shawnee would catch up with us and exact their revenge for what I had done.'

Having emptied her heart, Angelina could not stem the grief and anguish that burst from her in a sea of tears and emotion. Slowly she crumpled down on to the carpet as if her weight and the weight of her anguish she could not sustain. Alex let her weep, hoping that by doing so she would cleanse her soul of all the ugliness that had defiled it for so long.

When her weeping subsided, she rose. Alex was standing beside the bed and the pull of his gaze was too strong for her to resist. It was as though he were looking into the very depths of her heart and soul. She felt the touch of his empathy like healing fingers touching and soothing her pain like a balm. She had seen in his eyes the reflection of her torment, and now, as though he were God's own advocate, he was offering her re-demption.

Like a celestial being she moved towards him. She lay on

the bed and Alex knelt beside her in reverence. Her fear was like a cutting edge and yet sublime, and when it left her she was wide open to a flood of wondrous new emotions. When she tasted the warmth of his lips, she felt all the love, the compassion and respect he carried for her in his heart, and when he finally took her the pleasure transcended anything she had known before.

Later, little remained of the girl who had been a victim of the Shawnee. She was a creature of the past. The mysterious alchemy of her inner self, mixed with elements inside Alex, had worked the miracle of transformation. The change in her was clear, and for the first time in three years Angelina felt at peace with herself.

Alex wrote to Henry from Tonbridge to inform him of their arrival. He also thought it best to warn him that Angelina had discovered that her grandmother was alive and had insisted on paying her a visit.

'You will not be too hard on Uncle Henry, will you, Angelina?' Alex said as they journeyed to Mowbray Park. 'I do not want this subterfuge on his part to cause a family rift. After all, he was only abiding by your mother's wishes.'

Angelina met her husband's eyes calmly. 'I am not angry, Alex. I am more concerned about how Uncle Henry feels now he knows I have found out that he lied to me. I do realise he was honour bound to my mother to keep the promise he made before she died. Did you know that he was in love with my mother?'

'Yes. But I did not find out from Uncle Henry.'

'Then who?'

A coldness entered Alex's eyes and his jaw tightened. 'My mother.'

'But—I don't understand?' After she had spoken Angelina suddenly recalled a conversation she'd had with Aunt Patience at Arlington, and that she had told her that Alex's mother had been in love with Uncle Henry. Alex's next words confirmed this.

'My mother had her sights set on Uncle Henry from an early age. Whether she had any deep, abiding affection for him or merely had her eyes set on his ducal title we will never know. Uncle Henry did not reciprocate her feelings and she took his rejection badly. To spite him she married my father, and went out of her way to punish him for Uncle Henry's rejection. In those days it would seem Uncle Henry had eyes for your mother and no other. However, both sets of parents considered the relationship incestuous, which was why they parted, but the fact that Uncle Henry never married tells me he never got over losing her.'

'It seems that one way or another we have both been touched—and damaged—by the love my mother and Uncle Henry bore each other.'

'That must have hurt you, knowing how much your father loved your mother.'

'It did. Deeply. My mother's and Uncle Henry's hearts and minds were so clearly entwined, even after all the years in between. I sensed it when Uncle Henry came to America. It was as if I had stumbled on a secret, but I didn't want to think about it, because to do so would, in some peculiar way, be a betrayal to my father.'

'Didn't your grandmother tell you anything about what happened to cause the rift?'

'No—and I could see it was all too painful for her to remember. I believe it all stemmed from my grandfather being unforgiving in his attitude towards my mother's determination to thwart his authority. Grandmother told me that he strongly disapproved of my father—he had neither breeding nor substance, you see. My grandfather severed all ties with my mother—even though it broke my grandmother's heart. When she asked me if Uncle Henry was with my mother when she died and I told her he was, in a way she seemed relieved, as if a great burden had been lifted from her heart.' A sadness touched her eyes and she sighed. 'I'm rather glad I didn't know my grandfather. I don't think I would have liked him very much.'

'I think it wise that when you speak to Uncle Henry you don't probe into the past, Angelina. Let it be over.'

She looked at him, her eyes soft with love. 'Of course. That's what I want.'

After receiving them both, Henry faced Angelina, encouraged by the fact that she looked relaxed and was smiling her usual sweet smile.

'I'm sorry you had to find out about your grandmother like this, Angelina. Believe me when I tell you that I did not want to keep it from you, but your mother left me with no choice. I gave her my word, you see. I'm sorry if I hurt you.'

He held out his hand to her, his face pleading for her understanding. She took it in both her own, and she felt her heart go out to him.

'I don't blame you, Uncle Henry. I do understand why you didn't tell me. You couldn't break your word.'

Henry wondered how much she knew, how much her grandmother had told her. Did she know that the abiding love he and Lydia had felt for each other had been an affair doomed from the start, but while it lasted was filled with exquisite joy for the two lovers involved, who knew it was to end in heartbreak?

'Angelina, if you knew—'

'No, Uncle Henry,' she said quickly. 'You don't have tell me anything.' Reaching up, she tenderly placed a kiss on his cheek. 'I love you.'

They looked at one another, and smiled. Angelina's was one of love and understanding, Henry's one of gratitude.

Basking in naked splendour after a glorious night of love on their first night back at Arlington, nestling in the crook of her husband's arm, Angelina glanced up at him adoringly. With his head against the pillows and his tousled black hair falling over his brow, she could not believe how handsome he was. Sated and relaxed, he was the epitome of absolute, masculine contentment. Her heart abounded with love. When she placed a kiss on his chest he opened his eyes and let his silver gaze rest lovingly on her upturned face.

'What's this?' he whispered. 'Have I not tired you out, Angel?'

'Not quite,' she murmured, nestling her head against his shoulder and letting her hand wander over his chest in a leisurely caress. 'I feel too happy to go to sleep.' With a sigh she tipped her chin up so that she could gaze into his eyes. 'Have I told you how much I love you, Alex Montgomery?'

A lump of emotion swelled in Alex's chest and his heart lurched, as it never failed to do when she said those words to him. For the first time in his life he was filled with a sense of well being. She was the first woman to tell him that she loved him and mean it, and it filled him with wonder, gratitude and love.

'I have heard you mention it, and I don't want you to ever stop saying it,' he murmured in the gentlest voice Angelina had ever heard. 'I want to hear you say it every minute of your life. I can only count myself fortunate that you share my life and will continue to do so for many years to come.'

'It is my most heartfelt wish,' she whispered achingly.

'I love you too, my darling, and since you are the one who has shown me how to, no one has a better claim to it than you.'

Angelina sighed deeply, pressing her lips against his chest, her sweet-scented hair spilling over him. 'And I have triumphed against all the odds. I have you to thank for unlocking the door to my past. Now I am free.'

'No, you're not.' Alex raised her up and placed a hand on each side of her face, forcing her to look directly at him, looking at her with a combination of awe and reverence. 'You, my love, belong to me now—as I belong to you. We are pledged to each other—you and I—body and soul. We are partners for life, bound together for good or ill.'

For Angelina the world seemed to tilt when his mouth, hot and hungry, claimed her own. 'I would have it no other way, Alex,' she whispered against his lips, knowing the truth of it.

* * * * *

From Governess to
Society Bride

HELEN DICKSON

Chapter One

1820

The young woman paused to look around. It was early morning and most people were still abed. There was not a sound in this great London park, shrouded in the kind of thick fog the city was famous for. It was as if she were alone in the world. This was the time of day she loved best.

But then, somewhere in the distance, she could hear the pounding of a horse's hooves. She could almost feel the ground tremble beneath her feet. She resented the sound, that anyone should disturb her solitude. Turning full circle, she strained her eyes, listening to the thundering crash coming ever closer, when suddenly a sharp shout rent the air and a huge black shape of a horse and rider descended on her.

She cried out for him to stop and threw herself to one side, landing on the grass in a tumbled heap. The rider jerked at the reins and the beast reared, its hooves flashing like quicksilver, its coat glistening as the muscles beneath it rolled and heaved. Flared nostrils and blazing eyes gave him the look of a demented dragon. It missed her by mere inches.

The woman saw the man as if through a long tunnel. A small cry came from her throat as she saw the black apparition swing himself from his mount in one quick, effortless bound. With his cloak flying wide behind him he resembled a huge bat swooping down toward her. Seized by terror, she scrambled to her feet; brushing down her skirts she glared at him, her heart pounding fit to burst.

'You damned fool,' he roared. 'What the hell are you doing on the track? I could have killed you.'

'I beg your pardon?' she retorted sharply, setting to rights her bonnet, which had been knocked sideways, and trying to smooth away the mixture of terror and anger that had taken hold of her. He was so tall she was forced to look up at him, and she found herself confronting pale, snapping eyes. Black hair accentuated lean cheekbones and a resolute jaw, and his mouth was compressed into a stern arrogant line.

'If you had been any closer you could have been trampled to death. Is there no room in that brainless skull of yours for common sense?'

'Why, how dare you?' She was incensed, her face pink with indignation. 'And will you please not wave your crop about like that as if you were going to thrash me.'

The stranger slapped the offending weapon to his side without relinquishing her eyes. 'I am sorely tempted. Don't you know not to walk on the track? It's for horses, not ladies to stroll on.'

She raised her chin belligerently. 'I do know that, but I didn't think anyone would be foolish enough to be out riding with the fog as bad as this. And I was only following the track so that I wouldn't become lost.'

'Which is a dangerous thing to do at the best of times.' Abruptly the man interrupted his tirade to say with a touch of concern as a thought occurred to him, 'Are you hurt?'

She glowered at him accusingly, her face showing no sign of softening. 'No—no thanks to you. If you had been riding with more care and attention, this would never have happened—or perhaps your horse got the better of you and you haven't taught it who is master.'

'I assure you he knows who is his master.' He looked at her closely, seeing a gloriously attractive young woman whose whole manner spoke of fearlessness, of her need to let him see that she was afraid of no one, and certainly not of him. Even if she had not jumped out of the way as she had done, he would not have run her down. He was too good a horseman for that, but it had been a close shave. He smiled lazily. 'What a firebrand you are. Are you sure you stumbled and didn't just swoon at the sight of me and my horse?'

His hollow chuckle held a note of mockery. A flush of anger spread to the delicate tips of the woman's ears and icy fire smouldered in her deep blue eyes. 'Why, you conceited, unmitigated cad. You are arrogant if you believe I would ever swoon at your feet. Thank God I'm not afflicted by such weakness.' She stepped away from him, finding his closeness and the way he towered over her a little intimidating. 'Good day to you, sir.'

Not yet ready to be dismissed, he touched her arm to delay her. 'At least let me escort you to your home.'

Her chilled contempt met him face to face. She slapped his hand away. 'Do not touch me. I am quite capable of taking myself home. Go away and take that vicious beast with you,' she snapped, glancing irately at the black stallion that had begun to snort and stamp impatiently, its vigorous temperament reminding her so very much of its master.

'Aren't you taking a risk? You might be set upon by footpads or worse. Anything could happen to a young woman walking alone at this hour.'

'It just did, and I'm of the opinion that I'm in less danger of being set upon by footpads than I am from you. At least they may have better manners.' Turning her back on him, with her head held high she began to stalk away.

He sighed in feigned disappointment, slowly shaking his head. 'Such ingratitude.'

She spun round. 'Ingratitude?' she gasped. '*You* call me ungrateful? You almost trample me to death and I am supposed to be grateful?'

His eyes gleamed with amusement. 'Have it your way.' He set his tall hat securely on his head and swung himself back in the saddle on his prancing beast. 'Good day to you.'

He kicked his horse into motion. His laughter drifted back to her, his mockery infuriating her yet further. She stamped her foot and glared after him, muttering all kinds of threats under her breath. She had never met a man who had irritated her as he had just done and it chafed her sorely to consider his flawless success.

It was a glorious spring day. The sun had risen out of a broad expanse of opal mist, and scraps of cloud floated like spun gauze in the sky. Ash and sycamore, cherry and lilac trees were bursting into full flower, and trumpet-headed daffodils and clusters of primroses filled beds and borders. The air had a trace of freshness in it, a breeze blowing across Hyde Park from the river beyond. The park was quiet, save for a skylark singing high above and a few people taking an early morning constitutional, including a young woman walking aimlessly along the paths with two small girls trailing behind her.

Seated on a bench watching her five-year-old daughter, Estelle, running happily between the flower beds pursued by Jasper, a Labrador pup that was a recent addition to the Seagrove household, Eve sighed and looked down at her hands in her lap. Why did she feel so despondent? What was the matter with her? Why did her life seem to be so limited? She had her health. She had a good friend in Beth Seagrove. She was not unattractive and, thanks to her dear deceased father, eventually she would have more money than she would know what to do with. She was reasonably clever and had a broad base of interests. Everyone was always telling her how lucky she was to have Estelle, whom she adored. That should really be enough for anyone—but it wasn't. There had to be more that she could do with her life, something else to absorb her time and energies.

Tonight she was to attend a private party at Lady Ellesmere's house in Curzon Street. These affairs where most of the faces were familiar were more to her taste than the more established venues, and she really did enjoy attending them with Beth and her husband. However, Eve was determined to find something to do to earn her keep until her father's money was made available to her and she could look for somewhere else to live.

Turning her head, she looked at the young woman with the children. She was perhaps eighteen or nineteen. Her clothes were of good quality, but plain grey and unadorned—the same clothes a nursemaid would wear. Her face was pale and dark rings circled her eyes—she really didn't look at all well. She was seated on the bench adjacent to Eve's and her head was lowered on to her chest. Her shaking shoulders indicated that she was weeping very quietly.

The two little girls, her young charges, stood in front of her and stared at her. Their faces showed confusion and they were clearly anxious and frightened. The youngest child picked up on her mood and started to cry and shrank into the girl next to her.

'Don't cry, Sarah,' the eldest girl said to the woman on the bench. 'It will be all right.'

Her words seemed to calm the young woman, not because she was able to believe them but because of the sweet unselfishness of the child uttering them. Raising her head, she smiled at the child but her shoulders remained drooped in dejection.

Eve stood up. Fishing a handkerchief out of her pocket, she went to the unhappy trio. 'Can I be of help?' she asked, directing the question at the woman while bending down and smiling at the weeping child. 'Here, let me wipe your face.' Gently she dabbed at the tears of the child, who was looking up at her with solemn light blue eyes that reminded her of a wounded puppy. 'What are your names?' she asked.

'I am Sophie,' the older girl replied politely, 'and this is my sister Abigail. Abigail is three, nearly four, and I'm five.'

'Is that so? Well, I'm pleased to meet you both,' Eve said, thinking what pretty children they were. Both had heart-shaped faces and glossy dark brown curls and were dressed in identical blue dresses. Looking towards where Estelle was playing, Eve waved her over. 'Estelle, while I sit and talk to…?' She looked enquiringly at the young woman.

'Sarah, Sarah Lacy,' she provided quietly.

'While I talk to Miss Lacy, why don't you take Sophie

and Abigail to play with Jasper—would you like that?' she asked the two little girls. They nodded, looking shyly at Estelle, but not moving until Sarah had given them her permission.

'It's all right, children. You can go. I can see you from here.'

Typical of Estelle, who was accustomed to playing with Beth's two boisterous boys, she held out her hand to Abigail, and the three of them chased over the grass after a staggering Jasper, who stopped suddenly and sat down in a heap of tumbled legs.

Smiling, Eve sat next to the young woman. The poor girl was obviously not well. Her skin was pale and her soft grey eyes had a wild, almost desperate look about them.

'I hope you didn't mind me suggesting that your charges play with my daughter. The puppy is quite harmless.' The young woman shook her head. 'My name is Eve Brody, by the way.'

'No, I don't mind. I'm their nursemaid. It's good for them to be with other children. They so rarely are, poor mites.' Lowering her head, she stifled a sob. 'I'm sorry…' she began, then broke off miserably.

'It's all right, Sarah,' Eve said, moving closer to her. 'Are you ill?'

Unable to meet the kind stranger's eyes, Sarah looked down at her fingers twisting her handkerchief in her lap. 'I've just got a bit of a headache, that's all,' she answered shyly.

'Have you seen a doctor? Perhaps he can give you something that will help to make you feel better.'

Sarah shook her head and sniffed. 'I'll be all right. I feel better than I did.'

'Then why are you crying? You look quite distraught.'

'To tell you the truth, miss, I've been at my wits' end these past weeks. I don't know what to do. Really I don't.'

'Why is that?'

'Mark, my young man, lives and works as head grooms-man at a big house in Surrey. He's asked me to marry him, but it would mean leaving my job—and the children.'

'What's so terrible about that? Surely there is someone else to care for them—their mother?'

'They have no mother. My master, Lord Stainton, the children's father, is in the middle of closing down the house, which is why I'm out with them so early—to get them away from the upheaval. Workmen are all over the place and his lordship isn't in the best of tempers. Apart from myself and the housekeeper, most of the servants have been dismissed, and very soon we are to move to Lord Stainton's country estate in Oxfordshire. I haven't told Mark yet and I'm dreading it. He doesn't understand, you see, the bond I have with the children.'

'If your position means so much to you, then why doesn't your young man go with you?'

'Lord Stainton can't afford to take on more staff. His lordship's affairs really are in quite a bad way, which is why he has to sell his London house.'

'Even so, his problem is not yours, Sarah. Lord Stainton must find someone else to look after his children. It shouldn't be too difficult. I'm sure there are lots of young ladies with the right credentials who would jump at the chance.'

'I know—but there has been so much heartache in their young lives that I hate the thought of deserting them. They've been in my charge since Abigail was a year old. I can't bear to leave them. It will break my heart—and theirs—but I know I must.'

'Your concern is commendable, Sarah, but you do have to think of yourself.'

Estelle's laughter came to them from across the grass. Eve's eyes were drawn towards the sound, seeing her daughter rolling on the grass with Jasper on top of her licking her face, while Sophie and Abigail looked on, reticent to join in, but smiling none the less. Concerned, she fixed her attention on the young woman by her side.

'You really do look quite poorly. Perhaps you should go home and lie down for a while,' Eve suggested.

Sarah shook her head. 'That's impossible, although I really should be getting back.' She stood up, putting one hand to her head and the other grasping the back of the bench as she swayed slightly. 'Oh, dear. I do feel quite dizzy.'

Standing up, Eve took her arm. 'Come, I'll walk back with you. I can't let you go by yourself.'

'Oh, no. You've been very kind, but I've imposed on your time long enough.'

'I insist. Besides, I have nothing better to do. Where do you live?'

'Not too far away, just across the park in Upper Brook Street.'

'Then it is not far from Berkeley Street, which is where I live. Come, children,' Eve called. 'Estelle, you must carry Jasper.' She smiled as she watched her daughter bend down and pick a wriggling Jasper up off the grass and tuck him beneath her arm.

Stainton House was certainly in a state of upheaval. Workmen swarmed about all over the place and furniture was being either covered with dustsheets or loaded on to wagons in the street. Holding the children's hands, Eve and Sarah went inside. The size of the house surprised and impressed Eve. With its white-and-gold décor, she could well imagine how elegant it must have looked before the work-force moved in.

Eve was about to say her farewells to Sarah and the children when Jasper broke free of his captor and landed on the floor. Excited by the new environment and noise, the little dog bounded yelping loudly up the broad sweep of the staircase rising gracefully from the centre of the hall.

'Don't worry,' Sarah said, having recovered a little from her earlier discomfort. 'I'll go after him.'

The three children went and sat halfway up the stairs, watching the workmen with rapt expressions on their faces. Eve stepped aside to let two men pass carrying a gold-and-green striped sofa in the direction of the street, and turned when a voice barked out, 'Bloody hell, man, be careful! That portrait is worth a small fortune. Any damage and the buyer will refuse to take it.'

Eve strode over to the owner of the remark—a jacket-less, dark, forbidding figure, his grey breeches moulding his muscular legs and thighs, his white shirt open at his tanned throat, and his hair as black as a panther's pelt. Her face was a mask of indignation.

'Do you have to swear in front of the children?' she remarked haughtily. She saw his shoulders stiffen at the sound of her voice and when he spun round and his eyes sliced over her, she could almost feel the effort he was exerting to keep his rage under control. The man had ramrod posture and an aura of exacting competence, and Eve almost collapsed when she saw his face—it was as hard and forbidding as a granite sculpture and he was looking at her as if she were a mad woman who had invaded his domain.

She also recognised him as being the man whose horse had almost trampled her to death the day before.

'I'll swear when I like in my own house…' Suddenly he froze and his eyes widened. 'Good Lord, it's you—'

'Unfortunately that is so. And do you have to shout? My hearing is perfectly sound and you're frightening the children.'

'Children? Don't be ridiculous. I'm their father.'

'Precisely, and for that reason alone you should have more control over your temper,' Eve snapped, having recovered from the shock of meeting the rude and thoroughly obnoxious gentleman for a second time.

Lord Stainton turned his dagger gaze on the terrified servants, who had ceased what they were doing and stood frozen to the spot, their eyes agape. 'Who the hell let this emotional woman into my house without consulting me first?'

'I am not an emotional woman and, as I have already told you, I am not deaf, so kindly lower your tone.' Turning on her heel, she strode to the stairs to collect Estelle.

'And what's that supposed to mean?' he thundered, striding after her irate figure with the silent sureness of a wolf, stopping in his tracks when he saw three apprehensive young faces peering down at him from the stairs instead of the usual two. Placing his fists on his hips, he glowered from the extra child to the angry young woman. 'Miss Lacy,' he shouted. When Miss Lacy failed to appear, he cursed softly and pinned Eve with his gaze. 'Where has that child come from,' he demanded, pointing a long narrow finger at the offending child, 'and what the hell is she doing in my house, today of all days?'

Eve's eyes flew to the children while still feeling

concern for Sarah. After all, it was the purpose for which she had walked into the lion's den just minutes before.

'The child you are referring to is my daughter.'

'Then do you mind removing her from my house and yourself along with her? As you can see—'

'You are moving out,' Eve snapped.

'Do you always make a habit of stating the obvious, Miss…?'

'Mrs—Brody, and, yes, I do,' she said, her eyes flashing as cold fury drained her face of colour and added a steely edge to her voice.

He returned her gaze steadily, studying her as though she were some strange creature he had just uncovered in his home. He had already noted her slight American intonation; her Scottish name was another fact that intrigued a rather bemused Lord Stainton. There was a moment of silence in which he tried to calm himself.

At thirty-two years of age, six feet four inches tall and with amazingly arresting eyes he was a strikingly handsome man. Rugged strength was carved into every feature of his bronzed face, from his straight dark brows and nose, his firm and sensually moulded lips, to the square, arrogant jut of his chin. Just now he was also formidable as he glared at the young woman who stood before him on his black-and-white marble floor. Every line of his face was set with disapproval.

'Have you had an edifying look at me, Lord Stainton— I assume that is who you are?'

'You are correct in your assumption, Mrs Brody.'

'You are also the most ill-mannered, arrogant, inconsiderate man I have ever encountered,' she upbraided him coldly.

His eyes narrowed and his lips tightened. 'I dare say I am all you accuse me of. It goes with the title.'

Eve was in no mood to be mocked, and she could see by the gleam in his eyes he was doing exactly that. 'Then with you as an example, I can only hope you are the last titled Englishman I shall ever meet. Yesterday I fervently hoped and prayed I would never have the misfortune to set eyes on you again. Nothing has changed. Such an outward display of temperamental frustration is regarded as a sign of bad breeding where I come from.'

Ramming his fists into his waist, leaning forward, he stared at her in blank fury. 'Really! You really are the most infuriatingly outspoken woman I have ever met. How dare you come into my house and say these things to me—things you know nothing about.'

'Oh, I dare say a lot of things to a man who scares his children half to death and terrifies each and every one of his servants so they creep about in fear of you. The whole house vibrates with a tension that springs from you, Lord Stainton. It's a wonder you have any servants at all to order about. By the look on your face I would wager I've hit a sore spot. Please don't disappoint me by holding your temper. I would hate to see you explode with the effort.'

'Believe me, Mrs Brody, you would not want to see me explode. I have a temper, I admit it, a violent one when I am driven to it. And how I raise my children and choose to live concerns only myself.'

Eve had made her point with an icy calmness. Lord Stainton was so taken aback by her outburst and her forthright way of speaking that his superiority evaporated as he stared at the attractive young woman whose fury turned her dark blue eyes beneath gracefully winged dark brows to violet. Framed by a heavy mass of auburn hair arranged neatly beneath her bonnet, her face was striking, with creamy, glowing skin, high cheekbones, and a small round chin with a tiny, intriguing cleft in the centre. Her nose was straight, her mouth soft and generously wide. His gaze moved over her slender body with a familiarity that brought a rush of colour to her cheeks.

Mrs Brody was a young woman in her early twenties, and she moved with a natural grace and poise that evaded most of the women he knew. Despite being a married woman, she exuded a gentle innocence that he found appealing. Beneath this he sensed an adventurous spirit tinged with wilfulness and obstinacy.

Appalled that he could find the time to scrutinise a complete stranger who had entered his home uninvited and chastised him so forcefully, when all around him there was complete and utter chaos, in sheer frustration he turned from her.

'I've had enough of this charade, Mrs Brody. I have to get on. No one invited you here. There is the door. Use it.'

Eve could feel her face flaming in response to his rudeness. Her momentary shock gave way to a sudden burst of wrath. 'You're right, they didn't. I came to make sure your children's nurse arrived home safely. She was taken ill in the park and I considered it an act of human kindness to see that she made it home without mishap. Now that is done, it will be my pleasure to remove myself and my child from your house—when I have retrieved my dog from all this chaos, that is.'

He spun round to face her once more, and for the first time Eve saw his hard façade crack. 'Dog? What dog?' he echoed blankly. There was more than irritation in his question—there was stunned amazement.

'The one that disappeared up your stairs when we came in.'

'Are you telling me that there is an animal running loose in my house?'

'That is exactly what I'm saying—but don't be alarmed,' she said, her voice dripping with sarcasm, 'it won't bite. Ah, here it is now,' she said, thankful to see Sarah coming down the stairs with Jasper in her arms. Meeting her halfway, she took the pup and got hold of Estelle's hand, impatient to get out of the house as quickly as possible.

'I see Lord Stainton is out of sorts again,' Sarah whispered softly, looking at Eve with quiet concern. 'Are you all right?' She glanced over her shoulder. 'Have a care. His lordship is not a man to listen or be reasoned with when he's in one of his infamous adverse moods.'

With her back to Lord Stainton, Eve smiled at Sarah. 'Oh, I think I can manage his lordship, Sarah.'

'Unfortunately his temper rules his head. He will soon calm down.'

'No doubt so will I—when I am out of this mad house. Now you take care of yourself, and marry that young man of yours before too long.'

Confronting Lord Stainton for the last time at the bottom of the stairs, she lifted her chin, in no way intimidated by this man. 'Seeing that you are in the middle of a self-destructive rage cycle, Lord Stainton, I'll get out from under your feet. I'm only sorry that I subjected my daughter to the rantings of a very rude lord.'

'You have caught me on a bad day, Mrs Brody.'

'Considering I have encountered you on two occasions, Lord Stainton, judging by your behaviour it would seem that you have a bad day most days.'

'Not at all, Mrs Brody. If your daughter has been in any

way upset by my "rantings", then she has a small measure of my sympathy—the remainder of it must go to your long-suffering husband.'

Eve looked at him directly. 'I am a widow, Lord Stainton, and my husband's suffering was of short duration. He was killed outright by an English bullet in New Orleans. Now,' she said, grasping Estelle's hand tighter and clutching Jasper to her bosom with the other, 'I have no wish to detain you any longer. Good day to you.' She swept out of the house like a galleon in full sail, too angry to say one more word.

In a state of suspense, Lord Stainton stared at the open doorway through which Mrs Brody had just disappeared, feeling as if a hurricane had just blown itself out. He also felt bewildered and extremely angry with himself and a complete idiot, his expression holding more than a little dismay and remorse at what Mrs Brody had just divulged. From an early age he had been taught by his parents and his tutors to project a veneer of civilisation, regardless of how he was feeling, particularly when his emotions were incensed. He had just failed dismally.

'Miss Lacy,' he called, halting the nursemaid as she climbed the stairs to take Sophie and Abigail to their rooms. 'Mrs Brody? Who is she and where does she live?'

'Apart from her name I—I don't know who she is, Lord Stainton. She never said. Although she did say she lived on Berkeley Street.'

'I see.' He was about to turn away when he remembered something Mrs Brody had said. 'Miss Lacy.'

'Yes, sir.'

'Mrs Brody did mention that you weren't feeling well,' he said on a softer note. 'Do you need to see a doctor?'

'No, sir. I'm feeling much better now.' She bobbed a little curtsy. 'Thank you for asking.'

'Good.' With the skill he'd perfected when his wife had left him, he turned away and coldly dismissed Mrs Brody from his mind.

Disturbed and upset following her encounter with the insufferable Lord Stainton, and feeling a headache coming on, with a morose sigh Eve sank on to the sofa in the drawing room of the Seagroves' elegant house on Berkeley Street, unable to believe the furious altercation had happened at all. Her anger had evaporated somewhat on her walk back, but she was still shaken. The dejection that had replaced her fury was completely uncharacteristic of her.

With the children happily ensconced upstairs in the nursery and William, Beth's devoted husband, at work at the Foreign Office, glad to have some time to themselves, Beth poured them both some tea and sat back. She cast a sharp, searching look at her friend's exquisite features.

'What has you looking so grim, Eve? Tell me.'

'I met someone today.'

'Did you? Well, there's nothing so unusual about that. Is it someone I know?'

'I would think so. Lord Stainton, and I have to say he is the rudest, most conceited man I have ever met in my life.'

Beth laughed. 'Then that explains it. What happened?'

In no time at all Eve told her everything that had occurred, from the moment she had met Sarah Lacy in the park to being ordered out of Stainton House like one of the criminal fraternity. She didn't tell her about their previous encounter in the park, since Beth was always chiding her for going off by herself. When she had finished Beth looked stunned.

'Dear me! It sounds to me as if you have upset that illustrious lord.'

Eve grimaced. 'I didn't mean to—although I suppose I was somewhat rude and outspoken, and in his house, too. Do you know him, Beth?'

'My dear Eve, the whole of London knows Lord Stainton.'

'What do you know about him?'

'He's devastatingly handsome for one thing—you must admit that.'

Bringing the image of the tall, lean and superbly fit Lord Stainton to mind, Eve could not deny that despite his stern, finely chiselled mouth and the arrogant authority stamped in his firm jaw and the cynicism in his cold, light blue eyes, he was breathtakingly handsome. 'Yes, I suppose he is.'

Beth sighed almost dreamily. 'I do so like handsome men.'

'I know. That's why you married William,' Eve commented teasingly.

'Oh, no,' Beth said, chuckling softly as she took a sip of her tea. 'William is sensible, reliable and conscientious, but also sensitive, gentle and idealistic. *That* is why I married him.'

'I agree, he is all those things. William is a paragon among men, and not a hardened cynic like Lord Stainton. What else do you know about him?'

'Well, on a physical and intellectual level there's none better. He inherited the title from his brother, who died several months ago. He lives quietly and isn't often seen in society these days, although I have seen him on occasion at the more sedate affairs. He's been the object of gossip ever since he divorced his wife Maxine about a year ago. She's the daughter of the Earl of Clevedon—Lord Irvine. At the time the divorce created a scandal that set the *ton* on fire.'

Eve stared at her in shocked amazement. 'Divorce? He divorced his wife—the mother of those two lovely children? Why on earth would he do that?'

'I don't know all the details, but what I do know is that his wife caused complications from the day he married her. Compounded in her many faults, apparently, was the fact that she was exquisitely beautiful, elegant and clever and attractive to other men. A man of Lord Stainton's character would not tolerate infidelity.'

'She had an affair?'

'Several, apparently. After the birth of her second daughter it's rumoured she indulged in one affair after another, the most intensive being with Lucas Stainton's own brother. Her behaviour really was quite scandalous. She actually walked out on Lord Stainton to live with his brother in the country.'

'She left her children?' Eve gasped, appalled that any woman could do such a thing.

'Yes, she did. Apparently the divorce turned out to be extremely expensive—it virtually ruined him. Of course Lucas's brother didn't help matters, being an inveterate gambler. The Stainton coffers were depleted long before he died.'

'Then Lord Stainton will have an unenviable task on his hands replenishing them.'

'Indeed he will.'

'Is he ostracised because of his divorce?'

'On the contrary. It all adds to his mystery and charm. The *ton* positively pander to him and no one would dare give him the cut. Of course he is free to marry again, but the aristocratic mamas on the look out for suitable husbands for their darling daughters do not consider an impoverished, divorced lord at all suitable. However, he's favoured for his looks and every hostess in the *ton* has been trying to lure him back into society, but he declines their invitations.

'I believe he's selling his London house and moving to the country.'

'Yes, I know. Laurel Court. It's close to William's parents' house in Oxfordshire and it's very beautiful, although sadly neglected. If he's selling his house in Mayfair, then hopefully it might help pay some of the debts. If not, who knows what he will do. If he wants to keep the estate, then he might even resort to marrying an heiress—and why not? He won't be the first impoverished nobleman to marry for money and he won't be the last.'

'That seems rather drastic, Beth.'

'To you, having lived almost all your life in America, I suppose it does. In English society, marrying for money is considered a perfectly acceptable undertaking. However, pride is a dominant Stainton trait and Lord Stainton will find it extremely difficult and distasteful having to resort to such extreme measures. But that said, I do believe he might honour us with his presence tonight with Lady Ellesmere being an old friend of the family and the occasion being a rather sedate affair.'

Eve's eyes snapped open as a blaze of animosity and a shock of terror erupted through her entire body. 'Lord Stainton will be there?'

Beth laughed, in no way sorry for her friend's consternation. 'Don't be alarmed, Eve. He may decide not to go.'

'On the other hand he might.'

'Try not to worry. By now perhaps he looks back on the incident with amusement.'

'If he does, then he has a warped sense of humour, Beth.

He will not find the incident amusing, believe me. In fact, I might stay at home. Lord Stainton will not want to see me any more than I wish to see him. Besides, I have developed this terrible headache in the last hour. An early night suddenly seems most appealing.'

'Nonsense. You are going. With a room full of matrons and *grandes dames,* I am relying on you to talk to me. As for the headache, I'll give you a couple of my powders to alleviate it. Take one before you go and another before you go to bed.'

By the time Eve was ready to leave for Lady Ellesmere's party, her head was aching quite badly. Having taken one of Beth's powders and feeling no effect, she took the one she was supposed to take before she went to bed. After tucking Estelle in bed and kissing her goodnight, she went to join Beth and William.

Lady Ellesmere's house was a blaze of light when the carriage drew up outside. A liveried footman stepped aside as they swept into the marble-floored hall. Entering the salon, they paused and Eve's eyes swept the assembled guests dressed in their finery, the ladies beautiful in silks and satins fashionably cut.

With an eye for comfort, luxury and fashionable elegance, the walls were hung with ivory silk delicately worked with a gold-and-green design, the colours reflected in the upholstery and the heavy curtains hung at the windows. Expensive Turkish rugs covered the floor. The room was aglow with the dazzling radiance of myriad candles, the delicate crystal pendants of the chandeliers splattering the walls with prisms of light. Soft music being played by a string quartet could be heard in the background and for those guests who sought entertainment two adjoining rooms had been set aside for gaming. The French doors were set wide to catch the coolness of the night and to allow guests on to the wide lantern-lit terrace.

It was an informal affair. Lady Ellesmere, a striking middle-aged widow, was seated on a gold-coloured *chaise longue*. Like a queen, bedecked in sparkling jewels and her richly coloured silk skirts spread about her, she reigned supreme.

Taking two glasses of champagne from a silver tray, William handed them to his companions, then took one for himself and surveyed the glittering company.

'Rather splendid, isn't it?'

'As usual,' Beth answered. 'It's what you expect at Lady Ellesmere's affairs. How is your headache, Eve? Has the powder I gave you helped?'

Eve smiled. Relieved to see no one she would rather not, she began to relax. 'Yes, I believe it has—although I did take the other one just to be on the safe side.'

Beth stared at her in shock. 'You took them both? Oh, Eve, you really shouldn't have. They really are quite strong. I wouldn't drink too much champagne on top of them if I were you.'

William chuckled softly. 'Just one of Beth's powders is enough to send the sufferer off to sleep for a week, Eve. Two powders and you can guarantee being rendered unconscious for a fortnight.'

Feeling perfectly all right and in no way concerned, Eve laughed and took a sip of her champagne. 'I never drink more than two glasses anyway, so worry not, you two. In fact, I think when we've spoken to Lady Ellesmere

I might partake of some refreshment,' she said, her eyes straying to the connecting salon where tables had been laid out with delicious delicacies.

Lucas saw Eve the instant he entered Lady Ellesmere's salon. Seeing her made him stop, shocked into inaction. His brows drew together in disbelief that she was here, and that the harridan who had invaded his house earlier was the glamorous red head strolling casually through the roomful of wealthy elite with William Seagrove and his wife.

Lucas was with his good friend Henry Channing, who was easy to please and the most amenable of men. Henry revelled in London life, which was a change from the backwoods of Newcastle he'd been brought up in. With his looks and his father's wealth he was well received everywhere, his trade origins being conveniently forgotten.

Henry followed his gaze, interest lighting his eyes when he saw the delightful object of his friend's attention. 'That absolutely divine creature is Mrs Eve Brody,' he provided, 'born in England and raised in America. Her father passed away recently, leaving her immensely rich, I believe.'

'Is that so,' Lucas drawled drily, staring at the champagne in his glass.

'Mrs Brody, who is a widow, has received numerous offers of marriage in America. Since coming to England, she has attracted a great deal of interest, but she discourages those suitors as soon as their intentions become apparent to her.'

Lucas turned a baleful eye on his friend. 'You seem to be extremely knowledgeable about Mrs Brody, Henry.'

'My sister is a close friend of Beth Seagrove.'

'Then that explains it. However, I am not remotely interested in Mrs Brody, Henry.' Turning his back on Eve, he smiled at Lady Ellesmere, who was beckoning him over, and began walking towards her, abandoning a bemused Henry.

Later Lucas's eyes were drawn to Eve again, standing near the refreshment room, the light from the chandelier bathing her in a golden glow. From across the room he studied her stunning figure and flawless beauty. Her heavy, fiery auburn hair had been twisted into burnished curls at the crown. Her gown was pale green with a tightly fitted bodice that forced her breasts high and exposed a daring expanse of flesh.

Having been aware of his presence for some time and feeling his razor-sharp gaze on her, Eve found the memory of their angry altercation still very much on her mind. It made her feel quite ill at the same time as pride forced her to lift her chin and rebelliously to face him across the distance that separated them, meeting his ruthless stare. For the second time within twelve short hours her dark eyes beheld another's in mutual animosity.

Lord Stainton's tall, athletic frame was resplendent in black jacket and trousers. In contrast, his shirt and neck-cloth were dazzling white. He looked unbearably handsome. He also looked utterly bored.

Eve stood in resentful silence while his gaze slid boldly over her, from the top of her shining deep red curls to the toes of her satin slippers. She was accustomed to the admiring glances of gentlemen, but there was nothing gentlemanly about Lord Stainton's insolent, lazy perusal of her body. Incensed she turned her back on him to listen to what Beth was saying to her.

'If the weather is nice tomorrow, I think we'll take a

picnic to the park. Would you like that? There's to be a balloon ascent during the afternoon. The children would love that.'

'I wouldn't mind seeing it myself and it will certainly do the children good to get out of the house and let off some steam. How long will it be before your house in Camberwell is finished?' Eve enquired. There was great excitement in the Seagrove household over the large house being built for them in Camberwell, south of the river. Like many businessmen, William was moving his family out of the centre of the city, yet close enough for him to drive in to work.

'Another two months—and I cannot wait. Eve, I'm glad Estelle's settled in so well. When you arrived, I confess to being worried that she would miss New York.'

'Your brood have made it easy for her, Beth. In fact, at the moment life is one huge adventure for my darling daughter.'

Beth smiled, hiding her dismay that the same could not be said for her friend. Since Eve's arrival, she had quickly become a popular figure on the social scene. Several eligible bachelors had been plaguing her relentlessly to allow them to pay their addresses to her, but she politely shunned them all, seeming to have no interest in forming that kind of relationship with any man.

Glancing across the room at Lord Stainton, Eve watched him prowl among the guests. He seemed to radiate barely leashed strength and power. There was something primitive about him, and she felt that his elegant attire and indolence were nothing but a front meant to lull the unwary into believing he was a civilised being while disguising the fact that he was a dangerous savage.

When he began moving into their vicinity, Eve's urge

to flee promptly overpowered every other instinct. 'If you will excuse me, Beth, I would like to visit the ladies' room.'

Having seen Lord Stainton arrive and the shock register on Eve's face, Beth laughed and placed a restraining hand on her arm. 'Oh, no, you don't. I think you should be properly presented to Lord Stainton and forget your earlier encounter.'

When Beth drew her forward, mentally Eve braced herself.

Unable to avoid a confrontation, Lucas stood his ground and bowed graciously to Beth. 'It's a pleasure to see you again, Mrs Seagrove. Your husband is here?'

'He is indeed, although I fear a game of faro has caught his interest. Lord Stainton, may I present my good friend, Eve Brody.'

Eve looked at Lord Stainton's shuttered eyes. She could find no trace of gentleness or kindness anywhere in his tough, ruggedly chiselled cynical features. His slashed eyebrows were more accustomed to frowning than smiling, and he had a hard mouth with a hint of cruelty in it. It was a face that said its owner cared nothing for fools, and in the light blue of his dark lashed eyes, silver flecks stirred dangerously, like small warning lights.

'We've already met,' she stated, toying with the glass of champagne she held between her fingers.

William chose that moment to emerge from the gaming room; seeing him, Beth hastily excused herself, determined to reach him and coax him away from the game of whist that was about to start in the other room.

Lucas nodded to her and again fixed his gaze on Eve. 'That's right, Mrs Brody, we have met. I'm flattered that you remember me,' he replied, keeping a good distance between them.

Determined to appear calm and unaffected by their early encounter and not indulge in a public display of temper, Eve forced a smile to her lips. 'I've tried to forget our unpleasant encounter, Lord Stainton. It's difficult.'

'Well, here's to your future success.'

He lifted his glass in a mocking toast. Eve did the same. Unfortunately her head chose that moment to spin. Her hand shook and the champagne sloshed out of her glass and spilled down the front of her dress. Lord Stainton jumped to the wrong conclusion as to why her eyes looked glazed and, raking her with an insulting glance, his mouth curved scornfully.

'Didn't anyone tell you about the perils of drink, Mrs Brody?' he remarked contemptuously. He saw her flinch, but her gaze never faltered.

'I don't,' she bit back, resisting the urge to snatch his glass and toss its contents into his arrogant face.

'It is obvious to me that you do and that you cannot hold it,' he said imperturbably.

Desperate to appear normal, Eve was thankful when a solicitous footman was already lowering a tray of champagne to come to her aid. With a grateful smile pasted on her face, she handed him her glass and took a napkin he offered with shaky fingers. She proceeded to dab at her dress and handed it back.

'Thank you,' she said, glancing around to see if they were being observed, relieved to find the incident had gone unnoticed.

'Perhaps you would like some more champagne,' Lord Stainton said in a silky voice.

'No, thank you,' she replied tightly.

'It's a very wise person who knows when to stop.'

She glared at him. 'Go away, Lord Stainton. You really are the most provoking man alive and quite insufferable.'

Instead of being insulted or angered, he looked at her with amusement and shook his head. 'What were you expecting to find, Mrs Brody? A socially accepted gentleman? A rake or a dandified fop? I am none of these.'

Before Eve could react to his words, in a mockery of another toast, he said, 'Enjoy your evening.' And he walked away to join Henry Channing.

Chapter Two

As the evening wore on Eve was finding it more and more difficult to stay awake. What was the matter with her? All she wanted to do was go to sleep. And then it hit her. She knew what was wrong. It was those wretched headache powders she had taken. Perhaps some fresh air would help. Where was Beth? Her eyes swept around the room looking for her friend, but there was no sign of her.

Snaking her way round obstacles, she eventually came to the French windows that led out on to the terrace. Stepping out, she crossed to a low wall and placed her hands on it for support, breathing hard. The terrace was dimly lit and she did not see the tall dark-haired man, a thin cheroot he occasionally enjoyed clamped between his even white teeth, his features in shadow, quietly conversing with Henry Channing until it was too late, otherwise she would never have ventured outside.

'I say, are you all right?' Henry remarked, having watched her come outside. He was concerned when he saw her place her hand to her forehead.

Eve swayed, seeing the look of unconcealed disgust

on Lord Stainton's face. Before she could reply, his icy voice said,

'I believe the lady is completely foxed, Henry. You can expect to have one hell of a hangover in the morning, Mrs Brody.'

'I would expect it had I been drinking, but I haven't, and if I had it would be none of your business. How dare you?'

'I dare say a lot of things to you, Mrs Brody, but I won't waste my breath.' Catching her by the arm as she rocked to one side, he thrust her rudely down on to the wall. 'Sit there while I summon your friends. I think they should take you home before you disgrace yourself and them with your undignified behaviour.'

Eve raised her head and stared up at him, unable to focus properly. 'You don't understand…'

'I understand all too well,' he said scathingly, his accusing eyes dropping to the damp stain on the front of her dress.

'I resent that,' she gasped, trying to get to her feet but falling back and having to close her eyes when her head began to spin in a dizzy whirl.

'She's going to swoon,' Henry predicted.

'I am not,' Eve protested, defying her pronouncement by almost toppling off the wall.

'Oh, for God's sake!' Lord Stainton thundered, casting the cigar to the ground. Grasping her about the waist, he scooped her up into his arms and headed for a bench further along the terrace. 'Find Mrs Seagrove, Henry, and ask her to come at once—and find some hartshorn or whatever it is that brings one out of a swoon. And for heaven's sake be discreet. Should anyone come outside and find me with a senseless woman in my arms, gossip will be raging through London like wildfire before breakfast.'

Henry rushed off to do his bidding while Lord Stainton carried his helpless burden along the terrace.

Coming to her senses and blisteringly aware of her close proximity to Lord Stainton's broad chest, fury and indignation shot like red-hot sparks through Eve's body. 'How dare you?' she cried, squirming against him, trying to break his hold. 'Will you put me down? No matter what you think, I do not deserve such treatment.' Her struggle only seemed to make him angrier.

'Be quiet and keep still,' he ordered, going a little further before dumping her unceremoniously on to a bench.

Eve fought the lethargy that was stealing over her and snapped her head up, intending to launch into a tirade, but looking past her tormentor she saw a figure in a pale pink gown rushing towards her.

'Beth,' she cried. Never had she been so relieved to see anyone in her life.

'What on earth has happened?' Beth bent over her friend, her face creased with concern. 'Is your headache worse, Eve?'

'No, no, it isn't, and none of this is my fault. Beth, will you please tell this puffed-up lord who has the manners of a barbarian and who is bent on assassinating my character that I am suffering nothing more serious than an overdose of your headache powders and not over-indulgence of champagne.'

'Headache powders?' Instead of looking guilty because he'd made a mistake, Lord Stainton looked infuriatingly amused. 'You are prone to headaches, Mrs Brody?'

'No, as a matter of fact I rarely suffer minor ailments, but earlier today I had the misfortune to meet you, Lord Stainton.'

'Then what can I say?'

'Sorry would be a start,' Eve bit back.

'Very well. The mistake was mine. I apologise most humbly.'

'Humble? You?' she gasped, unable to believe her ears. 'You couldn't be humble if you tried.'

'Contrary to what you obviously think of me,' he drawled, 'I was merely coming to your rescue. Your actions, like on our previous encounter, led me to believe you were in danger of swooning.'

'And I seem to recall telling you that I never swoon— and I was not in any danger,' Eve lied coldly, avoiding Beth's questioning eyes, knowing full well that she would have to give her a full account of her encounter with Lord Stainton in the park.

Lazy mockery lit his eyes. 'And you are sure of that, are you?' he asked, as amusement seemed to drain the tension in his body.

'I most assuredly am.'

'To show you how wrong you are, Mrs Brody, I suggest that when you get up off that bench you will allow me to assist you.'

Eve opened her mouth to make some suitably scathing remark about his outrageous conceit, but his bold smile was too much for her. Swinging her legs on to the ground, she got to her feet unsteadily. When Lord Stainton reached out to take her arm, she snatched it away and glared at him.

'Don't you dare touch me. I wouldn't let you touch me to save me from drowning,' she retorted furiously.

'I understand,' Lord Stainton drawled mildly.

Placing her hand on Beth's arm, Eve completely ignored Lord Stainton. 'I would like to go home, if you don't mind, Beth. I really must go to bed before I make a total fool of myself and fall asleep in Lady Ellesmere's salon. That would never do.'

Seeing the funny side of the incident, Beth suppressed a smile. 'No, it would not. It's almost time to leave anyway. We'll find William and say goodnight to Lady Ellesmere.' She turned to Lord Stainton and Mr Channing, who was looking totally bemused and holding a bottle of hartshorn in his hand. 'Goodnight, Lord Stainton, Mr Channing, and thank you for your assistance.'

'Good Lord, Lucas,' Henry uttered after a long moment of silence, staring at his friend in disbelief. Grown men rarely dared to challenge him, yet here was this young American widow—an exquisite, extremely ravishing American widow—who had done exactly that. 'She actually accused you of having the manners of a barbarian. Mrs Brody is one angry lady,' he said, shaking his head in disbelief. 'I doubt she will forgive you in a hurry.'

Lucas glanced toward the closed doors through which the aforesaid lady had just disappeared, and in the space of an instant, Henry watched his lazy smile harden into a mask of ironic amusement.

'I'm sure she won't. But that's Mrs Brody's problem, Henry. Not mine.'

Beth insisted on picnicking away from the crowds of people who poured into Hyde Park to watch a French aviator's ascent in a huge balloon, which was the cause of much excitement among the Seagrove children and Estelle. The event had generated so much interest that it had disrupted the usual cavalcade of handsome equipages that congregated daily in the afternoon. It consisted of men mounted on fine thoroughbred horses, colourful and elaborately clad dandies and women in the best society, the carriage company some of the most celebrated beauties in London. The sun was pleasantly warm, and people were laughing and joking, all talking about the giant, hissing balloon that had taken off successfully.

Accompanying the carriage carrying Miss Lacy and his children on horseback, Lucas came upon the picnic scene by chance. It was one of complete enchantment, of a small group of people—three adults, one of them a nursemaid or governess, and three children, two boys and a girl. The adults were sitting on the grass in the shade of the giant beech trees, a white cloth spread on the ground on to which baskets of food had been unpacked. The children, in high spirits, were running about trying to catch one another, shrieking with laughter.

It was the woman, dressed in a delightful lightweight blue-sprigged dress with a wide sash of deeper blue tied in a bow at the back, on whom his attention was focused. He looked at the sunlight glinting on the flaming strands of her glorious wealth of auburn hair that tumbled on to her shoulders in a mass of curls, the sides drawn to the back of her head and secured with a blue satin ribbon. Her feet were tucked under her dress, her face upturned to the sky. She looked about sixteen, though her figure was mature. She was watching the balloon, which had just become airborne, soar up beyond the clouds, causing much excitement among the crowd.

Taking her eyes off the balloon, she turned her attention to the children, a serene smile on her face as her eyes settled on the little girl. Beth's two boys, boisterous and as audacious as a barrowload of monkeys, were a bit too much for Estelle, and she found it hard to keep up with them. But determined not to be left behind, she persevered.

Suddenly Estelle stood stock still and her face broke into a bright smile at something she had seen further away, and then she was running in a fever of excitement to Eve.

'Sophie! Mama, it's Sophie and Abigail,' and before Eve could stop her she was scampering off across the grass as fast as her little legs could carry her to where a carriage had halted so the occupants could watch the balloon.

Eve scrambled to her feet and ran after her, smiling delightedly on seeing Sarah Lacy and her young charges.

'Sarah, how lovely to see you again.' She looked at the children. 'Have you come to watch the balloon?'

'Yes,' Sophie said, her eyes shining with glee, clearly having enjoyed the spectacle. 'It was ever so exciting.'

'And it made a hissing noise like a dragon,' Abigail babbled happily, at three years old already having a good command of the English language.

'The children were so excited,' Sarah said, returning Eve's smile. 'They've never seen a balloon before.'

'Neither have I. It was quite a novel experience. Sarah, why don't you come and share our picnic? It would be lovely for Sophie and Abigail to play with Estelle—and there's ample food.'

'I don't think so, Mrs Brody. Thank you for your kind offer, but Miss Lacy and the children must be getting back.'

Eve whirled round at that familiar deep voice, and looked into the face of Lord Stainton. She knew by his expression that he was not as stunned as she was. For some inexplicable reason her heart set up a wild thumping. His face was still, but his eyes were a brilliant, quite dangerous pale blue. He lounged indolently against the back of the open carriage with the ease of a man discussing nothing more serious than the weather. The remembrance of their previous encounters, all of which had been angry and bitter experiences, touched her deeply.

He wore a plum-coloured cutaway coat and buff knee breeches tucked into highly polished black riding boots, and his neck linen was sparkling white. His gaze was sharp and penetrating and he radiated the same strong masculine appeal. Eve watched him warily, experiencing the depth to which her mind and body were oddly stirred whenever she was in his presence.

Pushing himself away from the carriage, he bowed his dark, shining head. 'I trust your headache is much improved today, Mrs Brody?'

'Yes, thank you for asking,' she replied stiffly.

'I didn't expect to meet you at such a gathering,' he remarked, his expression unreadable.

'I can't think why not. I enjoyed watching the ascending balloon enormously—almost as much as the children.' Distracted by Estelle, who was jumping up and down beside her, better to see Sophie and Abigail in the carriage, she said, 'Please let your daughters play with Estelle—just for a minute.' Lord Stainton's face became cool with the compelling arrogance she associated with him.

'I told you, we have to be getting back,' he uttered sternly.

Eve looked at his daughters. Their little shoulders were slumped in dejection and her heart went out to them. There was something rather timid about Sophie and Abigail, something cowed and contrary to the normal exuberance of children.

'Children need to run about and shout and laugh once in a while, Lord Stainton,' she said calmly, trying to speak to him without the abrasive tongue of an enemy. 'There's no harm in it.'

'Please, Papa,' Sophie whispered tentatively, 'can we play with Estelle for just a little while?'

Eve looked straight at him, waiting for him to reply to Sophie's quiet plea, hoping he was not inclined to inflict his bad temper on his children. She was relieved when she saw his expression soften.

'Very well, Sophie,' he conceded. 'Miss Lacy, please don't let them out of your sight.' Instructing the driver to wait with the carriage, he opened the carriage door and lifted his excited offspring down on to the grass, before striding back to his horse.

With Estelle and Sophie scampering on ahead, Eve took Abigail's hand and walked with her to the picnic. Lord Stainton watched them from atop his horse and he began to smile, for their laughter was infectious. His face was soft and his eyes were warm. He had a strong sense of responsibility and felt a deep affection for his daughters.

It worried him greatly that they were growing up without the influence and love that could only come from a mother, but when his wife had walked out on him, she had also callously abandoned her children. Turning his horse away from the delightful picture of the picnicking group and feeling a knot of envy that he was not a part of that group, he trotted over to speak to an acquaintance.

Settling herself on the grass beside Sarah, Eve glanced at her with concern. Her expression was strained and apprehensive and Eve suspected things weren't well with her. 'You look pale, Sarah. Are you all right?' she enquired with quiet concern. 'It can't be easy for you working for a man as formidable as Lord Stainton.'

Sarah smiled, watching her young charges as they laughed and chattered over their jellies and buns, happy to see them fitting in well with Mrs Seagrove's two boys, Thomas and David. 'It must seem like that to you, but his bark can often be worse than his bite. I've given much thought to what I told you yesterday—about leaving my employment.'

Eve looked at her expectantly. 'And?' she prompted. 'What have you decided?'

'I'm going to marry Mark. It's what we both want—but it will break my heart to leave Sophie and Abigail.'

'Have you told Lord Stainton?'

She nodded. 'This morning. I will carry on working for him until he leaves for the country—perhaps two or three weeks. I haven't told the children yet. I—don't know how to.'

Eve reached out and squeezed her hand comfortingly. 'I know just how difficult that will be for you, but I'm sure you'll find a way—and Lord Stainton will be sure to find someone who will care for his daughters.'

'Yes—I'm sure you're right.'

Their attention was drawn to the children who, having finished eating, with cries of delight scampered off across the grass, Sophie and Estelle hand in hand. Not intending to be left behind, Abigail shouted, 'Wait for me,' and ran awkwardly after them. Unfortunately, she was so intent on catching the two older girls that she didn't look where she was going, and the next instant she had run straight into a tree. There was a howl and Eve and Sarah turned simultaneously to see Abigail on the ground, her skirts tipped up in a froth of white lace petticoats and drawers, and a horrified Sophie running back to see what had befallen her sister.

Observing the incident from a distance, Lucas cursed beneath his breath and dismounted. As he strode towards what was quickly becoming a mêlée, an expression of immense concern clouded his face, anxious and not at all pleased.

Sophie, her eyes huge and brimming with tears, stood looking down at Abigail, her hand still clutching that of Estelle. 'Abigail was running and bumped into the tree and banged her head,' she wailed, crying even louder when she saw the graze and the swelling bump on her sister's head, almost choking on her tears.

Eve immediately scooped the injured child up into her arms to comfort her while Sarah tried to console Sophie.

'I knew this would be a mistake,' Lord Stainton thundered, glowering accusingly at Eve. It was as if she had physically pushed the child into the tree.

For a full five minutes the picnic area was filled with the voices of crying children, the concerned voices of Beth and Sarah, and Lord Stainton's deeper, alarmed and irate voice.

Eve looked at him coldly. 'Will you please be quiet,' she said, trying to keep her voice as calm as possible. 'Shouting like that will only upset the children more than they already are and make the situation worse.'

Inconsolable, Abigail continued to sob loudly, her hand on the already swelling lump on her forehead. She was frightened and bewildered by the sharp anger of her father and she cried fiercely. Completely ignoring the glowering Lord Stainton, whose mouth had clamped shut at her firm reproach, Eve sat on a bench with her young burden and cradled her on her lap, hugging her tightly and murmuring soft, soothing words against her wet cheek.

'Does it hurt very much?' she asked the sobbing child. 'Did that nasty tree get in your way?'

She nodded. 'Yes,' she wailed, 'it did.'

'Here, let me see.' Eve wiped the hair from Abigail's wet face.

'I bumped my head,' Abigail said between sobs, 'and it hurts.'

'I know it does, sweetheart,' Eve murmured, hugging her once more, 'and when you get home I'm sure Miss Lacy will put something very special on it to make it better.'

'And will that hurt?'

'No, of course it won't. It will make the horrid bump go away in no time at all.'

Eve would have been surprised if she had looked up and seen Lord Stainton's face as he watched her cradling his daughter, her cheek resting on the child's dark curls. Looking on, he felt as though he was an intruder, a stranger, and that the two children belonged to someone else.

Mesmerised by the lovely picture the woman and child created, his expression had softened. He listened intently to her trying to sooth Abigail, which was something that came quite naturally to her. Gradually the child became quiet and ceased to cry, looking at the face of the woman with something akin to adoration and responding to the warmth in her voice.

Both the scene and the words of comfort Mrs Brody murmured bewitched him and reached out to some unknown part of him that he had not been aware he possessed. It touched and lightened a dark corner for a brief instant and then was it was gone.

Aware of Lord Stainton's presence, Eve looked at him. Abigail saw her father and was shy of him, hiding her face in Eve's neck. Standing up and carrying the child, Eve murmured, 'Come, Abigail. Let's go and find Miss Lacy, shall we? And perhaps you would like to take some of those pretty pink fairy cakes home with you that you liked so much. We shall see if we can find a fancy napkin to wrap them in. Would you like that?'

'Yes, please,' Abigail whispered, having enjoyed the warmth and the cuddle the kind lady had given her and beginning to feel better already.

As Sarah settled the children in the carriage, with Abigail clutching the fairy cakes to her chest as if they were the most precious things in the world, Eve walked back to Lord Stainton. He was about to mount his horse and paused to look down at her.

'I do not believe Abigail will suffer any adverse affects from her fall, Lord Stainton, but if you are worried unduly perhaps a doctor could take a look at her.' A slow smile curved her lips. 'In the rough and tumble of growing up, children trip up all the time.'

'I sincerely hope you are right, Mrs Brody, and Abigail suffers no ill effects. However, Sophie and Abigail are not in the habit of running about like young savages.'

'Then perhaps they should be. It's far healthier for them to be out of doors and running about. They can still be in a stable environment without being cooped up in the house all day.'

'My children have all the stability I can give them. They have had a secure upbringing and they are happy in the affection of a nursemaid.'

'Nursemaids are all very well for infants, Lord Stainton, but for growing girls—'

'They need their mother,' he interrupted in a soft, blood-chilling voice as he loomed over her, stopping her abruptly, his face taut with some emotion Eve did not recognise. 'I couldn't agree with you more, but they don't have a mother—at least not the kind of mother you are familiar with.'

'I'm sorry. If you had let me finish what I was about to say, I was going to suggest a governess.'

'If I wanted your advice, I would ask for it. My children are my responsibility and I will guide them as I see fit.'

'Then I would say that, with the attitude you've got, you will not make a very good job of it.'

'Don't you dare lecture me on how to raise my daughters, Mrs Brody. They are nothing to do with you, so I would be obliged if you would mind your own business.'

Eve stood back as he hoisted himself up into the saddle and without another word rode after the carriage. Her heart softened—she was not cruel, and she could well imagine how difficult it must be for him raising two young daughters alone. Sarah's resignation must have come as a terrible blow and she sincerely hoped he would find someone who would care for his children as much as she had.

As he followed the carriage carrying his daughters, Lucas stopped every now and then, his eyes glancing back at the young woman with the deep red hair walking back to her party. Finally he turned his head away as if she didn't exist.

The household was in bed and Eve was alone. She was tired after going with Beth and William and the children to visit their new house across the river, but she was restless and unable to sleep. Seated before the dressing table mirror, she was staring into space. She loved England and Beth's spacious elegant house in Berkeley Street was a balm to her spirits, but she felt so alone. Instead of distracting her from her grief over her father's death, being here in this alien country with a loving family was compounding the unreality and isolation she had felt since his funeral.

Her father had died suddenly just three months earlier. They had always been close and his parting had left her bereft. Lonely and lost without his support, with her daughter she retreated with her grief into her home, though it wasn't long before potential suitors, aware of the vast wealth she had inherited, began arriving at her door like a swarm of locusts.

After weeks of turning her back on each and every one of them, she had emerged from her twilight world and, when a letter arrived from her good friend Beth Seagrove inviting her to come and stay with her and her lovely family, she had set sail for England. She and Beth had been close friends since childhood. Both their families had lived in New York and Eve had been sad when Beth had married William Seagrove and had gone to live in London.

Eve envied Beth her easy relationship with this lovely, supportive man, and dearly wished things had turned out like this for her. Sadly it was not meant to be. Andrew Brody, her husband of six months, had been killed in sordid circumstances, leaving her alone and pregnant with Estelle.

With a sigh she pushed her melancholia aside and studied her reflection in the glass. Decisions had to be made about what she was going to do next. No matter how much she loved staying with Beth and William, she knew that she couldn't stay with them for ever. Besides, as yet she was unable to access her father's money; according to the solicitor she had employed here in London, his affairs could take some considerable time to sort out.

Eve was quietly concerned about this because her available funds were limited, but her lawyer had assured her that it was only a matter of time before a conclusion was reached. So for the time being, in order to be self-sufficient, she must find some kind of employment to tide her over.

One thing she was quite clear about was that she did not want to return to New York and had already decided to settle in England, but not London. The city was too big, too noisy. She had no remaining family in England, so Eve was free to settle where she chose.

Ever optimistic, the three bitter encounters with Lord Stainton two weeks ago was forgotten, but not the gentleman himself or his beautiful children, and not for the first time she wondered if he had found a replacement for Sarah Lacy. She had not heard otherwise and, if this was indeed the case, had thought of a scheme that could prove beneficial not only to her but to Lord Stainton, if he would but listen to her and consider it.

The following morning as she left her room to go down to breakfast, Eve tried to recapture the emotions she'd had last night, emotions that had made it completely appropriate and perfectly right for her to see Lord Stainton and try to persuade him to consider her as a nursemaid to his children. In the cold light of day, however, what she was planning to do seemed completely insane.

Beth was incredulous and appalled when Eve told her what she intended. Lifting a spoonful of steaming porridge to his lips, William glanced across at her. Diplomatic as always, he was prepared to listen to what their guest had planned in more detail before voicing an opinion.

'You are going to ask Lord Stainton to employ you?' Beth gasped. 'But, Eve, that's preposterous. You dislike him intensely.'

'In all honesty, I don't know what I think and it's absolutely insane I know, but I'm going to ask him just the same.'

'What? After he almost trampled you to death beneath his horse and berated you and unfairly accused you of being drunk?'

'It wasn't his fault. I suppose that's how it must have looked to him. He jumped to the wrong conclusion, that was all. He can be forgiven for that.'

'Eve, you are a very wealthy woman,' William stated calmly. 'You have no reason to work for your living.'

'I have yet to receive my inheritance, William, as well you know, and I can't possibly go on living with you and Beth indefinitely. No, I have made up my mind to do this.' She raised her hand to silence Beth as she was about to protest. 'I have to seek temporary employment.' She smiled at the concern clouding Beth's eyes. 'You need not look so worried. Feeling as he does towards me, Lord Stainton might well show me the door.'

'Oh, dear. No good will come of this, I just know it. Have you not considered remarrying, Eve? Several gentlemen have shown considerable interest in you since your arrival in London—all eminently suitable and available.'

A darkness entered Eve's eyes and she shook her head emphatically. 'No, Beth. At this present time marriage is the last thing I want. Marriage to Andrew taught me many things—most of them unpleasant—and I am in no hurry to repeat the experience.'

Beth had always suspected that Eve's marriage had not been happy, but Eve had never spoken of it. 'But what you are doing—you, the most sensible woman I know—alarms me. Had it been anyone other than Lucas Stainton you were to approach for employment, I would not be so concerned.'

Eve laughed brightly. 'Don't be. I have made up my mind. It is the best solution—and only temporary. It will be perfect for me and enable me to keep Estelle close at hand. I also find myself concerned for Lord Stainton's children—they are going to miss Sarah Lacy dreadfully. If their father is still in need of someone to take care of them, I hope to persuade him to consider me for the position.'

Beth frowned and carefully considered her words. 'Well, he is a very proud man and he doesn't have the inclination to make himself liked, which is something we both know. His character has many contradictions and, I suppose, if you are set on going ahead with this madcap scheme, then it's as well you know what you are letting yourself in for.'

Eve frowned. 'You speak in riddles. I don't follow you, Beth.'

'There is another side to the scandal his divorce created. You see, he is a popular figure, but there are drawing rooms where he is admitted, but not welcome—although no one would dare give him the cut direct. At the time of his separation from his wife, some people took her side, saying he was heartless and cruel to divorce the mother of his children.'

'But she left him to live with his brother. Surely he cannot be blamed for that.'

Beth lifted her brows. 'Can't he? You see, some of her friends said he drove her away, that she found it impossible to live with his black moods and that she was afraid of him. Some of the more vicious gossips even went so far as to intimate that he refused to let her see the children.'

'And was this true?'

'This piece of slander was repeated, but never credited,' William was quick to say. 'However, it has been noted that she is estranged from her children. Some regard Lucas Stainton as a cold, frightening, unapproachable individual—and you have accused him of being cold and aloof yourself, Eve. He is an exacting master who demands only the very best from those he employs—at least such was the case before he had to thin out his servants.'

Eve was thoughtful for a moment. 'He does become angry easily, but I believe there is good reason for this. He can't be happy with his situation and because of it he can be just as easily hurt as anyone else. But—did he really deny his wife access to the children?'

'I don't know the truth of it, Eve, but I do know that I shall worry about you if you go to live in his house,' Beth said, reaching out to take Eve's hand.

'You needn't, Beth. I am not afraid of him and I can take care of myself.' Eve gave Beth's quiet, fair-haired attractive husband an enquiring look. 'I believe he's in the process of selling his London house to move to Laurel Court.'

'Yes. I don't believe he has a buyer yet, although it is a fine house and in a prime location, so I have no doubt he will soon have it off his hands.'

'And he is having to sell because of his brother's gambling debts?'

William nodded, reaching for a piece of toast. 'Sadly, Stephen Stainton exhibited a proclivity towards all manner of expensive vices. He gambled all the time—it had nothing to do with having fun, it was an addiction. He lost the astronomical sum of one hundred thousand pounds on one hand of piquet at White's and offered his estate in payment of the enormous debt. Fortunately his brother stepped in and paid it.'

'He could afford to?'

'My word, yes. At that time Lucas Stainton was a wealthy man. He's a brilliant head for business and was making enormous returns on every investment. Unfortunately it wasn't the first time he'd had to bail his brother out, but this almost ruined him.'

Eve felt a stirring of admiration for Lord Stainton. 'Clearing up his brother's mess while said brother was conducting an affair with his wife was definitely a kindness on his part, and I realise I shall have to reassess my opinion of him. He appears to be rather unapproachable and capable of giving the kind of crushing set-downs that make one cringe. Why, when he accused me of being intoxicated at Lady Ellesmere's party, so convincing was his attitude that I thought I might be until I remembered taking Beth's headache powders. It was most humiliating and embarrassing.'

'And I don't suppose you can see what women see in him either,' William teased gently.

'Yes, I can,' she responded laughingly. 'I'll do him the justice to admit he's terribly attractive. What is your opinion of him, William?'

'I like and respect him—I always have. But make no mistake. Whatever that man does, he does on his terms. There isn't a woman alive who wouldn't be impervious to him.'

'There you are, then,' Eve said, laughing lightly. 'You are one of the most sensible people I know, William, so I would believe you above all others.'

Beth smiled. 'Bless you for that, Eve, and I do agree with what you say about my husband. Lucas Stainton is one of the most attractive men on the social scene, a man who stands out among his fellow men. Wherever he goes women strive to please him, for despite his cynical attitude—although some more sensible members of the *ton* have remarked that he has good reason to be cynical where women are concerned—there is an aura of virility about him that does dangerous things to their hearts.'

'And how does Lord Stainton react to these adoring females who simper around him? Is there not one among so many who is capable of thawing his cold heart?'

'Not to my knowledge. Oh, he is no more immune to a pretty face than the next man, but since his divorce he has conducted his affairs with absolute discretion. There are those who know him well, like my own William, who say he inspires esteem and respect because he represents a rare specimen of a nobleman *par excellence*. On the other hand, there are those who accuse him of being a brute and intolerant of others, and with his droll replies in conversation and stunned expressions, he makes people feel that they are utterly stupid.'

'Perhaps that's because they are,' Eve murmured with a half-smile. 'As you have just said, Beth, perhaps if they knew him well they would perceive that he is much nicer than he appears.'

Beth looked at her curiously. 'Eve, what is this? You aren't enamoured of him after just three encounters, surely?'

'No,' Eve replied, laughing at the very idea. 'Quite the opposite, in fact. My encounters with Lord Stainton were anything but friendly—in fact, I found the man quite insufferable—but I have seen some of the qualities you speak of and I'm willing to take a chance on him—as he might with me.'

Chapter Three

Mrs Brody had been shown into the drawing room. Lucas would have known it was her the moment he entered, even before his eyes lighted on her. It was the perfume she wore—that was the thing he remembered about her—a subtle smell, hardly noticeable at all, but nevertheless a part of her.

Dressed in open-necked shirt and light grey silk waistcoat, Lucas stood surveying her from beneath frowning dark eyebrows.

For a moment Eve stared at him blankly. He watched her in silence, fixing her with a gaze so hard that she quailed. What a strong presence this English lord had. It filled the room, momentarily distracting her from her reason for being there. His bearing was proud and he was a man of uncertain temperament. Eve wondered what dark secrets lay behind that handsome visage.

Normally she was unimpressed with exceptionally handsome men because they were either vain or after her money, but this man was neither. He was thoughtful, intelligent and thoroughly male, positively emanating masculine sensuality. All of these attributes, combined with the fact that he had two adorable motherless children, made Eve decide that he was in every respect the right man she wished to work for. His words brought her back to reality with a jolt.

'Mrs Brody! You seem to have a propensity for invading my home. What is it this time?' he asked with mock civility. 'A mislaid child or dog, or another dressing down?'

'None of those.' She could hear defiance in her own voice, which she tried to moderate. 'How is Abigail? None the worse for her encounter with the tree, I hope?' she asked in an attempt to ease the situation between them.

'Abigail is very well considering, Mrs Brody.'

'Then I'm relieved to hear it.'

'I suspect you are not here to ask about Abigail. This is a surprise.'

'And not a very pleasant one, I take it, Lord Stainton?'

'That remains to be seen, though I must admit I had not taken you for a lady who indulged in afternoon calls to gentlemen's homes. Does visiting friends not keep you busy? I imagined you to be fully occupied from morning till night on the frivolous pastimes with which you ladies fill your days.'

His tone was caustic and his gaze ironic and Eve longed to tell him to go to the devil, but with everything balanced on this interview, and not wishing to antagonise him until she'd told him the reason for her visit, with great self-control she managed to smile politely.

'As a matter of fact, I prefer to fill my time with more worthwhile pursuits, but I hardly think you would spend your time light-mindedly thinking of what I do with my time, Lord Stainton.'

'Oh, and why is that, Mrs Brody?'

'It is merely an impression you give. The picture I have

of you in my mind is of a man who does not employ himself with useless thoughts of other people.'

'Really. I had no idea you had any picture of me in your mind at all, Mrs Brody. In fact, as we have only seen each other on four occasions, I fail to see how you have had time to form any opinion at all.'

'Oh, I can be charitable when I want to be, Lord Stainton—although I am certainly no saint. Far from it, in fact. My father was for ever telling me that I am not a lady, for I have this awkward habit of arguing when I should be listening and speaking my mind when I should be quiet. Our previous encounters have been unfortunate, and the one at Lady Ellesmere's a misunderstanding. We—do seem to have got off on the wrong foot.'

'Don't we just.'

Not to be put off, she ploughed on. 'I…have given our unfortunate encounters—and your predicament—some thought, Lord Stainton.'

'Indeed!' With narrowed, shuttered eyes focused on her face, he moved closer, looming over her. 'My predicament! And you know all about that, do you?'

'I know that Miss Lacy is to leave your employment very soon and that you must be concerned for your children's future well being.'

The muscles of his face tightened and a hard gleam entered his eyes. 'Prying into my affairs is a tasteless invasion of my privacy, Mrs Brody. I am very grateful for your concern, but I can assure you I don't need it.'

Eve began to feel her spirits drop. 'I see. So you have already found a replacement.'

'No, as a matter of fact I have not—at least not yet.' Lucas was becoming extremely frustrated at the difficulty he was having trying to find a suitable nursemaid. There were plenty of available women well qualified in looking after children, but none of them seemed willing to take on the position of working for the formidable Lord Stainton. Only two had approached him. One had the hard features of a harridan he would never consider letting close to his children, and he was sure there had been the smell of drink about the other.

'Then perhaps I can be of help.'

'You? Mrs Brody, am I supposed to be impressed or flattered by your show of interest in me and my affairs? Dear me, what a persistent busybody you are.'

'I have a proposition to put to you, Lord Stainton,' she went on, ignoring his sarcastic diatribe and looking him straight in the eye, 'a proposition that may be of benefit to us both.'

Resting his hips against a rather splendid walnut desk, the only piece of furniture left in the room, he regarded her coldly. 'I am intrigued.'

Eve wasn't sure how to interpret his tone. She waited for him to ask her to go on, but instead he folded his arms and stared at her, looking oddly impatient. She'd gone over what she wanted to say to him so many times that she was afraid it was going to sound like a well-rehearsed speech, and now the moment had arrived it came out in one sentence.

'I would like to apply for the position as nursemaid to your children.'

'What?' His amazement was genuine and he looked at her incredulously. 'You?'

Eve felt a wave of desperation as she strove for control and to calm her mounting fears. 'As mad and impossible as it seems to you, yes, me.'

'Mrs Brody! Is this your idea of a joke?'

Eve stiffened and lifted her chin. 'A joke? I find nothing amusing, Lord Stainton. I have given the matter a great deal of thought and it's a solution I am sure would suit us both.'

Recovering from the shock her suggestion had caused, Lucas burst out laughing unpleasantly, his reaction telling her that her application was not only ridiculous, but laughingly so. 'You, of all people, want to look after *my* children?'

Eve flushed violently. This arrogant Englishman had a habit of crushing her with shame and anger, but she refused to retreat now she had come so far. 'There is nothing unusual in it, Sir. I like children—indeed, I have one of my own, as you know. I am eminently suitable to be a nursemaid and have the advantage of having met Sophie and Abigail. They are two beautiful girls and I get on with them well.'

'Yes, I saw that in the park,' Lucas was forced to concede, having dwelt on the charming picture that had remained in his mind of Mrs Brody comforting Abigail with soft words as she held her close. 'But—forgive me if I seem somewhat perplexed. You see, I have been led to believe that you are a wealthy woman, Mrs Brody, in which case I am bewildered as to why you should be seeking such lowly employment.'

'I do not consider looking after children to be a lowly occupation, Lord Stainton—quite the opposite, in fact. It is a worthwhile and rewarding profession. It is true that my father was a wealthy man—and as his only child that wealth will pass to me. Unfortunately, there are legal matters to be taken care of in America, and until such time as the money is made available to me, I find myself in—unfortunate circumstances. I also have a daughter to raise. It is a situation that makes it necessary for me to seek employment.'

He looked at her hard, and after a pause he snapped, 'Temporary employment by the sound of it. I am not interested in setting someone on who will see it only as a short-term post, Mrs Brody, someone who will up and leave when she no longer has the need to stay.'

Eve felt hesitant, slightly uncertain, as well she might, in the face of such cold regard. 'Yes—I suppose it would be temporary, but this might be the case with whomever you employ. I can assure you that I would not leave until you had found someone else. Of course, I realise you will need time to consider my proposition.'

He spoke through gritted teeth, his eyes hard. 'I have. It took precisely one second. The answer is no.'

Their eyes locked.

'I see. Won't you at least consider it?'

'There is no question of it.' Biting down visibly on his impatience, he brought himself to his full height. 'I have no place in my house for a woman of volatile temperament and who has no regard for her employer or his children that she would leave without a thought of how it might hurt their tender feelings. That said, the interview is concluded and I think it would be better for us both if you left.'

Eve clenched her hands tightly. When she had come here, her objective had seemed close within her reach, but now was as remote as ever. 'Really, Lord Stainton, my proposition cannot be as dreadful as all that. I would not intentionally do anything to hurt your children. I am offering to look after them, to give you the perfect answer to your dilemma, and you are reacting as though I have suggested I commit murder.'

'As I might, if you remain here a moment longer. So, before you insult me further, Mrs Brody, with any more of your outrageous proposals, I would be grateful if you would leave my house.' He saw the banked fires leaping dangerously into flames in her eyes, and he deliberately threw verbal oil at her. 'I am sure after your time in America you are ignorant of such things as etiquette, but the English place great importance on such matters. Take my advice and learn the rules before you go knocking on any more doors and offering your services. You may get more than you bargained for.'

His volatile anger was tangible, frightening and completely incomprehensible to Eve, who had never met anyone like him. Shocked into stricken paralysis, she stared at him as the insult hit home. Then her temper exploded and she silenced him with the only means available—she slapped him so hard his head jerked sideways, then she took an automatic step back from the ice-cold fury in his eyes.

'How dare you insult me when I came here with nothing but good intentions? I will not tolerate it. Contrary to what you might or might not think of me, sir, I am not a savage. Perhaps my fellow Americans are to you. If so, then that might explain how we managed to beat you in the war we fought for our independence.'

Lucas's jaw tightened and his eyes were glacial. 'Try anything like that again and I will personally throw you out on to the street while your hand is in the air,' he said, icily and evenly. 'I am a survivor, Mrs Brody, and I have an ugly temper when roused. Don't test me any further.'

His tone was implacable and left no room for argument. 'Very well. I'll go. I'm sorry to have inflicted myself on you.' Still fuming, taking a card from her reticule she held it out to him. When he made no move to take it, she slapped it down on the desk, refusing to give up on him or his children just yet. 'However, when you've had time to come to your senses, to calm down and think more rationally, you may see things differently. This is where I am staying—should you change your mind.'

With nothing more than a quick nod, with her head held high and a swish of her skirts she took her leave. As she left the house she understood that his decision was irrevocable.

'Well, what did he say?' Beth asked, having waited impatiently for Eve to get back from Upper Brook Street. 'Did he agree to your application, or did he think you were mad?'

'I'm sure he did think I was mad, Beth. He refused. Absolutely.' In frustration Eve strode past Beth into the drawing room. 'He accused me of being an ignorant American, saying that my proposition was quite outrageous—and a great deal more that I won't offend your sensibilities by repeating. The man's an overpowering, conceited beast.'

'And what did you say?'

'I slapped his face.'

Beth stared at her in shocked disbelief. 'You slapped Lord Stainton?'

'He deserved it.'

Beth watched Eve pace distractedly across the room. 'And no doubt he was furious and asked you to leave.'

'Nothing so genteel, Beth. He didn't ask, he ordered me out.'

Perturbed, Beth sighed. Histrionics weren't in Eve's character and in all their lives she had never seen her friend so put out. After a time she ventured, 'So—that's it, then. You won't be working for Lord Stainton.'

'It doesn't look like it. I doubt he'd even consider taking on a woman who had the temerity to slap his face.'

* * *

For the next two days Lucas immersed himself in the usual duties and matters of business, firmly believing that it was the only way he could put Mrs Brody's visit from his mind, which had unsettled him more than he cared to admit. When Henry Channing arrived, he was grateful for the distraction as he tore his gaze from the letter that had just been delivered.

'Dear Lord! You call this a house, Lucas?' Henry remarked, glancing around the almost empty salon. 'This place looks like a mausoleum—all walls, pillars, statues and space.'

'What do you expect? I've sent most of the furniture and artefacts to be auctioned off.'

Never able to stand still for long, Henry helped himself to a brandy and began to wander about the room. 'There were some rather fine pieces, as I recall. I may even buy some myself.'

'Feel free. There are plenty to choose from at Sotheby's. What brings you here today, Henry? A social call?'

'Of course. You know how I like your company, dear boy. Although,' he said, his face losing its jocular expression and becoming serious, 'I did hear some news at my club in St James's earlier that might be of interest to you—not good news, I hasten to add.' When Lucas gave him his full attention, he said, 'Those two shipping yards on the Thames have gone under, Lucas. I'm sorry.'

Genuine concern for his friend clouded Henry's eyes. They had known each other since their Cambridge days. Henry had always admired Lucas. He was so controlled, so disciplined and determined, forthright and dynamic, driven in everything he put his mind to. As a businessman he was resourceful. He invested his money wisely, buying stock in new inventions and anything he thought promising with confident expectation of future gains. They usually paid off, again and again.

Unfortunately his brother Stephen had not been so clever. Lucas had told him he could not be expected to subsidise him indefinitely, but, unable to curtail his brother's extravagance, he bailed him out every time, selling stock until his own affairs had reached the point of crisis. He went from a man of substance to being branded a bad risk, and when some of his own investments went under, losses he could normally have withstood, he accrued tremendous personal loss.

And now the news that two of the shipping yards he had invested in—practically the last thing he had to hold on to—had closed, was the final straw.

'Good grief, Lucas. You look as if I've just handed you a death sentence.'

'Perhaps you have.'

'What do you mean by that?' Henry realised that this was the worst possible time for Lucas. Suddenly alarm sprang into his eyes. 'I say, you're not—I mean, you won't—'

'What? Shoot myself?' A cynical smile curved Lucas's lips. 'Nothing so easy. I have my daughters to consider. Their mother may have deserted them, but I will not.' Looking down at the letter in his hand, he became thoughtful.

'What is it about that letter that seems to hold your interest, Lucas?'

'I'm not sure. It's just arrived from my brother's solicitor along with the deeds to some land in the north-east.'

'I didn't know you owned land in my neck of the woods.'

'I don't. Apparently it's a parcel of land Stephen won off a landowner up in Newcastle—who is now no longer with us.'

'I see. It sounds interesting. As you know, my own family have been making a profit from coal for decades in those parts. What will you do? Sell it? My father might be happy to make you an offer.'

Lucas shook his head. 'I won't sell it, not if there's coal to be got—at least not until I've made some enquiries. I'll contact a mining engineer to have it checked out.' His lips curved in an ironic smile. 'You never know, Henry, it might put me back on the road to recovery.'

'I sincerely hope so, Lucas. You always did find making money easy. I have no doubt at all that you will soon be over this present crisis and back on your feet. I wish you luck, and if you do go up there then my home is at your disposal. In the meantime, are you able to carry on?'

'Not for long—but at the moment my prime concern is finding a new nursemaid for Sophie and Abigail before I leave for Laurel Court.'

'Which is when?'

'As soon as possible. I haven't been to the old place since before Stephen died. Eventually I intend moving there permanently, but first I must go and inspect the place. Lord knows what condition it's in, although any repairs that need doing will have to wait until I'm solvent.'

'I would have thought you'd have no problem getting a nursemaid.'

'So did I, but it's proving to be more difficult than I thought it would be. I've seen several, but none that was suitable—although, perhaps there was one.'

'Then ask her to come again and see how she gets on with the children.'

'Oh, she gets on with them—and they adore her.'

'Then what's the problem? Who is she?'

'Mrs Brody.'

Henry almost choked on his brandy. Uttering a sound of disbelief, he stared at him. '*The* Mrs Brody?' he asked, astounded when Lucas nodded. 'You're jesting, Lucas. You have to be. Tell me the truth.'

'On the contrary, Henry, I am in earnest.' He went on to tell Henry about the American widow's visit.

'But—I thought the two of you were at daggers drawn?'

Lucas shook his head. 'We were, but her application could be of benefit to both of us.' He smiled wryly. 'You might say she could be the answer to all my prayers.'

'But she is an extremely wealthy woman in her own right. Why the devil would a woman like her want to become a hired help?'

Lucas shrugged. 'She has her reasons.'

'And will you take her on?'

'I haven't decided. I confess that after giving her application a great deal of thought—and needing someone to replace Miss Lacy within the week—I am sorely tempted, if not desperate.'

Suddenly his gaze lighted on the card Mrs Brody had put down on his desk. Picking it up, he looked at it for a long hard moment. Her face came to mind. She was certainly attractive enough. Indeed, from the moment he had set eyes on her his baser instincts had been stirred. In fact, he couldn't understand why she could evoke a combustible combination of fury and the desire to know her better in him within minutes of meeting her. Slowly and methodically he began reviewing the American widow's serious proposition, making two lists in his mind—one for accepting her offer and one against. The former won.

* * *

By the time Lucas reached the Seagrove residence and was shown inside, frustration and suspense had twisted every muscle of his body into knots. His voice, demanding to see Mrs Brody, echoed through the house from the hallway, his presence like a strong wind blowing through the quiet rooms, bringing everything that was masculine and loud into the un-ruffled and well-ordered running of the house.

Eve came out of the drawing room to see who the visitor was, and in a flash her tranquillity was swept away. She could feel the very air move forcefully and snap with a restless intensity that Lucas Stainton seemed to discharge. Clad in an immaculately fitting dark-green coat that deepened his swarthy complexion and turned his eyes to the colour of light blue steel, he looked lethally handsome and incredibly alluring.

'Lord Stainton!'

'I would like a word with you, Mrs Brody.'

Lucas strode across the hall and walked straight past her into the drawing room, skirting the hovering servant as if she were not there. 'Leave us.'

His command was peremptory and the servant stepped back in shock. She glanced at Eve, seeking permission to leave, but Eve was not looking at her. Her eyes were fixed on her visitor. When the drawing-room door closed, shaking her head, the usually slow-moving servant slipped away at a faster pace.

'We have to talk,' Lucas said without preamble, striding into the centre of the room where he turned and looked at Eve. 'There are things we have to discuss.'

Eve raised her brows. His arrival indicated that her proposition had pricked his interest, providing her with the opportunity to chip away at his defences. Her spirits were lifted a little. 'We do?'

'Whatever I thought of your audacity to come to my house and offer yourself to look after my children, I should have had the courtesy to listen to you.'

'Yes, you should. It was most ungentlemanly of you to order me out of the house the way you did.'

A wry smile added to his hard features. 'According to your blistering tirade, I haven't done anything to give you the impression that I am a gentleman.'

Eve stared at him, her anger forgotten. 'No, you have not. Are you apologising?'

He looked puzzled for a moment, then he nodded. 'Of course.'

'Then I apologise for slapping you. It was most undignified of me and I should have known better.'

'Do you regret it?'

Eve lifted her brows, eyeing him with an impenitent smile. 'No. You deserved it.'

'You're right,' he admitted, 'but don't push your luck.'

A sudden smile dawned across his face and Eve's heart skipped a beat. Lord Stainton had a smile that could melt an iceberg—when he chose to use it.

'When you had left, I was afraid I might have been too harsh and it was unforgivable of me to ask you to leave so abruptly.'

For a moment Eve was too stunned to speak. 'And now? Are you willing to listen to me and consider seriously my application?' she managed to say in response.

'Yes, I am, but I am a cautious man and there are many aspects to consider.'

She shot a glance at him beneath her lashes, and

because he seemed to be genuinely interested and approachable for the first time, she continued haltingly, 'Before…we go any further, I… would like you to know that I don't usually go around knocking on gentlemen's doors. Yours was the first and will definitely be the last.'

He grinned, his features relaxing. 'I'm relieved to hear it.'

Lucas folded his arms casually across his chest. She was standing with her back to the door, surveying him with a steady gaze. For a moment he was taken aback by the sheer magnetism of her presence. She was dressed in a riding habit of midnight blue velvet, her hair arranged in glossy twists and curls about her well-shaped head that made it look like a beacon of light, and in that room of gentle shades she was a vibrant reminder that life went on.

Hers was a dangerous kind of beauty, for she had the power to touch upon a man's vulnerability with a flash of her dark blue eyes. Holding his gaze with her challenging stare and quietly determined manner, she crossed towards him with a smooth fluid grace and he felt suddenly exposed. He was staring at her, he realised, but he couldn't help himself. He was unsure why he was so quick to anger when he was with her. Perhaps unlike so many other women—excluding Maxine—she refused to be intimidated or impressed by him. Maybe she even disliked him a little. The thought hurt.

Their eyes met, measuring each other up, thoughtfully, calculating, aware of the differences in their backgrounds, but aware, too, of a personal interaction.

'It seems I am in your debt, Mrs Brody, and I apologise for not having thanked you before now.'

'Thanked me? For what?'

'You took care of Miss Lacy when she was feeling

unwell, the day you met in the park, and took the trouble to see her and the children home safely.'

Eve smiled. 'I merely did what any caring citizen would have done.'

'It was a kindness. Thank you. Now, about our last meeting—'

'You were angry and harsh,' she cut in. 'But now you have had time to consider what I proposed, I hope you realise there was some sense in it.'

He nodded. 'What you propose does make sense—even though it would be a temporary arrangement. In that I thank you for being honest with me.'

'That is my way. I come from a proud family with background and tradition, and respectability.' She smiled slightly. 'I do not underestimate your intelligence and knew full well when I went to see you that you wouldn't agree to my proposition outright. Anything you wish to know about me you only have to ask Beth and William Seagrove.'

'I would like you to tell me why you think I should employ you, Mrs Brody, what desirable attributes you possess that makes you so certain you are capable of looking after my daughters.'

'Well, I am intelligent and sensible and I excel at whatever I put my mind to. I am well read and speak French and Latin and a little Greek—and I sew a fine seam.' She smiled, a smile that lit up her eyes. 'I am also good with children, which surely is what you are looking for in the person you employ. I would look forward to getting to know them. They are quite adorable.'

'They are?'

He seemed surprised by her remark, which Eve thought strange. 'Don't you think so?'

'Children are children, Mrs Brody.'

'Not when they are your own.'

He looked at her with narrowed eyes. 'You—know that I am divorced from their mother—that she walked out on both me and her children?'

'Yes, and for what it's worth I am sorry. It—must have been a very difficult time for you.' Her look was one of understanding. 'I am offering you a way out, Lord Stainton, and I promise that if you are willing to admit me into your household, when the time comes for me to leave it will be done in such a way as to cause Sophie and Abigail minimum distress.'

Lucas was studying her with interest. He had seen the smile flicker across her eyes and the expression had caught his full attention. For a moment they considered each other thoughtfully before Eve looked away. He was a very handsome man.

'When can you start?' Lucas asked suddenly.

'Start?'

'Your full-time employment.'

It was said diffidently, but the effect it had on Eve was quite dramatic. Her face, as she stared at her new employer, was young, full of disbelief and a shining hope, showing how much she had wanted this position. 'Why—I—I hadn't thought,' she uttered haltingly, 'but I suppose I could start right away. When is Sarah—Miss Lacy leaving?'

'Two days, so it does not give you much time. Come to the house tomorrow—we will discuss your wages and Miss Lacy will familiarise you with things you need to know. You will have full charge of Sophie and Abigail. I want to leave for my home in Oxfordshire four days hence, so there will be preparations to make. It will be a short visit—time enough for me to assess what needs to be done since I have not visited the estate for some time.'

'And the children?'

'Are to come with me. A jaunt in the country—the country air and all that—will do them good. You, of course, will accompany them.'

'And my daughter?' Eve asked tentatively, realising that she had failed to mention Estelle and that he might consider it inappropriate for the nursemaid's daughter to be in the company of his own. 'As much as I want to look after your children, Lord Stainton, I will not be parted from my daughter.'

'And I would not expect you to be. She can occupy the nursery with Sophie and Abigail. I remember they got on rather well.'

'Yes—yes, they did.'

'Good,' he said, striding to the door, where he turned and looked back at her. 'Good day, Mrs Brody. I shall expect to see you at my house in the morning at ten o'clock.'

Eve arrived at Lord Stainton's house the following morning with Estelle. They were expected and admitted by a footman, who immediately went to inform his lordship of their arrival.

The tap of decisive, familiar footsteps warned Eve of Lord Stainton's approach. Turning quickly, she watched him cross the hall towards her. He smiled, a smile that took her breath away, his pale blue eyes meeting hers.

'I hope I'm not late,' she said hurriedly, nervous now he was her employer.

'You are on time. I always make sure I am punctual for appointments, Mrs Brody, and I expect punctuality in others.' He shot a look at the footman. 'Fetch Mrs Coombs. She can show Mrs Brody what's what.'

'Mrs Coombs is your housekeeper?' Eve enquired, holding Estelle's hand tight.

He nodded. 'She is, although many years ago she was my nurse. At present I employ eight members of staff. Bennet is my butler of long standing, and Mrs Coombs is my housekeeper and cook, with Nelly the kitchen maid. There are two footmen—not forgetting Miss Lacy and my valet. There is also Herbert Shepherd, my carriage driver. He looks after the few horses I have left. When I decided to sell the house I had to let most of the servants go. There was no point in keeping them on. But here's Mrs Coombs,' he said, beckoning the elderly housekeeper who was looking at the new nursemaid with interest.

'Mrs Coombs, this is Mrs Brody, who is to replace Miss Lacy. Be so good as to show her up to the nursery. I'm sure she'd like to see the children and familiarise herself with everything before Miss Lacy leaves us.'

Mrs Brody's name was not unfamiliar to Mrs Coombs. She had heard all about the furore between this young woman and his lordship from Miss Lacy and it had caused much talk and laughter among the meagre staff. She had nothing but admiration for the young lady. There weren't many people who would dare stand up to Lord Stainton, and Mrs Brody had tested both his patience and his temper—which was volatile at the best of times—fearlessly giving as much as she got. Jolly good luck to her, she thought with a pleased little chuckle.

As she entered the nursery, Eve smiled at Sarah, who was looking at her curiously and with great interest. Eve noted again how tired she looked, her young faced strained with anxiety. 'How are you, Sarah? And how's that young man of yours?'

Sarah sighed. 'Glad that we are to be married at last. In truth, I haven't seen much of him—it's so difficult getting time off, you see. I have to arrange it so that Mrs Coombs or Nelly can look after the children, which isn't very often, them both being so busy with chores.'

'But you are to leave tomorrow and I have come to take over. I expect you are surprised to see me here.'

'I am that. Oh, Mrs Brody, I can't tell you how relieved I was when his lordship told me it was you. I feel so much better about going. Sophie and Abigail are so taken with you.'

Going over to a window seat that overlooked the garden, Eve sat down and patted the space beside her. 'You must tell me everything you think I should know, Sarah.'

'I will, although I must say there haven't been any changes in the children's lives since their mother walked out like she did.'

'That must have been a terrible time for the children—and Lord Stainton.'

'Oh, yes, it was. His wife behaved quite wickedly—leaving him for his own brother. She told everyone about her husband's abominable treatment of her as her excuse for walking out, but I never believed any of it. Lord Stainton has always treated me with kindness and I think he is a man of admirable restraint.' Realising she might have been too outspoken, she bit her lip. 'I'm sorry. It's not for me to criticise.'

'Tell me, Sarah, how is Lord Stainton with the children?'

'He—he doesn't take much interest in them, miss—which is a crime when you see how lovely they are. Oh, he comes to the nursery every day to see them and it's plain that he has great affection for them, but he doesn't give much time to his daughters. They adore him, but…'

Eve put her hand gently on Sarah's arm. 'He sees his visits as a duty rather than a pleasure. I think that is what you mean. It's all right, Sarah, I understand. All I can say is that hopefully there will be a change for the better in the future.'

'Oh, Mrs Brody, I do hope so, because him being like he is makes it so much harder for those poor motherless mites. I feel so guilty about leaving them.'

Eve rose, smiling down at Sarah's worried face, wishing she could tell her for certain that everything would be all right. 'Don't worry. I promise I shall take good care of them.'

It was a hectic time as preparations to leave London began in earnest. The children were excited to be going to the country and Eve was looking forward to seeing Laurel Court and to putting London behind her. She informed Beth of what was happening, and she also sent a letter to her solicitor, Mr Barstow, informing him where she could be contacted.

Everyone was relieved when the following day dawned fine and warm. Having completed the packing the night before, Eve had the children fed and dressed and ready for the long journey by nine o'clock prompt. The servants were assembled in the hall and were to follow on in one of the large travelling coaches stacked high with baggage.

Lucas appeared at the specified time. He was to travel on horseback for much of the journey. Eve had seen little of him since taking up her position.

She was glad when they left London behind and the beautiful English countryside slid past the windows. The journey passed relatively calmly. She kept the children occupied by reading them stories and playing games, but after a while the lolling of the coach sent Estelle and Sophie to sleep. The same could not be said for Abigail, who became fractious and tearful, complaining of being hot. No amount of cajoling could pacify her and her crying began to unsettle her sister.

In desperation, Eve called to the driver to stop the coach and climbed out.

'Come on, darling, out you get,' she said, lifting a red-faced Abigail down into the road. 'Good girl.'

'Is something wrong?' A concerned Lucas rode towards her.

Faced with her father's dark countenance peering down at her, Abigail burst into fresh tears. 'I don't want to go back in the coach,' she wailed. 'I—it's too hot and I feel horribly sick.'

'Just take some gulps of fresh air, Abigail, and then you must get back inside,' Eve told her.

'But I don't want to,' she cried, gulping on her tears.

Eve looked up at Lucas. 'It's most unlike her to be difficult. Perhaps you could take her in front of you for a little way.'

Abigail immediately caught on to the suggestion and her little face became alight with hope. Looking up at her father, she raised her arms. 'Papa—can I ride on your horse?'

Eve thought this to be the best solution, but one look at Lucas looking down at Abigail with the suave indifference with which he generally treated his children, and she thought he was about to refuse. However, she was pleasantly surprised when his expression softened and he reached down and hauled the delighted child up on to his horse and settled her in the saddle in front of him. The transformation in Abigail was immediate. A wide, happy smile stretched her pink lips and she giggled happily, her little legs dangling on either side of the horse.

Lucas cocked a dark brow at Eve. 'How I wish I could pacify all the women in my life as easily as I can my youngest daughter.'

Eve responded with a wry smile. 'Perhaps if you didn't go around with a face as black as a thundercloud and barking at everyone like a bear with a sore head all the time, you wouldn't find it such a problem,' she dared to say, amused when she turned away and heard him chuckle softly.

Climbing back inside the coach, she watched him canter on ahead with his precious bundle sandwiched between his arms. They trundled along country lanes, winding onwards at a steady pace, passing charming, sleepy villages and fields where uninterested cattle and sheep grazed.

It was late afternoon and the clouds were gilded with sunshine as they approached their destination after stopping several times to take refreshment and stretch their legs,

Huge wrought-iron gates bearing a family insignia stood half-open and Eve's eyes lighted on a beautiful house at the end of a long curving drive lined with giant elms. She leaned forward to see it better. A park spread out in front of the property and a stream at the base of a gently falling hill was flanked by weeping willows. Lilacs and other flowering shrubs bloomed unhampered and untamed beside giant trees, their soft colours blending together in natural splendour. Beyond was a panoramic view of fields and forests and the gently rolling Chiltern Hills. The whole place had an air of sorry neglect, but this did not detract from its beauty—in fact, in a strange way it enhanced it.

It really was quite the most beautiful place Eve had ever seen. A brief shiver passed along her spine and she experienced a surge of joy when the coach passed through the wide gates and swept along the gently arched driveway to the house. The coaches stopped at the front, the tired horses wearily hanging their heads.

Eve stepped down and stood looking at the house. The breath caught in her throat with a gasp as she stared up at the magnificent edifice with its diamond-paned leaded windows glinting in the sunlight and the soaring roof.

'It really is quite beautiful,' she breathed, oblivious to the way Lucas had paused to look at her and the children's cries of delight on escaping the confines of the chaise.

In that first encounter with Laurel Court, Eve was irrevocably touched by the timeless splendour of the house. She felt helpless in the grip of something she could not name, or escape. As if spellbound, she turned and looked at the lush green acres spread out before her, impressive and heartbreakingly beautiful in its neglect. There was a fresh breeze in her face, warm and soaked with the fragrance of the countryside. She smiled with a feeling of content. It was like nothing she had experienced before and she felt herself ensnared by this lovely old house that seemed to be closing itself around her and claiming her for its own.

She was unaware that Lord Stainton had come to stand beside her until he spoke, his voice soft and warm to her ears.

'The house never changes,' he murmured. 'It smiles, it beckons, it invites and welcomes. I have loved it since I was a child. There is nowhere quite like it.'

'I know what you mean,' Eve answered without turning to look at him. 'I am a stranger here, yet I feel it too. Who could resist it?'

'Who indeed!'

At that moment she had no doubt at all that Laurel Court was part of her destiny, that she belonged here, that she could be happy here. Coming back to awareness, she shook herself, telling herself that these were fanciful thoughts and such things were not possible, that things did not happen like that, but then when a woman was as wealthy as she was, perhaps it was possible to make such things happen.

Chapter Four

From inside the house sounds of bolts being drawn could be heard and then the door swung open and Mr Evans, the caretaker, emerged.

Lucas took him aside and had a word with him and then turned to Eve.

'You will be relieved to know the house has been kept in a state of readiness. Take the children up to the day nursery to settle in.' He glanced at the second coach, which was already being divested of baggage. 'I'm sure Mrs Coombs will know what to do. If there is anything you need, ask Evans.'

Everyone piled into the house. Some of the servants had worked at Laurel Court when the previous Lord Stainton had lived there, and were glad to be back in familiar surroundings.

Eve looked about her in awe. Doing a quick sweep of the cavernous hall, which was filled with warmth and sunlight, she glanced through open doors, seeing the luxury of the rooms beyond. Taking a deep breath, she absorbed the atmosphere of the great house. It seemed alive but dormant, quietly waiting for the return of a family to fill its rooms with the voices and laughter of children, to make it a home again.

The nursery, which had housed generations of Staintons with its connecting bedrooms, was a lovely room; large, light and warm since it faced south. The children immediately began to explore. They were thrilled with the toys they dragged out of boxes and Abigail claimed the rather splendid rocking horse for her own.

Everything was chaotic as fires were lit and baggage unpacked and Mrs Coombs became more and more frustrated as she set about familiarising herself with the layout of the kitchen. Eve was to occupy a room that adjoined the nursery. It was of reasonable size, simply and elegantly furnished, the walls hung with cream silk, patterned with peach and pale green coloured flowers. Eventually things quietened down and the children were fed and all in their beds but too excited to sleep. Eve doubted they would drop off in a hurry.

'Will you tell us a story, Mama?' a bright-eyed Estelle asked, pushing back the covers and kneeling on the bed.

Sophie sat up in her bed and Abigail, not to be left out, copied the other two.

'Get back into bed, Estelle,' Eve ordered gently. 'I think you've had enough excitement for one day.'

'Oh, please, please,' Sophie pleaded. 'Estelle says you tell her a story about a princess who rides on an elephant covered in jewels—and another one about a dragon. Please tell it to us.'

Eve looked at the three expectant faces and relented. 'Very well, but you must promise to go to sleep when I have finished.'

Sitting beside Estelle, she patted the bed and immediately Sophie and Abigail scrambled out of their own and climbed into Estelle's. Eve put her feet up and, resting her back against the bed head, she gathered the children around her. The story had the children enthralled.

This was how Lucas found them when he pushed open the door. The unfamiliar scene in the dimly lit, warm room made him stop short and catch his breath. He had never seen anything more delightful or touching than Mrs Brody's closeness to his daughters, who clearly thought Eve was the best thing to come into their young lives. She had kicked off her shoes and her hair was unbound and rested on her shoulders. Abigail had fallen asleep, but Sophie and Estelle were cuddled up close and listening avidly, their faces flushed and rapt with wonder.

All three were in the circle of Eve's arms as she finished telling them a story about dragons and castles and a knight on a snow white charger rescuing a beautiful damsel. It was a beautiful tableau, one of homeliness and content and something deep and profound stirred within Lucas.

At the end of the story Sophie spoke importantly. 'I like the story about the princess best. I want to be a princess when I grow up and Papa will find me a prince to marry— a handsome prince who is very, very rich with lots of jewels.'

'And an elephant?' Eve asked, her expression as grave as Sophie's pronouncement.

Sophie thought about it for a moment, then said, 'No. He doesn't have to have an elephant. I think it would look silly in London and I don't really want to live in India.'

'Then I think a fine horse would do just as well, don't you—like the snow white charger in the last story?'

She nodded. 'But I still want to be a princess.'

Eve would have laughed, except that she could see that Sophie was deadly serious. 'You can be anything you want to be, Sophie,' she said, lightly kissing her brow, 'and I am sure when the time comes for you to marry, your father will find you the perfect prince.'

Sensing Lord Stainton's presence, she looked up. With his shoulder propped against the door, he was a towering, masculine presence in the children's bedroom. He had shed his neckcloth, but otherwise was dressed in the same clothes he had worn for the journey. He was watching her intently. 'Lord Stainton?' Her voice was quiet.

'I came to say goodnight to the children and to make sure you have settled in.'

'Yes, thank you.'

Sophie and Estelle immediately went to their beds. Gently disentangling a sleeping Abigail's arms from her waist, Eve tried to sit up.

'Here, allow me to put her to bed.' Lucas quickly crossed the room and tenderly lifted the child into his arms.

'Of course. She is your little girl, after all.'

Momentarily their eyes met and then he looked away and carried Abigail to the vacant bed. Pulling the covers over her, he gazed down at the fragile features of his daughter, and for the first time in months he placed a kiss on her soft cheek, inhaling the sweet innocence of her. Sophie, not to be outdone, held out her arms. He went to her and, after tucking her in, kissed her nose.

Sophie gazed up at him adoringly. 'Will you really find me a prince to marry when I grow up,' she whispered, 'just like the one in the story?'

His face had a satisfied look about it and he smiled into

the upturned face of his child. 'If I can find one who is handsome and rich and will love you with his whole heart, then I promise, sweetheart.'

Sophie sighed and, closing her eyes, snuggled beneath the covers, clutching her favourite, a rather battered stuffed cat. 'Thank you,' she murmured sleepily. 'You are the best papa in the whole world.'

Lucas smiled. He loved his children and felt a profound need to protect them both. He was about to turn away when Sophie whispered, 'Don't forget to kiss Estelle goodnight too, will you, Papa?' Without looking at Estelle's mother, Lucas went to her. The little girl was looking up at him shyly, much in awe of the dark, forbidding man. Ruffling her hair, he smiled and gently kissed her brow. 'Goodnight, Estelle. Sleep tight.'

Eve watched him, her throat tight with emotion. She could see that his daughters' need of him as the father they had never really had, the man in their lives to protect them against bad things, was a role he would relish. There were times when she thought he didn't even know his children existed, but now, struck by the various emotions playing over his features, the love reflected in his eyes could not be concealed.

'They are quite exhausted, poor lambs,' she whispered when he came to stand beside her, 'as I am.'

'Then you must go to bed.'

'Yes, but first I must speak to Mrs Coombs about the children's breakfast.'

She accompanied him out on to the landing where, seemingly reluctant to leave her, he fell into step beside her.

'I can see why you love this house,' she said by way of conversation, already feeling very much at home herself.

'I always have. Laurel Court means a great deal to me and it feels good to be back. I have been absent too long.'

Looking at his handsome face, curiosity stirred inside Eve. She didn't want to pry into information Lord Stainton didn't want to offer, but she would like to get him to open up and tell her something about himself.

On the assumption that if she offered personal information about herself, he might be inclined to follow suit, she said, 'Have you ever been to New York?'

'No—never. Have you always lived there?'

'Yes, until my father died. He wasn't ill, he—he just collapsed and died. The doctor said it was his heart. It came as a terrible shock and I felt his loss deeply. Nothing was the same any more. Suddenly the house seemed too quiet and too big—too empty. That was when I decided to come to England.'

'You have no other family?'

'I was an only child. My mother died when I was ten.'

'And you were close to your father?'

'There was no one like him. He was always there for me. He took care of me—and Estelle. When he wasn't working we went everywhere together, and when he wasn't there any more I became uncertain about a lot of things.'

Lucas looked at her with interest. 'I am surprised to hear that. You always come across as being a level-headed, confident young woman who knows her own mind.'

'I do have a soft side, but I am no weak-willed female to be shunted around by fate and circumstance.'

'That is something I found out about you the moment we met,' he said softly, amused by the memory of how he had almost run her down in the park and how angry she had been. 'Tell me about your father. How did he come by his wealth?'

'He was a speculator and financier. He invested money in ideas of other people who had a talent for running businesses.'

'And how did he decide which people he should invest in?'

She shrugged. 'Instinct, I suppose. Whatever it was, he was successful.'

'And your husband? I recall you saying he was killed.'

She wanted to be evasive, but that wasn't possible with his rapier ice-blue gaze pinning her. 'Yes—in New Orleans. We had been married just six months. Later I found I was with child,' she confided, forgetful that she had intended to draw Lucas out and not the reverse.

'I'm sorry. It must have been a difficult time for you, to find yourself a widow at such a young age,' Lucas said, so gently that Eve could hardly believe it was he speaking.

Strangely comforted by the deep resonance in his voice, she studied his hard, sculpted features. With her normal reserve greatly diminished by her memories of Andrew, tipping her head to one side she said softly, 'I was just eighteen when he was killed. You must have lost someone you were close to.'

Before her disappointed gaze, his expression became aloof and she deeply regretted asking the question.

'I was too young to remember my mother. My father was as unapproachable as I am, and my brother didn't give a damn.' He turned to face her and inclined his head slightly. 'I hope you have a comfortable night, Mrs Brody. I'll see you in the morning. Goodnight.'

Over the days that followed their arrival, Eve fell in love with Laurel Court. She saw little of Lord Stainton during those early days. He came to the nursery each afternoon and night, but mostly he was busy riding about the estate seeing what needed to be done after so many years of neglect. As he went about his affairs he smiled little. Clearly his worries were many.

She often drove into the village with the children and sometimes Lord Stainton accompanied them on horseback. She observed how relaxed he had become and that he cut an exceptional figure. He knew most of the local people, calling them by name, and he was the very soul of kindness and consideration. Comments passed reinforced her opinion that Lord Stainton was well liked by all.

It would surprise Eve if she knew how often Lucas's thoughts turned to her. He found as he went about his work on the estate that he anticipated seeing her when he returned to the house. Then it crossed his mind that he was looking for her, looking forward to seeing her. He found himself wondering about her husband, what sort of man would appeal to her.

Good Lord! What was he thinking of?

In spite of his initial reservations about employing her to look after his children, he found himself increasingly drawn to her as the days passed and he got to know her a little better. There were a number of reasons for this. One was that she displayed no hint of disapproval in respect of his own divorced state. In Eve Brody he thought he recognised a kindred spirit, albeit one whose non-conformity had taken a different direction from his. He was also relieved by the fact that she genuinely cared for his children, and in that alone he was thankful.

One day brought an unexpected and unwelcome visitor to Laurel Court. When Lucas walked into the drawing room, the woman who had been his wife and was the mother of his children turned to look at him, the arrogance in her demeanour by no means diminished by the eighteen months they had been apart. Lucas stopped dead, looking at her with the cold, speculating expression of a long-standing opponent.

Beautiful, seductive—Maxine was both these things, but as Lucas eyed her coldly, he wondered not for the first time why he had ever felt attracted to this woman with her pale hair and eyes and her vicious temper. He could still feel the anger and every second of his helpless fury when she had turned her back on him and their children and gone to live with his brother at Laurel Court.

Her voice sounded exactly as he remembered it—forceful and cool. Her gaze slid warily over his tall frame and in her well-remembered deep, throaty voice, with a tight smile on her lips, she said, 'It's been a long time, Lucas.'

'Not long enough,' he snapped. He tore the freezing blast of his gaze from her face and passed a contemptuous glance over her, his face tightening with distaste as he looked at the glittering necklace spread across her swelling breasts above the daring bodice of her ruby-red gown. 'Say what it is you came to say and then get the hell out of my life and stay out.'

Maxine was doing her best to remain steady in the face of what she knew would be a battle. She could see it on Lucas's face and in his eyes, which were as hard as iron. Resentment of her former husband wasn't an unusual emotion for her these days. After putting her through the bitter humiliation of a divorce, she hated him. Slowly she moved towards him, a sneer on her lips. 'Still the same old Lucas, I see—like some black bear waiting to pounce on a poor defenceless creature.'

'Defenceless? You? What do you want, Maxine? If you are here to gloat, then you can get out.'

She didn't flinch. 'Gloat? Nothing could be further from my mind. Since you failed to answer my letters, I realised the only thing left to me was to confront you. I intended going to see you in London, but when I learned you had come here I thought I'd come and take a look at the house in which, it might surprise you to know, I was happy for just a short time. I find myself somewhat financially embarrassed. I've come to ask you for some money, Lucas.'

He smiled thinly. 'Now why doesn't that surprise me,' he sneered. 'You always were greedy, Maxine, the greediest woman I have ever met. For one mad moment I thought you might have come to see our children—although you have probably forgotten you have two daughters.'

'Children,' she scoffed wrathfully. 'Are they still all you care about?' Anger flared in her eyes. 'I have not come here to discuss the children, Lucas, and I will not pretend anything different. I'm sure they are in good health and being well taken care of.'

'The children were never real to you, were they, Maxine? Just burdens you were forced to carry around for nine months, fetters that kept you chained to the house, stopping you doing what you enjoyed doing most— pleasure seeking. May God help them when they are older and discover why their mother walked out on them, that she is a woman without character or decency who thought money and flaunting herself in society was all that counted. Stephen was stupid and short-sighted and you reeled him in just like all the others before him. If he'd had any sense, he'd have kicked you out.'

For a moment Lucas thought he saw hurt or some other

emotion flicker across Maxine's enigmatic face, but it vanished almost as soon as it had appeared. 'The grass was greener—initially. Stephen was fun to be with. His death was—unfortunate.'

'Wasn't it?' he bit back. 'Leaving me with one unholy mess to clear up.'

'For what it's worth, Lucas, I am sorry. I never meant things to turn out like they have.'

'Sorry? I do not settle for apologies for what is unforgivable, Maxine. Try saying you are sorry to our daughters—if you can. I allow you into my house because you are their mother and for no other reason. Isn't it time you moved on with your present lover—Sir Alfred Hutton, I believe—who is not only old enough to be your father, but also penniless, I hear? Perhaps you should go home to your parents. Would they want you back there? Are you not still their precious daughter?'

Her eyes narrowed. 'You know I was never that. My sisters, yes, but not me. Father will not allow me back.'

Lucas raised an eyebrow. 'And can you blame him? The damage your scandalous behaviour brought to the respected Irvine name almost drove him to his grave. You were an adulteress, and when I caught and sought to dispose of you, you decided to hound me to extort money out of me at every turn.'

'Oh, for God's sake, don't drag all that up again. I am the mother of your children. Your treatment of me was harsh, to say the least.'

'You lied, deceived and cheated on me—with my own brother. What did you expect? Forgiveness?'

Maxine scowled at him. 'No, never that, but no one treats me like you did and gets away with it. Forcing me to go through a humiliating divorce, having my friends laugh at me—it is beyond tolerable!'

'You pushed my tolerance beyond all bearing with your faithlessness and your duplicity. You'll get nothing more from me, Maxine.'

Maxine stood white faced, watching him as he turned on his heel and walked away from her. Refusing to be thwarted, she hurried after him into his study.

'You will pay for what you did to me,' she said in desperation to his retreating back. 'Do not think that a divorce will release you from your debt to me.'

He spun round. 'Debt?'

'Oh, yes. You would not have your precious children were it not for me. I mean it, Lucas. You have to give me some money. I am in daily danger of being arrested for debts. It is this dire state of poverty which brings me here. I need it.'

Lucas gave a short hard laugh. 'You are not alone, Maxine. Had you come to see me in London, you would have seen an empty house—and all thanks to that worthless brother of mine, who drank heavily, gambled even more heavily so there was no money left, and seduced my slut of a wife. Why do you think I should give you anything, had I anything left to give, after that?'

Maxine moved ever nearer and thrust her face close to his, her eyes glittering and mean, her words vicious. 'I'll tell you why, Lucas,' she hissed, her voice shaking with suppressed rage. 'So that your brother's bastard won't be raised in poverty. That is why.'

Rendered silent, Lucas looked at her with blind incredulity. 'A child? Stephen fathered a child—with you? For the love of God tell me you are lying,' he demanded, grinding the words between clenched teeth.

'No, I am not lying. The child—a girl—is thriving. I have placed her with a woman who will look after her. Give me some money and I'll leave you alone. You'll never hear from me again.'

'And the child?'

She shrugged. 'I told you. It's being looked after by a good woman. I don't wish the child any harm. I just wish it had never been born. I thought you might like to keep it in the family.' She smirked. 'Your nursery is big enough. One more won't make any difference.'

'You callous, heartless bitch,' he ground out, his eyes alive with some dreadful emotion he was unable to conceal—Maxine felt the need to recoil from the expression she saw in them. 'I am disgusted by your behaviour. You have come here to try to extort money from me and compel me to raise your bastard child as a Stainton. Good God, Maxine, it beggars belief.'

'It is Stephen's child. I swear it.'

'Do you seriously believe that after what you have done I will give you anything? You could have come back to see the children at any time, but you chose not to. And now you come tricked up like a whore hoping to fleece me of money. Well, Maxine, you can go to hell—to the hell in which I have been confined these past two years.'

Maxine backed away from him. 'I can see there's no talking to you when you're in this mood, Lucas.'

'You're damned right there isn't,' he said, his face hard with contempt. 'Now get out, Maxine. And don't come back.'

Her expression was vicious. 'Oh, I shall leave now, but I will come back, Lucas. You see, I know you, Lucas, and you will not rest easy knowing there is a child out there that has Stainton blood in its veins. If you want to know where the child is to be located, then you will find me at Sir Alfred Hutton's house in London. But remember, Lucas, it will cost you. As far as I am concerned, divorce alters nothing between us. I didn't ask for it and I didn't want it. I'm the mother of your children and for that reason I demand recompense.'

Lucas's eyes narrowed dangerously. 'I will not be blackmailed, Maxine. If there is a child, then I shall find it—with or without your help. Now get out.'

When the door had closed behind her, Lucas raked his fingers through his hair. Dear Lord! What a mess. Just when he thought matters couldn't get much worse. And now there was the added burden of another child that Maxine had abandoned as callously as the first two. If the child was Stephen's, then he could not in all decency turn his back on it. But with two children to raise already, his situation was even more dire than it had been before Maxine had arrived at the house. He couldn't raise them on fresh air.

After putting the children to bed, Eve rested in the gathering darkness, listening to the night sounds beyond the open window. Too restless to sleep, fully clothed, she lay on her bed willing her body to relax as she waited for Lord Stainton to return.

She knew his former wife had visited Laurel Court earlier—indeed, the whole house did and could talk of nothing else. When Eve had been mounting the stairs she had heard voices raised in anger coming from the drawing room, and when Maxine had left the house some perverse instinct had drawn her to the window of the nursery, where Sophie and Abigail were happily engrossed in playing with their dolls, blissfully unaware of their mother's visit.

As Eve had watched her carriage disappear along the drive at speed, she felt that in the brief time she had been there, the ugly reality of Lord Stainton's marriage to Maxine had invaded the cosy atmosphere of Laurel Court. A short time later a horse and rider galloped across the park as if he had the devil riding on his tail.

As yet he had not returned and Eve could not rest until he did. It was some time after dark when she heard the weary clop of a horse's hooves on the gravel below. Relieved that Lord Stainton had returned home safely she drifted into a light sleep, to be woken when she heard a loud crash, the sound coming from somewhere downstairs.

Driven by a compulsion to know that her employer was all right and blind to everything but her intention, she left her room and moved silently along the landing and down the stairs. On the bottom step she paused and listened. No one else had been disturbed by the noise. A light shone from beneath the drawing door that was slightly ajar. Trembling with her own apprehension, she moved towards it and, pushing the door open, took a few cautions steps inside.

In the dim light of the room she saw Lord Stainton. He had his back to her. The light fell on his strong, strikingly beautiful hands braced against the mantelpiece. He had discarded his coat, waistcoat and neckcloth and above his biscuit-coloured breeches and top boots, his fine white linen shirt was stretched taut across his powerful shoulders. His head was bowed, his hair tousled, a heavy lock falling over his brow.

Eve might have stood there for a long time without moving if some animal instinct of Lord Stainton's had not made him sense someone's presence.

'Leave,' he snapped harshly.

Eve paused and summoning all her courage, said, 'Lord Stainton?'

At the sound of her voice he turned his head slightly and she saw the stern pride stamped on that lean profile, his jaw as rigid as granite. In agonised silence he looked at her for several seconds, his face preoccupied and stony—he looked like a man in the grip of a nightmare.

'I'm sorry,' she murmured softly, turning away from him. 'I—heard a crash and thought we might have an intruder… I'll leave you. I did not mean to disturb you.'

His head came up and he peered at her. Clothed in a dove grey gown, her hair bound with a ribbon in a single heavy fall down her back, she was like a pale ghost haunting the night.

'Wait,' he said, striding towards her as she turned away. 'Please—don't go. I apologise if I sounded harsh. It's been a long day.'

'And a long ride. I saw you leave,' she explained when he lifted a questioning brow. 'You were a long time coming back.'

His lips twisted in a tight smile. 'Don't tell me you were worried about me, Mrs Brody.'

'I—yes, I suppose I was,' she murmured, an embarrassed flush springing to her cheeks at what Lucas thought to be a touching confession. 'She—your wife must have upset you.'

'Maxine is no longer my wife,' he retorted curtly.

'Yes, I know. I'm sorry if you would rather not talk about this for some reason,' she said, sensitive to his changing mood. 'There's no need to do it.' It was not her place to pry into the personal affairs of this tall, powerful man looming in front of her.

'If I don't talk about it, it's because I find it very unpleasant,' he retorted, rubbing the muscles at the back of his neck. 'Much as I would like to forget that Maxine came here today, unfortunately she has presented me with a situation that has to be dealt with right away, and I have no choice but for us to return to London sooner than I intended.'

Disappointment overwhelmed Eve. She loved being at Laurel Court and had no desire to leave for London just yet, if at all. 'But—is it necessary for the children to leave? We would be perfectly all right here.'

'It is a delicate matter—and I may require the assistance of a woman. In short, you, Mrs Brody. It is a situation that is entirely too vexing and I should not trouble you with it, but suddenly things have become—complicated.'

'Oh?'

'Another child—a two-month-old baby to be precise.'

Eve looked at him closely, noting the worried frown that creased his brow. 'You seem overly concerned about the child. Is it kin to you?'

'It's a girl, and, yes. I believe she is my niece,' he replied tightly. 'If what Maxine told me turns out to be true, the child is Stephen's—my brother's child. She is also a half-sister to my daughters and Maxine has abandoned it in the same callous manner as she did Sophie and Abigail.'

'I see.' Suddenly Eve glimpsed in his eyes the pain of a man deeply wounded by what he saw as his brother's betrayal of his trust. She tried to conceal the shock she felt, unable to understand how a woman could abandon her child, but without success. 'I am not unaware of what went wrong between you and your wife, Lord Stainton. However, it is not my concern. My concern is for the children, and to my mind a two-month-old baby should still be with its mother.'

Lucas's lips curled scornfully. 'Normally that would be the case, but nothing Maxine ever did was normal.'

'No, I'm beginning to realise that. Does she not realise that what she is doing is sheer wickedness?' Eve burst out, unable to conceal her anger at the woman.

'Maxine is aware of that. She simply does not care. I can't fathom what goes on inside that head of hers, what makes her like she is. She was never satisfied. Perhaps it was the frustration of being married to me,' he murmured with a resigned shrug, 'or maybe it's some unknown flaw inherited from her family that has made her like she is. It is a question I have asked myself many times.'

All of a sudden he looked vulnerable—vulnerable and hurt. He was a decent man, Eve knew that now. It was always the decent ones who agonised this way, always the decent ones that suffered.

'It wasn't your fault. Your wife caused a great deal of trouble that beset you and your children. It must have been difficult for you. I can see that. I can also see why you don't have a very high opinion of women.'

'That's not quite true and I apologise if I have given you that impression. It's only Maxine I have an aversion to. God knows where she has placed the child—probably on some lice-infested slag heap in Covent Garden or the like. Heaven knows what diseases it might be exposed to. I cannot leave it there. I have to find the child before it's too late.'

Eve frowned up at him. 'Too late? But—you don't think anything awful could happen to her? She's only a baby.'

'It makes no difference. There are some cruel people out there, Mrs Brody, people who would think nothing to using children for their own disgusting ends.'

She looked at his proud, lean face and she felt as if her

heart would break. The more she saw of him and got to know about him, the more she understood why he was like he was, that the bitter experience of being married to a woman who had callously left him and their children had yielded up this bitter, unpredictable man, with his hard opinion of people and the world at large. His life with his wife and his brother's betrayal had not been a happy one, yet he had got on with it because he had tremendous strength of mind and will. He felt things deeply, but he rarely showed it.

'Then I can understand the need for haste. I would be happy to be of help—if that is what you want.'

Lucas looked down at her. Her face was rosy and lovely and her eyes glowed into his. He was known for a hard man, a stubborn, iron-willed man, but he stood before Eve Brody—his children's nurse—immensely shaken by what Maxine had divulged, and Mrs Brody was making him feel more than he should feel.

'You have helped me already.' He looked down at her for a moment and Eve fancied there was a strange expression on his face she had not seen before, but it was fleeting and soon gone. 'I swear Sophie and Abigail have never been so happy and it is all down to you. Now go to bed. I have inconvenienced you enough by knocking over the table and waking you. Could anything be more disconcerting? We have much to do before we leave in the morning.'

'Yes, yes, I will. Goodnight.'

The following morning, with a small brood of disappointed children who were only placated with promises of an early return to Laurel Court, they went back to London.

Lucas became a man with a mission. He mobilised

himself into finding his brother's child and he was awe inspiring to see in action. From the side lines, Eve watched him at his desk writing letters to anyone who had known his former wife. He would leave the house for hours at a time and arrive back exhausted.

Knowing he needed to keep a cool head for what lay ahead, Lucas did his best to stay calm and in control. It was not like him to get worked up, but the thought that somewhere Stephen's daughter might be at the mercy of some evil woman was almost more than he could bear.

He had to think where Maxine might have taken her, where the most likely place could be. She was devious, black-hearted and clever. He must put his brain to working out how he could find out—the trouble was his mind had been snarled up of late, barely able to function as he had sought a solution to the crisis in his life brought about by his lack of finances, let alone deal with this.

The answer to his dilemma came from the maid who had attended Maxine before she had left Laurel Court. At first the maid was reluctant to speak to him, but, convinced that she was concealing something, he persisted, his questioning becoming more of an interrogation, and by the time he had finished with her, she had told him everything he wanted to know.

She recalled that when Stephen had died Maxine had made enquiries about women who looked after babies when their mothers were indisposed—in other words, unwanted. The woman she had sent her daughter to was in St Giles.

Lucas felt a familiar quickening in his veins when Mrs Brody joined him in the hall. Her pelisse and the dress beneath were charcoal grey and deceptively simple, and a black bonnet covered her hair. A shawl was draped over her arm. He searched her features as she walked towards him and he saw nothing but a deep concern.

'You've found the child?' Eve asked quietly.

'Her name is Alice. Are you quite sure you are willing to come with me?'

'That is why I'm here.'

'I do know that I shouldn't be burdening you with all this.'

'I want to help, and if I am to look after the child then I'd like to start from the beginning.'

Narrowing his eyes, he locked them on hers. 'I must warn you that where we are going will not be pleasant.'

'I can take it. The important thing is the child.'

'I would rather people didn't know anything about this, that my useless first wife is capable of doing anything so vile as to farm her daughter out to a woman who goes by the name of Mrs Unwin. I shudder to think of the conditions she is living in, but I am compelled to do something to remove her from that.'

'And—you are certain it is your brother's child?'

'As certain as I can be. I managed to locate Stephen's valet and one of the maids that attended Maxine when she resided at Laurel Court. Both of them knew of her condition—Stephen, also. Apparently he was looking forward to the birth, but he died six months before Alice was born.'

'That is so very sad. I'm sorry. I—suggest we leave now.'

'I agree. Come.'

In no time at all they were leaving the well-structured world of the gentry in Lucas's carriage for the less wholesome district adjoining Soho and Covent Garden—St Giles. Everyone knew it was an area that was home to some of the most brutal and depraved people in London.

They left the carriage at the entrance to a narrow street, Lucas telling his driver to wait until they returned. Eve's heart was thumping with trepidation as they made their way through the rabbit warren of narrow, stinking alleys, hampered by an assortment of laden handcarts, people and animals.

Lucas had told her that what she would see would not be pleasant—indeed, she knew St Giles was a dreadful, hideous place—but even so she hadn't imagined anything as bad as what she now saw. With the accumulated dirt of years, it was grim. She was disgusted by the filth, appalled by the number of men and women slouched in the sagging doorways, and barefoot, malnourished children with empty eyes playing in the gutters. It was the smell that almost overwhelmed her. It was the smell of poverty, the foul, unacceptable smell of humanity at its lowest level.

Even though she was dressed in her oldest clothes she still felt conspicuous, and Lucas, also dressed in his plainest clothes, attracted as much attention as if he had worn a crown and ermine cloak. A group of women gathered in a doorway gossiping turned to look at him with sharp, suspicious eyes, and the same kind of interest the sight of him always kindled in the eyes of the more well to do.

He stopped to ask directions from a passer-by, who pointed to an alley ahead of them. Hurrying on, they entered the alley, which sloped slightly towards the centre to make a central drain, in which festering rubbish and things unrecognisable lay stagnant. Having the presence of mind to lift her skirts out of the filth, Eve's heart sank lower with each step she took. They seemed to be penetrating into a noisome slum, but when at last they reached the end it opened out into a space with better houses on three sides and they both gave a sigh of relief.

Seeming to know which house to approach, Lucas rapped loudly on the door, stepping forward when it was flung open by a woman dressed noticeably better than those they had seen so far.

'Well?' she asked, crossing her arms over her sagging bosom as she surveyed them, recognising them immediately as gentry but not intimidated by them.

'Mrs Unwin?' Lucas asked curtly.

'Who wants to know?'

Lucas's eyes narrowed and his jaw tightened. 'I am looking for a child and I have reason to believe she is here,' he said, ignoring her question

Mrs Unwin peered at him. There was about him a handsome, eye-catching arrogance and authority that kindled alarm in her and she stepped back. 'I look after a lot of children. Does this child you're looking for have a name?'

'Alice Stainton. I have been sent by the child's mother.'

Mrs Unwin looked at him doubtfully. 'And how am I supposed to know that?'

'You don't.' Raising his cold, glittering eyes to the woman, he said in an ominous voice, 'If you value your living, you will hand the child over to me—the right child, for I have ways of discovering the truth you won't like,' he warned softly.

Hearing the cold voice of authority and looking into eyes that were alight with the brilliance of a demon, Mrs Unwin instinctively knew better than to argue. Before she could say anything else, Lucas pushed her aside and stepped inside. Incensed that he thought he had the right to come barging into her home, uttering angry words of protest she followed after him.

After her came Eve, her nervousness increasing as she emerged from a passage into a dimly lit room. She stopped, rooted to the spot. The room was barely warm, the small fire having difficulty in maintaining the feeble flames. Several pans were hung on nails on the wall at the side of the fireplace, and an unappetising smell leaked from one that was balanced on the bed of embers.

The walls and ceiling were damp, and the floor was beaten earth. A dresser stood against the wall and a battered old armchair was set at an angle beside the fire. In the centre of the room was an old table on which the remnants of a meal on chipped and greasy plates stood. Around it was an assortment of wooden boxes to seat what appeared to be a multitude of children who stood about the room, their faces white and thin. Eyeing the newcomers warily, they moved together to form a protective, anxious circle, and from a box in the corner came a thin wail.

Lucas studied the squalid room from the threshold. His face showed no expression as his gaze swept over the children, while inside him a storm of such proportions raged he felt he might explode with the fierceness of it. 'Where's the child?' he demanded.

'Over there,' Mrs Unwin grudgingly replied, already seeing the weekly money the child's mother sent running out. 'I've taken good care of her, like I told the lady I would. Said she was in difficulties—that she would come and get her or send someone else when more permanent arrangements could be made.'

'I'm sure she did,' Lucas ground out. He could not bear to think of the fate that awaited this child if he did not remove it from this house. Many unwanted babies were left out in the streets to die. Those that survived were put out to parish nurses, most of them gin drinkers, who were known to maim or disfigure them before turning them out to beg by exciting pity. Others by the age of eleven or twelve, already eaten up with disease, were forced into prostitution, which would perhaps be the fate of many of these that were looking at him with hunger and fear in their eyes.

Looking past Lord Stainton, Eve's gaze did a quick sweep of the room. It fell on a box on the floor in a corner. Brushing past him, hesitantly she went towards it and, leaning over, she peered inside the makeshift cradle. The child was a small scrap of a thing. She knew instinctively that this was the child of Lord Stainton's first wife, but whatever its relationship to Lord Stainton, they could not abandon it to the miserable life it would be consigned to here.

'This is the child we are looking for, isn't it?' Eve asked of the woman, thinking there might be other babies in the house and wanting to be quite sure they had the right one.

'That's Alice,' Mrs Unwin replied, nodding.

Reaching into the cradle, Eve picked up what looked like a bundle of rags. As she wrapped it in the shawl she'd had the presence of mind to bring with her, she had no doubt that the child was alive with lice—already she could feel the itching begin on her flesh.

'I've done me best with the bairn,' Mrs Unwin said. 'Although it's not easy with so many mouths to feed under one roof, as you can see. Mothers come and dump their offspring, leaving a bit of money to pay for their keep and promising to come back with more, but that's the last I see of 'em.'

'Then how do you manage to feed them all?' Eve asked, deeply moved by the pathetic faces of the children. 'And why do you agree to take them in? Would the parish not take them?'

Mrs Unwin smiled scornfully at Eve's naïvety. 'The children beg on the streets—some pick pockets, some do better than others and what they get helps feed those that don't. As for the parish—children are a burden. The children you see here may not have enough food in their bellies, but they're not knocked about like some.'

'What will happen to these children, Mrs Unwin?' Eve asked, suspecting that nearly all of them would turn to crime in desperation as they struggled against poverty and the misfortunes of the world.

She shrugged. 'They'll leave, I suppose—like all the rest.'

Eve turned and looked beseechingly at Lucas's stoic features. Reading what she was thinking, he reluctantly delved into his pocket and brought out some loose coins—not a large sum, but more than Mrs Unwin had seen in a year.

'See that they get something to eat,' he said.

Without another word Lucas took Eve's elbow and led her outside.

When they emerged into the light Eve saw that his face was ashen and she thought he was trembling. He was a strong man, but what he had just been through had burdened him and his shoulders were slumped.

'Come,' he said to Eve. 'Let's get out of here. Are you all right carrying the child?'

She nodded, clutching the tiny bundle within her arms, as eager as he was to leave this place behind. With Lucas close by Eve's side, they hurried back the way they had come, and not until they were in the carriage and it lurched forwards did they both breathe a sigh of relief.

Chapter Five

Settling the bundle on her knee and holding it in the crook of her arm, Eve turned back the corner of the shawl and peered inside. What she saw brought a stabbing pain to her heart and tears sprang to her eyes, for the baby was awake, her gaze solemn and steady as she looked straight at her with pale blue eyes surrounded by sweeping black lashes. She was a dear little thing who seemed to sense that she had had a poor beginning and seemed not to know how to raise her voice in protest.

Her eyes held a shadow as though some anticipation of the future, unknown and mysterious, held her fast. Her little face was thin, her skin never having been into contact with water, and her hair, laying in a swirl of flat curls about her skull, was as black as coal. Remembering her own Estelle when she was this age—a bonny, spirited, healthy baby with bright eyes and rounded cheeks and plump limbs of the well fed—a lump came to her throat and her heart turned over with pity.

Leaning back into the corner of the carriage, Lucas studied Mrs Brody's face as she looked down at the child, noting that her high cheek bones were tinted pink, her expression one of melting softness. The longer he looked at her he reluctantly faced the fact that Eve Brody was a far cry from being an ordinary woman. In reality she was intelligent, spontaneous, courageous and naturally sensual. As the sun had penetrated the overhanging roofs of St Giles and he had looked down at her upturned face, he had been astounded to see how beautiful she looked surrounded by all the rot and filth—like a rose on a dung heap. He had been wrong to think of her as a bad-tempered, interfering woman. She was proving to be more unexpected than that.

Raising her head, Eve looked across at Lord Stainton, her eyes shining with unshed tears, surprised to see him staring intently at her. She was prompted to ask him why, but instead she said, 'Who could treat a baby in this way— to discard it as though it were nothing at all? How could anyone be so heartless or so cruel?'

'Maxine. She is a selfish wretch. I never knew how much until today. Is the child all right?'

Eve nodded, smiling down at the beautiful, solemn little person she hardly knew. 'She is malnourished and in desperate need of a bath, but she's beautiful. It's easy to see she's a Stainton.'

'It is?'

'She takes after her Uncle Lucas, with her black hair and light blue eyes. Poor little thing. She's had an awful time of it.'

'God knows what harm it's done her.'

'Possibly not much. They're very resilient, children. All a baby needs is food and warmth—and love, if it's available.' Eve took the baby's small hand in her own. She grabbed at her finger and held on, making a small baby noise that sounded like a gurgle. 'She's going to be strong. Look how she's holding on to my finger.'

Lucas looked, but said nothing.

'Do you intend to keep her with you?'

'What else can I do? There is no decision at all to make. This is Stephen's child, and my own niece—my daughters' sister. I intend to keep all the girls together.'

'What if Alice's mother decides she does want her? What will you do then?'

'After abandoning her other children and now this one, without a trace of compassion or remorse, there isn't a court in the land that would grant her custody. But what of you? The Stainton nursery seems to be increasing at an alarming rate.'

She smiled. 'And you know how much I love children.'

Eve held the little girl up for Lucas to see. She began sucking noisily on her fist. Fixing his gaze on the huge enquiring eyes staring at him out of a pathetically thin little face, a wave of sickness overwhelmed him, not only at the sight of the pathetic child, but because its mother, the woman he had married, had inflicted this on her own flesh and blood, a small defenceless child.

He looked at Eve but said nothing. What could he say? Dear God, he had never been a violent man, but now he felt violent. He hadn't believed in retribution, but now he did. At the first opportunity he would pay Maxine a call, but to begin with he must ask Eve for her silence.

'There is something I must ask of you.'

'What is it?' she asked, making the child comfortable in the crook of her arm.

'Do you think you can keep this to yourself, that you will never mention what happened today?'

'Yes, of course.'

'Not even to Beth Seagrove.'

'No, of course not. I am not given to gossip. I leave that to others.'

'Thank you. I ask you as a great favour to me.'

'But what will you say to the servants when we arrive back at the house? Look at the state the child's in. Questions are bound to be asked.'

'I'll deal with them in turn. I'll also deal with the one who took her to that—that hell hole.'

'It's the child's good fortune you found out where she was. Why did her mother not tell you?'

'Because she thought to blackmail me. She wants money—and a lot of it.' But more than anything else, Maxine had done this for revenge, Lucas thought bitterly.

On reaching the house, Lucas helped Eve out of the carriage, then ran up the steps to the front door, holding it open for her and the child.

'Mrs Coombs,' he called, and from the nether regions of the house the small woman emerged. She was dressed in black except for a snow-white starched frilly lace cap and apron tied about her stout waist.

Mrs Coombs waited. She asked no questions and showed no surprise. It was as though his lordship turned up every day with the nursemaid holding what she assumed was a baby. However, as she took one disapproving look at the soiled hem of Mrs Brody's dress and their boots caked with something quite unmentionable, her expression stiffened with distaste.

Aware of what the housekeeper must be thinking, Eve stepped forward with the child. 'Mrs Coombs, I'm sorry about this. Lord Stainton, please hold the child for a moment.'

Before he could protest, to both Lucas's and Mrs Coombs's amazement, with complete unconcern for the damage the soiled bundle might do to his lordship's jacket, Eve had thrust the child into his arms. A look of consternation flickered across his face and, standing awkwardly, he wrinkled his nose at the stench that rose from the soiled rags, while Eve sat on a chair, and, to Lucas's and Mrs Coombs's astonishment, removed her boots and placed them beside the door. Standing straight in her stocking feet, she looked at Lucas.

'In respect to whoever it is that scrubs the floors, Lord Stainton, I think you should show some consideration and do as I have done. I'll take the little one.' Eve turned to Mrs Coombs and smiled as Lucas sat on the chair Eve had just vacated to remove his boots. 'Will you please heat some water, Mrs Coombs. I am sure you will agree this poor little mite desperately needs a bath and some clean clothes—perhaps some of Miss Abigail's have been put away somewhere.'

Mrs Coombs looked from Eve to Lord Stainton bemusedly.

'Do as Mrs Brody says, Mrs Coombs.'

Mrs Coombs smiled at Eve. 'There's plenty of hot water and I'm sure some of Miss Abigail's baby clothes can be found. I'll go and take a look, shall I?'

'Thank you, but we must hurry. The baby is hungry and I'm afraid I have no idea when she was last fed.'

'I'll see to it. Some fine oatmeal soaked in warm milk should do the trick. Shall we go up to the nursery?'

'If you don't mind, Mrs Coombs, I don't want the baby to come into contact with the other children until after she has had her bath.' She cast the housekeeper a conspiratorial look, which Mrs Coombs understood perfectly.

'There is a room next to the kitchen we can use. It's warm so the child won't be chilled.'

'Mrs Brody.'

As she was about to follow Mrs Coombs, Eve turned to Lord Stainton, unable to suppress a smile when she saw him scratching the back of his head.

'Is there anything else you might need?'

'I think we can manage perfectly well with what we have.'

'If you say so. Meanwhile I'll arrange to have the crib that was used for the children brought down from the attic.'

'Thank you, and after that I would instruct your valet to prepare you a bath. You may find some of Alice's small associates have hopped on to you.'

Amusement touching her gaze, she watched as he slowly absorbed what she said, and when the realisation hit him, his expression was so comical that she laughed.

Eve followed Mrs Coombs through the kitchen and into a laundry room. The housekeeper was a good-natured, middle-aged, bustling sort of a woman. Taking to the baby instantly, she fussed over it like a mother hen, stripping the poor mite and discarding what could only be described as infested rags into a bin to be burned.

'My goodness, what a thin little thing she is!' Mrs Coombs exclaimed, horrified on seeing the thin little body, chafed raw in places.

'She is, isn't she, but I have every faith that in no time at all she will begin to put on weight. Apart from being undernourished, she looks healthy enough.'

'She's staying, then?' Mrs Coombs asked bluntly.

'Yes, I believe so.'

'Then she's going to need a wet nurse.'

Eve looked at her hopefully. 'Do you know where we could find one at such short notice, Mrs Coombs?'

She nodded. 'Leave it with me. Lady Carstairs along the street had to employ a wet nurse, a Mrs Price, since she had no milk to feed her last baby. As far as I know the child is almost weaned, so I might be able to persuade her to come here.'

'It would be a relief if you could.'

Eve carefully lowered the baby into a large bowl of warm water. Her thin little body and cap of ebony curls were soaped and sluiced and Alice seemed to enjoy rather than object to this new experience. Without so much as a whimper she gazed at these two people and about the room, and, as she kicked and flapped her arms, she gurgled and grinned. Afterwards, she was smoothed all over with rose powder and wrapped in a large fluffy towel.

Leaving Mrs Coombs to tidy up, Eve carried Alice up to the nursery where Nelly, the kitchenmaid, had been looking after the three girls in her absence.

The children were mesmerised by the new addition to the nursery and watched wide-eyed as Eve dressed her in some of Abigail's small baby clothes. Mrs Coombs brought some fine oatmeal soaked in warm milk, and the children moved close to watch as Eve slowly spooned it into the baby's mouth. She was hungry and slurped it all up. Then, after being put over Eve's shoulder to be winded, unable to keep her eyes open, sticking her thumb into her rosebud-shaped mouth Alice fell asleep, the curve of her long dark lashes casting faint shadows over her cheeks.

Standing up, Eve hugged the little body close, before placing it in the crib and pulling the covers over her. She stood back and sighed. As yet neither Mrs Coombs—who had disappeared to the kitchen—nor Nelly had asked anything about the child, and Eve had offered no explanation. It was for Lord Stainton to tell them. The three girls were leaning over the crib, unable to take their eyes off the baby. Kneeling between them, Eve smiled warmly and put an arm around each of them.

'She's a lovely baby, isn't she?'

They nodded in unison, causing their curls to bounce about their faces. Their eyes were dreamy, soft and glowing, and Sophie whispered so as not to disturb this wonderful little creature who been thrust into their lives, 'Is she going to stay with us?'

'Would you like her to stay, Sophie?'

'Oh, yes, we all would. She's so pretty.'

'What do they call her?' Abigail asked.

'Alice.'

Sophie smiled. 'That's a pretty name.'

'So it is. And will you and Abigail and Estelle help me to look after her?'

'Oh, yes,' they said in unison.

'Good.' She looked at Nelly, who was tidying the room. 'Stay with them, will you, Nelly. I have to go and speak to Lord Stainton—and then I must take a bath.'

Eve found her employer in his study—a solitary brooding man standing with his shoulder propped against the window, staring out into the street, but seeing nothing. Compassion swelled in her heart as she realised that although he appeared cold and unemotional in front of her, he had come in here to worry in lonely privacy. His very presence dominated the room. Having had a bath and a change of clothes, damp curls clung to his nape and around his face.

Suppressing the urge to go to him, she quietly said, 'Lord Stainton?' He turned and looked at her, his face impassive. He looked tired and Eve could just make out the fine lines beginning to form at the corners of his eyes. She didn't know his exact age but thought him to be thirty or thirty-one, although on the occasions when he smiled he did look younger.

'How is the child?' he asked, pushing himself upright and strolling towards her.

'She's settled and is sleeping soundly. I think that young lady will end up being thoroughly spoiled. Already Sophie and Abigail are her devoted slaves—not to mention Mrs Coombs and Nelly.'

Mrs Coombs chose that moment to bring them some tea. Neither Lucas nor Eve had asked for it—she placed the tray of wafer-thin bone china on the desk.

'Here you are. You'll need a cup of tea, I don't wonder, now the infant's been taken care of—bless her heart. Pretty little thing, too.'

'Thank you, Mrs Coombs,' Lucas said bluntly.

Ignoring the dismissal, Mrs Coombs turned an appraising look on Mrs Brody. 'I should think you'll be wanting a bath and a change of clothes yourself, Mrs Brody.'

'Most certainly, Mrs Coombs. I'll just have a cup of the tea you've so kindly brought and then I'll do just that.'

'Will there be anything else?'

'No, thank you, Mrs Coombs.' Lucas had raised his voice, but his expression was tolerant.

Unperturbed, Mrs Coombs turned her back on him and smiled at Eve. 'He's a proper gentleman is Lord Stainton,' she told her, 'for all his blusterings. He was born yelling as lusty as the best of them and never stopped—and I should know because I delivered him.' On that note, casting Lucas a fond look, she left them alone.

Lucas had looked on with some amusement while he watched Mrs Brody's expression throughout Mrs Coombs's appraisal of him. Having removed her bonnet, her hair seemed to glow with every different shade of red and gold in the sun's rays shining directly on her through the window. He watched her with fascinated interest, amazed by the gracious ease with which she conducted herself and the way she fitted into his household and effortlessly charmed Mrs Coombs.

There was a natural sophistication about her that came from an active mind and a genuine interest in others. He smiled to himself, remembering her courageous penetration into St Giles to assist him in his search for Maxine's child. He had known a few men with true courage in his lifetime, but he had never met a courageous woman until now. She was full of surprises, full of promise, he thought studying her surreptitiously, with beauty moulded into every line of her face.

'Mrs Coombs has obviously taken to you. You should feel honoured. She doesn't take to people easily. No doubt you find her overwhelming,' he said with a short laugh.

Eve liked to hear him laugh, which gave his stern features a tranquil benevolence she had once not thought possible. 'I think she's very nice and she has gone out of her way to make things easy for me—and it is clear she is extremely fond of you.'

'Mrs Coombs says and does as she pleases. She's been here for more years than I care to remember and has the idea that I won't dismiss her because I cannot do without her. And she's right—although she can be quite unmanageable at times.'

Eve poured the tea, placing a cup and saucer on the desk for Lucas, who accepted it with a brisk 'thank you'. Sitting in one of the two padded leather chairs on either side of the desk, the hot tea helped to soothe her.

'Will you be able to manage in the nursery?' Lucas asked, his tone expressing some concern.

'With a baby to take care of I shall need some help. Nelly is all very well, but Mrs Coombs needs her in the kitchen. Would you object if I looked for someone suitable—a girl, perhaps, and a wet nurse for the baby? Mrs Coombs says she knows a woman who might be glad of the position. It would only be for a short time and of very little expense.'

'Since it is you who will have to deal with them, I have no objections. All I require is that they are honest, trustworthy, reliable and hard working.'

'I understand.' On a sigh, with some dismay Eve glanced down at her soiled dress. 'I think I should go,' she said quietly. 'I desperately need to bathe and change my clothes.'

The following morning Eve received a letter from Mr Barstow informing her that she could expect to have access to her inheritance very soon and that he was only awaiting a letter finalising this from her father's solicitor in New York. This forced her to consider seriously what she must do next.

One thing she was sure of, she did not want to abandon her care of Sophie and Abigail and now Alice, but how could she remain working as a hired help when she was an heiress in her own right? Suddenly she had the stirrings of an idea, a faint hope that began to rise. The idea was perhaps ridiculous, and if she had any sense at all she would cast the notion aside without giving it a moment's consideration, but all her feelings were heightened.

The more she thought about it, the more it seemed the only plausible solution. Lord Stainton and his children had been a consistent part in her life for some considerable time. Sophie and Abigail seemed always to have been there. She now wanted them to be there always in the future, too. She only had to think a minute and she could see Laurel Court laid out like a picture, and Lord Stainton's presence there, strong and vital.

Feeling more relaxed and in control of her feelings, she had made her decision and would throw every caution to the wind. She wanted to live at Laurel Court. She wanted to raise Estelle at Laurel Court with Sophie and Abigail and Alice, and now she only needed Lord Stainton to agree. The thought suddenly invigorated her beyond all reason.

Knowing Lord Stainton to be in his study working at his desk, knocking on the door, Eve went in without waiting to be told to. When she looked at his head bent over some papers, a wave of apprehension swept over her. There was a tightness around her throat, a hollow in the pit of her stomach.

'Yes, what is it?' he asked without looking up.

'Lord Stainton, would you spare me a moment? I— there is something I wish to discuss with you.'

Lucas raised his head and wary eyes looked back at her. He pursed his mouth, a dimple playing about his cheek. Noting her lovely eyes, richly lashed under excellently marked eyebrows, and the way in which she looked at him, she suddenly looked so young and defenceless. She seemed uneasy. Clearly something of a serious nature was on her mind.

'Oh? Is it important?'

'Yes—very.'

His eyes brightened a merest fraction as he motioned her to a seat across from him. 'Then you'd better sit down.'

'No,' she said quickly, twisting her hands nervously in front of her. 'I would rather stand, if you don't mind.'

Lucas pushed back his chair and standing up, walked slowly round the desk to stand in front of her. 'As you wish. What is it, Mrs Brody? Is there something wrong with the children?'

'No,' she was quick to assure him. 'It's nothing like that.'

Folding his arms across his chest, he rested his hips against the desk and tilted his head to one side, looking at her intently. 'Then don't you think you'd better get to the point?'

Eve turned her back to him and walked to the window. Looking out, she knew her next words could be the turning point in her life—that it could be for the better or she was about to make a complete fool of herself.

Lucas found himself wondering if she had forgotten he was there. Then at last she turned and looked at him and smiled as if she knew an amusing secret. She had kept him waiting long enough to intrigue him. He had grown tense.

'I have a proposition to put to you, Lord Stainton, a proposition that may be of benefit to us both.'

'Mrs Brody, the last time you had a proposition to put to me it was to apply for the position of nursemaid to my children. What is it this time?'

'Well—I—I would like to ask you, in all humility, to marry me?'

'What?' He was incredulous. The startling pale blue

eyes swept over her face. 'Mrs Brody, I think you must have taken leave of your senses.'

'I assure you, Lord Stainton, I have never been saner.'

'Then it's the strangest marriage proposal I've ever heard. You! Asking me to marry you in all humility? You could not be humble, Mrs Brody, if you tried. You are without a doubt, a most unprincipled, impulsive creature— the most impulsive creature I have ever met.'

Eve straightened up and walked towards him. 'Please have the good sense to take me seriously.'

'I do,' he ground out, angry now and insulted, 'and the answer is no.' It was an instant response. Unconsidered. Automatic. His wife's infidelity and the costly divorce had strengthened him, and the bitterness had left him mistrustful. He had iron in his soul now, something this American woman would know nothing about.

'Whatever you expected to find when you came in here, I am not a charity case, nor am I a beggar or some brokenhearted, jilted husband who is so impoverished that I will grab the offer of a proposal of marriage from a woman in my employ and sink to my knees with gratitude. Why, if it weren't so serious it would be laughable.'

Eve stiffened. 'Laughable? I find nothing amusing to laugh at, Lord Stainton. I have given the matter a great deal of thought and I have decided that it is a solution that would suit us both,' she went on hurriedly before her courage and confidence deserted her. 'I have a lot of money coming to me very soon—money that doesn't risk being lost as a result of a poor harvest. My father had good, sound business sense and affairs that will go on increasing.'

Recovering from the shock her proposal had caused,

Lucas burst out laughing unpleasantly. 'Have you any idea how ridiculous this sounds? I? Marry an American?'

Eve flushed violently and stiffened with indignation. She refused to retreat now she had come so far. 'I was born in England and come from good stock and I am proud of who I am. One might think I am suggesting mingling common stock with blood royal. My blood is as pure as yours, sir, and just as ancient, for my family on my mother's side descends from the English nobility.'

'Really,' he drawled coldly. 'And what happened to this noble line, pray?'

'The title was entailed to the male line and when there were no more males it passed out of the family. If you were to marry me, you will have a secure family environment for your children—which is the most important thing of all—and all the money you want. Come now, you won't be the first Englishman who finds himself down on his luck and required to marry an heiress. I am not ignorant of the fact that in the upper classes large sums of money and extensive estates are involved in such marriages.'

Eve met his eyes. This man was sharp, intelligent and observant. Her thoughts had been guarded as she had spoken so matter of factly, but it occurred to her suddenly now that he understood her far better than she had realised. The thought was not reassuring.

Lucas gazed at her unblinkingly—a sudden interest seemed to appear in his eyes, and then it was gone. 'So, in exchange for my illustrious family name and title, you will bring with you a nice fat dowry.'

'Yes.'

'It cannot be. There are too many differences between us.'

'I don't care about differences. They don't matter. Circumstances have changed all that. Can't you see? I know how you worry about your children's future. I shall take good care of their well being—it will be as if they were my own.'

'But you do that already—and admirably so, so nothing will change there.'

'It will when my inheritance is made available to me, very soon—and then I must leave. I am reluctant to do so, having become extremely fond of Sophie and Abigail. Alice, too, so recently come, will have a place in my heart. When I applied for the position of nursemaid to your children, I told you then that when the time came for me to leave I would do it in such a way as to cause them the minimum distress. If we were to marry, they would suffer no distress. They would be delighted.'

Lucas studied her gravely for a moment and then his mobile mouth curved in a smile. 'I can see you have it all worked out—and you are an extremely attractive woman, Mrs Brody, I grant you that. You also have money and money gives you power. If one has those, one can do anything.'

'It may seem that way, but it is not true. I may have the means to do whatever I please, but, being a woman in a man's world with a child to raise, I do not have the opportunity.'

'So why me? If it is a husband you require, then surely London is full of gentlemen who would prove to be far less trouble than me—although in exchange for your wealth you will obtain a title if I agree to the marriage.'

'Titles are meaningless to me, and the men who come hoping to court me have no opinion whatsoever about my looks. It is my father's money that attracts them to me and nothing else—I know this.'

'Then I am no different from them—an impoverished lord who would be marrying you for your money.'

'That's where you are wrong, Lord Stainton. You see, *I* chose you,' she said, with a little smile in an attempt to lighten the tension. 'That is the difference. I see marriage to you and being able to reside at Laurel Court a good way of investing in my own and Estelle's future happiness. Besides,' she murmured with a little quirk to her lips, 'I would rather face a firing squad than marry any one of the gentlemen who came to offer their suit to me in New York. I am also a good judge of character and I see you as the most needy.'

'Thank you,' he quipped drily. 'Now that remark really does make me feel like the worst kind of charity case.'

'I didn't mean it to sound that way. You should know that I have no intention of returning to America. I wish to settle in England, and I have quite fallen in love with Laurel Court,' she told him with a softening of her features and a glow to her eyes. 'It is very beautiful. The perfect place to raise a family, and Sophie, Abigail and Alice would be stepsisters to my own Estelle.'

'And I would acquire a stepdaughter.'

'Yes, you will, and your children's future will be secure in a settled family environment. I am not naïve regarding my worth, Lord Stainton. Is it not an accepted fact that in England society is full of marriages of convenience and political and financial alliances?'

'It is common—although I am surprised you can be so matter of fact about an issue that is supposed to be the most important event in a woman's life. My world is so very different from yours. We may not be compatible.'

'I'm not overly concerned with compatibility. I have been married once—and so have you.' His expression chilled the moment she referred to his marriage, but, undeterred, she went on. 'I must tell you that I am not used to being idle, so I have no intention of being a full-time lady of leisure. If you do marry me, I shall look forward to playing my part in the restoration of Laurel Court.' She tilted her head and gazed at him enquiringly. 'Do you still intend to sell this house?'

'That is my intention. Unfortunately, Laurel Court, as you will have seen for yourself, has become sadly neglected. It will need some money injected into it right away if it isn't to fall into ruin.'

Already Lucas could feel his pride and self-respect being stripped away bit by agonising bit. When Maxine had left him for Stephen there had been no deliverance from his seared vanity and the wound continued to fester. His peers, who seemed to thrive on scandal and others' misfortunes, had watched with amusement his fall from grace. Meeting their sneers with his head held high, he had projected an artificial image so no one would see his helpless fury, his deep-rooted resentment and sorrow and his immense fears as he had watched Stephen and Maxine squander the Stainton assets until there was nothing left but insurmountable debts.

'Then it would seem my offer is timely. I have received a letter from my solicitor here in London telling me that my inheritance should be made available to me any day now. A bank draft will be handed over to you on the day we marry to enable you to begin restoring the house to its former grandeur right away. If you wish to retrieve any articles of furniture and paintings you sent to the auction, then you can have them returned.'

Turning sharply, Lucas strode away from her, loathing himself for prostituting himself like this, selling himself to this American woman so he could restore his estate and secure his children's future, but their well being and Laurel Court were important to him and he would strive to keep hold of them with his dying breath.

Eve stared at his rigid stance and smiled and said with understanding, 'I do understand how difficult this is for you, Lord Stainton.'

Spinning round, struggling to keep the irritation out of his voice, he said, 'Believe me, Mrs Brody, no part of this dilemma is remotely easy for me. Wealth gives you an advantage over me I don't like, but I know I will have to accept—for the time being at least.'

She tilted her chin up ever so slightly, meeting his eyes squarely. 'Yes, I suppose you will, just like I will have to accept that you want neither my respect nor my kind regard, only to ensure that your children have continued security in their lives—and, of course, my money. However, there will be three conditions you must agree to if you decide to accept my proposal.'

A gleam appeared in Lucas's narrowed eyes. 'Conditions?' he said, deliberately mocking the very idea.

'First you must promise to treat my daughter with kindness and take as much care of her as you do your own children and Alice. She is the most important thing in the world to me and I do not want a union between us to cause her any unhappiness.'

Lucas nodded. 'You have nothing to fear. Estelle is a delightful child. I would not do anything to harm you daughter, Mrs Brody. And the second condition I must adhere to?'

'My daughter must never know of this arrangement between us. I—would be embarrassed if I had to explain how I proposed marriage to you and I doubt she would understand.'

Lucas gave a brusque nod. 'I see no problem with that. And the third condition?' He waited rigidly, not feeling particularly complimented by her insistence that he should promise not to harm her daughter—as if she saw him as some kind of monster. He was even less flattered when she continued.

'You will accept on the grounds the marriage is considered a business arrangement. You need someone to look after your children and financing. I need a home for myself and Estelle and respectability. It will be a marriage in name only—an affair of convenience.'

'I see,' Lucas replied caustically, feeling more humiliated and degraded than he cared to admit. Having listened as she told him of the conditions he would have to agree on, he was fascinated by the rules of conduct that she'd recited with such absolute certainty. 'You appear to have thought of everything.'

'I told you, I've given it a great deal of thought.'

When Lucas next spoke his expression was resolute. 'Then before we go any further, I want to be sure you don't have any illusions about me. I'm telling you this because, if I agree to your proposition, I never want you to look back on our marriage with any kind of regret.'

'Go on,' Eve urged when he paused to let the words sink in.

'By your own admission you are a wealthy woman— and a very capable and attractive one. I am destitute— which is a fact that you already know. I am also arrogant, which you have accused me of being, and I am given to moods, temperamental and difficult to live with.'

Eve tilted her head on one side. 'Are you trying to discourage me, Lord Stainton?'

'Not at all. I am merely pointing out the flaws in my character and trying to establish some ground rules of my own.'

He stepped closer, and Eve almost retreated from those suddenly fierce eyes. But she steeled herself and held her ground before his glare.

'As long as we are totally honest with each other in advance,' he went on, straightening his spine and squaring his broad shoulders, his eyes holding hers in bondage, 'and make sure we have no false illusions or unrealistic expectations, it should not be a problem. However, if we marry on your terms our life will be a whole series of charades and false fronts. Do you really think you will be strong enough to keep it up when we are sharing the same house, living together, being watched day in and day out by all and sundry, including the children?'

'I—would hope so.'

'I'm sure you would—having given it a great deal of thought,' he said, quoting her own words and noting the slight doubtful hesitancy in her reply. 'However,' he said on a softer, more provocative note, 'it would be interesting to see if the arrangement would outlast the testing of the flesh.'

Feeling that he had turned the tables on her, restlessly Eve moved away from his searching eyes. She was becoming less and less sure of her reasons for wanting to marry him. The way it looked, if the marriage did go ahead, the two of them were unlikely to lead a docile life. 'I can see you are a man proud beyond measure, Lord Stainton…'

'Lucas.'

'What?'

'My name is Lucas. Lord Stainton is far too formal in the circumstances.'

'Very well. Lucas. I suppose if it were to be any kind of proper marriage I don't see how I could keep myself apart from it, but ours would not be a bond of marriage, but an arrangement, and I hope you would not bend local ears with matters personal to us.'

'It will not be a temporary arrangement, Mrs Brody…'

'My name is Eve.'

He nodded ever so slightly. 'As I was saying, it would be a permanent arrangement. One divorce is enough for any man, and I have no intention of living the life of a monk. Would you expect me to remain faithful to you?'

'I—I—yes, I would.'

He smiled thinly. 'Then you had better rethink our arrangement, otherwise I may insist on a few conditions of my own.' He turned and strode to the door where he stood and held it open for her, indicating that the interview was over. 'I shall give it serious thought and give you my answer tomorrow.'

'Thank you.'

Making time to consider Eve's proposition, suddenly Lucas remembered how it had been when he had married Maxine. Successful in his business life, he had turned to finding a wife, wanting a beautiful woman by his side, to grace and light up his home, a woman to warm his bed, to fill his arms, a woman to give him children—a son. He had succeeded in all those things except two—the woman he had married and her failure to bear him a son and heir. When he had divorced Maxine he had known that one day, if he was not going to die without an heir, he needed to marry again. The prospect was distasteful, but perhaps it was time that he considered it.

Like a caged tiger he prowled the length of the room, cursing fate and himself. Heiresses were few and far between and the idea of placing himself in the hands of the American widow was anathema to him. But if he agreed to Mrs Brody's proposition, he wouldn't come out of it too badly. It could be the answer to a problem he could see no other way of solving—a means to an end.

Besides, Maxine's visit to Laurel Court and her attempt to blackmail him had left him with a deep feeling of unease. To ensure his children could never be taken from him by his greedy, selfish wife, marrying Mrs Brody would be an excellent way of making sure that they remained with him in a secure and loving family environment.

But for now he was furious at not having the upper hand. He was considering trading his aristocratic lineage for the sake of his children's future security and Mrs Brody's money—a commonly accepted practice, but it made him feel less of a man for doing so.

Chapter Six

The following morning Eve was summoned to the drawing room. With a rustle of skirts and more than a little trepidation, she went in. Lucas spun round from where he was standing by the window and fixed her with his hard gaze.

'You asked to see me,' she said, amazed that she could speak without her voice shaking with nerves. Moving towards him she managed to smile. 'Have you considered my proposition?' she asked without preamble.

'I have.'

She waited for him to continue, the silence scraping against her raw nerves as he stared rigidly at her, his profile harsh, forbidding. She knew he must have thought hard for some way out of marrying her, and she also knew that beneath that tautly controlled façade of his there was a deep anger that he had failed to do so. But she also knew that he must see the sense of what she had proposed, and that it would be beneficial for them both.

'And?' she prompted. 'Have you decided against marrying me?'

'On the contrary,' he said, each word laced with bitter

regret as he felt the noose of matrimony once again tightening inexorably around his neck. 'You will be doing me a great service. I agree to the marriage. The main reason being to secure my children's future security and happiness—the other reason is to ease my present circumstances. I should tell you that my financial embarrassment is only a temporary affair and I anticipate acquiring wealth in the future. I promise in time I shall rectify my circumstances and pay you back every penny borrowed with interest.'

'It is not a loan, Lucas. I am not ignorant of the fact that everything a woman possesses at the time of her marriage belongs to her husband as a matter of common law. I know you will use it wisely.'

'Nevertheless, that is how it will be—a business arrangement. I still have several irons in the fire, so to speak, and in time I foresee them making me financially solvent once more. Unfortunately, the returns will come too late to see me over this present crisis.'

'Then I sincerely hope you acquire some profit from your investments, Lucas, and I am glad I am able to help just now.' Eve's lips curved in a little smile and she did not pursue the matter, for, no matter how hard she argued, Lucas Stainton was a fiercely proud man and would refuse to allow a woman to take on his debt unconditionally.

'Why do you smile?'

'Because I knew when I chose you that I was not mistaken in your character. You are a man of honour, Lucas, and pride, and I admire that. I also trust you. Loan or otherwise, I am well satisfied with the arrangement.'

As he turned and slowly walked away from her, with a slight nod of his head, his eyes became shuttered, his expression thoughtful, inscrutable.

'Is there something wrong?' Eve asked, feeling a small *frisson* of alarm.

'No, nothing is wrong—although you might not see it like that when I tell you that the "arrangement" is not as cut and dried as you would like to think. I too have certain expectations of this marriage. I have a condition of my own that I would insist upon—one that may not meet with your approval. It may even make you consider changing your mind about becoming my wife.'

Feeling suddenly nervous and unsure of herself, Eve swallowed. 'What is that?' she asked, peering at his well-chiselled profile, trying to fathom his mood. 'Tell me.'

Turning to face her, he looked at her long and hard before saying, 'I want an heir, a son to carry on the Stainton name and preside over Laurel Court when I am gone.' His eyes locked on to hers.

Stubbornly Eve shook her head, rejecting his statement. She felt the heat rise to her cheeks with embarrassment at having to repeat one of her own conditions she had put to him on their previous encounter. 'But—I said…'

'I know what you said, that ours would be a marriage in name only, but that is not acceptable to me. Should your feelings toward me border on anything that resembles love, then forget them. Love is a silly, romantic notion that has no place in my life. I don't want to be loved and I have no love to give. I don't need you. I don't need any woman. Give me a son and afterwards you can do whatever you want—within reason, of course. Should you become homesick for America, then you can return there—on an extended visit, if you so wish. You can even set up house on your own here in London. But whatever happens, you will remain married to me—and one thing I will make clear is that I will not tolerate you taking a lover.'

Dumbfounded, Eve stared at him in appalled disbelief. 'Return to America? And if I were to do so, would you permit *our son* to go with me?'

'No. I would expect him to remain with me.'

'And if I decide to set up house on my own?'

'The same would apply.'

Speechless with dismay and horror at that heretofore unthought-of idea that he would come up with something like this, that he had considered everything with the cold and calculating brain of a man who was used to making his own decisions and doing everything his way, Eve simply stared at him, her cheeks flushed, as he casually paced the carpet in front of her.

'I'm sure you understand that it would have to be that way.'

'And what sort of mother do you think that would make me if I agreed to such a preposterous, cruel and completely heartless suggestion? Why, I would be no better than your first wife. A child is a commitment. It needs its mother from the day it is born until it comes of age.'

'I agree absolutely and I would be happy for you to remain with me permanently, but that will be entirely up to you. Who knows? I will endeavour to make myself agreeable to you, in which case you might find being married to me is what you want and have no wish to leave.' He ceased pacing and moved to stand close to her, his penetrating gaze locked on hers once more.

'Moreover,' he continued, 'I shall expect you to grant your favours to me in bed without resentment. In other words,' he finished lightly, 'you will co-operate willingly until you conceive.'

'And if the child is female, what then?'

'We shall continue sharing a bed until I have a son.'

'But—that could take years—or I may never give you a son.'

His eyes narrowed and gleamed with a look that was positively wicked. 'In which case, think of the pleasure we will have—trying.'

Having given little thought to the intimacies of marriage Lucas would be entitled to, Eve's mouth dropped open in disbelief at what she was hearing. 'Have you any idea how cold and heartless your proposition makes you sound?'

Lucas's brows snapped together over ominous light blue eyes. 'Quoting your own words, Eve,' he said, his voice dropping to a low, icy whisper, 'you said that ours would not be a bond of marriage, but an arrangement, and as such that is how I am treating it. It also suits me perfectly.'

What he said was true, and Eve was beginning to regret ever saying those words. He really was discussing the terms of their marriage as he would a business arrangement— cold and without emotion.

'Will you not reconsider that particular condition?' Lucas continued. 'It is ridiculous to expect us to go through married life without carnal knowledge of one another.'

Eve remained silent, not with acquiescence, but she was determined not to let her emotions get entangled with being his wife. She was becoming less and less sure of her reasons for asking him to marry her. The way it looked, the peace and contentment she craved would be beyond her grasp with Lucas as her husband.

'Does the idea of sharing a bed with me strike you as distasteful?' he asked harshly.

'It's what might happen in the bed that worries me,' she replied quietly. Somewhere deep inside she could feel an uneasy stirring of something that had lain dormant for the five years she had been a widow. She often thought about Andrew, whether she realised it or not, and the memories of their union were not pleasant.

She had hoped her union with Lord Stainton would be a union of convenience and that their relationship would be conducted outside the bedroom. The humiliating details of those nights with Andrew came back in painful clarity and she cringed. He had used her as if she were a dumb animal, without feeling or emotion, unworthy of tenderness. It had been an ugly and humiliating thing, and she never wanted to experience anything like it again.

There was always the possibility that because of her memories, she would experience some understandable revulsion when she was again faced with the intimacy shared between man and wife, and if she did react to those intimacies with fright, was the experience Lucas had gained with women enough to be able to handle any problems of that sort? Feeling as vulnerable as a child, she lowered her gaze beneath his close scrutiny that was making her feel uncomfortable.

Lucas's jaw tensed. 'You play the reluctant virgin to the hilt, when both of us know you have no cause. You have been married once—you have a child, so you know what to expect—unless,' he said as a sudden thought struck him, thinking he might have found a chink in her armour-plated skin, 'you found marriage to your first husband so repugnant that you have no wish to repeat the experience.'

The colour in Eve's cheeks deepened. 'No—I—of

course not,' she said, flustered, trying her best to avoid his penetrating gaze. 'It's just that I—I thought you would prefer it if we didn't...'

'What? Make love?' A smile touched the corners of his sensual lips and a gleam entered his eyes. Ever since he had met Eve Brody she had stood up to him coura- geously, defying him to his face. Recalling how harshly he had berated Eve when she had proposed marriage, how she had defiantly set her chin against him and angry pride had blazed in her eyes, now, her lovely face mir- roring her confusion, she looked vulnerable and much younger and she had the innocent appeal of a bewil- dered child.

'What will you do if I say no to your terms?' she asked quietly.

'Turn you down,' he replied bluntly.

'Even though you are quite desperate?'

'Even so.' As he shoved his hands into the pockets of his snug-fitting trousers, one dark brow lifted, knowing what he was about to ask her would challenge her. 'The question is, Eve, how desperate are *you*? Just how desper- ate are you to marry me?'

Impaled on his gaze, Eve stared at him. Perilously close to losing her composure but unable to shake his, she sighed and moved away from him, turning her back as she con- sidered the matter. She had already decided there was more to Lucas Stainton than she had realised. Beneath the hard veneer there was an aloof strength and a powerful charisma that had nothing to do with his good looks or that mocking smile of his that was locked away behind an unbreachable wall. That was his appeal—the challenge. Despite their volatile beginning, Lucas made her want—and probably every woman of his acquaintance—to penetrate that wall, to find the boy he had been.

'Would you consider a compromise?' she murmured at length.

Interest kindled in his narrowed eyes. 'A compromise? I might. Go on. I'm listening.'

'I will agree to your condition, but I ask you to give me time, not to make demands on me immediately.'

Lucas thought about it for a moment. 'How long? One week—two—a month?'

'When—when I am ready,' she said hesitantly. 'When I think the time is right.'

He looked at her hard for a moment and then he nodded. 'Very well—as long as you realise you will eventually become my wife in every sense—and no longer than six months.' His eyes softened. 'You won't find me a cruel husband, Eve, I promise you that.'

With her pride somewhat soothed by that, Eve hesitated and then nodded slightly, noncommittally. 'It's a highly irregular proposition…'

'But not an unreasonable one,' he pointed out.

'No, I don't suppose it is, but all of a sudden I feel that the risk is all one-sided.'

A gleam of amusement lit his eyes. 'Not all. Consider the risk I am taking. I might lose my head completely and become enslaved by you. Then where would I be?'

Eve stared at this cold, dispassionate man before her. He looked so unemotional, so completely self-assured. It seemed impossible that he would want her, or anyone.

A slow smile curved her lips. 'If such a thing were to happen, where would either of us be?'

'Indeed. So what is your answer? Have we reached an agreement that is satisfactory to both of us?'

She nodded. 'Very well, but I will not be manipulated by you, Lucas, for you to dictate what is to become of me and my lovely Estelle.' Tilting her head to one side, she smiled at him softly.

'Then I shall strive not to be a dictatorial husband.'

'Of course you will have to take on more staff,' she said. 'And what will you do about this house? You might like to keep it now.'

'I could take it off the market, I suppose—but not until after we are married.'

Eve raised a brow, meeting his penetrating gaze. 'Just in case something goes wrong to prevent it—that I might withdraw my offer, perhaps?'

'Exactly.'

'I won't,' she told him firmly. 'We have both agreed to the arrangement and I shall not renege on it.'

'I may prove to be a purchase you will regret.'

'Whatever your failings, I doubt they will be different to any other man I may marry, and what good is wealth if one cannot use it to one's advantage?'

'When would you like the ceremony to take place?'

'Whenever you wish? When it is convenient.'

'There is just one more thing we have to discuss. It is usual for two people who are to be married to become engaged first.'

'Oh! I hadn't thought…I suppose you're right. What do you suggest?'

'I have been invited to Lord Gradwell's ball in Piccadilly next week. We will go together.'

'Would you care very much what people might think if

we just went ahead and got married without becoming betrothed first?'

'You're mistaken if you think I give a damn about what other people think, but after being married to a woman who didn't have any principles whatsoever, one thing I have come to realise in the short time we have known each other is that they are important to you. It's only right that we do everything that is proper and that we are seen together in public. To make it official I shall see to it that our betrothal is announced in the papers on the day of the ball so that everyone will be prepared.'

'How will they react, do you think, when they learn you are to marry your children's nurse?' she asked with a teasing smile. 'Do you think there will be a storm of protest from your friends and the rest of society who will think you are marrying beneath you?'

'If they don't already know that you are an American heiress, then they soon will.'

'They must have been terribly confused when I came to work for you. It's not exactly how things are done, is it? It must be a matter of fierce conjecture. I...don't want any fuss, Lucas—about the wedding, I mean.'

'There won't be any. After the ball when everyone has had an edifying look at us together, we will set a date for the ceremony and shortly after that we will leave for Laurel Court with the children. Do you have any objections?'

She smiled. 'Not to the last part.'

He grinned at the enthusiasm that always lit her eyes when Laurel Court was mentioned. 'I knew you wouldn't. So you have no objections to me proceeding with the arrangements without delay?'

'No—none whatsoever, although for propriety's sake I

think Estelle and I should go and live with Beth and William until the wedding.' She frowned, suddenly thoughtful. 'Providing I can sort something out for someone to look after the children.'

'Do you have anyone in mind?'

'Yes, Sarah Lacy.'

'Sarah? Is she not settled in a new position?'

'I don't think so. She wrote and told Mrs Coombs of her marriage, but as yet I don't believe she has taken up any employment. Perhaps she could be persuaded to return.'

'And her husband?'

'Well, that depends. You see, he is head groom on a large estate in Surrey. It is a good position, but I recall Sarah telling me he isn't happy working there. However, he would not want to leave unless it was for a position of equal status and pay.'

'The man would be a fool to do that.'

'Exactly.'

Lucas fixed his penetrating gaze on her face. 'What do you suggest?'

'That—you offer her husband a position here.'

'Make him my head groom, you mean.'

'Well, you don't have one.'

'Because I had to shrink my stable when my circumstances took a turn for the worse, I do not have the need for a head groom—and nor can I afford one.'

'That won't be a problem when we are married.' Eve's expression became earnest. 'Lucas, think how delighted Sophie and Abigail would be to have her back. I've seen Sarah with your children. She loves and understands them and she is a good worker. For your children's sake, please allow me to write to her.'

He nodded. 'Very well. Although you must be prepared for her to refuse. She might not want to come back.'

Eve's smile was one of immense relief. 'Oh, I think she might.' It was going to be overwhelming living with this man and she felt a nervousness at the new responsibilities she would have to take on as his wife. But as she looked into his pale blue eyes, she made a pact with herself to never show him her fears and to encourage his children to love and trust her. 'In the meantime it would be nice if we were to get to know each other a little better before we marry, Lucas. After all, I know very little about you or your family.'

Abruptly Lucas moved to the window. Eve followed him and impulsively laid her hand on his arm.

'Lucas,' she began. He turned his head and looked down at her, his gaze narrowing on her long fingers resting on his arm. 'I sense you don't like talking about your family—or any matters that are of a personal nature, but if we are to marry, then I would like you to feel that you can confide in me.'

Lucas looked down at her expectant face and a small rock tore loose from the wall of indifference he'd erected and maintained against beautiful women since his divorce. His conscience suddenly developed a voice after years of silence on the subject of sexual ethics, and it was disturbed over the true picture he'd just formed of Eve.

At Laurel Court she had told him about her family and her closeness to her father, and he had noted the softness that crept into her voice and the glow that lit her eyes when she spoke of her daughter. As she spoke it had been obvious even to him, who had little knowledge of loving family relations, that Eve had loved her father deeply and was still grieving over his death.

'Why are you staring at me?' she asked.

Lucas was staring at her because she had the deepest blue eyes, the smoothest skin, and the softest, most beautiful mouth of any woman he'd ever known. And if the tender way she had spoken about her daughter was any indication, she also had the softest heart.

'I'm having an attack of conscience,' he said with disgust, 'and I'm trying to deal with it.'

She smiled. 'Is this an unfamiliar occurrence for you?'

'In these circumstances, it's unprecedented,' he said bluntly. 'I realise that you instigated the situation, and I despise myself for taking advantage of your offer.'

'You needn't feel that way,' Eve replied, confused and uneasy and becoming more so by the moment.

'I do, but Maxine's visit and her blackmail attempt has hastened my decision to remarry. It would be a sensible thing to do at this present time.' He suddenly smiled, surprising her. 'I was also thinking that you are really quite charming.'

The unexpected compliment filled Eve with pleasure. 'I hope you continue to think so, but it does concern me that now you have agreed to my proposition—and I to yours,' she said, her cheeks colouring a soft pink, 'you will resent what marriage to me has gained you.'

'Don't. If my children are secure, there will be no resentment.'

'Very well. And now I think I'd best be getting back to the children, otherwise Mrs Coombs will scold me for keeping Nelly from her duties in the kitchen.' She went to the door where she paused and glanced back at him. 'Earlier you said you didn't need anyone. You were wrong about that. Everyone needs someone. They may not know it, but they do.'

* * *

'You know, if you'd asked me to name the last man on earth I would have expected you to marry, it would have been Lucas Stainton,' Beth said, having been told by Eve a week ago and still finding it hard to believe .

Eve and Estelle had returned to live with them at the house on Berkeley Street until her wedding. A delighted Sarah had returned to look after Lord Stainton's children, and Mark, her husband, had been made head groom now circumstances had taken a turn for the better.

'I have to confess that in the beginning I felt exactly the same,' Eve replied as they strolled arm in arm in the garden. 'When I took up the position to care for his children and I went to Laurel Court, everything changed, Beth. Be happy for me, won't you?'

'I am, Eve, and so is William, but I just hope Lord Stainton will make you a good husband. Even though he seems very civilised on the surface, there's a ruthlessness about him, a forcefulness. In business he has developed a reputation—that he stops at nothing when he wants something. At this moment he wants your money, but I can't help worrying about what he will do when he has it.'

'Lucas is convinced that his financial embarrassment is only temporary, Beth, and if he really does have the golden touch in selecting the right ventures to invest his money in, then I am sure he is right.'

'I just hope you know what you're doing is right. You really do wish to marry him, don't you, Eve?'

Seeing Beth's concern for her—which she always gave to others, and was a quirk in her nature that made her the most loyal of friends—Eve was quick to reassure her.

'I would never have suggested it if I didn't. Please don't worry about me, Beth. It is what I wish to do.'

Beth gave a sigh of relief and her countenance brightened. 'I'm so glad. Have you decided how soon you will be married?'

'Not yet, but it won't be long—and nor will it be a grand affair. I want as little fuss as possible and afterwards to disappear to the country.' Seeing an excited, calculating gleam enter Beth's eyes, Eve laughed and hugged her to her. 'I'm perfectly serious, so don't make any plans without my say so.'

Lucas cast an amused glance at Henry and handed him a brandy. 'I assume you have heard the news and are here to take me to task on the subject of my choice of bride, Henry.'

'As a matter of fact, you could have knocked me down with a feather when I heard the rumour that you are to marry your children's American nursemaid, a woman you know practically nothing about—apart from the fact that she is an heiress.'

'As a matter of fact, Eve was born in England and raised in America. So you see, Henry, I do know something about her—and she likes children.'

'After your disastrous marriage to Maxine, I suppose that's a relief. But doesn't it bother you that you will be marrying out of your class? After all, she has been your hired help. The gossips will have a field day and the scandal will be enormous.'

'Personally I don't give a damn what people say, in particular those members of society who believed I was to blame for my divorce from Maxine. What does concern me is if the scandal hurts Eve, but she is strong and I believe will weather the storm, so to speak.'

A thoughtful frown suddenly creased Henry's brow. 'Lucas, I have long passed the point where anything you do surprises me,' he said, but his irritated tone completely denied his philosophical words. 'I have been a detached observer of your marriage to Maxine and your affairs before and after, and because I've always avoided marriage you might think I am inexperienced in dealing with the female mind.'

'What are you getting at, Henry?'

'I have gathered that you are going to marry the delectable Mrs Brody for her money. I find it strange that with half the males in London, rich and poor alike, available to her, she chose you. You are not in love with her nor she with you. So, what is in it for her? What is it that she wants?'

'Security for her and her daughter. She has also become particularly fond of Sophie and Abigail, and I can't tell you what that means to me. She has also fallen in love with Laurel Court.'

'She said that?'

Lucas grinned. 'She didn't have to. You should have seen her face when she saw it for the first time. She was smitten.'

'It's a fine place, there's no denying that.' Henry's eyes narrowed as he regarded his friend. 'You really are going to marry her aren't you, Lucas?'

He nodded and a soft smile curved his lips as he perched his hips on the edge of his desk in a relaxed pose. 'Actually she's quite beautiful and seems very young to have a five-year-old daughter. Like I said, she adores children, which I find quite endearing. I want a son, Henry, an heir to my estate,' he said, making no attempt to conceal the yearning in his voice. 'I intend to work damned hard rebuilding it and I want to see it passed on to the next generation.'

From the moment Henry had heard the rumour that Lucas was to marry Eve Brody, he had been both shocked and surprised—not unpleasantly so, since he considered marriage might be just what Lucas needed at this time. Ever since his divorce from Maxine, Henry had tried from time to time to broach the subject of remarriage, but Lucas was not a man to listen or be reasoned with when in one of his infamous adverse moods—which was most of the time.

'I believe you. You've got yourself a treasure in Mrs Brody—a pile of money and a bride and a mother for your children into the bargain.'

It was the evening of the ball when Lucas and Eve would appear for the first time in public as a betrothed couple. The announcement in the papers had appeared that morning, causing great excitement in the house. Eve had explained to Estelle as best she could that she was going to be married, but the excited little girl was more interested in knowing Sophie and Abigail were to be her stepsisters than in her mother's impending marriage to the formidable Lord Stainton.

Undecided about what to wear, Eve searched through her wardrobe, surveying her fashionable gowns she'd had made on her arrival in London with Beth.

Beth considered them with an experienced, appreciative eye. 'I have to say you have exquisite taste, Eve. You haven't worn any of these, have you?'

'Until now I've had no occasion to wear them.'

'Well, now you have. Let me see,' Beth murmured thoughtfully, completely absorbed in her task of selecting Eve a suitable dress to wear for what Beth considered to be the most important occasion in her friend's life. She was twenty-three, so it had to be something mature yet simple so as not to detract from her youth and her fair skin, and her hair was of such vibrancy that she needed a colour that would throw it into prominence.

They both agreed to discard the creams and pastel shades, finally deciding on a peacock-blue gown that matched the lustre of Eve's eyes and clung to every curve of her slender body. With only an hour to go before Lucas was due to arrive, Beth and Cassie, the maid who had taken care of all Eve's personal needs since she had come to live in the Seagrove residence, began making Eve look presentable.

The high-waisted dress of shot silk had a scooped bodice and the hem was delicately embroidered in a deeper shade of blue and gold thread. When Cassie produced a petticoat, Beth shook her head, determined not to spoil the shape of Eve's figure and the outline of her long slender legs.

Eve considered this to be rather daring, feeling only half-dressed, but Beth obviously knew what she was about so she made no comment.

Reading her thoughts and sensing her unease, Beth smiled. 'There's no shame in showing your beauty, Eve,' she said, standing back and admiring her handiwork. With Cassie's assistance she had managed to transform a beautiful young woman into a magnificent goddess. Her appearance could not be faulted. The dress complimented her lustrous hair, which was caught up at the crown in a mass of thick, glossy curls. A small and elegant gold-feathered headdress, satin slippers and elbow-length gloves which matched her dress completed the effect.

'There, are you not pleased with the way you look, Eve?' Beth asked, standing her before the cheval mirror.

Checking her reflection, Eve's lips parted in pleasure and disbelief. She was unable to believe the transformation. 'You've performed miracles, Beth—you, too, Cassie. I can't believe it's me.'

'Nonsense, you were beautiful to start with, now you look spectacular. You will eclipse every other woman present,' Beth teased gently. 'When you arrive at the ball on Lord Stainton's arm, all heads will turn and conversation cease—and you will be the envy of every female who has ever coveted your betrothed.'

But it wasn't the other women Beth was concerned about. It was Lord Stainton, and she hoped to see if Eve, in all her finery, would have any noticeable effect on the way he looked at her.

From the window in the hall, Beth watched Lord Stainton's shiny black carriage draw up in front of the house. Immediately she went to inform Eve and was surprised to see her coming down the stairs.

'Lord Stainton is here,' Beth announced, her cheeks flushed with excitement.

'I know. I saw him from my bedroom window.' Eve took a deep, fortifying breath, taking the fan Beth handed to her. 'Wish me luck. I'm going to need it to get through tonight. There will be those members of society who will think Lucas is marrying beneath him. But I refuse to let it get to me. It doesn't matter what people think. What matters is that Lucas and I will be married and the children will be in a stable and loving environment.'

'Of course they will and you will be just fine. How I wish we had been invited to watch you make your entrance. The whole of London will be humming with talk of your engagement by now and dying to set eyes on the woman who has managed to snare Lord Stainton.'

'Snare being the appropriate word, Beth, because that's precisely what I have done. As for the gossip—it will be short lived when something else occurs to pique their interest.'

Beth's delighted enthusiasm, which had been increasing all day, was so contagious that Eve couldn't help smiling as she walked towards the door, nor could she suppress the unexplainable joy that surged through her when Lucas was admitted. His flowing crimson-lined evening cloak rested lightly on his shoulders, and his black evening clothes beneath matched his hair and contrasted sharply with his snowy frilled shirt and accentuated the long, lean lines of his body.

Eve noticed again how incredibly piercing his eyes were. It was impossible not to respond to this man—his masculine magnetism dominated the scene.

Lucas looked automatically in Eve's direction, and what he saw caught his breath. The exotic creature in a peacock silk gown and shining hair and high, delicately moulded cheekbones, generous lips and a perfect nose and a warm glow in her deep blue eyes, looked provocative and sensual and he could not take his eyes off her. He could well imagine the *ton*'s reaction when she appeared at Lord Gradwell's ball and he introduced her as his betrothed.

From where she stood, Beth felt a surge of relief and gladness as she observed Lord Stainton's expression. His face was soft as he gazed at Eve, the softness melting away the defiance, the stubbornness and the headstrong, overbearing determination to do and to shape everything to Lucas Stainton's liking. Despite the businesslike arrangement of their marriage, these two had much in common. Hopefully it would work out well for them both.

Without taking his eyes off her face, Lucas took her gloved hands in his own, his eyes gently appraising. 'You look beautiful, Eve,' he said, his voice low.

Eve favoured him with an eye-teasing, twinkling appraisal of her own. 'You look rather splendid yourself, my lord.'

Turning to Beth, Lucas inclined his head and held out his hand to William, who emerged from his study to greet him. They exchanged pleasantries, William and Beth offering their congratulations on their betrothal.

Lucas turned to Eve, placing her gold satin cape that Beth had handed to him over her shoulders. 'Are you ready to leave?'

Eve nodded, then, with solicitous care, he ushered her out to the waiting coach. Caught in the spell of his compelling light blue eyes as he handed her inside, Eve yielded to the temptation to let herself enjoy the evening, which had the promise of enchantment.

When the door had closed, Beth gave a wistful sigh. William placed an arm around her shoulders and drew her close, affectionately placing a light kiss on her cheek.

'Stop worrying about her. She knows what she's doing, and I am confident that she's in good hands.'

'I know you're right, William. I'm just worried that she might lose her heart to Lord Stainton and that she will be deeply hurt in the process.'

'Whatever happens, Beth, it's for them to sort out. Eve is a grown woman who knows her own mind. It is not for us to interfere.'

Eve sat back and relaxed as the carriage lurched into motion. The setting sun trailed its golden hues across the roofs and trees and gave off a warm glow, softly illuminating Lucas's handsome face and making her aware of his casual gaze.

'How is Alice?' she asked. 'Has she settled into the nursery?'

He nodded. 'Without any difficulty—and thriving. Sophie and Abigail adore her.'

'Does she resemble her mother in any way?' Eve dared to ask.

He shook his head, his expression hardening. 'She's more like Stephen.'

'I—do so look forward to seeing the children again. I have made enquiries for a young woman to help Miss Lacy in the nursery. One of Beth's chambermaids has a sister who would like to be considered for the position. Her name is Miriam Clegg. She has worked as a nursemaid, so she is no stranger to children.'

'Then I shall leave it to you. If you think she is suitable, then you can employ her.'

Content to be in his company, Eve hardly noticed when he left his seat to sit beside her. When she turned her head and looked at him, he caught her brief, anxious glance and smiled.

'I have something for you. I would like you to have it before we reach Gradwell House.'

In his hand he held a black velvet box. Opening the clasp, he withdrew a diamond necklace, with one large single-drop diamond in the centre. It was the most beautiful necklace Eve had ever seen. Dangling it through his fingers, he held it up so that it caught the light.

'Do you like this?'

'It is very beautiful.'

'Turn around.'

'What?'

'I said turn around and I will put it on. This necklace is my engagement present to my future wife—to seal our bargain.' Noting how her features stiffened, he smiled apologetically. 'Our betrothal,' he corrected. 'Now turn around.'

Wordlessly Eve turned her back to him and pulled down the neck of her cape. His long fingers on her nape sent tiny tremors down her spine as he fastened the diamond clasp. The single diamond settled just above the creamy flesh swelling invitingly above the low bodice of her gown, feeling cool against her skin. Turning back to him, she fingered the jewel and smiled awkwardly.

'Thank you, Lucas. I've never seen a necklace quite as beautiful.'

'It is a family heirloom,' he explained. 'The necklace was my mother's and my grandmother's before that.'

Eve stared at him, uneasy about receiving a gift that must have sentimental and family value. 'Then you should not have given it to me. I cannot accept it. It should be given to—'

'My wife.'

'I was about to say your eldest daughter, Sophie, when she is of age.'

'Do not deprive me of the pleasure of giving you gifts, Eve. There are other heirlooms to be handed down to both Sophie and Abigail—and it is you they have to thank that they haven't had to be sold to pay my brother's creditors. I want you to have this particular necklace,' he said, lowering his eyes to the single-drop diamond, and Eve was deeply touched that he thought her worthy of such a priceless gift on so short an acquaintance.

'Then what can I say?'

Lucas smiled lazily, having the perfect answer, for with her beautiful face turned towards him, the sweet scent of her and the sensation of her alluring body next to his acted on him like a powerful aphrodisiac. Later, on reflection, he was uncertain what happened next. All he knew was that he desperately wanted to hold her, to feel her lips on his. It never occurred to him to ask himself if this was prudent.

'You—could thank me with a kiss,' he suggested softly.

Her eyebrows rose a fraction and her lips twitched with nervous humour. 'A kiss? Lucas, it seems I must remind you of our arrangement, which we both agreed to and which I hoped you would properly observe, and yet here you are trying to use your subsequent gift to seduce me.'

The expression in his eyes changed for a heartbeat, then darkened again. 'You are to be my wife.' His voice was soft, though his smile was knowingly chiding. Reaching out, he touched her cheek in a careless, intimate gesture, unaware of the inner turmoil his sudden request had brought. 'It is not so unusual for two people who have just become betrothed to seal their pact with a kiss—especially when the groom to be has just presented his bride-to-be with a beautiful diamond necklace.'

Only for a moment did Eve hesitate, a moment in which she recalled the brutal kisses Andrew had forced on her, but for some strange reason she didn't feel any revulsion at all with Lucas. 'Very well, a kiss in exchange for a necklace.'

As she leaned towards him, her eyes focused on his mouth, on his sensuous and slightly parted lips. A curious sharp thrill ran through her as the force to her senses seemed to ignite. He was watching her, silently challenging, his eyes alert above the faintly smiling mouth, and she promptly forgot her reasons for marrying him.

She shook herself, willing herself not to give in so easily to the pull of his seduction and lean, hard body. Self-consciously she pressed a kiss on his smooth, freshly shaven cheek, the smell of his cologne sharp and pleasant. Sitting back, she looked at his scowling countenance.

Tilting her head to one side, coquettishly teasing, she asked, 'What's wrong? Wasn't that what you're used to?'

'Your kiss was pathetic, Mrs Brody,' he reproached, his gaze on her mouth. 'I'm sure you can do better than that.' He ran his thumb along her lips, the touch warm and soft, and Eve stopped breathing in anticipation and fear of the kiss she knew he would give her.

'What are you doing?' she whispered, seeing something primitive and dangerous flare in his eyes. Her voice was unsteady and she wondered if he could hear her heart beating with trepidation.

'I'm going to kiss you as you should be kissed,' he answered, placing his hands on either side of her face. 'And, please, no protests,' he murmured as he felt her try to draw away from him.

Before Eve knew what was happening he had pulled her close and taken her lips with sudden, demanding insistence in a hot, hard kiss that stunned her into frightened immobility. She tried to break free, but his strong hands held her fast, and before she knew what was happening, heat ran down her spine, warming her in delicious places she was certain she could not tell him about.

It was a hot, deep, plundering kiss and he kissed her with a sure expertise, his lips moving on hers with hungry ardour. Eve was powerless to resist and she found herself wondering whether other women felt so intoxicated, so overwhelmed by his attentions. Dear Lord, let them reach their destination soon, otherwise she didn't care to think what liberties he might take with her on the carriage seat.

It was one thing to be attracted to the man she had proposed to and insist on a temporary arrangement of abstinence—to admit she was attracted to him would be as good as announcing that the arrangement they had made was null and void and allow him free rein to do just as he pleased, which was unthinkable to her. A kiss was one thing, but anything of a more intimate nature she could only think of with abhorrence at this present time.

After what seemed like an eternity, Lucas relinquished her lips. Drawing a long, audible breath, he sat back against the upholstery. Soft and flushed and with shining eyes, Eve stared at him.

'I apologise,' he murmured. 'I should not have done that. It was a mistake.'

'One you regret?'

'Not in the slightest. And you?'

She shook her head. 'No, but our arrangement still stands. The kiss was in payment for this beautiful necklace,' she said, gently fingering the shining jewels, 'and nothing more. Besides, I was in no danger of being seduced,' she said assuredly.

Lazy mockery lit his eyes. 'And you are sure about that, are you?'

Eve wasn't at all sure and she tried desperately to control her raging emotions and match his casual mood. 'Absolutely.'

'Then I suggest you remove that appealing look from your eyes and move away from me before I am tempted to show you how wrong you are.'

Eve slid farther away from him and glanced out of the window. She smiled, seeing they were approaching Piccadilly. 'I'm afraid not. We're almost there.'

His mouth curved in a wicked smile. 'I could instruct Shepherd to drive on by.'

'I don't think so. Think how disappointed the *ton* would be if we failed to appear.'

'At least it would give them something to gossip about.'

He sighed and relaxed into the corner of the carriage. His eyes moved over her with unhidden masculine appreciation. Pride and ownership were evident in his possessive gaze and Eve's stomach clenched. He had never looked at her like this before—as if she were some tasty tit-bit he was planning to devour at his leisure.

'You know, Eve, you have the most disconcerting ability to look and act like a termagant one moment and an incredibly alluring and vulnerable young woman the next.'

'Thank you,' she said uncertainly. 'At least I think so. Was that meant to be a compliment?'

'It was,' he assured her. 'But perhaps it did not come out as I intended. I shall be more careful the next time.'

Eve was touched by his indication that he intended to try to change to please her, but she doubted his decision to do so would outlast the night.

In no time at all their equipage joined a steady stream of dignified carriages disposing only the cream of London society at the splendid portals of Lord Gradwell's mansion. The evening light was suffused evenly with gold and peach and pale blue, the trees dark splashes of colour. Eve sat forward in the seat, immediately tense and nervous. Lucas caught her brief, anxious glance and reached out to take hold of her hand.

'Don't be nervous. You'll likely set them all agog,' he said softly.

A smile wavered on her lips. 'I sincerely hope not. I'm not one for parading myself. I hope to remain as inconspicuous as possible—preferably in a corner and behind curtains.' He laughed softly and she watched as he brought her fingers to his lips to kiss their tips slowly. Even though she was wearing gloves the gentleness of his gesture did strange things to her heart and stirred a bittersweet yearning which she instantly quenched. His gaze softly caressed the delicate visage.

'That will never do. I think we'd better go in before I really do decide to forgo the ball and instruct Shepherd to drive on by.'

Eve waited as he stepped lightly to the ground, then he turned back, offering up a hand. Though any contact with him sent the blood racing through her veins, she accepted his assistance to the door of the mansion. Within the large and impressive hall, he removed his cloak and drew the cape from her shoulders, handing them to a footman. Taking her hand, Lucas led her in the direction of the ballroom. Long French windows were thrown open to the evening air and spacious gardens, where small lights had been hung and twinkled in the trees.

In the entrance the major-domo stepped ahead of them and decorously announced them. Two hundred men and women dressed in silks and satins and with jewels glittering in the light of the chandeliers turned to look. There had been much talk of Lord Stainton's betrothal and speculation about his intended. Quizzing glasses were raised by guests anxious to appease their curiosity about this woman who had been in his employ and managed to capture the cool, cynical and unapproachable Lord Stainton, and curiosity was matched by envy from the women and open admiration from the men.

Eve saw a sea of faces. She wondered if it was her imagination or did the babble of conversation from the guests already assembled in the huge white-and-gold ballroom really go quiet as she appeared on Lucas's arm? Lucas allowed himself a look of approval at her, his eyes lingering on the auburn curls and lovely features. All the other women paled into insipidness beside her vivid beauty and vitality.

Keeping her proudly and protectively by his side, Lucas strolled nonchalantly into their midst. Eve noted with amusement the number of women that were following his every move, and she couldn't blame them. With his thick black hair, piercing light blue eyes, and tall, athletic physique, Lucas Stainton was magnificent.

Aware of the tension in Eve's body, Lucas bowed his head to her. 'They are all dying of curiosity. Word of our betrothal has spread, as I knew it would. The first rule of social survival at these events is to always present a calm and united front, so smile,' he murmured, 'and enjoy yourself.'

'That's easier said than done,' Eve murmured, but in keeping with that rule, she smiled at him as if there were nothing in the least extraordinary about her arriving conspicuously on the arm of the elusive, devilishly handsome Lucas Stainton, a man who treated her with the possessive familiarity of his betrothed. 'Between us we should be able to put on a show for them.'

Chapter Seven

Every neck in the ballroom craned to see Eve, tall, proud and very lovely, walk beside Lucas. The folds of her gown clung to her slender body, down to her exquisite slippered feet, and her necklace gleamed with prisms of sparkling light.

Impressed and amused by Lucas's supreme indifference to the excited curiosity their appearance was generating, Eve watched as he bowed to acknowledge friends and acquaintances, introducing her to what seemed like hundreds of people. An admiring coterie of young bucks gathered round her, and half-heartedly she wrote their names on her dance card, recognising those who had left their calling card at Berkeley Street when she had come to England in the hope that she would accept their suit.

Lord Gradwell, a widower who seemed in no haste to remarry, was a middle-aged, imposing man with a relaxed congeniality that came from leading a privileged lifestyle and being descended from an illustrious blood line. His parties and balls were always popular and informal, with people clamouring to be invited.

Taking two glasses of sparkling champagne from the

tray of a hovering footman, Lucas handed one to Eve, clinking his glass to hers in a toast.

'To the future, Eve.'

For the benefit of their audience she gave him a dazzling smile. 'To the future,' she murmured, taking a hasty swallow, aware that her hand was shaking slightly. As she met his gaze she thought back to the kiss he had given her. She should never have let that happen. What a foolish, uncharacteristic, impulsive thing for her to do. But it had been such a wonderful kiss—awkward for her as she came into close contact with another man after five years. His mouth had covered hers with casual expertise and increasing demand, and when he had raised his head, ending the kiss, he had stared into her eyes with an unspoken promise of seduction.

Eve's cheeks reddened with embarrassed heat and without warning she knew a moment of blind panic. Somewhere in her mind a voice cried out that she was making a dreadful mistake and that what she was doing was madness, committing herself for the rest of her life to a man she did not love, a man who had told her in no uncertain terms that he didn't want to be loved, that he had no love to give, that he didn't need her and never would.

This was the beginning, and after they had said their vows, there would be no turning back. Lucas said something to her and she looked at him, meeting his gaze, and she wondered if he felt as she did, a sense of being caught up in an implacable destiny, that whatever the future held, they had to endure it together for the rest of their lives.

'I'm sorry, Lucas, I wasn't listening. What did you say?'

'That you look exquisite and are by far the most beautiful woman here tonight.' His eyes flicked about the room, taking note of the men who were eyeing her. He guessed their thoughts were not so different from his own. Decorously he presented his arm. 'Come, people are staring, and I would have this dance before I find you swept away by some overzealous swain.'

He led her forward on his arm and the guests parted to let them through as the musicians struck up a waltz.

Caught up in his arms, that was the moment the chill in Eve's heart and her doubts disappeared and the dance passed in a euphoric dream. She glanced up at Lucas's disciplined, classical face, her features soft and warm with gratitude, and the light blue eyes regarding her from beneath half-lowered lids seemed preoccupied and thoughtful.

'Has anyone ever told you that you are rather gallant and kind hearted?' she said, feeling quite reckless after her fortifying glass of champagne.

'Certainly not,' he replied, pretending offence. 'The general consensus is that I am cold, heartless and ruthless—in fact, I do recall on one occasion a certain lady taking me to task in my own home and accusing me of being an arrogant, inconsiderate, puffed-up lord—oh, and that I have the manners of a barbarian.'

Eve's reply was an irrepressible giggle, knowing full well that she was the lady he was referring to, but pretending ignorance. 'Why, I am aghast at the injustice of that. It is clear to me that you must be the most maligned, misjudged and misunderstood gentleman alive.' The deep blue eyes flashed with puckish humour, and the barest hint of a smile curved her lips to mock him. 'How could anyone accuse you of being anything other than kind, considerate and—sweet?'

He looked stung while trying to bite back a smile. 'Sweet? Sweet is one thing I am not. Ruthless and arrogant, not forgetting the barbarian bit, I can live with—but sweet? Never in a thousand years,' he said, sweeping her across the room in a swirling rhythm that dazzled her and made other couples seem clumsy in comparison.

One only had to look at them to see that they were in accord. In fact, it gave rise to considerable amusement when the cream of fashionable society beheld the formerly aloof, austere Lucas Stainton smiling almost affectionately at his betrothed as he waltzed her around the room.

Aware of the attention they were attracting, Lucas smiled down at Eve's face upturned to his. 'You do realise that the announcement of our betrothal will bring forth invitations from all and sundry, don't you, Eve?'

'It will?'

'Absolutely, so prepare yourself to be invaded. Tomorrow morning the Seagrove household and my own will be awash with calling cards and invitations to this and that.'

Eve wrinkled her nose. 'One of the most dispiriting aspects of my introduction to London society was that I found it an ordeal. The Season that excites so many people, to me resembles an obstacle race of so many events that, to respect the custom, they must be got through and must be dreadfully arduous to the participants. Personally I have found some of the events excruciating and a dreadful bore.'

'New York isn't so much different in the upper echelons of society. Your father must have moved in such circles.'

'Yes, he did and I accompanied him on occasion, but on the whole we lived quietly. Before I came to England I must confess that I tried to familiarise myself with everything English by immersing myself in a study of your newspapers in order that I might talk about current affairs and British politics—with William being attached to the Foreign Office I thought it inevitable that I would meet politicians, you see.'

'And have you? Met many politicians, I mean.'

'Some, and all they seem to want to talk about is America. I even spent hours poring over whatever I could find about the English peerage in an attempt to familiarise myself with the aristocracy, but I found it so complicated and confusing that in the end I gave up.'

Transfixed, Lucas stared down at her sagely, strangely moved as he listened to her confession of how she had tried to learn about everything English before leaving America. 'That was a very wise thing to do, since the English aristocracy is confusing to even the best people—even to the aristocracy.'

'Even you?' she asked, gazing into his unfathomable light blue eyes, seeing the cynicism lurking in their depths.

'Even me.'

'Thank goodness. Then we shall make a pact never to discuss that particular topic when we are wed.'

His eyes gleamed with amusement. 'I promise I shall make a note of it,' he said laughingly, 'and the subject will never pass my lips.'

They spent the rest of the dance talking about anything and everything, and for his part Lucas confirmed what he already suspected about Eve—she was extremely well read, intelligent and witty, and yet there was a naïvety about her that he found appealing.

The waltz ended all too soon and Lucas was about to take her on to the floor for the next dance when an elaborately attired young dandy by the name of Sir John Forsyth appeared and bowed before her.

'Excuse me, Lord Stainton, but this is my dance, I believe,' and before Lucas could object Eve had been whisked away from him.

Momentarily thwarted, leaning his shoulder against a pillar, Lucas was content to watch her swirling about the floor in a lively country dance. Beside him Henry Channing observed him with amusement.

'Your future bride is proving to be a popular distraction, Lucas. Congratulations, by the way. I read it in the *Times* in case you're wondering.'

'Nothing like making it official, Henry,' Lucas replied drily, without taking his eyes off Eve.

'And you have come to Lord Gradwell's ball to celebrate.'

Lucas smiled sardonically. 'Marriage is not high on my list of reasons to celebrate. You should know that.' He frowned with disapproval when the dance ended and Eve remained on the dance floor to partner the same young man in another country dance. 'I'll be damned if she isn't going to dance with Forsyth again. Clearly she is ignorant of the impropriety of dancing with the same gentleman twice.'

'And you are beginning to sound like a jealous beau,' Henry remarked, slanting him an amused look.

Lucas ignored him.

When Eve finally left the dance floor, seeking sanctuary to catch her breath, she fled to the designated ladies' room and closed the door. After freshening up and checking her appearance in the mirror, satisfied that she looked poised and relaxed, she was about to leave when she heard two women in the room adjacent.

'Who would have thought Lord Stainton would be here tonight,' one voice remarked, 'and just as handsome as ever, don't you agree?'

Eve paused. She hated eavesdropping, but she felt compelled to wait to hear what would come next.

'He certainly is. Pity he's penniless though. I haven't seen anything cause quite a stir as his betrothal since his scandalous divorce from Maxine. No one thought Lord Stainton would ever marry again and I was positively shocked when Mama read it out of the *Times* this morning—and to an American of all people, who has been nursemaid to his children. Of course Mama has always said he never got over Maxine.'

'Then he shouldn't have divorced her. Poor Maxine. He made her look an utter fool. The humiliation she suffered was quite dreadful. She never thought he would go through with the divorce.'

'What could he do? Continue turning a blind eye to her affairs? I have no sympathy for her—despite what your mama says. Lord Stainton's too proud to be branded a cuckold.'

'Nevertheless, the divorce was granted pretty quickly— often it can take years.'

'That's because Maxine's adultery was proven without any difficulty and he refused to bring charges against his own brother. He was the innocent party and there is no reason why he can't remarry.'

'I suppose not, and the American woman is stunning, don't you think, despite her unfashionable red hair?'

'Perhaps next week red hair will be all the rage. Fashions come and go. She's very rich, too, by all accounts—although what she was doing caring for his children is a mystery, but I'd wager her money is what attracted him to her.'

'I'm sure you're right, although there was no mistaking the gleam in his eye when he looked at her—and the look he gave Sir John Forsyth when she stayed on the floor to dance another dance with him was hot enough to reduce him to a cinder. I think Maxine has yet to meet her. It will be interesting to see what happens when she arrives with Sir Alfred. Fireworks, I shouldn't wonder.'

'They are invited?'

'Of course, but you know what Maxine's like—always one to make a grand entrance. It wouldn't surprise me in the slightest if she tries to get her husband back.'

Having heard quite enough, with burning cheeks Eve quietly opened the door and went out, her spirits slightly dampened by what she'd heard. Lucas was standing on the edge of the dance floor close to the open doors leading on to the terrace. Crossing towards him, she was waylaid by Henry Channing, whom she remembered from Lady Ellesmere's party. Hearing her name, she spun round.

'Have you decided to conquer the *ton* as you have my temperamental friend, Mrs Brody?'

Eve laughed into his boyishly handsome face. 'Hardly that. I think it's virtually impossible for anyone to conquer Lucas. I'm happy to meet you again, sir—in more favourable circumstances, I hasten to add. Have you just arrived?'

He nodded. 'A little while ago. However, I have just heard that a particular lady Lucas will be far from pleased to see has just this moment arrived.' He chuckled softly. 'I think Lord Gradwell only invited them both to cause mischief.'

'Oh? What lady?' Recalling the conversation she had just overheard, Eve paled. 'His wife?'

'His former wife, and, yes, I'm afraid so, and I have a feeling that she's going to be difficult to deal with as usual.'

Together they turned and faced the door.

Maxine made her late and daring entrance. A small, confident woman, she glided into the room, her arm possessively looped through that of the lacklustre Sir Alfred Hutton. All eyes automatically turned in her direction. A gown of the sheerest emerald green silk enveloped her voluptuous body, flowing about her and revealing more than a hint of her cleavage. She sailed forth, very much aware of the stir she had created and obviously enjoying it. Eve glanced at Lucas. If he was at all embarrassed by her arrival, he gave no sign of it.

Maxine's eyes latched on to her former husband immediately and her eyes narrowed. Like everyone else in London she had read about his betrothal to an American heiress and her anger towards him had seethed to great heights. That Lucas would marry again was not what she had expected. Not at all. She moved towards him, swaying slightly, with an uneasy-looking Sir Alfred trailing in her wake.

'Well, well, Lucas. Here we are.'

Lucas stiffened and looked at her, an ironic twist to his finely chiselled lips in an otherwise cold face. 'Maxine.' His eyes passed over her contemptuously. 'You've been drinking.' Turning his back on her, he stepped out on to the terrace, away from prying, inquisitive eyes and scandal-mongering tongues.

Maxine smiled thinly and followed him. 'So I have, and I intend to drink some more before I leave.'

Eve watched, seeing a woman whose eyes were turned up to Lucas. She was an incredibly beautiful blonde, with diamonds twined in and out of her shining curls. That woman had been his wife, had known him intimately and borne him two children. Her heart sank.

'So, that is Maxine.'

'I'm afraid so,' Henry confirmed.

'They make a striking couple.'

'Once, perhaps, but that's in the past.'

'Is it?' Eve murmured, her eyes clouding over as she recalled one of the women in the retiring room saying that Maxine might try to get him back. She felt a stab of painful jealousy as she watched them together. But, she reminded herself, Lucas had divorced Maxine and he was going to marry her. 'There is no denying that she is very beautiful.'

Henry's eyebrows rose in amused mockery. 'In Maxine's case, beauty really is only skin deep. If you don't mind, I think I'd best intervene and try to alleviate a situation that could become embarrassing to all concerned.'

Curious to meet the woman whose children would very soon become her stepchildren, Eve followed him. As she approached she was subjected to a searching scrutiny by Lucas's former wife, her cold eyes set hard and uncompromising. She stood beside Lucas. He was a proud man whose marriage had been full of acrimony. She knew how angry he felt towards Maxine, and she could see how he restrained himself with great difficulty from losing his temper completely.

'And you must be Mrs Brody,' Maxine remarked without bothering to wait for Lucas to introduce them. Her pale eyes did an insolent sweep of her rival, and she said, as if Eve didn't exist, 'Why, Lucas, the lady looks positively divine—and I expect money increases her desirability. She's extremely wealthy by all accounts. Her father left her a large fortune—is that correct, Mrs Brody?'

Maxine's eyes took on a new gleam. Eve was well acquainted with people, men and women, whose only pretence of friendship was the lure of her wealth and she recognised the cold avaricious greed in Maxine's eyes. 'He might have,' she replied, equally as cold as the woman she was addressing. 'That's for me to know and everyone else to speculate on.' She smiled. 'Although I do manage a few creature comforts.'

Maxine's eyes narrowed and her lips curled. 'You're sharp, Mrs Brody, but would you be sharp enough, I wonder, to hold a man like Lucas without your money.'

'That's enough,' Lucas snapped, his fists clenched tight as he took a step towards her.

Eve placed a restraining hand on his arm. 'No, Lucas. Let her have her say.' She took a deep breath, but her eyes did not flinch as they held Lady Irvine's. 'Let me assure you, Lady Maxine, that I do have other assets that are attractive. It is Lady Maxine, isn't it? I believe you reverted to your maiden name on your divorce.'

Maxine made no attempt to hide the cool smirk in her smile. 'Naturally.' Her gaze shifted to Lucas. 'One Lady Lucas Stainton is enough for anyone. I'm really surprised, Lucas. Who would have thought that you would tie yourself to an American?'

He looked at her, his eyes hard as his face moved from grimness to intense anger. 'You are making a spectacle of yourself, Maxine, as well as being most indiscreet and immature and extremely rude to Mrs Brody. Leave before any fresh scandal blows up. I had hoped we'd done with all that.'

Maxine glared at him from two stormy eyes. 'I might remind you, Lucas, that you do not order me to do anything any more—not now, not ever. You know what it is I want from you and I will give you no respite until I get it.'

Eve's glance shifted to Lucas and she saw that his expression had become positively savage. 'Go to hell, Maxine.'

'Then I shall continue pestering you. Don't think I won't. I told you on our divorce that I would not go quietly.'

'I made adequate restitution to you in the divorce settlement. If you have squandered it, then that is your misfortune. I am no longer under any legal obligation to hold myself responsible for what you do.'

'Legally, maybe not, but what of your moral duty? That is another matter entirely.'

'Because of the children? They are nothing but bargaining tools to you Maxine—all three of them.'

Maxine was thrown off guard and she looked in surprise, somewhat uneasy. 'Three? You speak as though you are already familiar with Stephen's daughter, Lucas.'

'She is in the nursery with Sophie and Abigail. I rescued her from a filthy hovel in St Giles.' He glared at her with absolute contempt. 'You might just as well have thrown her on the dung heap.'

'So you did your snooping, Lucas, and came up trumps. I should have known you wouldn't rest until you found her.'

'It wasn't difficult.'

'I saw your daughter,' Eve said. 'I was with Lucas when we found her—malnourished and riddled with lice. You are her mother. Don't you care?'

Maxine gave her a hard stare. 'No, Mrs Brody, quite frankly I don't. I didn't have the coin to keep her—and don't embarrass yourself by telling me you would have been more than happy to bear the expense, Lucas. You're penniless—remember. You haven't two halfpennies to rub together.' She turned her sneering face on Eve. 'So what do you do? You marry an American heiress—who, for some curious reason, has been looking after our children. How degrading for her and yet how sensible of you to marry her. Be wary, Mrs Brody. He divorced me. Once he gets his hands on your money, he might dispose of you in the same way.'

Eve hastened to allay the possibility. 'I shall, of course, release Lucas to whatever decision he might make. There is time for him to reconsider. But when we are married, he will never divorce me. I promise you that.'

'I know how difficult this is for you both,' Henry said, 'but you would do well to remember that you are Lord Gradwell's guests and people are watching. Besides, we are not here to indulge in the rights and wrongs of your first marriage, but to celebrate the imminence of your second, Lucas.'

Eve was impressed by Henry's intensity, by his knowledge of the situation, which proved to her how well he knew them both, and led her to wonder how many times he'd had to calm the situation between Lucas and his former wife in the past.

Maxine drew herself up and looked at Henry. 'You always were the peacekeeper, Henry.'

Looking apologetic, extremely uncomfortable and ill at ease beneath the glare of the superior Lord Stainton, Sir Alfred took her arm none too gently. 'Come away and let us take some refreshment, Maxine. Lord Stainton is quite right. You are making a spectacle of yourself,' he chided crossly. 'Nothing can be gained from this.'

She shook his hand off in frustration and glowered at him. 'How would you know, Alfred?'

Glaring from Eve to Lucas, Maxine tossed her head flippantly. 'I have plenty more to say, but for now I will wish you luck, Lucas. It will be interesting to see how you deal with being a kept man, totally dependent on your wife. It will be a whole new experience for you—and not a pleasant one.' Hooking her arm through that of her escort, she sauntered away through the crowd.

The musicians struck up another waltz, at which Lucas, his face dark and tense, turned to Eve and Henry. 'Henry, I would be grateful if you would partner Eve in this dance. I think I'll take a turn about the garden.'

Eve looked at him in alarm. 'But—would you like me to stay, Lucas?'

'No, thank you,' he answered tersely, avoiding her eyes, his body ramrod straight. 'I would appreciate some time by myself.'

'Very well. If you're sure.' She smiled at Henry. 'Come along, Mr Channing. Show me how well you waltz.'

He glanced at Lucas concernedly and then, thinking some time to himself was what he needed, he offered Eve his arm, smiling broadly. 'It will be my pleasure. I'm sorry about that unpleasant scene, Eve—I may call you Eve?'

'Of course you may. I'd like you to.'

'And you must call me Henry.'

They danced in silence for a while before Henry spoke again. 'What do you think of him, Eve? He's not the easiest man to get close to.'

Her smile became nervous. 'He's—better for knowing, I think,' she began with caution, 'and guarded about what he thinks and does.'

'And do you find him handsome?'

Eve gave an astonished laugh. 'He is extremely attractive. From the looks I've seen cast his way tonight, I'm not the only woman who thinks so.'

'It's always been the same. Wherever he goes, without

opening his mouth he draws attention to himself. You know, Eve, Lucas is a fine man—one of the finest. Before this he was a man most envied—always one to take risks—a gambler if you like—something I would never dare do. But it was his own money he gambled with on investments—some might say they were unsound, but he was always lucky.'

'Some would say far-seeing,' Eve said, a flash of pride in the man she was to marry putting a gleam in her eyes.

'This business with Maxine set him back considerably, but he'll get to where he was. I'm certain of that. He isn't the sort to stay down. He'll put the bad times behind him and get on with it. I admire him for that.'

'He has a good friend in you, Henry.'

'We have been friends for a long time, Lucas and I. He has tremendous strength of mind and will. I cannot match him in that, and he rarely meets with opposition from anyone.'

'Only Maxine,' Eve murmured quietly.

'Yes, only Maxine,' he agreed. 'She hurt him cruelly when she walked out without a word, leaving Lucas alone with the children. She made no attempt to hide the fact that she did not love her children. They were unwanted and a trial to her since the day they were born. Sometimes it's the case that when a woman leaves her husband she has no place in society, no future—Maxine is determined she will not be ousted. Lucas still finds that hideous affair between Stephen and Maxine difficult and painful, and it turned him irrevocably against marriage—which is why I was so surprised when I found out he was to marry you.'

Her curiosity won over her desire not to pry. 'What was he like, his brother?'

'Oddly enough, I liked Stephen—but Lucas must be the

one to tell you about that. It was a nasty business and it's not for me to divulge matters of a personal nature Lucas might not want to resurrect.' A smile flickered across his face. 'But I believe he will tell you some day. He told me of the circumstances that brought you together, Eve. I hope you don't mind.'

'No, of course not. I hope you don't disapprove, Henry.'

A smile drew Henry's firm lips apart as he expertly danced her away from a knot of couples to a less crowded part of the floor. 'If my humble approval can be of any comfort to you, Eve, I give it to you gladly.'

It was Eve's turn to smile. She knew she would see much of Henry in the future and she was glad. She would always come to an understanding with him. 'Thank you. It means a lot to me—and gives me courage to face an uncertain future knowing that in you I have a friend.'

'Whatever the reasons that brought you and Lucas together, I sincerely hope the two of you will be happy. Lucas deserves to be. He needs to be taught how to love again, and trust, and I think you are beautiful and sensible enough to stand a chance of winning both.'

Unconvinced of this, Eve gave a little ironic smile and said, 'Lucas and I are not marrying for love, Henry. I might even go so far as to say it is a forced marriage on his part, and that the feelings I inspire in him, far from resembling love, rather approach the feeling of anger and even resentment.'

'I think you are beginning to know Lucas and to read his moods. For the time being your position is strong, his is weak, and that is where his resentment lies. But it will not always be like that. I know Lucas. He will rise above it, I promise you.'

'I hope you're right, Henry, otherwise we are going to be horribly unhappy.'

'You must be optimistic. I think your marrying him is a good thing. Now it's a question of your union being a success. Your marriage is convenient to you both, but that does not necessarily mean that affection, tolerance and even love itself will fail to blossom once the deal is done. I would like to offer you some advice.'

'Oh? And what might that be?'

'After the ceremony, get him to return to Laurel Court. He loves that place. He's been working himself into the ground sixteen hours a day for months now, trying to get himself back on top—and he will eventually, I have every faith in that. But some time away from London will do him good.'

'I will bear that in mind, Henry, and thank you for being so open with me.'

'My pleasure.' On a lighter note he grinned down at her upturned face. 'You dance divinely by the way, Mrs Brody,' he said, swirling her round. 'In fact, you dance so well that I shall insist on partnering you in one more dance before we leave.'

When the dance ended Eve returned to Lucas on the terrace, a smile on her face that faded slightly as she beheld the hardness of his taut jaw and the cold glitter in his eyes. Her heart filled with compassion and understanding.

'Lucas? Is something wrong?'

At her soft use of his name, the muscles of his face clenched so tightly a nerve in his cheek began to pulse. 'Wrong?' he repeated cynically. 'The only thing that is wrong is me. Maxine was right.'

'What? Lucas, was it what she said about you being a kept man, because, if so, please ignore what she said.'

'I can't, Eve,' he ground out. 'That's the trouble.'

Startled, Eve's eyes flew to his, and took new meaning from the steely quality of his dark expression. Her mouth went dry and her heart began to beat in a heavy, terrifying dread as she sensed Lucas had withdrawn from her, as if the closeness they had shared so far tonight had never existed. Of course he was struggling to survive and was lashing out like a cornered animal.

'Are you telling me you won't marry me, because, if so, I do understand.'

'Our reasons for marrying are hardly the reasons on which to build the strong foundations of marriage.'

Eve took a deep breath, not knowing what to say, but she felt the bite of cruel truth in his words.

'God knows I don't want to marry you,' he went on. 'I don't want to marry anyone, but at this time I have no choice.'

'And you hate yourself for it, don't you, Lucas?'

When he looked at her, Eve stepped back in alarm from the unexplained violence glittering in his eyes.

'Yes, I do.'

The dark frown that accompanied his angry reply surprised Eve. She stood back to see his face. Without warning the dark side of his mood had returned, and she was already mourning the parting of the frivolous, capricious Lucas Stainton she had briefly glimpsed.

'Maybe you acted in haste when you agreed to my proposal.'

'No, Eve. I acted in greed.'

'Arguing over semantics will not gain you anything. Do you have to be so proud? This needn't be a disaster. Accept that you need my money. Of course, I could always withdraw my offer,' she said irately and hating herself for saying it.

The betrothal had been made official. The ridicule that would ensue should they retract it would be horrendous; besides, Eve could not forget there were children involved, his children, who had a father, and a mother who didn't want them.

'That is entirely up to you,' he retorted coldly. 'As far as I am concerned the arrangement still stands and I intend to make the best of it. Come. We will not talk of this now. It's neither the time nor place. Let us return to the dancing and try to get through the rest of the evening as best we can.'

Eve allowed him to escort her back inside and on to the floor of swirling couples. Suddenly she felt as though he'd erected a solid wall of rock between them. When she'd proposed marriage, she'd had it all worked out in her mind as to what kind of arrangement their marriage would be, naïvely believing Lucas would be so relieved that he would fall in with her plans, but somewhere between her proposal and their first kiss, she'd discovered she liked being with him, and she had an inbred urge to knock down that wall of rock and delve beneath the rubble and discover the man beneath.

When it was time to leave, Eve was coming out of the retiring room only to find herself confronted by Maxine. Eve was painfully aware of the other woman's close proximity as she stood her ground, determined that Eve would not pass. Eve looked into her face. She was a beautiful woman and carried a certain elegance and charm, but there was a coarseness in her manner and her eyes betrayed the truth of her nature. They were small and calculating, deep and dangerous and ever watchful.

'I see you are leaving, Mrs Brody? I hope it isn't because of something I have said.'

'Not at all, Lady Maxine. Please step out of my way. I don't think we have anything further to say to each other.'

'Of course. Don't let me detain you. Have you decided when the happy event is to take place?'

'Not yet.'

Maxine gave her a long measuring look and then she smiled, a calculating gleam lighting her eyes. 'You know,' she said, tapping Eve's arm with her fan, 'your marriage might just prove to be advantageous.'

'To you?'

'Who else? Lucas treated me very badly.'

Eve looked at her incredulously. 'Whatever happened between you and Lucas has nothing to do with me, but I am of the opinion that he was not to blame. You left him. You humiliated him, and I believe you almost ruined him. He has not done this to you. You have done it to yourself.'

Maxine looked at her. The American woman was too bold to be either threatened or cowed. Maxine's poise wavered before those merciless, bright young eyes.

'You are arrogant, Mrs Brody,' she hissed, beginning to sound erratic and breathing heavily, feeling the effects of the wine she had consumed throughout the evening taking hold of her. 'Don't think that marrying Lucas will be a bed of roses. It will be anything but. Remember that I am speaking from experience—and you must also remember that since you are to be step-mother to my children, I have no intention of letting you forget it.'

Eve's eyes met Maxine's, a silent challenge flared between them. This woman is not going to go away, Eve thought. She will cause trouble if she can. For what seemed like an age Maxine made no move. Instead her smile grew colder, more devious, and then she stepped aside to let Eve pass. Eve walked away, feeling inside the disturbance of something she didn't fully understand, and in the silence that followed, the unpleasant incident lived on in Eve's mind, filling her with the restlessness of many questions.

It was a different journey returning to Berkeley Street to the one coming. Lucas's face was turned away from her, his profile a hard, chiselled mask. His confrontation with Maxine had created a breach between them that might never heal. He was furious and Maxine's cutting remark about him being a kept man had been humiliating and had dented his pride, adding more tension to his already overburdened emotions, and he had turned his resentment on Eve.

It was the early hours when his coachman pulled the spirited bays up before the house. Neither Lucas nor Eve had spoken a word since leaving the ball. Lucas leapt out of the coach and held his hand out to her. She took it and climbed out and stood looking up into his face.

'Thank you for a lovely evening, Lucas. I'll wait until you contact me.'

'Goodnight, Eve. I apologise for that unpleasantness with Maxine.'

She shrugged. 'It wasn't your fault. You weren't to know she would be there.' Unable to bear the atmosphere between them another moment, she said goodnight and went inside.

Lucas watched her go up the steps and disappear into the house before getting back into the carriage.

Chapter Eight

Six weeks to the day that the arrangement had been struck between Eve and Lucas, they were married. When they had been told of the betrothal—that his lordship was to marry the new nursemaid—the staff at the house in Upper Brook Street were astounded, but, as the shock wore off, highly delighted. Mrs Coombs broke into her much guarded bottle of sherry and insisted everyone raise their glasses in a toast to the couple, declaring that after his lordship's last disastrous marriage, never did she think she would see the happy day when he would marry again.

The morning dawned sunny and warm—a good omen? Eve sincerely hoped so. In the Seagrove house grooming and preparations had taken most of the morning, the ceremony just ten minutes, which was performed before noon at St George's Church in Hanover Square. Both Lucas and Eve had agreed that it was to be a quiet affair without fuss, with just a handful of Lucas's friends and the Seagrove family. Anything more elaborate would be inappropriate under the circumstances.

Despite Eve's efforts to ignore it, her wedding had a

distinct aura of unreality and tension. On the brink of a new life, she couldn't understand why her feelings seemed to seesaw between excitement and gloom.

Standing in the open doorway to the church before the ceremony, William smiled at her in an attempt to dispel her serious expression. 'Headache bothering you again, Eve?' he murmured. 'If so, mention it to Beth. She's wonderful with things like that.' He winked teasingly. 'She might even give you one of her powders.'

Knowing William was trying to get her to relax, Eve was grateful. Her mood lightened and she laughed softly. 'Absolutely not. I mean to remain awake and upright when I speak my vows.'

With her hand hooked through the crook of William's arm, Eve walked slowly down the aisle to where Lucas stood before the cleric. Estelle, Sophie and Abigail—all three of them bridesmaids in their lavender dresses and with matching ribbons in their hair and carrying posies of summer flowers, identical to her own—were enthralled by the proceedings and the changes it would bring to their own lives.

Henry was among the guests, waiting to witness this strange union between the American heiress and Lord Stainton—a man she barely knew yet to whom she was still willing to entrust her life and all she possessed. Sarah Lacy, holding a babbling Alice, was dewy eyed with emotion, content in the knowledge that her new mistress would be as happy as she was with her beloved Mark.

Eve noted all this in the last moment as she moved closer to Lucas, looking magnificent in a splendid suit of midnight blue velvet and white neck linen. His tall body and broad shoulders threw a shadow across her path. There was an undeniable aura of forcefulness, of power about him.

He half-turned to look at her so that he might watch her progress towards him. His face was serious and it looked as if it had been sculpted from granite. Eve wasn't to know how he was fighting to control the strong rush of emotion that engulfed him at the sight of her, for, from the top of her shining hair to the hem of her gleaming ivory satin gown embroidered with ivory silk thread, she looked radiant.

However, he felt a certain amount of unease when he met her unwavering speculative gaze. It was as if she were studying the man she had bought and was wondering if she was getting value for money. The thought put a stiffener into his spine and he lifted his head to a lofty angle and squared his shoulders.

And then, incredibly, he found she was smiling at him and his heart and soul felt as though they were being lifted by that smile of astounding beauty. The unease of a moment before melted away. Never had he met a woman like Eve Brody, a woman who was about to give herself and all she possessed to a man she scarcely knew. A man she did not love—a man who did not love her and never would—at least not in the romantic sense.

Taking her place beside Lucas and handing her posy to Estelle, who was trying to look very grown up, for a moment Eve was transported back through time to her marriage to Andrew, when her father had placed her hand into that of the young man who was to disappear so quickly and so tragically from her life. Taking a deep breath, she thrust the memory aside and tried to bring back the smile Lucas had found so incredible, but couldn't. This was a different wedding, a wedding of her instigation. In a few minutes from now she would become Lady Lucas Stainton and there would be no going back.

The cleric was a quiet man and confused by the attitudes
of the bride and groom towards each other. He was used
to conducting marriage ceremonies, but this was the first
he had conducted between a widow and a divorced man,
a man who had already promised to love one woman until
death and was now about to do the same to another. This
marriage was not illegal, but it did not conform to what he
as a servant of God approved of.

The cleric faced them, seeming to look through them,
but not at them. In sepulchral tones he began reading the
words of the marriage ceremony, words that would bind
Eve to Lucas for ever and she heard Lucas repeat them in
his deep rich voice. He spoke sincerely, as if he truly meant
every word. And then he was looking at her, his eyes laying
siege to hers, with an indefinable expression, and then he
gently but firmly slipped the gold wedding band on her
finger, the same finger that, until she had become betrothed
to Lucas, had worn Andrew's ring.

When the cleric pronounced them man and wife, Lucas
leaned forward to place a light kiss on Eve's lips as a seal
to the marriage. Apart from taking her hand occasionally
to hand her in and out of the carriage when they attended
some event and to place the wedding band on her finger, it
was the first physical contact there had been between them
since he had kissed her on their engagement. His mouth
was gentle on hers, as befitted the formal occasion in front
of witnesses. The time for passion between these two would
not come just yet.

His duty done, the cleric mumbled congratulations and
watched the bride and groom depart in the waiting carriage
to the groom's house for the wedding breakfast.

At the house Henry bent and kissed Eve's cheek. 'Congratulations, Eve, and to you too, Lucas. I sincerely hope you will be happy together.'

'My dear Eve,' Beth enthused, rushing forward to embrace her as others began crowding round the newly weds. 'You make a lovely bride and I wish you both every happiness.'

'Seconded by me.' William pecked her cheek and shook Lucas's hand.

William didn't sound quite as certain as Eve would have liked. She knew he had qualms about what she had done and didn't fully approve. But he respected her decision, for which Eve was grateful. With Mrs Coombs ushering the servants about their business while telling them that their new mistress would make his lordship an excellent wife, Estelle came to give her a hug, her pretty face shining with excitement as Eve lifted her off her feet and hugged her back.

'You look lovely, Mama,' she whispered, her mouth against her ear.

'And so do you, Estelle—and you, too,' she said, drawing Sophie and Abigail towards her with her free arm and placing an affectionate kiss on each of their cheeks while Sarah Lacy, holding a wide-awake Alice in her arms, looked on fit to bursting with happiness. Unable to resist this lovely addition to her growing family, Eve gently kissed her plump baby cheek. 'All of you look like fairy princesses and I couldn't have wished for prettier bridal attendants. Now off you go. I think Thomas and David are waiting for you to show them the house, but don't be long. We will be sitting down to eat very soon.'

When they had scampered out of the room, with a strange sense of unreality Eve went to take her place beside her husband. Already so perceptive of his mood and able to read every nuance in his light blue eyes, she knew he would be feeling right now that he would rather be anywhere than here. Drawing her closer, he put his hand over hers, covering her wedding ring. He looked deeply into her eyes and she felt her heart turn over. Never before had she seen such a tender expression on his proud features. But both of them knew this was a business arrangement and should not be treated as something romantic.

Lucas had watched the tender scene with the children and was moved to an emotion he hadn't felt in a very long time. Eve seemed to have a talent for motherhood. She was warm and loving and physical and never afraid to show her feelings. He felt a pang of regret. He didn't have any memories of anyone kissing his children, or seeing their faces light up with joy as they did whenever they were with Eve.

Lucas looked at his bride as if he were seeing her for the first time. He smiled, his pleasant thoughts bringing a warmth and humour to his face, which had been lacking so far this day, and he was surprised at the answering response. Her mouth was full and a luscious shade of deep pink. He noticed too she had an unbelievable small waist and a long, lovely neck. Her eyes were the most brilliant, incredible shade of dark blue to be almost violet and were quite extraordinarily wide with a slight upward slant that emphasised her high cheekbones. Her skin was creamy smooth and rich with a translucency that had him wondering whether it continued beneath the ivory satin of the gown she wore. He speculated and the thought put a covetous gleam in his eyes.

In fact she was exquisite, this wife of his, and put all the pale, simpering, overeager English roses who came out each Season in the shade. When she had approached him with her outrageous proposal of marriage, wishing to know all there was to know about her before he committed himself, he had sought William out at the Foreign Office on the same day that he had spoken with Eve's solicitor.

William had told him that as soon as her period of mourning had ended, Eve had received proposals from several gentleman of note—a French count, an Italian millionaire—and had been showered with admiration from every eligible male in New York society, and yet she was neither spoilt nor pampered, and her father had seen to it that she had not been cushioned against all the vicissitudes of life. She was also so accustomed to wealth that fortunes meant nothing to her.

And if he were honest, Lucas would have to admit that he had admired her from the moment she'd taken him on in the park and then in his own home, a courageous, stubborn young woman, who did not fear him, and on being confronted by Maxine was scornful of her attitude. She was aware of the risk she was taking in marrying him, yet she was prepared to trust him, to risk everything her father had worked for. Suddenly he felt the weight of the burden she had placed on him and he knew it was up to him to make sure that Eve was always safe.

Ignoring everything else for the moment, there might have been only the two of them in the room as she met his gaze, and suddenly Lucas found himself actually looking forward to his future for the first time in a long time. In the beginning, as part of their arrangement, he was prepared to wait as patiently as it was in his nature to be for Eve to become his wife in the full meaning of the word, which, now he'd had time to reflect, if he had anything to do with it would not be long in coming.

'Well, here we are—married again, both of us.'

'But we were not married to each other.'

'Then we shall have to learn how to live together,' Lucas said gravely.

Eve looked down to where their hands were still joined, his strong fingers wrapped around hers. 'Which I hope will not prove too difficult—given your unpredictable temperament, my lord.'

'I promise I shall try to be patience personified in the future.'

Perhaps it was the occasion and all that it implied, or perhaps it was the odd combination of gentleness and solemnity in his light blue eyes as they gazed into hers, but, whatever the cause, Eve's heart quickened its pace.

'However our marriage came about, whatever differences there are between us, could we put them aside, do you think, and behave like any normal, newly wedded couple at their wedding feast?'

Mesmerised, Eve stared into his fathomless eyes while his deep, soft voice seemed to caress her, pulling her under his spell. For some reason, his request did much damage to her resistance. She nodded finally and softly said, 'As you wish.'

'You look very lovely, Eve,' he said, smiling crookedly and handing her a glass of champagne, 'or perhaps I should say Lady Stainton. How does it feel to be a titled lady?'

'No different to what I was fifteen minutes ago.'

'Plain Mrs Brody?'

She wrinkled her face. 'I would like to think Mrs Brody was never plain.'

That made Lucas chuckle, which went a long way to making Eve relax. It was the first spark of humour she had seen from him since the evening of their engagement.

'You're right. She was courageous, warm and kind and she had a beautiful smile.'

Her laughter bubbled to the surface like fresh spring water. 'Now you flatter me—and coming from you, that raises my suspicions and warns me to be wary.'

The blue eyes lightly swept her and catching her own, held them with a smiling warmth. 'Don't be. I never say anything I don't mean. You have many qualities I admire, Eve, and in particular I am delighted that you like children so much.'

'It's very hard not to when blessed with one of my own and three adorable stepchildren—if you count Alice. You have no idea how happy it has made Estelle having sisters to play with.'

He cocked a handsome brow as he gave her a knowing look. 'And in time a brother.'

Perhaps Eve should not have been standing so close. It was most difficult to subdue the deepening blush of embarrassment while appearing nonchalant, for her thoughts had become tangled in the fact that while she insisted on keeping her side of the bargain they had made regarding the terms of their marriage, he was reminding her of his side of the arrangement.

'I—I hope so. I know I am bound by my word, and I have every intention of fulfilling my part of the vows, but I asked for time and you granted my request.'

'I did, and be assured that you have nothing to fear from me. I accept the way things are between us, but you cannot blame me for hoping for a turn of fate. I want an heir, and I can think of no greater satisfaction than for you to bear my son.' His look through narrowed eyes was one of wicked mischief. 'You are now my wife. Have you not vowed to love, honour and obey me, sharing your life with me—as well as all your worldly goods?'

'And must I remind you that you have done the same, Lord Stainton?' An impish smile played on her curved lips.

He grinned. '*Touché!* Although I consider that I have come out of it with the best deal.'

'In monetary terms, maybe you have,' she murmured, her attention drawn to the door as the three girls entered, their faces rosy and shining with the pleasure of the day. 'But I am satisfied with my side of the bargain. The girls really do look lovely. It's the first time Estelle has been a bridal attendant.'

'And Sophie and Abigail. They've never had so much excitement in their young lives.'

'I have a feeling that all this excitement will wear them out and that by tonight we are going to have three tired children on our hands.'

The wedding breakfast had been prepared by Mrs Coombs. The long table was festooned with flowers and there was a wealth of food and champagne for the thirty or so guests. It would have been a subdued affair had the children not been present, which Lucas did not approve of but Eve had insisted upon. Their excited chatter and laughter lightened the atmosphere, coiling itself warmly about the adults.

All too soon it was over and the guests had left. The children were in the nursery and Eve was alone with her husband. They were about to partake of a glass of champagne before going to their separate beds when one of the footmen informed them that a Mr Edward Barstow had arrived to see them both.

'I've put him in the study, my lord.'

Lucas became thoughtful. 'Barstow?' He looked at Eve. 'Isn't he your solicitor?'

A shadow of apprehension crossed her vivid features. 'Yes. I wonder what he wants.'

'Let's go and find out.'

Mr Barstow was seated at the desk. When the study doors opened he rose swiftly to his feet, stealing a quick, appraising look at the dark-haired Lord Stainton and his beautiful new wife. With a pair of penetrating ice-blue eyes levelled on him, Mr Barstow swallowed nervously as Lord Stainton walked round the desk and gave him a curt nod, waiting for him to speak.

Eve, in whom patience had been a lesson painfully learned and not always completely, waited for Mr Barstow to speak. There was a hard knot in the centre of her chest, and try as she might she could not get rid of it.

Mr Barstow cleared his throat. 'Good evening, Lord Stainton—Lady Stainton. I apologise for presuming to call on you without first making an appointment—and today of all days—but I felt my news could not wait.'

Eve returned the greeting, finding it strange that he did not offer them his congratulations. 'Good evening, Mr Barstow. Will you take some tea?'

'No—no, thank you.' He glanced at Eve, then quickly away again, the weight of what he had to tell her heavy indeed. Placing his valise on the desk, he extracted a sheet of paper. 'I received this letter earlier today—from a Mr Pilger, who as you know is working on your father's affairs in New York.' He handed it to her. 'I thought, seeing the gravity of its contents, I should show it to you and Lord Stainton at once.'

Eve glanced at it in puzzlement.

'Please read it, Lady Stainton?' Mr Barstow urged as she gazed questioningly at him.

Eve began to read, and the more she read, the colder she became. Even when she had finished reading she couldn't comprehend the words so she read them again. Then she took a moment to stare down at the letter through horrified, disbelieving eyes, still unable to assimilate what she had read.

Concerned by the sudden pallor of her face, Lucas went to her. 'Eve? What is it?' Watching her intently, he held out his hand for the letter.

Eve's hands were trembling as she gave it to him. 'Please read it, Lucas. Perhaps you can make some sense of it.'

Lucas did. Other than the merest tightening of his expression, there was no visible reaction to the staggering news, or to all its serious and terrible implications. Regarding Mr Barstow in dispassionate silence, he handed him the letter.

Biting off an expression of sympathy he knew Lord Stainton would reject, he looked at his wife. 'I—realise what a dreadful shock this must be to you, Lady Stainton. I am so very sorry.'

'But—this cannot be right, Mr Barstow. There must be some mistake. There has to be. My instructions were simple. I informed you that my financial affairs were to be transferred to my husband on our marriage. He is now legally entitled to every penny I have.'

'You no longer have the money at your disposal—at least not nearly as much as you hoped there would be.'

Eve was aghast. 'But—my father was a wealthy man. He amassed a fortune. It—it cannot be gone.'

'It would seem a substantial amount of his holdings have folded, Lady Stainton.'

'But it cannot have disappeared overnight.'

'His assets have been dwindling steadily for some time, and, as you will know, all branches of the American economy have suffered grievously in recent months—which I feel is the reason why you have been unable to access his money. In its battle to save itself, the bank called in its loans so ruthlessly that many concerns, not to mention individuals, your father was one of them—are ruined.'

'Did he know of this before he died?' Lucas asked, surprised at the calmness of his voice.

'I believe so. He sold off some of his investments when things began to go under. Perhaps if he'd lived, being the kind of man he was, in all probability he would have recovered, but as it was—'

'He died,' Eve whispered. She looked at Lucas's taut features. 'Lucas, I had no idea. You must believe that. Are—are there any debts—creditors to pay?' she asked as Mr Barstow closed his valise.

'Not to my knowledge. Mr Pilger is winding down your father's affairs in America and will let me have the paperwork in due course.'

Lucas looked at him. 'Is there anything else?'

'No, sir. I'll see myself out.'

His retreating footsteps could be heard going through the hall. Not until the outer door banged to did Eve move towards Lucas. He stood with his back to her, his hands resting on the mantelpiece, his head bowed, his shoulders taut. Nothing could be heard but the rustling of her skirts. She came to a halt a few feet from him, pausing to gather her wits before she spoke. She tried to think how to begin, and because she was so overwhelmed with emotion she said the first thing that came into her head.

'You're angry, Lucas, and you have every reason to be.' She saw his shoulders stiffen at the sound of her voice and when he brought himself up straight and turned and looked at her, his expression gave her no reassurance. His eyes were slits of explosive rage in his grim face, and she could almost feel the effort he was exerting to keep it under control. His gaze snapped to her face, his pale blue eyes turning an icy, metallic silver.

'You're right,' he bit out, his mouth set in a bitter line, his black brows drawn in a straight bar. 'It would appear that you married me under false pretences, Lady Stainton.'

Eve flinched at his enunciation of her new title, which rang with a hollow note. 'It does look like it. I promised you a fortune. I can't believe there isn't one. That it's virtually all gone. You had no reason to marry me after all.'

'Right,' he snapped, striding to his desk, and dragging out the chair sat down. 'No reason at all. Why in God's name did I take your word regarding your wealth?' Why had he been so naïve? After everything that had happened with Maxine, had he not learnt his lesson?

'Lucas, you have to believe me when I say I had no idea and I do not understand how it could have happened.'

'What is there to understand? It's simple enough. Your father lost his money. Whether it was bad management or the state of the American bank makes little difference.' His lips twisted in a bitter, cynical smile. 'It would appear your father and I have much in common, my sweet. Before I met you I had only myself and my daughters to take care of. Now, with a wife and another child foistered on me, I find I have extra responsibilities I could do without.'

The vicious meaning of his words cut Eve to the heart. With a surge of genuine anger her jaw jutted with belligerent indignation and tension twisted within her as she quickly came to the defence of her darling daughter. 'Since you see us as pitiful nuisances—'

'Your words, not mine,' he interrupted harshly.

'Nevertheless,' she seethed, her voice like splintered ice as she took up a stance in front of him, 'that is what you mean—and as I was saying, if that is how you see us, then I shall remove myself and Estelle from your house forthwith.'

'Like hell you will. I will give you a warning, Eve, and heed me well,' Lucas said in a terrible voice. 'Do not even consider leaving this house with the intention of leaving it for good. You are my wife and you will not leave without my permission. You will remain here with me until such time as we go to Laurel Court, and do not dare disobey me.'

Fury was quick to flare in Eve's eyes. Moving forwards, she planted the palms of her hands on his desk and leaned towards him. 'How dare you, Lucas Stainton? I do not need your permission to do anything and if I want advice I would not ask you, and how dare you actually remind me of my vows—would you like me to remind you of yours, my lord?'

His eyes narrowed and a murderous glint shone out at her. No woman had ever dared to speak to him so defiantly or look at him with sparks shooting from her eyes. There was a deep and dreadful silence, a silence so menacing, filled with an unwavering determination of the two to hurt, to destroy one another, that the tension was palpable.

Lucas scraped back his chair, but Eve did not flinch. Their eyes locked together in awful combat. Neither was about to concede.

'Do not goad me, Eve, and do not defy me, because you won't like what will happen if you do, believe me,' her husband said perilously.

Eve's voice held nothing but contempt. 'I am not your chattel and I will not be treated as such. What has happened is unfortunate, but it does not necessarily have to be the end of the world.' The expression on her husband's face was difficult to read, but some new darkness seemed to move at the back of his eyes.

Combing his fingers through his hair in frustration, he turned from her as if he couldn't bear to look at her or be close to her and strode to the window where he drew a long breath, striving to get control of his temper. When he spoke again he seemed more composed.

'The damage, whatever it may be, has already been done. I'm to blame for this. Being fully aware of the state of the American economy, I should have investigated more thoroughly into your father's affairs before committing myself to this marriage. I can only hope that my banker will take a more understanding view. You may not care a damn about my feelings—'

'But of course I care,' Eve cried, wishing there was something she could do, something she could say to make things better.

His lips twisted scathingly. 'Do you realise what will happen if this ever gets out? It will cause the biggest scandal in London since my divorce from Maxine. It will bring further disrepute to my family.'

The utter helplessness of being a woman totally at the mercy of her husband struck Eve with full force. Then her dormant self-respect flared into life. His manner and his deliberate cruelty riled her. Did he think this was easy for her, that she wasn't suffering too?

'Your family is now my family, Lucas, so it affects us both,' she flared, her cheeks burning with anger. 'Dear

God in heaven, what do you want me to do? What do you expect me to say? I didn't know how bad things were. Have you any idea how hard all this is for me?'

'Yes—yes, of course I do.'

'Lucas...' she began, taking a step closer, then stopping when she got nothing from him but a blast of icy contempt from his eyes. 'I realise,' she began again, her voice trembling with emotion while she tried to think how to reach him, how to diffuse his wrath and keep her own at bay, 'that you must despise me for this, but do you think I could have stood by your side this very day and promised the things I did if I had known any of this—if I had even suspected this would happen? I would have told you.'

'I don't despise you, and I don't blame you. I blame myself.' Lucas saw little good in lashing out at her. She was feeling just as devastated as he was, but with all the qualified people her father had employed to take care of his affairs, why the hell hadn't she been informed that he was facing financial ruin?

Eve drew a shaking breath and braved another step closer. 'I know I've hurt you terribly and I am sorry, but there is nothing I can do about it. If you're expecting me to shout and weep, then you're wasting your time. I am not given to hysterics.'

Lucas looked at her, seeing the hurt and despair in her eyes. Feeling something inside him, some strange emotion that was unrecognisable to him just then, unconsciously his hand went out to her. His expression became one of mixed emotions, strangely gentle, and his light blue eyes softened and were filled with sorrow and compassion, telling her of his regret that this disaster should give her pain. But Eve would have none of his pity or of his concern and her cold, narrowed eyes told him so.

'Eve, I do know how distressed you must be feeling—'

'Do you, Lucas? Do you really? I don't think you do. This is not just about you, and if this is the way it has to be between us then I suppose I will endure it. The deed is done and we will have to find a way to live in harmony with it, because the only alternative is to have our marriage declared null and void or to divorce.'

Lucas froze, his eyes pinning hers as cold and hard as steel. He moved slowly towards her like a dangerous predator. 'Eve, let me make one thing perfectly clear. I will say this once and once only and you will listen to me and never, ever, mention divorce to me again. First, our marriage such as it is, will not be nullified, and, second, we will not get divorced. Divorce, as I found to my cost, is an expensive business and only undertaken by those who are wealthy. I am not. That aside, Eve, if I were the richest man in Christendom I would not put myself through it—or sully my family name further—by embarking on the enterprise again. Do I make myself clear?'

'Yes. Perfectly.'

'Good. Now go to bed,' he said between his clenched teeth, and while Eve was willing to stay and argue the matter further, Lucas's cold anger told her there was no point.

Eve tossed her head proudly and, turning from him, marched to the door. 'While you're in this present state of mind I think that would be for the best,' she threw back at him. 'We can discuss this whole thing reasonably and rationally in the morning. Goodnight, Lucas.'

Usually, her terrified mind reminded her, Lucas's temper was explosive, and he was so infuriated by the fact that the fortune he'd expected was not forthcoming, that instead of raging, he'd been coldly, murderously silent and that alarmed her more than his outburst would have done.

She felt physically ill when she left him. She went up to the bedroom that was to be hers on the first floor. Lucas had given her the choice of any of the rooms and she had chosen this one because it was close to where the children slept.

Passing the night nursery she looked in, relieved to see they were fast asleep. In helpless misery she entered her room, relieved there was no one there. It had been a long day and seeing the covers turned back on the bed and her nightdress draped over a chair, together with a fire burning in the fireplace, it all looked suspiciously inviting.

She was still in a state of shock as she began to undress, tugging at the innumerable hooks down the back of her dress and then unpinning her hair. She shook it out with both hands so that it tumbled like a thick dark snake down to the small of her back, and then climbed into bed.

Overwhelmed with the alarming news she had received and unable to believe it, she squeezed her eyes closed and held back her tears while her mind tormented her with more pressing problems.

In bed she lay awake for a long time, tortured with doubts about the future and with the awful fear that, despite what Lucas had said about not wanting to end their marriage, after he had considered it in the cold light of day, he might see it as the best option and do just that.

Lucas downed the glass of liquor in his hand and poured himself another, but no matter how much he wanted to drink himself into oblivion, there wasn't enough liquor in the world to douse the fury that was burning inside him like an inferno.

After all his experience, and what had happened with Stephen, he'd been taken in by a woman he'd thought would bring him a fortune, when, in fact, she was worse off than he was. Dear God, he thought, wanting to smash the glass into the hearth, if it weren't so serious he would laugh at his own gullibility. He took another swallow of his drink. If he'd had any sense at all, he would have thrown Eve out of his house before she made that damned proposition.

Rage boiled inside him like acid, destroying any tender feelings he had for her. Damn the woman. Damn her conniving female heart. She had brought nothing to the marriage, and to add insult to injury she was denying him the pleasure of her body until she felt like submitting to him. The hell with what she wanted, he thought, tossing back the rest of his drink. Since she couldn't keep her side of the bargain neither would he, and if she didn't bend to his will he would damn well break her to it.

He could think of nothing but his need to possess her, intent only on the conclusion of his own desire, to crush her, to hurt her, to claim her body in any way she chose to give it.

Eve was drifting on the edge of sleep when she had a strange feeling that someone was in the room watching her. Her eyes snapped open. A man—Lucas—was standing quite still at the bottom of the bed, the glow from the embers of the dying fire behind him. With his black tousled hair and dressed in shirt and trousers, his shirt open to the waist and the sleeves rolled up over his forearms, he was strangely threatening as he stood motionless as a dim statue, all his attention riveted on her.

With a gasp of indignation she sat up and got out of bed,

grasping a blue silk bed-gown draped over the back of a chair close to the bed.

'Lucas! What are you doing here?' Her mind was in complete turmoil. She couldn't imagine why he had come to her room. Without answering he moved towards her. Tall, lean of waist, belly and hips, with strong muscled shoulders, Lucas Stainton was undoubtedly a handsome man, but his face in the mellow light was too strong, his mouth too stubborn and his chin too arrogant for Eve's liking just then. In fact, the sheer power emanating from him brought a fluttering to her stomach. She could smell brandy and his eyes were piercing bright. He stopped a few inches from her, a mocking smile curving his lips.

'Why, Eve, who else did you think it would be on our wedding night?' he drawled. 'A prowler, perhaps?'

'I really have no idea. Lucas, it is very late and time you were in bed.'

His smile became a leer as his smouldering, insolent gaze swept over her, turning to amazement at the heavy mass of the auburn fox pelt that rippled down her back to her buttocks, crackling and alive in the light from the fire.

'I know—which is the reason I am here.'

Unconscious of the vision she presented in her clinging robe and her hair tumbling over her shoulders in loose disarray, Eve's cheeks flamed, but at the same time her heart missed a beat. The meaning behind his words was only too clear. She felt her modesty, intact for so long, was being invaded by this man, her husband, who was beginning to alarm her nervous, awakened senses.

'I meant in your bed, not mine.'

'I know what you meant, but I decided that your bed will be far more comfortable than mine, so here I am.'

His cool mockery snapped Eve's fragile self-control. Planting her hands in the small of her waist, she glowered at him irately. 'Aye, Lucas, and fortified with a considerable amount of your fine brandy and a good deal of natural stubbornness. Now please leave. You are drunk.'

'So I am—and with good reason. Now get into bed, and stop playing the outraged virgin when we both know you're not. You have been married. You have a child, so you are not uninformed about these things. Besides, it is customary for marriages to be consummated on the wedding night.'

A small knot of tension began to form in the centre of Eve's chest. 'But you said—'

'Forget it,' he ground out. 'A wife's vows require that she submit to her husband in all things, and that includes satisfying him in bed.'

'You? And what about me?'

His grin was salacious. 'I am confident of my ability to satisfy you too, Eve.'

'Must I remind you of our arrangement?'

He cocked a dubious brow. 'Ah—the arrangement. And are you still absolutely certain this is how you want it to be between us?'

She nodded. 'Positive.'

'And if I refuse?'

'Then I'll do as you ask and submit to you.'

'Submit?' he repeated, furious by her choice of word. 'I don't want you to *submit* to me—to give yourself with reluctance.'

Eve's eyes locked on to his and her response was emphatic. 'Then don't pressure me,' she flared on a note of desperation. 'You promised you would give me time. We made a bargain and I thought you were gentleman enough to keep it.'

'I'm no gentleman and that was before today's unfortunate events. Things have changed,' he told her coldly. 'The arrangement, my sweet, is off.'

'And you obviously think I am compensation for an unpaid debt,' she threw at him angrily.

'Precisely.'

He raised his head and Eve was alarmed by the predatory gleam in his eyes, which looked dark in the dim light. He took a step towards her and then another, and Eve retreated step for step, until the backs of her legs bumped the bed. Unable to go forwards and adamantly unwilling to fall back on to the bed, she stood in mutinous silence, her heart pounding in her chest. He paused and his dark brows pulled together.

'Now, suppose you tell me why the prospect of going to bed with me seems to frighten you?'

'I'm not frightened. I don't fear you—truly I don't. I just don't want you to touch me,' Eve uttered, uneasy with his boldness. Tendrils of alarm wrapped themselves round her heart. 'You are drunk, Lucas. Please go away. Don't do something you will have cause to regret in the morning.'

She turned to move away from him, but in sheer frustration as she continued to deny him, Lucas reached out and, with his hands on her waist, roughly spun her around and jerked her into his arms, drawing her against his hard, muscular length.

'Enough of this nonsense,' he murmured shortly, his male senses aroused and eager to get on.

Eve's heart crashed terrifyingly as he bent his head and took her lips in a hard, silencing kiss. Pressed firmly against him, she was a mass of quivering rebellion. She was aware of nothing but the vigour of him, the power of him, the faint scent of his cologne and the aroma of brandy on his breath that fanned her cheek. Bracing her hands against his chest, she tore her lips from his and averted her face, offended by the effrontery of him.

'Stop this,' she said, breathing hard, deeply shocked by his assault. 'Don't, Lucas, please, please don't, not like this—not this way. I don't want you to.'

'Be still,' he muttered, taking her chin between his strong fingers and turning her head back to his so that she was forced to meet his eyes. He met her wary gaze beneath the long curving sweep of her lashes and admired the soft blush on the creamy skin of her cheeks, the slim, straight nose, and the delicately formed lips, which seemed to beckon the touch of his own.

'I know only one way to kiss a woman, Eve,' he whispered silkily, his fingers becoming gentle on her jaw, sliding his parted mouth along the smooth satin fire on her slender neck, 'and I've never had any complaints before. I'm beginning to think you enjoy baiting me, for you do it better than anyone I've known before.'

The room was hushed and dark and still around them. His hands glided restlessly, possessively, over her. Her struggles excited him further, his hands going at once to her breasts, the small nipples quivering against his hard palms, sliding his hands down her back and over the gentle swell of her buttocks, aware that her trembling body was naked beneath her flimsy nightdress and desiring nothing more than to strip it from her and push her down on to the bed and lose himself in her.

Unable to relax her rigid body, still she struggled against him, jerking herself away, trying to fend off his inquisitive hands. She was becoming increasingly afraid, her natural reserve and modesty in the face of so much male aggression turning her cold and resistant, for what he was doing, without any thought to how she might be feeling, was a stark reminder of Andrew's cruelty and made her feel that history was about to repeat itself.

And yet even now something told her that, given time and patience, for him to allow her senses to become accustomed to this powerful being invading her female world she had protected for so long, she would become as he wanted her to be, and as gratified as he appeared to be.

'Lucas—I can't…' she protested, only to have the words silenced by his mouth.

As his passion built, so did his conscience and the awful, guilty premonition that what he was doing was wrong. As some semblance of reality returned, abruptly he dragged his lips from hers and stepped away from her, seeing that her face was a mask of tortured anguish. Deeply shocked, he flinched with pain and remorse. How could he have done this to her? How could he ever hurt her? Raking his hand through the side of his hair in angry self-disgust, unable to look at her one second more, he spun round and strode to the door. He paused for a moment before he turned and studied her in silence.

After a moment he said in a quiet, almost apologetic tone that startled Eve, 'The fault for what happened just now was mine and I apologise. It had little to do with your baiting me. The contents of Mr Barstow's letter cancelled out our arrangement and merely gave me an excuse to do what I've wanted to do for some time.'

'Lucas—if I've hurt you…'

'Eve, the only wound that's been inflicted tonight is to my pride. The failure of our bargain infuriates me, and it galls me beyond measure to occupy an empty bed on my wedding night. It doesn't have to be like this between us. Is your own pride so great that you can't set it aside for just a few hours—just this once?'

A lump of nameless emotion constricted her throat, and although she had not forgiven him for coming to her room and trying to force himself on her, she was moved by the way he had stepped back and apologised. She felt something stir in her breast, the feeling moving down to the pit of her stomach where it lay, warm and comfortable. Looking into his face, she was unable to look away, held by something she was unable to name, but which her female body instantly recognised.

She had seen the look once before when a man had wanted to take her to bed, but then she had feared the look—and with good reason. However, she felt it strange that she did not fear the way Lucas was looking at her— quite the opposite, in fact, for she found herself unprepared for the sheer force of the feelings that swept through her and she knew that she was in grave danger, not from her husband but from herself. The prospect of pretending for just a few hours that she was a beloved bride and he an amorous groom seemed not only harmless but irresistibly appealing and she was tempted to ask him to take her to bed, but something deep inside stopped her.

Finally, drawing a long, steadying breath, she said, 'Yes.'

The single word, spoken with such quiet conviction, hit Lucas in all its finality. 'Then I will bid you goodnight.' He turned from her and left her room, his heart twisting in agony at what he had just done—coldly forcing himself on her like the wretch that he was.

Like a sleepwalker, numb, stunned by what had just happened, Eve turned to the bed. Still in her robe, she crawled beneath the covers and curled herself in a tight ball, hugging her knees. Yet the haunting pressure of Lucas's lips and body pressed close burned in the depth of her being.

Chapter Nine

The following morning Eve dressed and went downstairs. The house was surprisingly quiet considering four children lived in it—so very different to the Seagrove household, where children's voices and laughter could be heard for most of the time. When she reached the hall she was informed by one of the footmen that Lucas would like to see her. As she crossed towards the study, she realised it was going to be more difficult than she anticipated greeting him with just the proper degree of casualness after what had transpired between them the night before.

When she had visited the nursery earlier, although Sarah had given her a quiet look, Eve was relieved that she was sensitive enough not to employ any indelicate talk concerning her wedding night—although what Sarah would think were she to tell her that both she and Lucas had slept in their own beds she really had no idea.

Lucas was working at his big desk amid a pile of folders and papers and did not look up, not even when she closed the door. He was freshly shaved, groomed and sober, but his handsome face was unreadable.

'Please sit down,' he said, his voice terse, cold and impersonal. Keeping his eyes lowered, with a wave of his hand he indicated a comfortable winged chair to the side of the desk. 'I'll be with you in a moment.'

Doing as he bade and perching straight backed on the edge of the chair, Eve wondered how he could look so utterly casual and composed after last night. He seemed able to dismiss it entirely. She sat quite still, hardly daring to move, practically holding her breath, the swift scratching of his pen across the paper invading the silence in the room. After a full two minutes he suddenly threw down his pen and looked up. Whatever thoughts of revenge and wounded pride had driven him to seek her out in her bed were forgotten, while she was struggling to look even a little normal in the aftermath of his assault.

On the other hand, she realised he no longer looked cold or cynical or angry, and that was a relief.

'You wanted to see me, Lucas.'

'Yes,' he replied blandly, shoving his chair back and standing up. 'You look pale, Eve. Did you not sleep well?'

'I did—eventually.' He offered no word of apology for having intruded on her privacy, even if he didn't mean it, and though his lips smiled, his eyes did not. Not that eager to refer to the matter, standing up, she said, 'What is it you wanted to see me about?'

'To tell you that I intend leaving for Laurel Court tomorrow morning. I intend to keep this house for the time being. With no one living in it, the upkeep will be minimal. Please see to it that the children are packed up and ready to leave by nine o'clock.'

For a moment, surprise left her speechless. This was the

last thing she had been expecting. 'Laurel Court? But—shouldn't servants be sent on ahead to get things ready?'

'There isn't time. We shall travel together. You liked Laurel Court, as I recall, so I don't suppose you have any objections.'

'There is nothing I would like better. But surely a few more days to prepare wouldn't go amiss.'

'No, Eve,' he said abruptly, 'and please don't argue. I have urgent business in the north-east and I don't want to leave you and the children alone in London.'

'But you are suggesting that we are to be left alone in the country.'

'Why not? You will be perfectly safe. Laurel Court is a hell of a lot better for the children than living in town.' When she didn't respond, he said in a bored drawl, 'At least at Laurel Court you will be spared my presence. Please tell me you didn't expect me to remain and play happy families. Tell me you aren't that naïve.'

Flinching from the chilling bite of his tone, Eve looked at the hard, handsome face. Mr Barstow's arrival yesterday had successfully destroyed any hope she might have had of meeting Lucas on any sort of common ground, confusing her and seriously diminishing her own sense of worth. Swallowing convulsively, she shook her head and answered him honestly.

'After the events of yesterday I didn't know what to expect, but I did not expect you to ignore what happened.'

'Good. At least we are in agreement on that. There's been enough deceit and misunderstandings between us.'

Suddenly Eve felt a burning annoyance at his attitude and all her resentment toward Lucas and the circumstances that had changed her life so immeasurably welled up inside her in a fierce anger.

'I did not set out to deceive you, Lucas. So if you are to continue punishing me for something that was beyond my control, then do so if it makes you feel better. For myself, I am relieved you are to put some distance between us. I only hope the north-east is far enough away.'

Lucas's eyes darkened in anger. 'I am not,' he insisted with straining patience, 'intent on punishing you and nor do I place the blame for what has happened at your door. I am doing my damnedest to come to terms with the unfortunate circumstances that have brought about this débâcle, while trying to work out what to do to save us from complete ruin.'

'And you think you can do that by going away?'

'It is possible.'

She put up her chin. 'Very well. If you will excuse me, I will go and inform Sarah there is some packing to do.'

Lucas watched her go with grudging admiration. The situation for her must be devastating, he realised suddenly. She too had lost everything and now she was forced to face a new way of life at the side of a husband who had made it clear he didn't want her.

But then, that wasn't entirely true. He did want her, that was the trouble. One part of him wanted nothing to do with her. And yet another—by far the greatest part—wanted to take her in his arms and awaken all the exquisite, undiscovered passion in that lovely body. She aroused carnal feelings in him that he had no business feeling if he meant to keep his distance from her, yet he knew how fragile his control was whenever he was near her.

Lucas got to his feet as Eve swept into the dining room on their first night back at Laurel Court. He had a glass of wine in his hand and had been swirling the deep red liquid round as he stared broodingly into the fire. He turned slowly towards her, placing his glass down while he poured her some wine and handed it to her.

'So, Eve, are you happy to be back at Laurel Court?'

'Yes, I confess I am. I have developed a fondness for it, and the children are excited about being back.'

The look he gave her was sharp and meaningful. 'You do realise that I am in danger of losing it if nothing is done to recoup my losses,' he reminded her, deliberately sowing the seeds of discontent.

Holding on to her temper with superhuman effort, Eve managed to speak calmly. 'The collapse of my father's finances have come as a bitter blow to you, Lucas. I do know that without you feeling that you have to remind me of it all the time.'

'And never fails to stir your temper,' he remarked, admiring the way anger turned her eyes to a deep midnight blue.

'And you have a talent for raising my temper to boiling point more than anyone else. As mistress of this beautiful house I will do everything to help in any way I can.'

'You will find plenty to do over the days and weeks you are here. The staff is small and we can't afford to set on more, so your duties will be many. Do you ride, by the way?'

'Yes,' she answered stiffly. 'I love riding.'

'Then I'll show you the whole of the estate in the morning—such as it is.'

'I'd like that. When do you intend leaving?'

'In two or three weeks. I want to make sure you are all settled in before I go.'

'And will you be away long?'

'As to that, I have no idea.'

He led her to the table when their food was brought in. Their places had been set together, Lucas at the top of the table, Eve beside him, so that they might talk without the length of the table between them. The candlelight gleamed on the polished surface and shimmered on the crystal glasses.

Eve ate in uneasy silence, but as the wine and the delicious chicken and onion soup began to have a softening effect on her, and looking forward to the braised beef and lemon soufflé to follow, she began to relax.

'With so few provisions, Mrs Coombs has excelled herself,' Eve commented as she spooned the soup into her mouth.

'Mrs Coombs is very much aware that we are dining alone together for the first time as husband and wife and she has gone out of her way to make this a memorable meal. So even though we both know it will not have the desired effect, enjoy it and be sure to thank her afterwards.'

'I do not need reminding of my manners, Lucas,' Eve told him tartly, 'but I think I should remind you of yours. Where I come from, it is considered ill bred to argue at the dining table.'

Her sharp reprimand filled Lucas with amusement, and, duly chastened, he said, 'You are quite right. I should know better and I apologise.' Having finished his soup, he put his spoon down. Leaning back in his chair, he looked at her speculatively. 'What is to become of us, Eve? Nothing between us is going as planned, is it? We have both lost a great deal and are paying the price. But there might be other options.'

Eve raised both brows, a little smile quirking her lips. 'You aren't, by any chance, thinking of robbing a bank?'

He grinned. 'Nothing so dramatic.'

'Has it got anything to do with your going to the north-east in such a hurry?'

He nodded. 'I shall be travelling to Newcastle. I've inherited a parcel of land up there. The land itself isn't worth much, but then again it might be. You see, there is a disused mine on it.'

Eve stared at him in amazement. 'A coal mine?'

He nodded. 'When it was brought to my notice shortly after my brother died, I employed the services of a mining engineer to take a look at it. He has surveyed what he can of it, although it is much flooded and the pit-head buildings in disrepair, as is the pumping system, he assures me there are still rich seams of coal to be got out.'

'But without the necessary capital to modernise, to make it safe and operative, how can it be reopened?'

'I shall go cap in hand to every banker and every businessman I can think of who might be willing to lend me the money, and don't forget I have this place as collateral.'

'But do you know anything about coal mining?'

'Not a thing, but I can learn. As fortune would have it, Henry's family home is close to Newcastle. He has kindly offered me his hospitality. He is to come here the day before I leave and we will travel together.'

He continued speaking of his journey north, falling silent when the next course was brought in, and not until they were alone did either of them speak.

'Have you selected rooms for yourself?' Lucas asked, slicing through the succulent piece of beef.

'Yes—a lovely suite of rooms overlooking the gardens. One of the reasons I chose them is because they are close to the nursery. Do you approve?'

His eyes narrowed and gleamed across at her and the

semblance of a salacious smile curved his lips. 'Most certainly,' he murmured softly.

Lifting a brow, Lucas regarded his wife for some time until she chafed at the unsuppressed humour she saw dancing in his bright eyes. Discomfited, Eve watched him narrowly, suspiciously. A queer feeling settled in her stomach as she wondered what he found so amusing about her selection of rooms.

'You clearly find my selection of rooms entertaining, Lucas. Would you care to share it with me? If you don't think they are suitable, then perhaps you would suggest something else.'

'I would not deprive you of the rooms you have chosen. They are the ones I would have selected for you myself. It suits me very well having you so close.'

With belated perception she realised what so amused him and she gritted her teeth at the thought of her own foolishness. 'Do you mean to tell me that of all the rooms in this huge house, I had to pick the ones next to yours?'

'Correct. And there is a door connecting your apartment to mine, so it is—convenient.'

She glanced at him sharply. 'Not too convenient, I hope. I sincerely hope there is a lock on the door.'

He paused in his eating and surveyed her dispassionately. 'There is, when I choose to use it. I do fear the nearness of you might completely destroy my good intentions—although if that should happen, I hope you would not object as strongly to my actions as you did last night. The last thing I want is for you to submit to me, but I don't think it would be too difficult to make you want me, Eve.'

Eve's colour deepened. The quiet emotion in his voice startled her and she looked away. It was a challenge, softly said, and Eve found herself gripping the napkin in her lap to keep her hands from trembling. His intention was to put on a grand front, and he expected her to do the same. But how easy it would be to let appearances slip into reality—if only this were not an arrangement between them.

Lucas was so attractive and she was drawn to him in a way she had never thought to experience. Even if none of the gentler emotions such as love were present, could they not have a good marriage? Yet the arrangement and Andrew's past callous indifference to her as a woman and his wife had set a barrier between them and her pride refused to let her cross it. She could only hope that Lucas's restraint would continue and her resistance would not be tested as it was last night.

Aware of her confusion, Lucas was unable to suppress a smile. 'When you have need of my services, feel free to knock on the connecting door. You will find your husband more than willing to share your bed.'

'I have no intention of doing any such thing.'

'Why? Would it be such an onerous duty?' His smile widened, which she found infuriating. 'Your cheeks are flushed, Eve. Are you unwell?'

'I am perfectly well, Lucas,' she snapped, 'If it is your intention to try and batter my defences with another assault similar to the one you tried last night, then please don't.'

Lucas smiled inwardly. He had got the measure of his lovely wife and knew that her demeanour was no indication of how she was inside. She was a clever woman, granted, but she had not yet learned that resistance, or indeed any kind of opposition, only turned Lucas Stainton in the other direction from the one which Eve wanted him to take.

'This is foolishness, you know, Eve.'

'Foolish?'

'To keep yourself apart from me. You are my wife and one day you must bear my children—however distasteful the idea appears to you now. Resisting the inevitable is like swimming against the tide. Some day you will have to abandon your resistance and let the tide take you where it will.'

'Then when that day comes, Lucas—whether it be tomorrow, next week or next month—I will be sure to let you know.'

Eve continued to eat in silence. Lucas had given her much to think about and the fact that he had such easy access to her worried her considerably.

Gazing at her as he ate his meal, Lucas was struck afresh by her loveliness. It was easy to forget he hadn't wanted to marry her. What was difficult was controlling his physical reaction to her nearness. An exercise in fortitude, he thought wryly, that was going to be exceedingly trying.

Eve's mind was working on similar lines. She too was experiencing a similar physical reaction to the one Lucas was experiencing. His dark green coat and close-fitting light grey trousers hugged the contours of his muscled torso and long, well-defined legs, making her fully aware of his overwhelming masculinity. She was finding it harder and harder to retreat into cool reserve when she was near him, especially when memories of his kiss, hot, wild and sweet, kept swirling around in her mind.

Chastising herself for allowing her thoughts to suggest what her body wanted to experience again, Eve was relieved when the meal was over. Pleading tiredness, she declined the coffee and excused herself. She hurried up the stairs, gaining the safety of her bedchamber. Only then did she pause to catch her breath. Whether it was from relief at having escaped her husband, the exertion of her climbing the stairs, or simple fear, her heart pounded in her breast, seeming to jolt her entire body with ever beat.

One of the maids was turning down the covers on the bed and stayed to help Eve out of her clothes and into her nightdress. She was discreet and went out quietly. Silence filled the room. Left alone in her apprehension, Eve stared at the offending door. Going towards it, she turned the knob. It was for all its ominous presence locked, but she had no doubt at all that the key was on Lucas's side of the door. Stepping away from it, she prayed desperately for the strength and fortitude that would be required to face whatever lay before her should he decide to exercise his husbandly rights and unlock that door.

If Lucas should find his way into her room and seek to finish what he had started last night, she was absolutely certain that she could not withstand his persuasive, unrelenting assault. What she had experienced in his arms had been new to her. He had aroused feelings and emotions Andrew never had, and she had no idea how to deal with them.

After a while she got into bed, her ears attuned to every sound in the great house. She heard Lucas enter his room and, holding her breath, she lay as stiff as a statue as she listened to his slow footsteps moving about, fully expecting him to come through the door at any minute. Eventually there was silence, but her husband was as easily dismissed from her mind as a wolf at her throat.

When Eve awoke, glistening bright sunlight filled the room in abundance as the maid drew back the heavy drapes. Rousing slowly, she blinked and huddled deeper into the covers, not yet ready to rise until she glanced at the clock on the mantelpiece and saw it was nine o'clock.

When Lucas came striding through the connecting door, bathed and attired, no evidence of her sleepless night remained. Seated at her dressing table brushing her hair, she stared at him in horror and disbelief that he should take such liberties as entering her room without knocking. In an immaculate white shirt, buff-coloured riding breeches and gleaming black boots, he looked incredibly handsome and at ease with himself. From somewhere in the depth of her momentary panic, indignation seized her.

'Good morning, Eve.'

'Good morning, Lucas,' she replied, tossing him a cool glance as the maid made a hurried departure. 'Don't you ever knock?'

His brows lifted derisively. 'On my wife's bedroom door? Never, so you'd better get used to it.' He grinned leisurely as his perusal swept her. 'Very nice,' he murmured, perching his hip on her dressing table and watching her in fascination as she brushed her magnificent wealth of hair. 'That colour suits you.'

Lucas's eyes captured hers and held them prisoner, until she felt warmth suffuse her cheeks. 'What do you want?' she asked bluntly as she continued to concentrate on her hair, trying to ignore the effect his presence was having on her heart rate, and not to look at the lean, hard muscles of his thighs as they flexed beneath the tight-fitting breeches.

'I came to see if the sights were better in here than they are in my room.' The corners of his lips twitched with amusement and his eyes gleamed into hers as he added, 'I am happy to report they are.' Idly he reached out and took a heavy lock of her hair, twining it around one of his long, lean fingers. 'You have beautiful hair, Eve. 'Tis a crime to confine it in knots and coils all the time.'

'Lucas, do you mind?' she snapped, snatching it from his finger and proceeding to twist and coil the rich mass and secure it with pins in her nape. 'It's just not practical to have it hanging loose all the time.'

'You seem to have suffered no ill effects from your first night as mistress of Laurel Court.'

'I slept very well as it happens.'

'Despite the presence of the big bad wolf on the other side of the door.'

'Yes, Lucas, despite that. It must be a long time since the house had a mistress.'

'It is. Stephen might have made free with my wife here, but as you know he never married her. My mother was the last mistress.' He smiled, 'She would have liked you. She set great store by family and would have seen in you a hope for its continuation. Indeed, she would have been anxious for us to produce an heir.'

Eve had the feeling he was laughing at her, but she was not amused. The subject was one she dearly wished to avoid. Her silence spoke for itself.

Lucas's mouth quirked in a half-smile. 'As I am. Of course every man wants a son and you seemed to fit the requirements of my son's mother admirably. You have beauty as well as brains, Eve. Our son will be well blessed.'

Incensed, Eve shoved a final pin into her hair. 'And is that supposed to be a compliment? Is that all you see me as—as some kind of—of brood mare?'

'That you should bear my son was part of the arrangement. With three children between us, I have no doubt of our ability to produce more offspring.'

Flushing furiously, Eve avoided his eyes. 'We have three daughters, Lucas, and your brother produced Alice, don't forget. Producing a son might prove to be another matter entirely. I shouldn't think you would want another girl.'

'On the contrary. I happen to like little girls. My self-esteem has need of consolation, of a sort, and I can think of no greater comfort than for you to bear my child—boy or girl.'

As quickly as it rose, the colour drained from Eve's face. 'I know I am bound by my word, and I will abide by it, but I ask that you give me a little time.'

His eyes held her gaze. 'Providing that's all it is. Things change, Eve—like the conditions to our…arrangement. I am sure your father would have wanted you to have a full, rich life and that is what I intend to give you.'

He spoke so seriously that Eve turned her startled gaze on him. 'Do you really mean that?'

He shrugged, lightly fingering her hairbrush. 'Why should I not? A marriage of convenience need not be doomed to disaster.'

'I hope not, although I doubt I shall ever be able to forget that this is exactly what my union with you is, and that you see me in less than a romantic light.'

'Do I detect a note of regret?' Gleaming whiteness flashed as he grinned down at her. 'Despite your American upbringing, there is a strong sense of the English in you. If you feel you have missed the incessant tradition of wooing before rushing into marriage, then we could pretend we are not yet married and begin the wooing process right here and now.'

Suspicious of everything he said and did, Eve stared at

him, unsure if he was teasing or not. 'I don't think so, Lucas. I agree a civilised relationship would be very agreeable, but I am not yet willing to forgo our arrangement.' She smiled sweetly. 'Now, shall we go down to breakfast and afterwards you can show me the wonders of Laurel Court.'

'I believe, my sweet,' he said solicitously, following in her wake, appreciatively watching her hips as they swayed with a natural, graceful provocation, 'that you have a penchant for testing me and my ability to withstand you. I shall be delighted to show you the estate, and the fact that you refuse to forgo our arrangement only spikes my interest—so I warn you to beware, Eve.'

Eve turned her head and looked at him, and she did not miss the meaningful sparkle in those pale blue eyes.

Eve was not disappointed in her expectation of Laurel Court, the ancestral home of several generations of Staintons, comprised of woods, parkland and fertile fields. This was Lucas's home, the place where he was born and where he'd grown to manhood.

When she was mounted, Lucas brought his horse alongside her dancing mare, eager to be off.

'Shall we go?'

The day was pleasant and warm with gusts of wind that billowed out the skirt of Eve's jade-green riding habit and loosened tendrils of hair about her face. Her horse was spirited and eager and needed a firm, attentive hand on the reins. She was deeply conscious of her companion as he rode beside her, letting his body roll easily with the surge of the powerful mount beneath him.

Lucas stole an admiring glance at his companion. He stared at her profile, tracing with his gaze the classically beautiful line of her face, the sweep of lustrous ebony eye-lashes, the delicate curve of her cheek. She represented everything most desirable in a woman. She rode well, assured, elegant and in control, apparently unconscious of his gaze. He felt a familiar quickening in his veins. How vital and alive she was, with the sun bringing out the vivid lights in her hair exposed beneath her fetching hat set at a jaunty angel, a white feather curling up from its shallow brim.

They stopped to rest the horses by a small lake beyond a grassy slope, dismounting and leaving their mounts to graze on the tender tufts of grass by the water's edge. The tranquil lake with willows draping their heavy branches in the water was a peaceful, perfect setting. Two swans went gliding by and water lilies rode the stillness of the water like white boats. They strolled along the bank, the warmth of the sun beating down on them.

Eve breathed deeply, soaking up the atmosphere. 'This is a lovely place. You were so lucky having all this on hand while you were growing up. New York was so very different. In the summer we used to go and stay with friends on Long Island, but it was nothing like this.'

Lucas turned his head and glanced at her. She looked lovely with a flush of health beneath her flesh and her eyes clear and vivid blue, the snapping colour of them brought about by the joy of being at Laurel Court.

'I suppose I was fortunate, although I suppose I took it for granted. I haven't been here for some time—it was difficult when Maxine left me and came to live with Stephen. It seems strange being back. There is much to be done but, until I can grasp back some of the capital I lost, things will have to wait.'

'I can understand how difficult it must have been for

you. You say you inherited the land in the north-east. Do you have relatives up in Newcastle?'

'Not that I know of. The deeds to the land were found in my brother's papers when he died.'

'Won't you tell me about him?' she asked quietly.

'You don't want to know, believe me.'

'As a matter of fact, I do.'

'You must already have heard what he was like.'

'I have heard things that have been said about him, but I cannot form an opinion about someone I didn't know. Was he much older than you?'

'Ten years.'

'And was he never married?'

'He was too busy pleasure seeking. We were not close. Years of heavy drinking did not deal kindly with Stephen. His health suffered and the poor condition of his liver often reflected itself in quick and severe changes of mood. Long periods of elation when he was drinking were followed by a slow decline into discontent and remorse to the depths of black depression. Yet for all his faults he still possessed his share of irresistible charm. The easy lopsided smile and twinkling blue eyes were capable of melting even the coldest female heart—and there was none colder than Maxine's.'

'What is she really like, your wife?'

'You've met her. You must have seen for yourself what she's like. I would spare you the more unsavoury details,' he answered, followed by a curt, impatient question of his own. 'Eve, are you always so inquisitive?'

It was a thinly veiled reprimand and a warning not to come any closer, but Eve couldn't accept that. 'I'd rather you didn't—and, yes, I'm inquisitive by nature,' she said, much to his surprise. 'But it's not just that. I would like there to be truth and honesty between us.'

'Very well. Maxine's attitude to marriage did not include the concept of fidelity. She succumbed to Stephen's charms, turning to him for the excitement she craved after the birth of two children in the mistaken belief that as the older brother he had no shortage of money in his pocket or his bank.'

'Was Stephen her only lover?'

He shook his head. 'I believe there were others.'

'I—thought that in most aristocratic houses adultery was taken for granted, always provided, of course, the affair is conducted with discretion.'

'Not in my house, and not when the other party was my own brother. Neither of them took the trouble to conceal the affair.'

'And—the children?'

'They are both mine. I am sure of that. When Maxine failed to provide me with a male heir, she ignored the two she had given birth to and thought she was free to amuse herself as she pleased. She walked out before Abigail was out of the cradle.'

He fell silent and Eve dropped her eyes in shamed remorse for forcing him to speak about his brother and his wife, reopening old wounds. 'I'm so sorry for asking,' she said quietly, 'but thank you for telling me.'

They continued to walk in companionable silence, watching a rather splendid kingfisher skim the surface of the water and hearing the cry of a curlew overhead.

'Tell me about your husband?' Lucas said after a while. 'Who was he?'

Eve turned her head and looked at him sharply. She

was very conscious of him studying her, deliberately and at some length, and her new consciousness of him made her avert her eyes. She was taken off guard by the question, but it was asked politely and with a subtle interest, and she saw no reason not to appease his curiosity. In fact, she was surprised he had not asked about Andrew before now.

'Andrew? Our families had been friends for as long as I can remember. He was older than me—almost ten years—and famous for his charm and good manners.'

'And how old were you when you married?'

'Seventeen.'

'A naïve and virginal seventeen,' Lucas murmured softly, his gaze on her flushed face.

'Yes, I was. I think he thought of me as a child.'

'And you loved him, of course?'

She turned her head and looked at him in helpless consternation. 'Why of course?'

'Isn't passion supposed to be characteristic of seventeen-year-old girls? Aren't all young ladies supposed to be in love at that age?'

'Passion, maybe. Clear thinking isn't.' She gave a rueful smile. 'I remember that very vividly. I didn't love Andrew. We were—friends. I respected him—but love? No.'

'Then why did you marry him?'

'Because our families were friends. It—was expected of us.'

'And did you always do things to please everyone else?'

'Yes, but where my marriage to Andrew was concerned, I should have listened to my head.' She smiled wryly. 'I don't suppose you can call six months a proper marriage, but at the time it felt like a lifetime. We were in New Orleans at the time with his business. He went out one night and was shot in a bar-room brawl with some Englishmen. Like your brother, Andrew liked to gamble—but he didn't like to lose. He couldn't take it. I realised afterwards how little I knew him.'

'And he was not entirely the charming man he seemed to be.'

'No. He was quick to anger—and—not very nice.'

Unexpectedly Lucas's expression darkened into a thoughtful scowl and he felt an unexplainable surge of anger at Andrew Brody. He stopped and gently took her arm, forcing her to look at him. A suspicion had entered his mind and, once it had, the rage he felt at the suspicion was so powerful he couldn't rest until he'd proved or disproved it. In her dark blue eyes he detected a terrible anguish.

'Eve, did Andrew physically abuse you?'

The light was harsh on her face, but she turned it up towards Lucas. It was as if he had seen through the very bones of her head into the secret places of her mind. 'No—he—he didn't hit me or anything—but abuse doesn't have to be physical,' she said quietly, turning from him and walking slowly on, wondering what he would say if she told him the truth, that in her experience, the ugly and humiliating way men and women expressed their love physically was agony.

Lucas glanced at her profile. Now her face tightened and shut, as if a door had been closed. Quite obviously her brief marriage had been a horrendous crisis in her life, and he wasn't sure that even after five years she had been able to surmount it. If not, it went a long way to explaining things about her that had puzzled him from the beginning. Had the physical side of marriage she had endured married to Andrew been so bad that she had been reluctant to enter into marriage again—with anyone? If so, there was little wonder she had insisted on the proviso that they slept apart.

'It's all right, Eve. I see I've embarrassed you.'

His voice was so gentle. Gentle and yet positive. 'My marriage to Andrew is in the past and belongs there, but one good thing came out of it—Estelle. She has made everything worthwhile.'

'I can see that, but there is something I would like to ask you. The question is of a sensitive nature, but if we are to proceed with our marriage it is one I shall have to ask you some time.'

'What is it?'

'Do you still have nightmares—problems—call it what you like, about what happened with Andrew?' Lucas asked. 'Because if you do—'

'No,' Eve interrupted quickly, embarrassed heat consuming her face. 'Of course I don't—at least…'

Once again Lucas stopped and she turned to face him, his expression grave, his gaze refusing to relinquish hers. 'The truth, if you please, Eve. We have to get to the heart of the matter. It is important to both of us.'

She swallowed audibly, suddenly nervous about talking about something that had lain dormant for five years. 'I know it is, but…well—I don't think so—at least I hope not. Afterwards, when Andrew died, having no one to confide in—not that I could ever talk to someone, however close, on such a sensitive matter—I tried seeking explanations in my own mind about what…you know, and I thought about it in such a way that reduced it to proportions my young mind could understand and accept.'

'And what conclusions did you reach?'

'That sexually I was illiterate. Perhaps if I'd had

someone to guide me, to show me what being a woman meant, then I would have been aware of what was to happen and it would not have been so bad. My mother died when I was quite young, you see, and although my governess was a good teacher and a fine woman, there were things she couldn't teach me because, being a spinster, I don't think she ever learned them.'

'And when you came to me with your proposition, insisting there would be no sexual contact between us if I accepted, did you honestly think I would meekly comply to your suggestion?'

'Yes,' she replied simply, 'if you were desperate enough for the money.'

'And you didn't think I might become sexually frustrated, spending the rest of my life close to a beautiful wife and being denied any contact?'

She sighed and moved to stand by the edge of the lake, looking out over the water. 'In truth, I don't think I thought about that side of it very much.'

Lucas moved to stand beside her. Eve forced herself not to turn towards him. 'Your trouble,' he said thoughtfully, 'is that you don't know what you're missing.'

Eve did look at him then and her eyes sparked. 'Yes, I do. Andrew saw to that.'

'It sounds to me as if Andrew was a bit of a bully who only thought of his own gratification. Your governess may also have been at fault, but on the other hand, maybe it would be better if I showed you what you have been missing.'

Before she could move, he had pulled her into an embrace that brought her right up against him so that her breasts were against his chest and his hips leaned hard and flat against her skirts.

His powerful, animal-like masculinity was an assault on her senses. 'Lucas! What are you doing?' she demanded.

An explicable, lazy smile swept over his face. 'Preparing to give you a lesson.'

'Please let me go, before you do something you will regret.'

'I won't. Neither of us will. I'm a good teacher. Relax,' he whispered when she struggled against him, relieved to see a look in her eyes that was not quite fear and not quite anger either. 'Despite how you perceive what happened when you were married to Andrew, marriage to me will not be the same. We are both adults and we both know exactly what this is leading up to. Do you want me to spell it out so there's no mistaking my motives?'

A heated blush stained her smooth cheeks and he deliberately pushed the point. 'My motives aren't noble, Eve— they're adult and they're perfectly natural, and it's already a foregone conclusion that I'm going to kiss you,' he murmured, lowering his head, his eyes fixed securely on her lips. 'This is a preliminary demonstration, not a full-scale initiation, I promise,' and before Eve could make any further protest he'd claimed her lips in a long, shuddering kiss.

Eve stiffened within his arms and tried not to jerk away from him, for there was nothing she wanted more than to be loved by this handsome, challenging husband of hers, to be loved as a woman should be loved by a man, but she wanted to give her love freely, not to have it taken. But when he deepened his kiss, her heart began to hammer like a wild, captive bird.

Shyly she slid her hands up his chest and around his neck, holding him close and shyly kissing him back. The kiss was disturbing, and it induced in her a whole new range of uncontrollable feelings. Her eyes, which had been wide open to begin with, slowly fluttered closed. All she was conscious of was Lucas's mouth and his body pressed to hers and what he was doing to her, and she wanted it to go on for ever. She had no thoughts, only feelings, and they filled her with such a sense of languorous pleasure that she seemed to be floating.

Lucas told himself to go slowly, to stop before he forced her down on to the grass and behaved like the sex-starved male he was instead of the leisurely lover he'd promised to be, but when her hands slid into the hair at his nape, her mouth yielding with tormenting sweetness to his intimate kiss, he felt a burgeoning pleasure and astonished joy that was almost beyond bearing.

Dragging his lips from hers and brushing a kiss along her jaw and down her throat, where a little pulse was fluttering with all the wild panic of a trapped butterfly, Lucas again sought her mouth, passing his lips over the soft contours. He traced the trembling line between her lips with his tongue, urging them to part, insisting, and when they did he plunged his tongue into the soft sweetness of her mouth and kissed her long and deep.

Long minutes later, Lucas finally forced himself to lift his head, and gaze down into her eyes. 'I think we're going to have to stop.'

Eve thrilled to the sound of his voice, the words he uttered and the touch of his fingers filling her with conflicting emotions. She struggled to free herself from the trance-like state induced by his intoxicating kiss, the heat of the sun, and by the glittering waters of the lake. She glanced around, suddenly conscious that they were in an open place and easily watched.

'I think so, too. Someone might see us.'

He chuckled lightly. 'Be at ease. Your virtue is safe with me. Who could be more concerned than your husband?'

She smiled somewhat shyly. 'Who indeed?'

'Do you still fear what will happen when you are in my bed, Eve?' Lucas questioned huskily, watching intently the myriad of emotions flit across her face.

It came with a slow dawning that in his arms most of her apprehensions had fled. Though the barrier of not knowing how it would be between them remained, it no longer worried her like it did and hopefully would soon be removed, but still she resisted on the strength of her old fear. 'We shall have to wait and see.'

'For what? You no longer have an adequate excuse to avoid my bed. The sooner you realise that, the better it will be.'

He continued to look at her, his eyes clearly expressing his wants. The bold stare touched a quickness in her that made her feel as if she were on fire. Her pulses raced and her heart took flight. She could feel his nearness with every fibre of her being, and she was less shaken by the sight of him than by his slow perusal.

'I—I think we should be getting back,' she said hesitantly, turning from him.

They walked back to where they had left the horses, moving more quickly than before and without speaking. Lucas cupped his hands for Eve's booted foot and hoisted her effortlessly into the saddle. Hooking her knee round the pommel and arranging her skirts, she tried avoiding his eyes, but her gaze was irresistibly drawn to them. He stood beside her, looking up at her, holding her eyes in a wilful vise of pale blue. His voice was soft as he continued, but it held a note of determination, which in a peculiar way both frightened and angered her.

'In the beginning when our bargain was struck I trusted you. I have had a taste of what you have to offer, the sweet warmth of your lips, and I am impatient to sample the rest of you, which is mine by right of wedlock. And I will have it.'

With a cluck of her tongue she reined the horse about and cantered off without waiting for Lucas to mount. With a satisfied smile parting his lips to reveal a flash of white, he was soon riding in her wake, her mare chafing against the control of the bit, her tail arched high and her full mane flowing. And on her back a vision of loveliness, cool and relaxed and controlling the horse with a practised hand, the full riding skirt covering both herself and the side of the horse.

Their pleasant interlude by the lake had given her much to think about, that he knew, and he sincerely hoped she would resolve her dilemma before it was time for him to leave.

Of late he was ever conscious of her, and whenever he was close to her he was aware of all her womanly attributes and he wanted her. The scent of her lingered on the perimeter of his mind. She was like a fire burning in his blood, a fire that was unquenchable, for the thought of other women became soured in his mind when he compared them to his lovely wife.

Chapter Ten

For the rest of the day Eve was noticeably quiet. When Sarah asked her advice about a matter to do with the children, she gave it, but without real interest, which brought a frown of consternation to Sarah's brow. That something was on her mistress's mind was obvious, but considering her recent marriage followed by a hurried departure for the country, it wasn't surprising.

Every time Eve thought of Lucas and the feelings he had stirred in her, she could feel the blood rushing to her cheeks. In frustration she put her hands to her heated face. This is ridiculous, she thought, furious with herself. If I'm going to blush every time I think of Lucas, I'm in terrible trouble. Ever since she had returned from their ride she had been fighting common sense and dreaming about what could be—that the roots of their marriage were beginning to take hold in the barren soil of their unfortunate beginning. For goodness' sake, she told herself scathingly, all he did was kiss you. Oh, if only there was someone she could confide in. If only she could talk to Beth, with her good, rock-solid sensible composure and sound advice.

In an attempt to calm her frustration and bring some semblance of normality to her thoughts and the problem her marriage was posing, she went out into the overgrown garden to pick some flowers to fill the empty vases. She was so absorbed in her task and her thoughts that she failed to notice the man observing her.

Lucas stood casually watching her through the open window of the study as Eve snipped some rampant white roses and placed them carefully in the basket she carried on her arm. His eyes passed over her shapely figure with warm admiration. The light breeze teased the rich locks of her hair tumbling about her shoulders. Her arms reached forward to snip a rose almost out of her reach, and for a moment the bodice of her gown stretched tight across the slim back. He enjoyed watching her. Despite her earlier marriage there was a graceful naïvety about her that intrigued him, and he thought he would greatly enjoy instructing her in the ways of love.

Eve suddenly paused, arrested by the intruding suspicion that she was being watched, and straightened up. Her eyes were drawn like a magnet to the mullioned windows of Lucas's study on the ground floor, catching sight of the tall, jacketless onlooker calmly watching her, and the shock that went through her made her catch her breath.

The evening meal was a strained affair. When Eve swept into the dining room she found her husband already there. Seated in front of the fire with his long muscular legs outstretched in front of him and crossed at the ankles, he looked disgustingly at ease as he sipped a glass of wine. At the elegantly set-out dining table he was far too close for her peace of mind, for he sat at the head of the table and she close on his right. His gaze never wavered from her.

He was bronzed from the sun, and in contrast his light blue eyes seemed to shine like bright gems. Why did his presence always affect her? Why didn't he just go away and let her be reconciled to his leaving? Why did he have to prolong her agony? There was a long night to be got through, when her self-control would be tested to its limits.

'You were watching me this afternoon, Lucas.'

'Do you mind?'

'How long were you standing there?'

A slow smile touched his lips. 'Long enough.'

Eve was in no mood for a game. 'For what?'

His smouldering gaze passed over her. 'Long enough to come to the conclusion that you're worth much more than any bargain.'

Eve stared at him in surprise, unconscious of the vision she presented in her gold-coloured gown, cut low to reveal her white shoulders, and wearing her hair loose, which was the way Lucas liked it. She shrugged casually. 'Oh, I don't know. A fortune for my companionship seems like fair trade to me.'

'I'm partial to more than companionship, Eve. Much more.'

'I suspect your interest is partial to a great deal of female companionship, Lucas. No doubt you've had plenty of ladies to choose from in your time.'

His smile was as smooth as his voice. 'I'm a gentleman, my sweet, and a gentleman never tells.'

Eve lifted her head haughtily. 'You rate yourself too highly, Lucas.'

He grinned. 'I've always held myself adaptable to the circumstances.'

'I think what you mean is that you're a cad,' she said with firm conviction.

'If a cad is a man who likes a woman to warm his bed, then I agree. I'm a cad.'

'And proud of it, too.'

His chuckle was low and deep. 'At this moment there is only one woman who interests me—only one woman that I want in my bed. After sharing a kiss, I think we should progress to the next stage, to something more intimate—in my bed.'

Eve flushed crimson. 'Lucas, we are having dinner. Please behave and control your lustful cravings.'

'That is becoming an impossibility, my love. We are husband and wife. How else should I behave?'

'With restraint. Now, if you don't mind, I think we should direct our attention to something less provoking.'

'What do you suggest?'

'You are to leave shortly. I think for the time that is left we should discuss what is to happen while you are away. The enormous task of running this house and employing more staff, doing what is best for four children and dealing with people I have never met I find daunting. So, if you don't mind, Lucas, I would be grateful if you would instruct me on matters before you leave.'

Lucas agreed and the rest of the evening was spent discussing less amorous issues, but when Eve left him to his brandy to go to bed, she knew it was still at the forefront of his mind and that he was not yet done with her.

With her new found duties as mistress of Laurel Court and living in a constant whirl of activity, Eve was kept busy from dawn until dark. Lucas was out for most of the time, reacquainting himself with his tenants and checking on the general order of things.

Laurel Court was a beautiful house and tastefully furnished. A long gallery hung with family portraits ran along the front on the first floor. Rooms entered into more rooms—bedchambers and withdrawing rooms and a vast study with book-lined walls and soft leather chairs. Impressive paintings—oils and watercolours, some painted by masters—adorned the silk-lined walls. When Eve thought about Lucas's struggle to revive his fortunes, she thought that a mere fraction of the contents of this house alone would solve his problems overnight, but she could understand why he was loath to part with any of the treasures Laurel Court housed.

After the first week word had spread that Lord Stainton was in residence with his new wife and neighbours began calling and invitations were issued for them to attend various affairs.

The children were blissfully happy and Eve was gratified that Estelle, a bold child with great charm, had adapted to her new life with her stepsisters better than she could have hoped. But Eve was concerned about both Estelle's and Sophie's education and made her concern known to Lucas on returning from church one Sunday morning.

'Estelle and Sophie are growing fast. They're both five years old and very bright. It's time they had a governess.'

Watching his eldest daughter fly up the stairs after a giggling Estelle, Lucas frowned and nodded. 'I agree. We'll have to look for someone suitable.'

'Can we afford it?'

He grinned down at her. 'I'll sell one of the paintings to cover her wages. It won't be the first. But you are right. I want to give them the kind of upbringing every child should have. A governess will bring some order to their lives.'

'I would like to start some foundation for us, too, as a family—for the children's sake, you understand, so they can grow up secure in an orderly environment. They are bewildered, you see. Neither Sophie nor Abigail can understand what happened to their mother and it must be explained to them as gently as possible—not the whole of it, since it will only bewilder them more—so they will not be hurt by gossip in the future.'

'I agree,' he said, his tone bitter, 'but when is a child old enough to be told that its mother abandoned it when it was in the cradle?'

'Like I said, they must be told as gently as possible. In the meantime, I'll begin finding a governess—someone reliable, kind and pleasant.'

'Who will not be too indulgent—'

'Like Sarah, you mean.' Eve smiled. 'She does tend to indulge them, but that's her way and I cannot fault it. She is so good with them and loves them dearly.'

Lucas looked at her, his expression soft. 'And that's important to you isn't it, Eve, that all the children are loved?'

'Of course, although the new governess must instil discipline. That is important too.'

'And she must also be intelligent,' Lucas added, happy to leave this side of his children's upbringing to her.

'That goes without saying. I'll write to Beth to see if she can help.'

Alice, who was assured of her welcome into this new environment, had been emaciated when she had arrived into the Stainton household. She had now acquired the glossy good health and plump contours that came with nourishment. Her hair was a fluff of dark curls. She was a pretty baby and what a delight she was turning out to be, smiling and laughing at everything that moved.

Sarah, who was thrilled to be living at Laurel Court with her beloved Mark, thought Alice was an absolute treasure and no trouble to anyone, she remarked fondly. There was a brightness and sweetness in her that was endearing, drawing members of the household to her like pins to a magnet. Whenever Miriam took her for a walk in the gardens, there was always one of the gardeners Lucas had set on—local men who had worked at Laurel Court in the past—hanging over the perambulator for a sight of her, and to tickle her tummy, which never failed to make her chortle happily.

Riding home after visiting one of the farms to see how the haymaking was progressing, on hearing the babble of children's voices and a high-pitched yell, Lucas had his attention drawn to a merry, colourful gathering beneath a giant horse-chestnut tree and beside a shallow brook that ran into a large pond in a dip just beyond the house's gardens. It was a particularly lovely day, one of those soft drowsing days of midsummer. Lucas turned his horse in the direction of the happy people.

Miriam was gently rocking Alice's perambulator; seeing Lord Stainton, she bobbed a respectful curtsy. Miriam was very much in awe of her employer and usually scuttled into another room when he came to the nursery—which was often since they had come to Laurel Court. Sarah said it was odd that he should suddenly start taking an interest in the children, and was quite baffled by it—although Sarah also said that maybe Lady Stainton had much to do with that, for she spent a great deal of her time in the nursery.

Lord Stainton was even-tempered with his daughters, sitting them on his lap and listening patiently to their little troubles, so that they gladly accepted their papa into their childish world.

Now, as Miriam looked up at him shyly, the warm glow of the sun turning his face to a deep amber and his eyes piercingly blue, she thought Lord Stainton was perhaps the most handsome man she had ever seen. His dark hair tumbled by the breeze curled vigorously, falling over his forehead. His gaze settled on his wife, who was standing on the bank watching Estelle and Sophie paddling in the brook, his eyes took on a hungry look and his teeth gleamed in a bold buccaneer's grin.

'Can anyone join the picnic?'

Until that moment Eve had been unaware of his presence. She froze into stillness, her back towards him. It was as if she was afraid to turn to see who intruded on their simple picnic. After a moment she turned and looked up at him, a smile on her lips and a warm welcome in her eyes.

'Of course, Lucas,' she said, remembering the last time he had seen her picnicking on the day the balloon had gone up in Hyde Park, and how different his attitude had been that day.

Springing athletically from the saddle, he let his horse loose to nibble the grass. His gaze was drawn to the two girls in the water, their skirts tucked into their drawers, squealing with laughter as they held on to each other for support on the slippery stones. The brook was placid, the reeds on the far side reflected mirror-like in its calm surface.

'They're obviously enjoying themselves,' Lucas remarked. 'Where's Abigail?'

'Over there.' Eve pointed to the little girl earnestly picking daisies and clutching as many as she could in her small fist. 'She insists on picking enough daisies to make a chain to go right round the tree. Now you're here you can watch Estelle and Sophie while I help Sarah set out the picnic.'

Lucas had no objections to this and, removing his jacket, he sat beneath the tree, leaning his back against the trunk and draping one arm over his raised knee. He was content to do as Eve asked, but, try as he might to concentrate on the two girls, his gaze was constantly drawn to his wife, and his thoughts had a habit of turning to lust whenever he looked at the woman who insisted on keeping him from her bed.

As he listened to the friendly drone of a browsing bee as it busied itself in a clump of sleepy dandelions, his heavy-lidded gaze feasted on the vision of the lovely creature in a pale sprigged summer dress. The richness of her loosely brushed back hair emphasised the creamy whiteness of her fine skin and her brilliant blue eyes. She looked enchanting. Eve was warm, loving and giving. She was made for love and having children and everything else a husband and wife could contrive in a successful marriage.

The restraints she had forced on his nature were in danger of breaking, and the force between them had grown powerful and impatient in its long captivity. Tonight would be his last night at Laurel Court for some time, and perhaps with a little candlelight and champagne—and that way he knew he had with a lovely woman, he would succeed in luring her into his bed. He would be his most charming, he decided, and hopefully he might recapture that passionate moment they had shared when they had ridden together the day following their arrival at Laurel Court.

Placing plates on to the shining white cloth spread out beneath the spreading canopy of the tree, Eve could almost feel her husband's eyes burning into the back of her neck and she turned slightly. The source of her discomfort sat smiling and unconcerned with Abigail, who had clambered on to his lap, as she did at every opportunity. His sensual mouth was curved in a soft smile, and his light blue eyes were speculative. Feeling the blood warm her flesh, she quickly looked away, hearing him chuckle softly, fully aware of the effect his presence was having on her.

Eve poured some lemonade into a glass and turned and handed it to him. 'Here. You look as though you need it. It's very cold and might go some way to…'

He lifted his brows, deeply amused. 'What? Cooling my—?'

'Lucas,' she whispered harshly before he could say 'ardour'. 'Remember where you are. This is a children's picnic, not a—'

'What? A—' In the face of her scowl warning him not to utter anything unmentionable, he laughed out loud. 'Worry not, Eve, I am fully aware of where I am and that little pigs have big ears.'

Abigail, her interest pricked, looked up at her father. 'Am I a little pig, Papa?'

'No, my pet. You are a little angel.' Ruffling her hair playfully, he laughed, lifting her off his lap and moving closer to Eve.

The picnic was all laid out and Eve called to the children to come and eat. Immediately they gathered round and like hungry monsters began tucking in to anything they could lay their hands on. To Sophie and Abigail it was a novelty seeing their authoritative father sitting on the ground joining in their picnic and seemingly enjoying the experience. At first his presence disconcerted Sarah and

Miriam, who kept as far away from him as was reasonably possible, but his relaxed manner and the ease with which he joined in the laughter and light-hearted banter put them at their ease.

Lucas sat cross legged next to Eve, watching Sophie munch in a most unladylike manner on a chicken leg and Abigail break pieces of bread into her napkin to feed to the ducks on the pond.

'How very uncivilised,' he remarked, amazed that not so very long ago he would have upbraided his daughters for their lack of manners.

'No, it isn't,' Eve was quick to retort. 'The children are having fun. I can see nothing uncivilised in that.'

'You spoil them.'

His tone of voice made her look more closely at him. She detected some indefinable, underlying emotion in it as his eyes gleamed beneath the well-defined brows. 'They should be spoiled now and then. They are children for such a short time. Did you never have fun when you were a boy, Lucas?'

His eyes danced with the joy of memory. 'All the time—in this very brook as it happens. And if the girls were of the opposite gender, I could show them some of the finest trees on the estate to climb.'

'And what, may I ask, is so very wrong with girls climbing trees?' Eve remarked with mock indignation, laughter lighting up her eyes. 'I will have you know that as a girl I climbed some very impressive trees.'

'And fell out of several, I'll wager.'

'I did too,' she confessed, not too proud to admit it, 'and I had the bruises to prove it.'

'That doesn't surprise me in the slightest. From the very first I could see you showed none of the restraint implanted into young ladies of my acquaintance. You do not tread with caution, more with an air of one who suspects that delightful danger lies ahead, but you are prepared to enjoy it nevertheless.'

Eve stared at him. 'Is that how you really see me?'

He nodded. 'I also see you as courageous and that you have a sense of adventure and a rebellion that strains against any chains that try to bind you against your will. You must have presented a nightmare to your father while you were growing up.'

'I did—often—but he was so lovable, like an old bear, and he didn't seem to mind.'

Estelle and Sophie returned to the brook, screeching with laughter as they splashed each other with complete abandon. Lucas went to bring some order to the antics of these helplessly laughing young girls, but, unable to quell their exuberance, he found himself drawn in instead, becoming the recipient of a shower of water. Unable to swallow his laughter and oblivious to his trousers and shirt front soaking up the spray, he knelt on the bank and splashed them back.

Smiling, Eve watched him. For the first time she saw her husband indulging in riotous fun and behaving with complete impetuosity with his children. She felt some exquisitely painful emotion squeeze her heart. She could deal with a morose Lucas, an angry and temperamental Lucas, but this was a new side she was seeing to her husband and harder to deal with.

How attractive he looks, she thought, conscious of some unwitting excitement. Her body was taut, every muscle stretched against the invisible pull that was for ever drawing her towards him. He hadn't told her in so many words what he expected of her tonight, but it was there in his eyes every time he looked at her, and she would have to be strong indeed to withstand him—if she wanted to.

The hour was late when Henry arrived. Eve was contemplating going to bed.

'I'm sorry I'm late. I was unavoidably delayed,' he said, shaking Lucas's hand and affecting a fine courtly bow to Eve. Taking her hand, he bowed over it in the best of old-world tradition while smiling broadly at her. 'It's a pleasure seeing you again, Eve, and may I say you are looking lovelier than ever.'

'You may,' she said, smiling graciously. 'In fact, you may say anything you like to me, Henry, if it's complimentary.'

'I'm happy to see you've survived marriage to my good friend here without scars.'

'So far, but it's early days. I'm sorry your visit is to be brief. You should have been staying a few days at least.'

'Next time I will.'

Henry followed them into the drawing room, feeling a deep admiration for this lovely woman who had taken on his friend in his hour of need. Pity about her inheritance, though. That was bad luck, losing it like that. Lucas had told him about it before he'd left London, and Henry had been worried about how his marriage to the young American widow would stand such a set-back. But now, seeing them together after just a few short weeks, they seemed to be getting on well enough.

'Your husband is anxious to get to Newcastle to survey his land—is that not so, Lucas?'

'Absolutely,' he answered, handing Henry a much-needed brandy. 'But not so much the land as what's beneath it.'

Henry winked at Eve good humouredly. 'We'll make a colliery owner out of him yet. This is just the start. He'll soon be taking up the reins of his business empire again, Eve, with all his old shrewdness—manipulating his investments, weaving his way through the intricacies of the stock market and buying shares in this and that. You'll see.'

Lucas glanced at him, a fierce gleam of anticipation in his eyes. He was excited about his trip to Newcastle and eager and determined to tackle his responsibilities, to take what he might find in the industrial north by the scruff of its neck and force it to his own will as he had done in the past.

'That is exactly what I intend to do, Henry, and I don't intend hanging about. You're right, this is the start of my recovery and I refuse to mess it up. The steam-engine has created an unprecedented demand for coal, which may become the main source of my income, but I shall soon have interests in other concerns.'

'Such as?'

'The railways—which, you mark my words, will eventually put the coach out of business. Every day miles of new track are covering various parts of the country, linking towns, cities and ports as never before. If a boom is coming, I mean to be in on it, Henry, and any other form of trade, be it glass making, copper-smelting—indeed, all the industries that go on in the north, in Manchester and Liverpool and anywhere else.'

Eve looked at him with admiration. She liked to hear him talk like this, to see him fairly snapping and crackling with energy, ready to attack whatever it was that came his way, to cast off the brittle, restless shell that had encased him since he had been stripped of his wealth, to smooth the sharp edges that had once cut not only those he dealt with, but himself. He would recover, she had no doubt, for was he not the most dominant, hard-headed, stubborn man she had ever met?

Henry raised his glass. 'I will drink to that, Lucas. I wish you every success.'

Suspecting the two men were about to fall into an in-depth discussion about coal mining, Eve said, 'If you'll excuse me, I'm just going to check on the children and then I'm going to bed. I hope you don't mind, but it's been a long day. Lucas will entertain you, Henry.'

She turned at the door and looked back. Lucas was watching her leave, and in his eyes was a look that told her he was not done with her yet.

Wrapped in her pastel dressing gown in the privacy of her bedroom and curled up in the chair by the hearth, Eve felt a deep contentment, believing that at last things might be starting to go Lucas's way and that their future would be secure.

Her thoughts wandered away from the subject of coal mines and industry that occupied her husband's mind, and her own became no different to what Lucas's had been by the brook. Her face was soft and wistful as she gazed into the glowing embers. Her arms hugged her slender waist, as if they sought to simulate a lover's embrace, which was but a memory of their kiss, which seemed more like it had occurred today instead of almost three weeks ago. Breathing deep and closing her eyes, she felt again the ache in her breasts when they had been crushed against Lucas's hard chest and the warmth of his breath against her lips, and once again she saw the urgency in his gaze as he lowered his lips to hers.

Suddenly a sound from behind the door intruded into her thoughts. Her eyes snapped open and she listened to the footfalls that were familiar to her now. She had listened to them every night and not since the morning following their arrival had Lucas entered her room through the connecting door. The warmth of the fire relaxed her body, and as she continued to listen to him moving about, again she felt the awakening of pleasure deep within her. It was strong and disturbing, flooding her body with a pulsing warm excitement.

Dear God, what was the matter with her? Why was she so afflicted? She had been Andrew's wife and had found no softening in her heart in his bed, yet now her mind envisioned the dark, handsome face of the man behind that door. She resented the hold he had over her so that she didn't know what to think any more, and she withdrew in horror from the bold, unmistakable urging of her body. She knew she would not be free of this torment until she had given him what he wanted from her.

What she wanted?

With each day he grew bolder and on each encounter he confronted her more openly.

This was no chaste marriage she had with Lucas, not with the outpouring of passion that had already been displayed between them. The footfalls fell silent, but a light still shone from beneath the door. Her husband was waiting for her on the other side like a big black spider intent on luring her into his web, this she did not doubt. He was challenging her, testing her, wanting her to go to him.

It was as if some mystical presence were embodied within that room, for she was caught for a moment by a yearning so strong and physical she found it hard to draw breath. Uncurling her body, she stood up and padded to the door. She looked at it long and hard before putting her hand on the brass knob and slowly turned it.

Was it locked?

Her heart lurched when it yielded. For a moment she wanted to turn and flee to her bed, but somewhere in her tormented mind, she knew Lucas was right, and that their marriage should be more than in name only. Gently she pushed the door and it opened silently into a room of large proportions and dimly lit.

Eve saw the shadowy shape of a huge bed on a raised dais, and there, very much at ease, seated in a large armchair by the fire was the room's inhabitant. The image of relaxed elegance, Lucas was calmly watching her, supremely confident in the hold he knew he had over her. He had discarded his coat and waistcoat and neckcloth, and his fine white linen shirt was open at the throat to reveal a firm, strongly muscled throat. His sinewy arms showed below his rolled-up sleeves. His eyes smiled at her, touching her everywhere, and the mocking grin gleamed with startling whiteness against his swarthy skin—in fact, there was a health and vitality about him that was almost mesmerising.

With her gauze dressing gown draped about her like a diaphanous cloud, and with her hair unbound in a single great fall down her back, Eve stood staring at him, her eyes dark and huge in her pale face, burningly aware of the reasons that had brought her here. All at once she knew there would be no going back, for the figure, which was already rising with a cool nonchalance that did not seem appropriate to greet her with a deep, profoundly mocking bow, had succeeded in luring her into his bedchamber.

'Come in, Eve. I was expecting you.'

'I know.'

'Although I did not expect you quite so soon. I thought the struggle with your inner self would have taken longer.' He met her expectant gaze with a cool, crooked smile of mild amusement. 'Thankfully Henry was quite worn out from his journey and eager to seek his bed—as I am, but for different reasons. I'm glad that you've decided to see sense. The law does not recognise chaste marriages.'

'My state of abstinence I intended to diligently pursue as my only means of escape from...'

'What happens in bed between husband and wife,' he stated calmly when she faltered. 'And yet here you stand, confronting your husband in his lair—a man you bought under false pretences, I might add.'

'Do you have to keep reminding me?' she snapped, her concern more with her own response than with his lingering, hungering gaze.

He smiled, leisurely, infuriatingly—sure of her. 'Do you recall me saying that it would be interesting to see if the agreement we made would outlast the testing of the flesh?'

She raised her head haughtily, tossing back her glorious mass of hair. 'What of it?'

'We have been married a mere three weeks and already you are showing signs of weakness.'

'And no doubt you think because I let you kiss me that day that you have found a chink in my armour?'

His chuckle was low and deep. 'No, my love, not a chink, but a massive hole.'

Purposefully he reached out and loosened the belt on her dressing gown. Eve put up no resistance. She met his gaze directly and her body tensed as his hands worked it off her shoulders and it fell to her feet, revealing a sheer white nightdress. One soft and lovely shoulder was temptingly bare. Her body was covered and yet revealed everything, and Eve saw the quickening of passion spark in her husband's eyes as they slowly perused her from head to toe. Stripped naked by his bold gaze, every bit of the courage she had strived so hard to erect was shattered in an instant. She was too close to that muscular chest, too close to the scent of him, of everything that was masculine.

For a moment she was assailed by the memory of Andrew and what he had done to her. Her flesh went cold. Then a darker fear pierced her terror. Had Andrew mentally scarred her, left her unable to respond to a lover's touch? Her mind rebelled, but a trembling set in. Seeing her hesitation, Lucas sensed it and questioned it with a frown. Reaching out his hand, he caressed her cheek with featherlike fingertips.

'You tremble. Do you fear me?'

Eve waited for the screaming denial to come from the dark recesses of her mind—and this time she was determined to quell its intrusion and the trepidation that had arisen and surged within her. Lucas was not forcing her as Andrew had done. He was awaiting her consent. The knowledge stilled her panic. When she met Lucas's eyes, she suddenly realised the moment was rapidly approaching that she had dreaded, and that it was too late to withdraw.

'It has nothing to do with fear.'

He drew his finger gently down the bare flesh of her slender neck. 'The time for talking has ended. Now it is time for loving.'

'It is my intention to be your wife in every way, but I have had little practice, so I ask you to show patience, Lucas.'

He raised a quizzical brow. 'And you won't run scared

and change your mind?' She shook her head, but he could see the uncertainty in her large dark eyes. His expression softened, understanding more about what was going on in her mind than she realised. 'I am not like Andrew. You will not find what we do either distasteful or undignified. This I promise you. You will find pleasure, not pain in my arms. Making love is a time for giving and sharing, not taking. I will not hurt you. But I must warn you that what happens between us—that what you will find and experience here in my bed—may bind you more eternally than anything else in your life.'

Lucas's long-starved passions flared high. Disposing her of her clothing and his own, he swung her up into his arms and carried her to the bed, his need to possess her paramount to all else, to claim her body and make her his own in every sense, to seduce her before the shuddering, rapturous invasion, making sure with his experienced hands and mouth that her climax would be as devastating as his own would be.

His eyes revelled in their freedom as they feasted hungrily on her naked body, on her beauty stretched out alongside him—her swelling, full ripe breasts, pink tipped and tantalising, the inward curve of her narrow waist, the seductive roundness of her hips, and the long, lithe grace of her limbs. He had already realised that beneath her clothes Eve was what every man dreamed of, but he was unprepared for this vision of incomparable beauty, of the soft, creamy satin lustre of her skin that contrasted against the darkness of his own. He wanted to look at her, to explore every inch of her, to taste and smell, to satisfy his male curiosity in the soft curves of the woman who was now his wife.

Nervous now and feeling like a child in a woman's body, Eve was unable to avert her gaze from her husband's splendid, naked body. It was powerful, lean and broad in all the right places, the gleam of his skin darkened by the generous covering of hair on his chest. She felt devoured and found it difficult to remain pliant beneath his probing eyes, but as his fingers and lips began their assault, she forgot everything.

Andrew's rough, careless handling of her on their wedding night and the subsequent months, had left her scarred, this she knew, but ever since she had met Lucas Stainton, ever since she had met the physical flesh and bone of the man, she had felt there was more to it than what Andrew had done to her. When Lucas had taken her in his arms he had made her breathless and aroused feelings inside her in the most startling way, just like he was doing now. But she was no starry-eyed girl. She was cautious now, wiser.

She found her lips entrapped with his, and though they tasted of brandy and were soft and gentle, they flamed with a fiery heat. She felt herself falling slowly into a dizzying abyss of sensuality and awakened passion. With a silent moan she slipped her hands around his waist, clinging to him for support, aware of the sudden increase in his ardour in each of his searing kisses. She shivered as his mouth left hers and traced a molten path over her cheek, her brow, and he nuzzled the sweet-scented tresses beside her ear, touching it lightly with the fiery tip of his tongue.

Hearing her soft moan and her faint inhalation, Lucas was satisfied and encouraged by her reaction. Purposefully he tightened his embrace, feeling her body shudder against his, and he realised with a surge of desire that her demureness and reserve hid a woman of intense passion. He wanted her, wanted to fill his mouth with the taste of her, to have those inviting hips beneath him, to have those long, lithe legs wrapped around him.

His eyes were translucent in the subdued light, his lean and handsome features starkly etched. A strange feeling, until this moment unknown to Eve fluttered within her breast, and a flood of excitement surged through her.

Lifting her heavy auburn hair aside, Lucas slid his warm parted lips to the point of her shoulder and along to the flesh of her throat, his mouth, hot and wet, searing the intoxicating ripeness of her breasts, his white teeth lightly nibbling the smooth silken skin of her belly. He felt her tremble at the intimacy of his touch, but instead of pulling away, as he expected her to do, she nestled closer. He turned her to him and they came together naturally, like two beings forged together by a common bond. His hand trailed down her spine, pressing her hips tighter against him, where the fire, a throbbing pressure growing in his loins, was already raging. He had played out his hand with patience, but now it was waning.

He knew he must be gentle lest her fear destroyed the moment, and so he held her and stroked her, and when he entered her he was ready to be as patient as she needed him to be, since he had won.

Eve's body reacted to his intrusion, to this indescribable, splintering feeling that built pulsing beats deep within her, with a mindless pleasure that mounted to such an all-consuming intensity she did not believe she could bear it. She became helpless with desire, allowing it all to happen, wanting it with primitive ferocity. She felt the thunderous beating of her heart. What Lucas was doing to her was stunning, expanding to a rapture that made her arch beneath him, the wild, soaring ecstasy fusing them together and sending her up in flames.

A shimmering bliss erupted in an explosion that tore a gasp from her throat, and together they were joined in sweet oblivion. Time seemed to verge on eternity before everything drifted back into place. Lucas raised his head and looked down at her. She was flushed and satiated with loving. Driven by a mindless compulsion to have her, he had taken her with a determination and hunger that stunned and aroused him. Her hair was spread out in shimmering waves across the pillows, and she was staring up at him with wide, searching eyes that had taken on a strange, deep hue, amazement etched on her flushed face.

The whisper of a sigh escaped her as she lifted her face to meet his, wanting to hold on to this moment in time lest she lose some portion of it to the oncoming forces of normality. Her trembling lips parted as his mouth possessed hers with a gentleness that was nothing like the fierce kisses of a moment ago.

'My God,' he murmured, his eyes smouldering. 'You are wanton beyond belief and quite magnificent, Eve.'

Completely captivated by the intimate look in his eyes, the way the hard planes of his face had smoothed out and the way a stray lock of crisp, dark hair fell across his forehead and the compelling gentleness in his voice, Eve swallowed and said, 'So are you.'

His hypnotic gaze held hers as his fingertips stroked her cheek seductively, sliding along the line of her jaw to her lips. From the first moment he had taken her in his arms he had known they were a combustible combination, and what had just passed had been the most wildly erotic, satisfying sexual encounter of his life. Whatever Eve had felt had been real and uncontrived, and, as he now knew, she was totally uninitiated.

'Would you like me to tell you what I like most of all?'

'Please.'

'I like the way your body fits into mine so perfectly, and that it is attuned to what I want. Are you regretful, my sweet?' he questioned huskily, his warm breath caressing her cheek.

Eve shook her head, and strangely it was no lie. All the doubts she had expected, all the qualms of gnawing shame she imagined would torment her, were not there. More unnerving and frightening to her was the strange sense of contentment, of rightness she felt being in his arms, as if it were where she was meant to be.

She thought how little comparison there was between what had just happened to her and her unpleasant experiences with her first husband. It was more than simply that Lucas could touch her heart while Andrew had meant almost nothing to her. The man to whom she had just given herself so spontaneously, with whom she had just shared the most intimate of experiences, had really become her lover in every sense of the word. Lucas's love making and not Andrew's clumsy, painful fumbling had made her blossom into a woman.

'Are you content now I have fulfilled my word?'

'Nay, Eve, far from it,' he murmured, nuzzling the hollow in her throat where a pulse was beating a tantalising fast rhythm beneath her soft flesh. 'The night is far from over. Tomorrow I must be away early and I intend to make the most of you while I have you in my bed.'

He moved against her, his body rousing, responding again to the softness of hers, and then she was his again, and he revelled in the sweetness of her, touching and kissing her with all the skill of a virtuoso playing a violin, as if he had all the time in the world.

When he finally raised himself from her, her slumberous, love-filled eyes gazed up at him adoringly, and that look, along with the way her arm was slung possessively around his waist, set alarm bells ringing. Gently he pulled away from her, feeling his blood run warm when she stretched with the suppleness of a cat and sighed with contentment, and the way her dark eyes were watching him languorously brought desire surging through him all over again.

She had a body that was created for a man's hands, and a mouth that positively invited his kiss. The woman in his arms had fire and spirit and she was also charming and innocent. She had given him exquisite pleasure, and when the moment of his release came, he couldn't have said who clung to the other most desperately. It was as though the very life source was being wrung out of him. He had turned her into a passionate, loving woman, a woman to fill his arms and warm his bed and banish the dark emptiness within him, a woman to fill his life with love and laughter and to help him fulfil his youthful dreams.

What more could a man want? What more, indeed?

What he didn't want was what she was capable of doing to him, and this thought brought him up short and restored his sanity. He was beginning to care for Eve in a way he was not comfortable with. He was furious with himself for wanting her, hating himself for that weakness, that same weakness that had almost destroyed him when he had married Maxine. How stupid he was being, how incredibly gullible to let himself fall into the same trap twice.

Sensing a change in him and that he had withdrawn

from her, suddenly anxious, Eve propped herself up on her elbow, the covers slipping off her shoulder to reveal her pink-tipped breasts that still throbbed from his kisses. 'Lucas? What is it?'

'Nothing,' he replied, trying not to look at her loveliness readily available to him for the taking. But he could not help himself, and, as his eyes devoured her, Eve felt the heat in her face, and then it spread, filling every part of her body at that nakedly desirous look, a need, and a certainty, telling her he was sure of her, as sure as he had been that she would want him when he had finally succeeded in luring her into his bed. 'Eve, if you don't mind I think you should return to your own bed. Tomorrow will be a long day, and as you know, I have to make an early start.'

Suddenly Eve's passionate lover had turned into a civil stranger. Bewilderment clouded her eyes. It was replaced by humiliation on being reminded of how things stood between them and being so casually dismissed from his bed. The passion, the magic they had spun in the privacy of his bed, had delighted her and it had seemed satisfying to Lucas. But in the full knowledge that Lucas did not love her, she did not deceive herself—they married for convenience, and this she must not forget. He had taken her only for her money and was trying to make the best of what they had—a man who might need his wife to warm his bed from time to time, but who would purposely and effectively keep her at arm's length and lock her out of his heart and mind as if she didn't exist.

Without a word she got out of bed and, self-conscious of her nakedness, slipped her nightdress over her head, wondering how he could look so absolutely casual after what they had just done. Picking her dressing gown up from the floor, unable to conceal the hurt she was feeling, she turned and looked at him.

'Shall I see you before you leave, or is it your intention to sneak away without saying goodbye?'

Overwhelmed with guilt, Lucas swung his long, lean body off the bed and strode towards her and caught her to him, his eyes alive with mirth at her obvious outrage. 'Oh, Eve, I apologise if my request sounded dismissive and I don't blame you for being furious, but it was never my intention to offend. But such is your allure, my love, that if you stay I shall be in no mood for sleeping and I shall be so worn out that I may have to delay my departure for another day.'

'Then why don't you?'

'Because you know very well that Henry has come here so that we can travel north together.'

Unconvinced by his excuse, Eve disengaged herself from his embrace. 'Of course. You are right. I should hate to be the cause of any discomfort you might feel in the morning.' Stepping away from him, she looked at his hard, handsome face. 'And you need not worry, Lucas. I did not know what to expect of anything that we did, but I did not expect you to make any undying declarations of love.'

Lucas read her every reaction in her expressive eyes and he was satisfied that he'd done his utmost to kill any romantic illusions about love she might have.

'I'm not that stupid or naïve.'

'I'm glad I haven't misread you. Eve, there is no reason why ours cannot be a happy marriage. You won't find me a cruel husband, and when I have made it back to where I was before, you will find me a generous one.'

It was a strange thing for a man to say, when such

thoughts should never need to enter a wife's mind. Eve gazed up at the cool, dispassionate man. 'How cold you make what is between us sound, Lucas. How matter of fact. Do you feel nothing for me at all?'

His features tightened and his eyes hardened. 'Of course I do. I have grown extremely—fond of you. Eve, I told you in the beginning that love is a romantic notion that has no place in my life, that I have no love to give—at least not the kind of love I think you are looking for—but there can be affection between us and who knows? After this night you may already be with child—my son—and if that is the case then after the birth you can do whatever you please. That is part of the arrangement we made that I will adhere to.'

Eve stared at him. His eyes were hard and uncompromising, watching her steadily. There was no doubt he meant every word he said. She was suddenly angry. All the happiness she had felt at the prospect of their future together and bearing him a son was quenched in outraged pride. What he had said enraged her and she looked at him with contempt.

'You haven't learned anything about me at all, have you, Lucas? How can you speak in such a callous manner, without feeling or emotion, as if loving someone and having a child can be settled with cold logic? I told you then and I will tell you again. I will never abandon a child of mine. Ever. So if that means having to live here with you for the rest of my life, then so be it.'

'I am glad, because I cannot think of anything that would please me more than having you in my bed whenever we are together.'

Eve was appalled. Was that all he was going to say? She waited, beginning to feel uncertain and more than a little afraid, because she now realised with cruel certainty that

she was in love with him—in love with her own husband—
and she would glory in it if she thought he felt the same,
but if all the love was on her side, she wouldn't humiliate
herself by telling him so and seeing the mockery in his
eyes. She was hurt and disappointed, for she had wanted
what had happened to have changed him as much as it had
her, but she could see it had not and never would.

'Goodnight, Lucas. In the morning I shall make sure the
children are up and ready so you can say goodbye to them.'

Closing the door on him, she walked to her bed like a
sleepwalker. She was too numb to feel and full of pain.
Shock had formed a merciful cushion around her which, as
it melted, would give way to suffering in all its sharpness.

Chapter Eleven

Lucas didn't see Eve alone again. The following morning he breakfasted early with Henry. When it was time to leave, as she had told him, the children were assembled to bid him farewell. Eve stood holding Abigail's hand. His eyes were drawn to her and he took a step towards her as though to put a hand on her, but she stepped back, her face blank, her eyes empty, a hard blue emptiness that told him nothing of what she felt, and at once his eyes hardened as he turned away from her.

In the coach bearing them northward, Henry gave his friend, who lounged morose and uncommunicative in the corner, a searching look. Sensing all might not be well at Laurel Court and he hadn't yet found connubial bliss, he enquired after Eve and asked how Lucas was settling down to married life again. Unsurprisingly his enquiry was met with a blank stare.

'Fine,' Lucas replied curtly, before fixing his gaze once more out of the window.

'You're a fool, Lucas,' Henry reproached harshly, feeling heartily sorry for Lucas's wife. 'Eve is an extraordinary young woman—ravishingly beautiful, too—and it is obvious that she adores your children. You should think yourself damned lucky to have her. I pity you—ignoring the one woman in a million who could make you truly happy.' He turned and looked at his friend. 'Are you listening?'

Lucas sent him an impatient look. 'To every word,' he drawled, remembering the moment when Eve had left his bed and how cold he had felt without her presence, and that when he'd driven away from Laurel Court he had suddenly felt totally bereft. 'How can I not when you are bombarding my ears. And if it's of any consolation to you, Henry, I agree.'

It was three weeks following Lucas's departure that Eve suspected she was pregnant. The thought pleased her and a smile of quiet joy lightened her face and her step. A baby was one good thing to come out of the night she had spent in her husband's bed that had been both wonderful and appalling. Of course, she thought wryly, Lucas would be delighted, especially if it turned out to be his much desired son, and if she provided him with a daughter she would have to go through the whole procedure again.

She tried not to dwell too deeply on that night and how much she missed him, the pain of their parting having seeped into her very bones. During daylight hours when she had the running of the house and the children to distract her, she succeeded, but when darkness came and the children were tucked up in the nursery and she was in her bed, the memories would come creeping out of the corners of her mind and she would relive all the glorious things Lucas had done to her and the dreams would pursue her all the way into wakefulness.

Beth responded quickly to her letter enquiring about a

governess for the children and told her she had asked a Miss Fraser—who was working in Bath with a good family and was seeking a new position now her charges had been sent away to school—to contact her. She was well liked, reliable and extremely knowledgeable about most subjects, and Beth thought she might be just the person Eve was looking for.

Beth was right. Miss Fraser was everything Beth had said of her and was eager to take up residence at Laurel Court and begin teaching Sophie and Estelle—and very soon Abigail—as soon as possible. More importantly, the children liked her, which meant a great deal to Eve.

She had letters from Lucas telling her of his progress in the north and she was touched that he could find time to think of her and write to her, although she was disappointed that there were no endearments in the letters. His news was about reopening the mine, which, according to his mining engineer, was rich in coal reserves and when it was up and working in the near future, promised to be a thriving concern.

He told her he had managed to secure the necessary finance without difficulty and went on to tell her of a new pumping system that would benefit the mine, what it was like down on the coal face, the people—hewers, hurriers and trappers he would have to employ to work the mine, viewers and under-viewers—and that he had already found a reliable manager, a Mr Christopher Dunlop who was married with a young family. Mr Dunlop also had an engineering degree in mining and a good head for business. Lucas was confident that he could leave him to oversee everything during his absence, for he had no intention of moving to the north-east.

One piece of news that delighted Eve and was so uplifting was in a letter from Mr Barstow concerning her father's affairs. It would seem that her father had assets not affected by the decline in the American economy after all and she was still a wealthy young woman—perhaps not as wealthy as she might have been, Eve thought, but with that and the colliery in the north-east, it would go a long way to helping Lucas back on to the road to recovery.

Apart from the dark cloud her relationship with Lucas had created, Eve was content at Laurel Court. It all seemed so unchanging, so safe and secure and immune to the changes of the outside world, so much nicer than London. So that when a carriage came bowling down the drive one day and stopped outside the house, she had no premonition of what was to come.

She had just taken a turn around the garden in mellow morning sunshine and, returning to the house, went to receive her visitor. Every vestige of colour drained from her face as she stopped in a shock of recognition. It was Maxine, and, whatever it was she wanted, Eve was sure she was not going to like it. Never had she needed Lucas more than she did just then.

Desperately trying to crush the apprehension that had stirred restlessly at her first sight of the woman, struggling to remain calm and composed and pinning a smile to her face, she crossed the hall towards her.

'Lady Maxine. This is a surprise.'

'And not a very pleasant one, I'll wager. I expect I'm the last person you want to see—and I am Lady Hutton now,' she informed Eve haughtily. 'Alfred and I were married last month—about the same time as you and Lucas, I believe.'

'Then congratulations are in order. Do come into the drawing room.' She smiled tightly at the hovering servant. 'Have refreshment sent in, will you, Tilly? Please, Lady Hutton, come this way.'

'I do know my way. I lived here long enough,' she retorted drily.

'Yes, I know.' When they were alone and seated opposite each other, Eve was aware that an atmosphere of disturbing, inexplicable hostility had entered the room that until a moment before had been filled with mid-afternoon quiet. Folding her hands sedately in her lap, she looked at her visitor squarely. 'Lucas is away just now, so you'll have to make do with me, I'm afraid.'

'I know. He is in Newcastle. It is you I've come to see.'

'Oh?'

'I would like to see my daughters. I have a right to see them, wouldn't you say, having been kept from them all this time?'

'I don't think that is correct, Lady Hutton,' Eve said coldly. 'No one has kept your children from you. You chose not to see them.'

'Do they ask about me?'

'Sophie does occasionally. Abigail—I believe was very young when you went away.'

'And Alice?'

'She is thriving.'

'Good. And you have become fond of them?'

'Extremely fond. They are adorable, lovable children. I have a daughter of my own who is Sophie's age. They have become good friends.'

'And you would not like to see my three girls removed from here?'

An icy tremor of alarm trickled its way down Eve's spine. Her heart skipped a beat as she met Maxine's eyes steadily, seeing something she did not care for glowing in their depths. 'Certainly not. There has been enough sadness and disruption in their young lives. At last they have some stability and they are happy with things the way they are.'

Maxine raised her head haughtily. 'Are they? We shall see about that. I would like to see them.'

Eve could feel a gathering of concentration, like shadows entering the bright, elegant room, like dark forces of will being directly focused on her. 'I'm afraid I cannot allow that—not without Lucas. Besides, your sudden arrival might—upset them. If you wish to see them, you must contact Lucas first. Where are you staying?'

'At the King's Head in the village—with my husband. But how dare you refuse to allow me to see my own children? I am their mother. Do not try to stop me seeing them.'

Eve straightened on the edge of her seat and looked Lucas's first wife in the eye. 'I'm afraid I must. But let's not play games, Lady Hutton. I find using children as pawns in adult games distasteful. Why don't you tell me the real reason that has brought you here? Lucas is away. You knew that before you came. You have asked him for money in the past and he refused to give you more after the divorce settlement. Perhaps you thought I would be more amenable—although now you are married, surely it is your husband who should provide for you.'

Maxine betrayed her exasperation with a sound of disgust. Getting money out of Lucas's new wife was going to be more difficult than she'd imagined. 'I do need money—but unfortunately Alfred is…financially embarrassed at present.'

'As you say, Lady Hutton, it is unfortunate, but that is not my concern.' Eve's tone was frosty. Maxine's blonde hair was exquisitely coiffed and her well-endowed body was gowned in costly good taste, which belied the impoverished state she was constantly pleading. 'Do you really expect me to give you some money?'

'Of course.'

'And if I don't?'

'Then I will have no choice but to take my daughters with me.'

Eve blanched and her body stiffened. 'If you intend to blackmail me, then you can think again. When I married Lucas, my wealth was given over to him—which is how things are done in England. You must know that.'

'Don't tell me you can't get your hands on it if you want. Your father was reputed to have been an extremely wealthy man. Are you refusing my request?'

'You seem to have the general idea. You will not get a penny out of me. Threaten me all you like, but it will not change a thing. I cannot allow you to see the children and I will certainly not let you take them out of this house. Lucas has left them in my care, and that is where they will stay. When he returns, the two of you can discuss in a civilised manner what is to be done with your daughters, but while he is away they are my responsibility, and I take my responsibilities very seriously, Lady Hutton.'

Feeling the sting of defeat, a wave of maddened colour washed over Maxine's face and her lips twisted contemptuously. 'Is that so? Well, we shall see about that. Obviously Lucas feels indebted to you for getting him out of a fix, but how does it feel knowing you hold a man by playing upon his indebtedness to you?'

Eve met the trembling rage of the other woman with assurance. She stood up. 'I don't have to discuss my feelings with you, Lady Hutton. I don't think we have anything else to say to each other, so I think you had better leave.'

The servant came in with refreshment. 'I'm sorry, Tilly. Please take it back to the kitchen. Lady Hutton is leaving.'

Maxine's face hardened to a frightening malevolence and her eyes narrowed to slits of pure loathing. 'You'll regret this, I promise you,' she hissed, her head high, her expression contemptuous.

'I don't think so. Good day, Lady Hutton.'

Without another word Maxine swept out of the room and the house. Not until Eve heard the carriage drive away did she realise she had been holding her breath. She was much shaken by what had transpired and sincerely hoped she wouldn't have to set eyes on Lucas's former wife again, but deep down inside her she knew Maxine wasn't done with her yet.

It was mid-afternoon the following day when Abigail was missed. The three girls had been in the garden with Miriam walking Alice. After playing their favourite game of hide and seek, Abigail failed to be found.

Miriam went to the nursery to see if the little girl had returned to Sarah, but she hadn't. Deeply concerned, Sarah asked everyone if they had seen the child, only to be met with shaking heads. Instructing everyone to search the house and gardens, she went looking for Eve, finding her in her room lying down after suffering a bout of nausea, which was one of the discomforts of her pregnancy.

'We can't find Abigail,' Sarah blurted out, breathless

after running up the stairs. 'I thought she might have sneaked in here for a cuddle or something, knowing how attached to you she has become.'

Eve stared at her, stunned by her words. 'No, I haven't seen her, Sarah,' she said, sharing Sarah's concern for the missing child. 'Who was the last to see her?'

'Sophie and Estelle. They were playing hide and seek in the garden. Oh, Lady Stainton,' she cried wretchedly, wringing her hands, 'I am so worried that something terrible has happened to her. I've asked everyone to look for her—to search all the places they know she likes to go.'

Eve felt a peculiar hollowness developing in the pit of her stomach. Immediately she went to question Sophie and Estelle, and by the time she had finished Sophie was sobbing tears of distress.

'She—she might have fallen or sprained her ankle or something,' she cried. 'You will find her, won't you? She can't be lost.'

Eve gathered the little girl to her and tried to be patient, speaking as softly as she could manage. 'We will find her, Sophie. Like you said she might have had a little accident. Was she upset or anything when you last saw her?'

'No, she was looking forward to going to see the kittens in the stable when we'd finished playing.'

'I see. Then we'll start by looking there. Now you and Estelle stay with Miriam while Sarah and I go and look for her. I'm sure she isn't far away.'

The hollowness inside Eve deepened as she left the nursery. She almost knew where Abigail had gone—been taken. Fear and doubt and then anger flared in her eyes, and suddenly she was all action. Grim faced, she turned to Sarah, giving orders in a confident and sure voice.

'We must be calm, Sarah. Get the staff together and search every inch of the house and outside, anywhere a little girl might hide—beginning with the stables. She might have gone to look at the kittens by herself. In the meantime, I'll have Mark take me in the carriage to the King's Head in the village.'

Sarah stared at her as though she'd taken leave of her senses. 'The King's Head? But—why on earth would you want to go there?'

'Abigail's mother—Lady Hutton as she is now—called to see me yesterday on the excuse of wanting to see the children. I think you know why she really came, Sarah. When I refused to give her what she wanted, she threatened to take the children. It's too much of a coincidence that Abigail should go missing now. I think Lady Hutton has taken her in the hope that I will pay handsomely for her return.'

Sarah was horrified. 'You mean she has kidnapped her own daughter?'

'I wouldn't put it past her, would you?'

Sarah shook her head, no longer knowing what to think.

'She is staying at the King's Head with her husband, so the sooner I get there the sooner I can find out what she's playing at and hopefully bring Abigail home. The poor mite must be so distressed. But just in case I'm wrong, see that every nook and cranny is searched.'

It took Eve half an hour to have the carriage made ready and to travel to the King's Head. It was a large and busy coaching inn, with a wall enclosing its huge yard. Stepping down, she hurried inside, oblivious to the stares she drew from ostlers and patrons alike. Her heart sank when the proprietor told her that Lord and Lady Hutton had left for London an hour ago.

'And the child? Was there a child with them?'

He nodded. 'Aye, and I thought it queer at the time—seeing as they didn't arrive with one.'

Eve thanked him and returned to the carriage, instructing Mark to take her back to Laurel Court and to saddle her a horse. Hurriedly she changed into her riding habit and woollen cloak as she told Sarah that her fears were confirmed, that Lady Hutton had taken Abigail and that she was going after her.

Sarah tried to argue, telling her it was madness to embark on such a mission when it was almost dark and that a summer storm threatened to break the long spell of hot weather. The wind was already rising and black thunderclouds gathering overhead.

'I have to, Sarah,' Eve said, pulling on her gloves as she hurried down the stairs.

'Then at least take the carriage.'

'I will make better progress on horseback. They have taken the road to London, so at least I know which direction to take. They'll probably pull in for the night somewhere so I'll stop at every inn I see.'

'But you might come to harm,' Sarah cried, hurrying after her as she strode across the hall.

Eve spun round, her face white and her whole body trembling. 'I have to do this, Sarah. I will never forgive myself if anything happens to Abigail. My husband left his children in my care and it's up to me to get her back.'

Sarah watched her gallop off with a terrible sense of foreboding. In desperation she picked up her skirts and ran to the stables to speak urgently to her husband. 'Mark, you have to go after her,' she cried in frantic haste. She was relieved to see he was already saddling a horse and that he intended doing just that.

Darkness shrouded the land and the wind rose viciously as Eve made the headlong journey after Lord and Lady Hutton. As the miles rolled past, above the noise of the wind she listened to the pounding hooves and terrifying pounding of her heart. Every inn she came to she stopped to enquire if Lord and Lady Hutton were staying, but to no avail.

Fear instilled itself into Eve's heart, fear and desperation. What if they had taken a different road and they weren't going to London at all. They might even have stopped to stay with friends. Just when she thought she would have to turn back, she struck lucky.

At the same time that Eve, pursued by a concerned Mark, rode in search of Abigail, Lucas burst into Laurel Court with all the turbulence of the threatening storm. No one was ever unaware when Lord Stainton had arrived, was present or had just left, such was the forceful vigour that went with his make up. Buoyed up with the success of his Newcastle trip and impatient to see Eve, rather than spend the night in Oxford he'd hired a horse and ridden the short distance to his home.

Home! He savoured the word with relish. He had not thought of Laurel Court as home since he was a youth, and now he did, and his beautiful wife waiting within its walls had made if feel so. Dear Lord, how he'd missed her. When he remembered the unforgivable way he had treated her on the night before he left, shame and self-disgust tore through him. How could he have done that? She was the dearest, the sweetest, most magnificent woman he'd known, and he loved her. Yes, he loved her so much he ached with it, and he meant to tell her tonight.

How long had he loved her? he asked himself curiously as he went inside, and the truth was that he didn't know. From the first moment he had seen her, probably, and he desperately wanted her love. He was greedy for it. Nothing made sense when he thought of her—of Eve, in all her audaciousness, defiant and brave, her eyes blazing as she prepared to do battle with him, and those same eyes docile and brimming with contentment after making love.

Glad to close the door on the dreadful weather, he strode briskly into the hall. Surprised to see everyone standing around, he stopped, looking from one to the other. Sarah, her face a frozen mask, was the one who moved towards him.

'Good evening, Sarah,' he said, smiling broadly. 'Where is my wife?' He looked around, expecting her to materialise at any second.

'Lord Stainton. Something has happened.'

Lucas looked at her hard. Something was wrong. Very wrong. The suspense hovered thickly and ominously. 'Tell me.'

The smile vanished as he listened. He was as calm as though Sarah was telling him about the weather. When she had finished, he looked over his shoulder to one of the footmen. 'See that my horse is saddled.' His voice was decisive. He expected to be obeyed at once. 'Which direction did she take?'

'The London road,' Sarah provided.

No more than a minute or two later, at the same moment that thunder rumbled overhead and lightning streaked across the sky, Lucas was racing after Eve and Mark. The thought that something dreadful had happened to Eve and his daughter tortured him. It consumed him and filled him with a torment worse than any soul could.

Eve was shown into the private dining room Lord and Lady Hutton had requested. They both looked towards the door when Eve entered. Maxine smiled slowly, unsurprised to see their visitor, and her husband—a nervous, quiet man of few words—rose, wiping his mouth on his napkin.

'Lady Stainton! Why, how delightful to see you.'

'I believe you are expecting me,' she said, her eyes on Maxine, noting there was an alertness about her, an interested, expectant gleam in her eyes.

Lord Hutton laughed uneasily. 'Expecting you? Why should we be?' Confused, he looked at his wife, his manner suddenly turning from confusion to suspicion. 'Maxine?'

Maxine raised her head in an imperious manner. 'Yes, I knew you'd follow when you missed the child,' she said impassively, her eyes taking on total uninterest as she calmly continued to eat her meal, as though Eve were a stranger who had somehow got past the proprietor and invaded her privacy.

Eve glared at her accusingly. 'I hope you're proud of yourself. Where is she?' she demanded, hardly able to contain her fury.

'Where every child should be at this time. In bed.'

Eve stared at her in shock and disbelief. 'In bed? Are you telling me you have put her to bed and left her alone?'

Maxine shrugged. 'What is so very wrong with that?'

Eve was incensed. 'I would like to see her. My first concern is for Abigail and I want assurance that she is all right.'

'She'll be asleep,' Maxine said coldly. 'I don't want her disturbed.'

Lord Hutton was looking from one to the other, scowling darkly. 'Maxine, what is this? Lady Stainton is clearly quite distressed. I was under the impression that she agreed to you taking the child.'

Eve drew herself up, her face set and white. 'I did no such thing. My husband left the children in my care. How dare you calmly come along and kidnap one of them?'

'Kidnap? I would hardly call claiming one's own daughter kidnap,' Maxine stated coldly.

'When someone abducts a child demanding money for its return, I think the word is appropriate,' Eve threw at her, so angry she had to clench her hands to keep herself from slapping the supercilious face of this silly, selfish woman.

'Maxine,' Lord Hutton chided harshly, 'is this true? What have you done?'

She glared at her husband, suddenly irate. 'Alfred, I would be grateful if you would learn to keep out of what does not concern you.'

'Not concern me?' His face became suffused with anger as he prepared to assert himself, which, being a man who wanted nothing more than a quiet, uninterrupted life, was a rarity. 'You think not? Listen to me, woman. You are married to me now. You live in my house and I shall say what goes on in it and who comes and goes.'

'I need no one's permission to take my own child,' Maxine flared, throwing her napkin on to her dinner and getting up forcefully from the table.

'Be that as it may,' Eve retorted, outraged, 'but you forfeited any rights you had over your children when you walked out on them. You abandoned Abigail when she was still in the cradle. You aren't fit to be a mother,' she seethed, unable to conceal her disgust. 'Have you no shame—no sense of responsibility, no idea what Abigail is going through at this very minute? Dear sweet Lord, what you have done is the cruellest thing. I am deeply concerned about Abigail, who, because of your greed, will suffer for it. Will you tell me where she is, or do I have to ask the proprietor?'

Lord Hutton stepped forward, glowering darkly at his wife. 'There is no need to do that. I will take you to the child myself.'

'Do that, Alfred,' Maxine hissed, 'but I will not allow Lady Stainton to take her.'

'We shall see about that,' Eve seethed, turning her back on the woman and following Lord Hutton out of the room and up the stairs. The inn was full, noisy and so smoky her eyes smarted.

Lord Hutton pushed open a door into a softly lit room. It was quite small. The covers on the bed were ruffled, as if someone had been lying on it, but the bed and the room were empty. Something inside Eve shattered and she began to move her head slowly from side to side in denial.

'She must have been so frightened and confused. Where can she have gone? I must find her,' she cried frantically.

'I'll have the inn searched.'

When no sign of Abigail was found, Eve ran outside to search the inn yard and stables, questioning ostlers and anyone she saw, but no one had seen her. Panic and fury rose in her breast as she ran from the inn. It was dark and raining, the moon appearing now and then between breaks in the cloud. The wind caught and swirled her hair about her head. She looked about her in desperation, wondering which way a little girl in her distress would be likely to take. Seeing a path leading away from the inn, she ran towards it, calling Abigail's name as she went.

Running on, she went into the woods beside the track, going deeper and deeper into the interior, still calling the little girl's name as she zigzagged in and out of the trees, branches and thorns tearing at her face and clothes. It was very dark. Fear dissolved into chilling terror when above the noise of the storm came the sound of rushing water— a river in full flow—and it sounded very close.

'Oh, no. Dear Lord, please don't let her have come this way.'

She ran on, losing all sense of direction, and then miraculously she saw a white, frightened face staring up at her. Eve's heart almost burst with relief. Falling to her knees beside the diminutive and forlorn little girl, she pulled the sobbing child to her breast, smoothing the wet hair from her face and shushing her and rocking her. Abigail was in such a distressed state she could scarcely get her breath.

'Hush, sweetheart. I'm here now. You're safe. No, hush…'

Eve's heart ached for the bewildered terror of this child who had been taken from her own safe and protected world into one that was an alien, frightening place by complete strangers. Hugging Abigail's trembling little body close beneath her cloak, she wrapped her in compassionate arms. After a while Abigail's sobs were reduced to hiccoughing. Sensing the river was very close and afraid to venture back to the inn in the dark in case she fell into the water, she decided to stay where she was—to wait out the night if necessary. Her clothes were damp, but it was reasonably dry under the trees and it was not particularly cold.

She bent her head, unable to stem the tears. She was exhausted and she wanted—wanted what? Lucas. At that moment she wanted her husband more than she had ever wanted anything or anybody in her life. She wanted him to take away the fear and dread, for him to tell her what to do, to feel his strength and his arms about her and his voice telling her that everything would be all right.

The noise of wind and water was so loud she didn't hear her name being roared in the darkness of the night.

When Lucas reached the inn he was met by Mark. The young man was pacing about, as though in a quandary as to what he should do. His relief on seeing Lucas was immense.

'Thank goodness you're here, Lord Stainton.'

'Where is my wife?'

'I wish I knew, sir. As far as I can make out, she's gone looking for Miss Abigail, who's wandered off and is goodness knows where.'

Lucas stopped short, horrified, as another rumble of thunder shook the ground. 'In this?'

'Aye, sir. Lord Hutton is quite beside himself. I've been out with others with lanterns from the inn looking for them, but—nothing.'

At that moment an extremely distraught Lord Hutton came outside. 'I can't tell you how terribly sorry I am about this, Lord Stainton. I had no idea what Maxine was up to. None at all. You have to believe that.'

'Oh, I do,' he ground out.

Lucas's eyes went to Maxine hovering in the doorway. At the sight of her he felt ice-cold anger settle in his chest, then spread to every part of his body, and yet it felt as though his thoughts were so maddened they would set fire to his mind. Quickly he strode towards her and looked directly at her, and she felt the need to recoil from the expression in his eyes. They were as hard as rock. They were narrowed with what looked like venom, and his mouth snarled in a cruel twist.

'You heartless, selfish, stupid bitch,' he hissed when he finally stood in front of his former wife. His eyes, narrowed to ice-blue slits, were alive with some dreadful emotion he could not keep hidden. Almost demented with anxiety, he could barely stand, the pictures of Eve and Abigail wandering about in the dark somewhere he could not shut out.

'After everything, you won't let me be, will you, Maxine? Not content with bleeding me dry, you try it on Eve—who is more of a mother to Sophie and Abigail, and Alice, than you ever were—and when she refuses to give in to your demands you take one of your children to blackmail her into giving you what you want. Well, I hope you're satisfied. God alone knows where they are.'

'They—may not have wandered far. The river—'

'River? There is a river?' He stared at her in horror. Combing the wet hair from his brow with his shaking fingers, he stepped away from her, hating her. 'Eve is the bravest, most generous-hearted woman I know, and by God, Maxine, if anything happens to either her or Abigail, I swear I will…'

'Enough,' thundered Lord Hutton. 'Lord Stainton, hurling insults at my wife—although God knows she deserves it—will not help find your wife and child.'

Lucas looked at him, trying to control his rampaging fury and dread. 'No, you're right. She's not worth it. I must go and look for them myself.'

Lord Hutton watched him turn, but not before he had seen those piercing eyes glare one last time at Maxine, the flame in them shrivelling her so that she fell back in alarm. What kind of woman, Lord Hutton wondered, was Eve Stainton, that could render a man to such a passion, to such a deep belief in his own conviction that she was alive somewhere out there in the dark with his daughter, and that he would not rest until he had them back?

Lucas stumbled about in the dark, turning this way and that in his desperation to find his wife and child. He stood on the edge of the wood calling her name, the words whipped from his mouth and borne away high on the wind. He searched for most of the night, before turning back to the inn. The sound of the river played ominously on his mind, but he refused to even contemplate that Eve or his daughter might have fallen in and been swept away.

He lowered his forehead on the trunk of a tree, his muscles in his throat working convulsively as he called her name one more time. This time it came out as a hoarse whisper, as waves of agonising pain exploded through his entire being. The appalling devastation of what her loss would mean to him was too dreadful to contemplate. He could not bear to lose her. Eve stirred his heart, his body and his blood to passion, to a love he could not have envisaged, and given the choice it would be eternal.

He could not face a world without her in it, without that special blend of humour and wit, of fearless courage and angry defiance, that passion he had experienced in his bed, her lips smiling at him, her deep blue eyes challenging him, the compassion and understanding she had for his children. All these things made up Eve, his wife.

Dawn was just beginning to break and Lucas was sitting by the fire in the tap room, his elbows on his knees, his head in his hands. Lord Hutton, who had fallen into an uneasy doze, was seated across from him. They were both about to resume the search.

Standing in the doorway holding Abigail's hand, Eve couldn't believe her eyes when she saw Lucas. As if in a trance, slowly she moved towards him.

'Lucas? Lucas?' she said again, her voice dwelling on his name.

She stopped short. Everything seemed to happen in slow motion as she watched his body stiffen. Slowly he raised his head and turned and looked at her, his face a ravaged and tormented mask, his eyes haunted. Eve was appalled at what she saw. Gone was the cynical twist to his strong mouth and the arrogant tilt to his head. He stared at her as if she were some kind of apparition. She stood there, her hair a tangled mass hung to her waist. She was almost un-recognisable to anyone but him.

'Eve?' He mouthed her name, his gaze going from her to his daughter and then back to his wife. 'Eve?' It was louder now and Eve watched him unfold his long lean body and then he was striding across the room and she was in his arms. He crushed her to him, his anguish so great, so tearing, that it carried him beyond all boundaries, as tears poured down her cheeks.

'I have been driven out of my mind. I thought you were dead and I could not bear it. I love you. Oh, God, I love you so much. I can't tell you what I thought. I looked everywhere but I couldn't find you—and the river… Oh, God, the river.'

'I know, I know, Lucas, but I am all right, truly.'

With her cheek resting against his chest, Eve smiled. Her suffering really had been worth it, just to be here in his arms, she told herself, feeling the fast beat of his heart beneath her cheek, and the rise and fall of his chest as he breathed, and to hear him say such wonderful things to her, things she had despaired of ever hearing from his lips. Her heart began to beat with such joy it quite alarmed her, that she could feel so elated after her terrible ordeal. It was just too incredible for words. She was safe now and nothing could touch her again.

Raising her head, she looked at him, loving him. 'I found Abigail and, not knowing where we were, was too afraid to move. It was dark and I was terrified that we might fall into the river, which seemed to be rushing all around us, so I waited until it was light enough to make our way out of the wood.'

He continued to hold her, trying to absorb her body into his. Placing his hands on either side of her face, he kissed her with a hungry violence. A shudder went through his tall frame as she arched into him and kissed him back. Only when she felt a tug on her skirt did she remember Abigail. So did Lucas and, releasing Eve, he swung the child off her feet and held her to him, kissing her cheek and murmuring soft, soothing words of comfort.

'Thank God. Thank God,' he murmured hoarsely, overcome with emotion. 'Everything will be all right now, my darling.'

'And I won't be sent away again? It was very dark and I was frightened and it made me cry,' Abigail mumbled, her soft cheek resting against his.

'I know, sweetheart, and I'm sorry I wasn't there, but no one is going to take you away ever again. I promise.'

'I want to go home now,' she murmured tiredly.

'And so you shall.'

Lord Hutton took Eve's arm. 'Come, Lady Stainton, sit by the fire. I'll summon the landlord and have him prepare you some sustenance. You look quite worn out. It must have been an ordeal.'

She nodded, sitting wearily in the chair Lucas had vacated a moment before. 'One I would not wish to repeat.' She glanced about her. 'Lady Hutton? Is she…?'

'In bed. Although I have to say she sees the error in what she has done and is—remorseful.'

'I'm sorry, Lord Hutton, but after everything Abigail has suffered at her hands—and my own harrowing ordeal—I doubt she knows the meaning of the word.'

A tired Abigail came and climbed on to her lap and Eve kissed her head, wrapping her arms around her protectively. 'At least she doesn't seem to have suffered too much from what has happened to her. A hot bath and a nap will do her good, although I don't want her to be left alone.'

Lucas looked down at them, unable to believe they had returned without mishap. 'A hot drink for you both, Eve, and then we must get you home. Mark should be here at any time with the carriage.'

'Mark?'

'He followed you last night and spent most of it searching for you. I sent him back to Laurel Court for the carriage.'

'And you, Lucas? Why didn't you let me know you were coming home?'

He grinned. 'I wanted to surprise you. Instead I was the one to be surprised when I arrived and found you were not there. Sarah told me what had happened and I came after you.'

Lucas turned and stiffened when he saw Maxine hovering in the doorway. Elegantly arrayed, tilting her chin in her usual proud manner, she slowly moved into the room. There was something new in her eyes, a hint of pleading—and, yes, remorse. But Lucas's first wife was not one to relent easily, and her gaze met his a little defiantly.

Tightening her arms about Abigail, who had her face buried in Eve's cloak, Eve looked at Maxine a little uncertainly. She was rather pale and the lack of colour made the small veins in her cheeks more visible, making her look older than her thirty years. Eve had not seen Maxine since she had left the inn last night and she did not really want to, but this matter had to be resolved before they left.

'Maxine,' Lucas greeted her in a chiding tone laced with sarcasm. 'I trust you slept well.'

'As a matter of fact, I didn't sleep at all, you see—I know it was a terrible thing that I did and I thank God that Abigail has been found unharmed. I admit I have not always thought in such terms, but there have been reasons for that.'

'Forgive me if I have difficulty believing you,' Lucas ground out. 'The reason you turned your back on your children was that you couldn't stand having them around you.'

'I know what I have done is wrong. All I could think of was myself. You were right, Lucas. I am not a fit mother. I never wanted children, you see.' She shrugged. 'Unfortunately, within marriage, one cannot prevent these things happening.'

'Too damn right you can't,' Lucas bit back, 'but when they do such things are dealt with reasonably and one does not evade one's responsibilities. It didn't take me long to realise you married me for my money and nothing else.'

'Money!' Lord Hutton cried, his face suffused with wrath. 'Why is there all this obsession with money?'

'It's a very useful commodity, Alfred,' Maxine stated coldly.

'Of which I have precious little, so you will have to get used to it, just like you will have to get used to living in Devon, Maxine, for I have lost all interest in London's pleasures. In fact, to be absolutely honest they sicken me. We will leave within the week.'

Maxine stared at him in alarm. 'No—no, Alfred, you cannot mean that. I have no liking for the country—I will suffocate and you know it.'

'Madam, after what you have done you will do as you are told.' It was said calmly, but there was no mistaking the steel beneath the words. Lord Hutton was a down-to-earth man who found it hard to show emotion, but he was overwhelmed by the enormity of what his wife had done. 'You took a child against the wishes of Lady Stainton—that she is your own child is beside the point, since you have not clapped eyes on her in God knows how long. To my thinking it was a criminal offence that caused immense and unnecessary distress to all concerned.'

Maxine paled and looked strangely meek and humble as she held out her hands to him in beseeching appeal. 'Stop it, Alfred—please. Do not speak to me like this.'

'If you say one more word, Maxine, I shall knock you senseless. You greedy, vindictive—' He took a shuddering breath, fighting to control his temper. 'Dear God, had I the means I swear I'd divorce you myself.'

Maxine blanched, horrified at the thought that she would be so humiliated twice. 'Alfred—you wouldn't.'

'Yes, madam, I would, but as it is I am stuck with you, so we will have to make the best of what we have.'

'Stop it, both of you,' Lucas interrupted. 'It's too late for any of this and I do not want to argue in front of Abigail. What is done cannot be undone, and I for one am sick of it. Maxine, I do not intend to see you again in the foreseeable future. Feeling as you do about your children, nothing can be achieved by it. But if you try anything like this again, I swear I will be the one to knock you senseless.' He looked at Lord Hutton 'Take her to Devon, Lord Hutton, and keep her there. And be sure to lock away your family silver, otherwise in the blink of an eye she will find a way to divest you of it.'

Lord Hutton nodded. 'Oh, I shall, Lord Stainton, most certainly. I have the full measure of my wife, and you may rest assured that this will be the last time she will come pestering you for money.'

Chapter Twelve

Arriving back at Laurel Court, Mrs Coombs and Sarah took charge, but when they tried to get Eve to go to her room and rest she refused and went to sit with Abigail, seeing that she was given a soothing drink and put to bed. The child napped fitfully and finally slipped into a peaceful sleep, confident that if she woke in terror she would be comforted by Eve's presence.

Not until Abigail had woken and was being fussed over by Sophie and Estelle and a doting Sarah did Eve go to her own room for a much-needed bath.

The early evening breeze stirred the curtains and in the silence of the house Eve could hear Lucas moving about in his room as she stepped into the warm scented water prepared by Tilly, and relaxed in the luxury of it.

Lucas let himself into Eve's rooms. His eyes did a quick sweep; on hearing a splashing sound coming from her bathing chamber, his smile was lascivious. Padding across the carpet in his stocking feet, he was met by a wave of rose-scented steam. Having just taken a bath himself, stripped to the waist he leaned against the door post, his eyes aflame. All he wanted to do was feast his eyes on her.

Eve was in a big brass tub with her back to the door, her head resting on the high rim. Her freshly washed hair was secured in a wild untidy knot on the top of her head, with damp tendrils curling and clinging to her neck. One slender leg suddenly emerged from the water and was raised skyward, sleek and glistening with droplets of water as her hands reached out to lather the firm white flesh.

An amused smiled twisted his lips. It was his most fervent desire to join his wife in the tub, but it was highly likely her maid would return at any minute and her embarrassment would be excruciating if she were find the master and mistress indulging in such antics.

Believing she had heard Tilly return, Eve said, 'Hand me the towel, will you, Tilly?'

Seeing a towel draped over a chair, Lucas shoved himself away from the doorframe, reached for it, then held it out. Without turning, Eve arose from the tub and stepped out. She started to turn and reach behind her for the towel—that was the moment she saw Lucas.

'Lucas!' His heated gaze seared her and in a moment of alarm it was in her mind to flee, but then her eyes warmed and her smile welcomed him. 'How silently you came. Are you here to share my bath or to tempt me with your own nakedness?' she whispered, wantonly trailing a finger lightly down his bare chest. 'It is obvious you have no excuse for spying on me.' She allowed him to drape her in the towel and, turning her back on him, she sauntered into the bedroom.

Lucas watched appreciatively her hips moving with an undulating grace beneath the towel, then followed her. His eyes devoured her when she dropped the towel and reached for her dressing gown, exposing her body to the full—the full, ripe, swelling breasts and the luscious roundness of her hips and long shapely legs.

Knowing full well the effect her nakedness was having on him and that she was rousing his senses to full awakening, and in no hurry to cover herself, still smiling, she slowly put her arms into the flowing sleeves and tightened the belt around her slender waist, but not before she had seen the hard glint of passion strike sparks in his pale blue eyes.

Her bare feet seemed to glide over the carpet, and her lips were curved upwards in a totally wicked smile. She gave a deep throaty laugh and placed the flat of her hands on his chest, sliding them upwards over his ribs, feeling the heavy thud of his heart beneath her questing hands.

'When are you going to tell me what it is you want?' she purred as his hands came round her waist. Slowly, deliberately, she leaned into him, the peaks of her thinly clad breasts pressed to his chest, rousing his blood to boiling as the heat of her touched him.

'Dear God, Eve, you know damn well what it is I want without me having to spell it out,' he rasped, his long-starved passions flaring high as he folded her in his arms, crushing her to him and covering her soft reaching mouth with his.

Her arms snaked around his neck and she returned his kiss with all the passion and longing that had been gathering force inside her since he had left her. Placing his hands beneath her knees, he swung her up into his arms and carried her to his bed, kicking the connecting door shut. Placing her on the covers, he leaned over her, untying the belt of her robe and removing it, before divesting himself of his trousers and revealing the naked male beauty of his body in its arrogant readiness to make love to his wife.

Eve waited for him, her breasts and her insides quivering in hot anticipation.

Lucas leaned over her, his hand leading her with purposeful intent, bold in his knowledge and gentle in his regard of her. There was a radiance about her he had never noticed before, something different, but he could not name it.

'How lovely you are,' he breathed. 'You have grown even more beautiful in my absence. Is it some kind of sorcery you practise, my love?'

She laughed softly. 'This is no sorcery, Lucas. Your eyes do not deceive you. You have been absent too long, that is all,' she murmured, pulling his head down to her lips.

There was between them a storm of passion that deafened their ears as greatly as the crashing of thunder. Each kiss and touch was fire, each word a caress, each movement in their union a masterpiece of music, a rhapsody of passion that played on their heart strings and united their souls, combining to become a consuming crescendo that left them sated and warm and pulsating with pleasure.

Eve lay exhausted and drowsy in her husband's arms, her breath softly stirring the furriness of his chest. How she loved him, and she gloried in being able to respond to him in their bed. Lucas, his dream fulfilled after the long, tortured weeks of being without her, turned his head and buried his face in her loosened hair, savouring the sweet scented fragrance of it.

A warm and gentle breeze stole in through the open windows and cooled their heated bodies. Some moments later Eve rolled on to her stomach and, leaning on his chest, looked up at him, her gilded tresses spread in thick waves of silk over him, her deep blue eyes dark and sultry.

'Did you mean it?' she asked softly.

His mouth twitched at the corners. 'Mean it? Mean what?'

'Earlier you told me that you love me. And don't you dare insult me by telling me you can't remember because I won't believe you. Was it said to placate me, in the heat of the moment—or what?'

His gaze met hers without wavering, promising everything. 'The answer to that is that I meant it. I do love you, Eve, beyond all else. I love you so much that it hurts.'

The relief was so painfully exquisite that Eve thought she would die of it. 'What? I have to ask myself is this the man who told me that love is a silly, romantic notion that has no place in his life, that you don't want to be loved and that you have no love to give.. What has happened to change your mind, Lucas?'

'You, Eve. You have changed my mind. I was a complete ass. Can you ever forgive me for saying those things to you?'

'There is nothing to forgive, Lucas. I know why you said them and why you couldn't accept my love. Until you made love to me I had not realised the full extent of how much your marriage to Maxine had damaged you emotionally. Now I fully understand. But things change, people change—and I believe Maxine has changed— as you have changed, Lucas. In fact I think you are rather wonderful and very clever.'

'No, I'm not,' he declared solemnly. 'If I had even the slightest intelligence, I would have taken you to bed on our wedding night—or before.'

'When was the first time you wanted to do that?'

'The day you arrived at my house and gave me a severe dressing down for shouting and cursing and doing all the things every bad-tempered, temperamental gentleman does when things aren't going his way,' he admitted, smiling at the memory. 'No one had dared do that since I was a child. I think I fell in love with you then—when you were holding Estelle with one hand and trying to hold on to a wriggling puppy with the other. It was when I went to Newcastle that the depth of what I felt was driven home. I missed you—Lord, how I missed you. You have no idea how much. But what of you, Eve? How do you feel?'

'Like your wife—your wife who loves you very much,' she said, her eyes aglow with love, 'you and your children, and one day I will give you a son.'

'Suddenly that no longer seems important. You see, I have come to realise that as much as I want a son, I want you more. So, my love,' he murmured, rolling her on to her back and beginning to plant tantalising, rousing kisses on her lips once more, 'feel free to fill the nursery with as many daughters as you wish, providing they all look like you.'

Nothing touched Eve more than this, which was all the proof of his love that she needed.

'The children have missed you,' she murmured between kisses. 'They are thrilled to have you back.'

Breaking off nuzzling her ear lobe, he looked at her from beneath hooked eyes. 'And the new governess? Is she suitable?'

'Miss Fraser. She's worth her weight in gold. You'll like her—and the children adore her.' She smiled teasingly. 'Have you decided which painting you'll have to sell to pay her wages?'

He gathered her close, his kisses urgent, warm and devouring as he continued with his seduction. 'It will no longer come to that, my love. Very soon we shall have enough money to employ a thousand governesses.'

She laughed softly, feeling the bold urgency of him once again. She pushed him away and he looked down at her in puzzlement, his eyes questioning. 'You must learn to be more gentle, Lucas.'

'Why,' he murmured, shoving back her hair and proceeding to kiss her gleaming shoulders, her breasts, his lips warm, devouring, fierce with love and passion, 'are you in danger of breaking, my love?'

'No, Lucas. I am strong enough to withstand our love-making, it's just…'

'Just what?' His mouth went lower, kissing her belly and becoming bolder still.

'You might hurt the baby.'

He stopped what he was doing and slowly looked up at her. The silence grew. Very slowly he brought himself up to lean over her. 'What did you say?'

'I said you might hurt the baby.'

He smiled. 'So that is what is different about you. I knew there was something, but I'm damned if I could put my finger on it.'

'Do you mind?' she breathed, watching his face.

'Mind? No. I am ecstatic. I love you. We love each other. Everything is as it should be.'

Lucas stood on the terrace gazing over the magnificent grounds at Laurel Court, which had been tended, pruned, planted and nurtured by an army of gardeners and brought back to its former glory. Things were going well for him. After all his determination and hard work, his business ventures were thriving and he was beginning to reap great rewards. The money bequeathed to Eve by her father as yet remained untouched in the bank. They had discussed at length what was to be done with it and they were in accord that it could be used to set up a trust for the children, in particular for Alice, since there would be nothing forthcoming from her mother.

Attired in a simple gown of lavender silk and lace trim, Eve came to stand beside him, linking her arm through his.

Master James Stephen Stainton was one year old. It was his birthday, a momentous day, and Eve wasn't going to let it go by without a party. Not that her son was aware of it, but he was enjoying all the attention that was being showered on him.

'Penny for them?' she murmured, following her husband's gaze.

Placing his hand over hers, he smiled down at her. 'I was just thinking what a lucky man I am—to have you and the children and all this. Don't they make a charming picture?'

Looking at their joint offspring scampering about with Beth and William's boys—the family having come on an extended visit—she agreed.

The gardens seemed to be full of children running wild on this lovely spring day, and Miss Fraser, a harassed expression on her face, was inclined to blame Miriam for that. The young nursemaid seemed to delight in encouraging them, even joining in their game of hide and seek, which entailed a great deal of activity and laughter and tumbling about.

Master James was sitting on the grass, his face rosy and smiling, and then he rolled onto his hands and knees and began crawling after Alice, who was toddling after Abigail. James was a beautiful child and there was very little of Eve in him. As young as he was, he even had the same arrogant jut to his baby jaw as Lucas, the same scowl, the same light blue eyes and an air about him of masculine fierceness.

Postponing his decision to go to the children and join in their games, Lucas slid his hand round Eve's waist, drawing her possessively close. He smiled and touched the deep red curls at her neck and then he bent his head and kissed her gently on the lips.

'What a fine sight. Do they not make you feel proud? Are you happy, my love?'

The kind of happiness he spoke of began to spread through her until she ached from it. 'Very.'

'Are you certain?'

'Absolutely.'

'For the first time in my life I finally know what it feels like to have a home and a family. It is you I have to thank for that. The bargain we made turned out to be a good one. You are a fine woman, Eve Stainton—an exceptional one.'

His wife tipped her face up to his and laughed. 'You are not bad yourself, Lucas—and I love you.'

* * * * *

The World of Mills & Boon

There's a Mills & Boon® series that's perfect for you. There are ten different series to choose from and new titles every month, so whether you're looking for glamorous seduction, Regency rakes, homespun heroes or sizzling erotica, we'll give you plenty of inspiration for your next read.

By Request
Relive the romance with the best of the best
12 stories every month

Cherish™
Experience the ultimate rush of falling in love.
12 new stories every month

INTRIGUE...
A seductive combination of danger and desire...
7 new stories every month

Desire
Passionate and dramatic love stories
6 new stories every month

nocturne™
An exhilarating underworld of dark desires
3 new stories every month

For exclusive member offers go to
millsandboon.co.uk/subscribe

WORLD_ M&Ba